Maddened by his nonchalance, Shana gripped his lapels and tugged him closer. "I am not the woman who's going to make your dreams come true."

Gabe nodded.

"I mean it."

"I know."

They were in an incredibly romantic place. She was a woman who did not get involved. This mesmerizing man seemed unaccountably attracted to her. More fairy tales. She wasn't a princess waiting to be rescued; she rescued others.

Gabe waited for her to prove him wrong. If she cured his belief in his dreams, she might cure the insomnia that plagued him.

Very well. She thought of the most unpredictable, unlikely, un-Shana-like thing she could do. She kicked off her snow-soaked pumps, dropped her coat, and threw her arms around his neck. The man wouldn't know what hit him.

Before I Wake

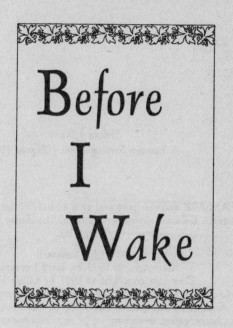

Before I Wake

Terry Lawrence

B A N T A M   B O O K S
NEW   YORK   TORONTO
LONDON   SYDNEY   AUCKLAND

Before I Wake
A Bantam Fanfare Book / August 1995

ISBN 0-553-56914-7

Published simultaneously in the United States and Canada

*Bantam Books are published by Bantam Books, a division of Bantam Doubleday Dell
Publishing Group, Inc. Its trademark, consisting of the words "Bantam Books" and the
portrayal of a rooster, is Registered in U.S. Patent and Trademark Office and in other
countries. Marca Registrada. Bantam Books, 1540 Broadway, New York, New York
10036.*

PRINTED IN THE UNITED STATES OF AMERICA

RAD   0   9   8   7   6   5   4   3   2   1

To Susann Brailey,
my editor

Acknowledgments

My sincere thanks to Dr. David Walker, D.O., and particularly to Marcia Rinal, manager of the Munson Sleep Disorders Center at Munson Medical Center in Traverse City, Michigan. Her helpfulness, cheerful attitude, and ready information made this book possible. Any fictional liberties or pharmaceutical inaccuracies are strictly my own.

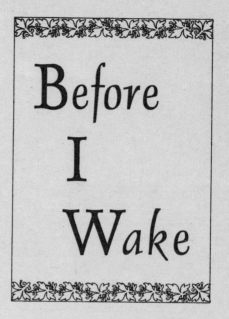

Before
I
Wake

BOOK ONE

Miles To Go Before I Sleep

I

The Vampire. That's what they called Gabriel Fitzgerald down at the brokerage firm. He worked all night, patching into worldwide trading boards, sending buy and sell orders to places on the planet where people were up and doing business—Japan, Hong Kong, Singapore. If the other traders glimpsed him at all it was on the rare occasions he attended meetings with fellow partner Brice Grier. At Grier/Fitzgerald, Gabriel Fitzgerald was a shadowy figure, more spoken of than seen. A legend.

Judging from the startled looks on the faces of the young traders as he walked into the office at nine A.M., the legend held. He strode down the aisle separating the banks of flickering computers and buzzing phone lines. The urgent bray of young men wangling deals instantly lowered to a hushed murmur. "He's here," they muttered into their telephone receivers. "Gabe Fitzgerald, the man who doesn't sleep."

He felt their gazes on him all the way to Brice's glass-enclosed office, admiring, mystified, envious. He had what they wanted. He worked his own hours and made the trading world dance to his tune. He'd circled the Pacific Rim the way a cowboy lassos a steer, the way a socialite runs her manicured finger around the lip of a crystal glass and makes it sing. Passably handsome, muscle-toned, and custom-tailored, he'd dated some of the city's most beautiful women. He'd also amassed a fortune beyond most people's wildest dreams.

He would have traded half of it for one night of uninterrupted sleep. Failing that, he'd trade the rest of his money for a woman who loved him the way he was. "Pathetic, isn't it?"

He'd spoken aloud. He stared out the window at the January snow. In the glass's reflection he saw his partner stop in the doorway and blink.

Brice complained Gabe always started conversations in the middle. He hurried to catch up. "What's pathetic?"

"People starving all over the world, and I'm pissing and moaning about a few hours lost sleep."

"So what else is new?" Brice lifted his chubby cheeks in a warm smile. He enveloped Gabe's hand in a comfortable grasp.

Gabe felt his tension ease. Brice was one of those men who'd gone straight from baby fat to middle-aged spread. Everything about him was comfortable, from his roomy crumpled suit to his backhanded take-a-seat gesture. Surrounded by the trappings of someone who'd inherited his first million before the age of twenty-five, he worked happily toward his tenth.

"Another sleepless night?" he guessed, slapping a file on his desk. On the highly polished mahogany, the manila folder looked as if it were floating on an inch of water. "How many hours this time?"

"Thirty-seven and counting."

Brice whistled low. "If it was anybody else, I'd say get thee to a doctor."

"For what, pills?" Gabe spat. "They make me feel like a drugged-out zombie."

"Instead we get the pleasure of your sunny company."

Gabe rubbed his eyes with his thumb and forefinger, pinching the bridge of his nose. It was all the apology Brice would get.

The young financier didn't seem to mind. He unbuttoned his suit coat and sat. His throne-sized leather chair squeaked rhythmically as he set it rocking. He was like a little boy who'd been told not to fidget and could do nothing else.

By contrast Gabe's intensity was entirely internal, a python coiled around its prey, squeezing harder and harder. He only succeeded in suffocating himself.

"So what's eating you?"

Gabe smiled grimly at the appropriateness of the phrase. "Mary Ann left me."

Brice stopped rocking. "Sorry, pal."

"Knew you'd sympathize," Gabe said in his tired drawl. Brice had all the heart he lacked.

"Hey, look, let's go out. We'll hit the bars. You'll meet someone new. Always do. Lucky dog."

"At this hour?"

Brice tilted his head toward the rows of traders on the other side of the glass wall. "Come five o'clock, we'll follow these guys. They'll know a place."

Gabe scowled at them. Even there in the company he helped found he was on the outside looking in. He felt like the lone wolf prowling the edge of the settlement, respected, feared, rarely befriended.

"Unless, of course, you want to go home and sleep," Brice said.

"Fat chance."

His lids felt like emery boards, scratchy and dry. His eyes were as hard and polished as ivory cue balls. His suit coat felt like a lead vest weighing him down as he stood. He squared his shoulders, fighting it. He could deal with the sleeplessness. It was this damn loneliness he couldn't shake, the sense the nights would never end and he'd be alone forever. The Vampire. Not a flattering image by any means.

"You look like death warmed over, y'know."

Gabe huffed and grinned again. "Gotta live up to my reputation." He slumped into a seat opposite Brice's desk.

Brice hit a switch and the blinds closed electronically, shutting out the traders' curious sideways glances. Freed from his role as boss, he dragged off his tie and threw it in his center drawer. An electronic game caught his attention. He snatched it up, sliding the drawer shut with his abdomen as he scooted his chair forward and set his elbows on the desk. Rapidly pushing buttons, he glanced at his partner over the tiny images on the screen. "So Mary Ann left."

"Packed up. Couldn't take it anymore."

Beeps alternated with miniature explosions as Brice breezed through the game's early sections. "You didn't keep her up nights, did you?"

"I'd never do that." Sleep was too precious. So was keeping a woman in his life. If he could manage that, he'd know he was normal. Despite all signs to the contrary, he thought grimly. He rubbed his eyes.

"Damn!" Brice's exclamation preceded the inevitable explosion signaling the end of the game. He tossed the box down and focused all his attention on Gabe. Eager to help, eager to do anything but endure his friend's unnatural stillness, he rocked back in his chair and steepled his fingers. He pursed his lips. His brows rose halfway up his forehead as if in search of his receding hairline. "So tell me about it."

Gabe's cynical glare broke the spell. "You playing psychoanalyst now?"

"Shit, Gabe, what am I supposed to do?" He shifted in his seat.

Gabe sighed. He had a knack for making people squirm. Brice said his stillness was creepy. Ninety percent of it was sheer exhaustion, the other ten intense concentration. A laserlike focus was the only way he knew to combat the foggy feeling, to keep his edge. You snooze, you lose.

He seemed to be losing everything anyway. Life slipped through his fingers like sand in an hourglass. He couldn't go on this way.

Apparently neither could Brice. While Gabe scowled at the shine on his shoes, Brice plucked a black rubber ball from what looked like a silver eggcup on the corner of his desk and began squeezing it in his fist. "Some kind of wrist exercise," he explained.

Gabe ruthlessly brought them back to the subject. "What's wrong with me?"

"Seriously?" Brice planted his elbows on his gleaming desk and shrugged, rolling the ball between his palms. "You aren't always the nicest guy in the world."

"Yeah?"

"A little snarly sometimes."

"Snarly." Gabe practically growled the word.

"Grouchy. Grumpy. Touchy. Testy." With every word Brice bounced the ball against his desk. Two balls ricocheted off the shine, one reflected, one real. On the razor-thin line of the surface the balls met, flattened, bounced back. Thwack, thwack, thwack. "Cranky. Crabby. Cantankerous—"

Gabe's hand shot out and snatched the ball in midair. Both men froze.

Brice sheepishly held out his palm. He set the ball in its executive eggcup. "Sorry."

"So I'm a son of a bitch to live with."

"Who isn't? With the amount of sleep you get I'm surprised you can carry on a normal conversation much less a relationship."

If Brice didn't stop ticktocking those suspended silver ball bearings against each other, Gabe was going to smash the entire pointless contraption against the wall. "So what do I do about it?"

"You refuse to sleep with one of the most beautiful women in Chicago, whaddya expect?"

"I can't *make* myself sleep."

"Hey, easy. I know."

Gabe clenched his jaw. He'd snapped again. Lucky for him Brice had the loyalty of a beagle and the attention span of a Mexican jumping bean. One minute he was a chubby adolescent enthralled with his toys, the next he was the friend Gabe had known since college.

Back then sleeplessness hadn't been a problem. Everybody pulled all-nighters. Guys prided themselves on driving straight through to Daytona on spring break. Life was for living around the clock.

Except Gabe's clock never wound down. The nights never stopped. The daylight hours dragged at him like quicksand. He fought to stay awake, stay sane, avoid the dreams. He wasn't succeeding.

He reached for the picture of Peg and the kids on the corner of Brice's desk. Brice slid a magnetic chessboard out of his way. Gabe traced his fingers down the walnut frame. "Do your kids have any toys, or are they all on Daddy's desk?"

Brice yanked the frame out of his hands with a friendly expletive. "You ever consider one of those sleep disorder clinics?"

"Checking in somewhere?"

"Peg cut an article out of the paper. Said I should give it to you."

"Did I look that bad?"

"You've looked better. When Mary Ann didn't come to dinner with you we kind of wondered." Brice bent a paper clip into the shape of a whale. "Nothing wrong with getting help, you know. Hell, if you're coming to *me* for advice, you must have a problem."

"If our clients heard about it, we'd all have problems. The last thing we need is a rumor going around that one of the partners checked into some kind of rehab center. They'll think I spent their investments on coke or covering the Cubs."

"If you're betting on the Cubs, you're sicker than I thought."

Gabe surprised himself with a rusty chuckle. He ran a hand over his face. The skin felt rubbery and slack. His eyes stung. He opened them with a shock. He'd zoned out again.

Brice had come around the side of the desk. His hand rested on Gabe's shoulder. "Your secret's safe with me, bud. Get some help."

Irritation sparked in Gabe like the lit end of a fuse. "For what? For something people do every night?"

"For something that's putting you in an early grave."

Graves. Gabe pictured a headstone of polished granite, the words "Rest in Peace." He almost envied the couple lying beneath it.

Brice clapped him on the shoulder. Gabe jumped and hoped it didn't show. Hiding his tiredness had become second nature. He let his friend walk him to the door, concentrating on holding it together, wondering how the hell that crinkled newspaper clipping got in his hand.

"Call 'em. And don't worry about us. This gang won't think anything if you disappear for a few days. It'll just add to the legend."

"I've had it with being a legend. I want a life."

Is that what he was supposed to write on the top line of the form: "I want a life"? What kind of loser was he?

He read it again. WHY HAVE YOU COME TO THE SLEEP DISORDER CLINIC?

"Insomnia" he wrote. *Chronic.*

HOW LONG HAS YOUR PROBLEM PERSISTED?

"Twenty years."

He stared at the words. They'd never believe him. He barely believed it himself.

CAN YOU DESCRIBE YOUR SLEEPING PATTERN?

He could count on the fingers of one hand the nights he'd actually slept with Mary Ann. He'd drop off for an hour or two, spent and comfortable after making love, then he'd get up, wearily, quietly, so as not to disturb her, so as not to be called on to explain. He felt like a thief sneaking out of his own bedroom.

If he stayed he'd only lie there in the dark, thoughts crowding his brain like onlookers at an accident, lurking, gawking, pointing out every mistake he'd ever made, the money he'd won and lost, the women who'd left him, fed up with his sleeplessness, his restlessness, the dreams he kept from them.

Sitting in the waiting room of St. James' Hospital, he recited the dialogue by heart.

"Aren't you coming to bed?"

"I can't sleep. It's nothing personal."

"Sleeping with me is nothing personal?"

"Just give me some time."

How many times had he used that tone, pleading for understanding while shoving it away? Love was like sleep, the harder he chased it the more he watched it recede.

His head tilted forward, chin sinking toward his chest. The motion startled him awake. He clutched the clipboard before it slipped off his lap. The ugly yellow walls of the waiting room momentarily stumped him. Faces came into focus, tired puffy faces with dark-ringed eyes, pent-up, irritable people, exhausted and lost. Apparently he'd come to the right place.

St. James' was a crumbling brick complex on the edge of a rundown section of Chicago. It was the last place mentioned in the newspaper article Brice had given him, hence the last place any of Grier/Fitzgerald's clients would spot him. A good choice.

He sat up straighter, deliberately drawing his shoulders back, keeping his posture rigid and alert, fighting the sluggishness, the brain-numbing weariness. He rubbed his forehead, a habit he'd developed to wean himself away from rubbing his eyes. Thirty-nine hours.

The last time he'd seen his bed, Mary Ann's suitcases had littered it. Her clothes lay scattered on the quilt like bodies strewn across an airfield after a plane crash. Reassembled, her wardrobe might add up to a person, a silk blouse here, a scrap of designer dress there, stockings shriveled at the foot of the bed like a snake's discarded skin.

He'd been discarded. He couldn't honestly blame her.

"Mr. Fitzgerald?"

He squinted up. A woman bent over him, coils of dark blond hair shading her face. His first impression was of a peasant madonna, full-bodied and earthy, sensible and square-jawed. Her cheeks were wide and full, like her lips. She had round brown eyes and freckles spattered across her cheeks, a sprinkling of cinnamon on pale creamy skin. There wasn't a sharp edge to her.

Gabe grimaced and tried to clear his head. He was there for help, not to gape at the nurses. Her dingy white lab coat featured a plastic name tag half hidden by a lapel. Glasses hung around her neck on a gold chain, librarian-style.

"Gabriel Fitzgerald," he said, hoping that answered her question, wondering briefly if she'd asked one.

"I'm Shana Getz. May I see?"

See what? God, he was losing it. The simplest things took immense effort. Processing information was like pushing toy trucks through molasses.

She held out her hand. She wanted the clipboard. He handed her the story of his life. Maybe she could rewrite it.

2

She perched on an empty seat beside him, clipboard slanted on her lap, glasses balanced on her nose. If he was lucky, she'd disappear to file it in some vast data base. He'd have time to get his act together before she led him to a doctor.

She read all the way to the bottom then lifted the page, craning her neck to read the back.

They should have thought of that when they printed the form, Gabe thought. A surge of aggravation braced him. The whole bureaucratic gauntlet irritated him. He was in no mood to jump through their hoops or answer their Twenty Questions. He had to stay awake.

You snooze, you lose.

You snooze, you dream.

The woman bent over his form like a mother over a cradle, concerned, protective, in love with his paperwork. Seated beside him, she bumped her knee against his thigh and stayed close. Did she think he was going to slide out of his chair, for chrissake?

The memory hit him with all the force of a dream, a voice right there, speaking in his ear:

"If you pronounce the t it's 'for Christ's sake,' and that's wrong."

He was eight or nine years old, at an age where he enjoyed testing out swear words on grown-ups. He enjoyed it even more when his grandmother dropped a cake pan and let fly with a few of her own.

" *'Chrissakes' is just a word,"* she'd explain. *"Like 'landsakes.' 'Geez' is another one. 'Geez' is okay as long as you don't make it 'Je-sus.' "*

The razor-fine distinctions she brought to her rationalizations fascinated him.

"Anything you say, Grandma."

"Pardon me?"

He gritted his teeth at the sound of the woman's voice beside him. Tilting his head to the side, he gave in and rubbed his eyes. Hard. "Just talking to myself."

He'd lived with his grandmother for five years. Even though he'd loved her, there'd been a barrier between them, a secret they never discussed. He wondered what the woman beside him would think of it.

She was pretty. Color flushed her cheeks a delicate pink. She shoved her glasses up her nose and flicked some of her tangled hair over her shoulder. Sneaking a finger under her glass frames, she smoothed the skin beneath one eye.

With a pang, Gabe realized she'd taken his "Grandma" crack to heart. Unfortunately, he was too damn tired to do anything about it. "Look, is there a doctor I can see? I don't have a lot of time."

"Twenty years," the woman in the lab coat murmured.

It took him a minute to make the connection. She meant twenty years of fighting sleep. For a moment he thought she was talking about his grandmother. It was twenty years since she died.

"You must have gotten *some* sleep along the way."

He cleared his throat, shaking the cobwebs from his brain. "Sometimes I get as much as six hours a day."

"How often is that?"

"Once or twice a year. It lasts a couple weeks. Then it's back to four hours or so."

"The season?"

"Huh?"

"Is it seasonal? When you sleep better?"

"I never noticed." He was usually so damn grateful, he took it where he could get it.

She made a note. "And the four hours, are they all together or fragmented? An hour here, an hour there?"

The question hung in the air, like motes of dust falling through the slanting light of a morning window. She knew. This woman knew what it was like.

"Fragmented." He tasted the rightness of the word, weighing the sensation. Was it possible someone understood what he went through? He looked at her more closely. Her brown eyes seemed undefended by lashes. Patience radiated from softly molded lips. She knew how long nights could be.

"Mr. Fitzgerald?"

He shut his eyes tight. He had to get with the program. She'd think he was nuts for staring at her that way. How could he explain it wasn't her, not exactly? It was all those years of feeling like a freak, a vampire. Finding someone who understood threw him, that's all. Even if he couldn't tell her the whole story.

"Normally"—he cleared the grittiness out of his throat "if you can call it normal, I get an hour of sleep at night. More of a nap. Then I wake up and work until dawn. Around ten A.M. I try sleeping. If that doesn't work, I give up and go running."

"Running."

"To wear myself out so I can sleep through the afternoon."

She chuckled. "I should think you'd be worn out already. When you're done running, do you fall asleep immediately?"

"I take a shower. After a couple hours I usually doze off."

"For how long?"

"Two or three hours. I wake up when—" He looked at his hands. "When the woman I was living with got home from work I'd wake up. We'd go out. She had a full social calendar. When we got home she'd go to bed and I'd go to work."

"For a grand total of four hours sleep per day. Is that enough?"

Not for Mary Ann it wasn't. "You wanted the routine. On a good day, that's how it works."

"And on a bad one?"

The hair on the back of his neck bristled. He didn't want her pity. "I haven't slept for almost forty hours."

"Forty, really!" She sounded thrilled. Her pen skittered down the margins, making a mess of his neatly printed form.

Her enthusiasm was like a splash of cold water, a buzzing, aggravating alarm. He'd worked on that form, rigorously keeping his writing on the lines, not allowing it to slant or wobble. His *y*'s were strict and straight, the dots over his *i*'s as precise as bullets hitting the bull's-eye.

She obliterated his meticulousness with slashes of curlicue shorthand. Obviously the woman didn't have a clue. If she did, she'd know what an effort it had been to fill out that form, how hard it was to act like a normal human being when he'd gone so long without sleep.

He took a steadying breath. It wasn't her fault his temper was frayed.

She concentrated on her work, punctuating her silent conversation with the paper by raising her brows, quirking a smile, narrowing an eye as she considered then wrote some more.

"All that from a few questions?"

She flashed him a smile. "Initial observations. Should've brought my notepad. It'll just be a minute."

He didn't mind. It gave him a chance to concentrate on something besides himself. He studied her as she pulled a handful of hair away from her face. She was somewhere in her mid-thirties, at an age where experience collected around her eyes in laugh lines and dimplelike grooves on either side of her smile.

Get to a certain age and everyone had baggage, Gabe thought. Even a smile had to be qualified by parentheses. All the same, he wanted to see her smile again. It was the only bright spot he'd had in days.

"So," she summed up, "an acute episode of sleeplessness brought you here."

"A newspaper clipping brought me here."

He tried to emulate her answering smile. His face felt as creaky as old leather.

Her fingertips on his knee rooted him to the spot. "Mr. Fitzgerald, insomnia isn't a character flaw. I know what willpower it takes to function in the world when all your body wants is sleep."

He tried to sit up straighter. Her hand stayed where it was.

"Some of the most courageous people I know fight this battle every day of their lives. I think you may be one of them."

The woman handed out reassurance the way Red Cross nurses handed out doughnuts. His emotions careened from anger to gratitude, from desperation to injured pride.

"I need sleep." Mortified to hear the slur in his speech, he bit off the rest of the words. "If I can get a few hours, I'll be okay. I can function on that."

"But can you function well?"

His body felt pummeled by lack of sleep. "If I can get through this period—"

"It's happened before."

Was that a question? Was he expected to answer? He

nodded, his head bobbing like a puppet with a broken string.

"Then it'll happen again."

"Probably." He needed help but he'd be damned if he'd cave in to his tiredness. "Look, is there anything you can give me?"

"We don't prescribe sleeping pills if we can possibly help it."

What did she think he was, a junkie? "I don't want pills, I want answers!" He told himself to lower his voice then forgot what he planned to say. He had to get out of there. He was too tired to deal with all the questions. If he'd gone home, hit the sofa, he'd be asleep by now.

Her fingertips splayed lightly on his leg, her presence gently drawing him back to reality. His jaw relaxed. His galloping heart slowed. A subtle heat penetrated his skin. The warmth crept up his body, comforting, stimulating, distracting.

When she had his attention, she stood. Her lab coat swung open. A splash of color caught Gabe's eye. With a self-conscious grimace she opened it the rest of the way. On her white T-shirt a quarter moon smiled. A comet's purple tail glittered from her left shoulder to her right breast. "Madam Sandman" it read. "A patient gave it to me."

"Cute."

She buttoned up her coat. "Will you follow me?"

Gabe lumbered to his feet. He felt like Frankenstein trying to walk a straight line. Concentrating on the scuffed bands of colored tape running the length of the corridor, he vowed not to stagger or weave. He got as far as ten steps. She led him around a corner. He veered so wide, he put out a hand. A chill ran through him as he touched the tiled wall. At least fear cleared his head.

They stepped into a creaking elevator.

Bing. "We're here." His guide sidled through the parting doors the moment they opened.

Gabe trudged after, picking up bits and pieces of her

monologue. Once she'd gotten him on his feet, she was off and running.

"We're on the second floor of the west wing of Building D. This section dates back to the nineteen twenties, when the hospital first expanded. The original building was rebuilt in eighteen seventy-three after the Great Fire. Building C and Building A were built in nineteen forty-eight and nineteen sixty-three respectively. Nineteen sixty-three was the last time St. James' had an expansion. Since then it's been strictly shrinkage."

Tired or not, a handful of his brain circuits still worked. "How could Building A come after Building D?"

"A is for Administration."

As if that explained everything.

"Not that I'm complaining."

About what? he thought, irritation nagging him like a sore tooth.

"If it weren't for empty hospital beds and woeful underfunding, the Sleep Disorders Clinic would've never gotten the space to operate. We have one whole floor of a wing of a building the board of directors were thinking of closing down not six months ago. They kept it open for our sake, to see if we could make a go of it. And make some extra money for the hospital, of course." Did she ever stop for breath? She trod ahead of him, body slanted forward, heels hitting the linoleum with rubber-soled thuds.

She would have been a beautiful woman, he thought, if she'd stood up straight, worn heels, combed her hair, and slowed her speech to a pleasant murmur. Instead she seemed blissfully oblivious to things like appearance.

A small voice told him he was being harsh. Another said he was coming to his senses. Depending on the hall lights, her hair was either dingy brown or glistening gold. He guessed she'd run a brush through it that morning; she hadn't touched it since. Long, lazy curls unfurled to her shoulder blades, bouncing as she walked, swaying as she turned a corner. Hypnotizing him. Aggravating him.

Why couldn't she have simple hair, blond, straight, chopped off at the chin? Or better yet, wound up in one of those chignons Mary Ann wore, carefully controlled, scrupulously pulled together.

Her lab coat needed a hot iron and a bottle of bleach. It sagged at the seat and wrinkled horizontally across the backs of her thighs. It looked as if she'd slept in it.

Maybe she was a night owl too. Nah, he couldn't be that lucky.

The thought brought him up short. He wasn't there to pick up women. His relationship with Mary Ann had gone downhill steadily the last year. He wasn't ready to start again. Never again. Not until his problem was solved. So far they'd barely scratched the surface. He hadn't even mentioned dreams.

If only he could sleep, he'd handle whatever dreams came his way.

They took another left in the hospital maze. "Madam Sandman" glanced back to make sure he kept up. She stopped before a door.

"B–two forty-one," he read.

"Building D used to be Building B. Don't ask."

He concentrated on her upturned face, that humorous, understanding look she had as if the joke were on them. Fluorescent lights turned her complexion pasty and flat. He hated to think how bad he looked. "Is this where people stay?"

"You mean the sleep lab? That's down the hall. But first a brief consultation." She unlocked the door and waved him inside.

He stopped on the threshold. The stuffy warmth of a hardworking radiator hit him in the face like a dry sauna. The air was thick with dust. Teetering mounds of paperwork and file folders covered a gray metal desk, its legs and top rounded on the corners.

"Army surplus, circa nineteen forty-five," she quipped.

She inched her way behind it, flipping through folders, looking for an empty one. Multicolored tabs identified how many times they'd been reused. Penciled notations were scribbled across their surfaces. Sticky notes stuck out of current files like yellow quills.

"Please have a seat." She indicated a green swivel chair. Gabe handed her the files piled on it. She swiped off the last clean corner of her desk, snatching up a bottle of Wite-Out. "Can you believe it? They gave us *typewriters* for our reports. Not even electrics. It'll be carbon paper and inkwells next. Parchment!"

"I thought the clinic was new."

"The clinic is; the amenities aren't." She settled into an imposing leather chair, swiveling left and right. "File cabinets would be nice."

Gabe knew by her one-of-these-days shrug the place would never be clean.

"Maybe when we've proved ourselves the administration will pony up. As it was, all our start-up money went into lab equipment. Cameras, monitors, electrodes. It adds up."

"I guess sleep isn't cheap."

"Ha! That'd make a good T-shirt." She jotted it on the corner of someone else's file.

Gabe doubted she'd ever find it again. All the same, her laugh meant his sense of humor hadn't completely deserted him.

"So!" She scooted her chair forward. Pushing her glasses up her nose, she slid his form inside an empty manila folder.

The snap of the metal clip against the empty clipboard set his teeth on edge. "I must've been nodding off back in the waiting room."

She waved his explanation away, dropping the Wite-Out in a drawer with a clunk. "Happens all the time. One of these days I'm going to walk in there and everyone will be softly snoring away."

"Wouldn't that eliminate your job?"

"It *is* our job." She slapped the surface of her desk for emphasis. A small mound of folders deadened the impact.

"It doesn't matter *how* you help people as long as you *help*. That's my motto."

"Is it."

"Maybe it's my philosophy." She took off her glasses, sucking on a stem and staring into the middle distance. "Sleep is like love; does anyone ever get enough?"

"Of which?"

"Both. Both are essential to life and yet mysteriously out of our control. We can't make sleep happen any more than we can make ourselves love this person instead of that one." She leaned forward earnestly, arms folded across her front as if embracing her theory. "Like love, you can't give someone a magic potion and make sleep happen. That's what I meant about pills; they don't work for long. The side effects, ugh, you don't even want to know about the side effects. The half-life of some of these drugs— But to get back to the subject—"

His head pounded.

"A life without a good night's sleep is like a life without love. Everything else can be there but when that one element is missing—" Her throaty laugh rumbled through the room. "I'm sorry. When I get going it's hard to stop." She reached across the desk and set her hand on the telephone as if it were his arm.

He remembered the way she'd touched his knee, the sense of reassurance, the automatic generosity some women had. He scooted his chair a little closer. By then she'd leaned back.

"Lecture over," she said with a laugh. "When it's something I feel strongly about, I do tend to run on."

And she'd seemed so soothing in the waiting room. "No problem." He actually envied her enthusiasm. He'd lost his somewhere along the way. He shifted in his seat, pinching the crease in his slacks, crossing one leg over the other. It was time to play normal and well adjusted. "I take it sleep is a subject you know a lot about."

"Don't even get me started!"

"And love?"

"What about it?"

Gabe wasn't sure why he'd asked. Maybe love, or his inability to maintain it, was the real reason he'd come. "Love and sleep don't always go together."

"Of course not. You can love someone without sleeping with them. Parents, friends, siblings—"

"Women?"

"Well—"

"If a man doesn't sleep with a woman, she might get the idea he doesn't love her."

She slid her glasses back on, taking careful aim at a delicate subject. "Have sleep problems caused other problems in your life? Sexual problems?"

"No."

"It wouldn't be unusual. There's nothing more debilitating—"

"No problems with my sex life. Period."

"Ah. Good, then." She smiled.

He frowned. How had he blundered into that mess? He hadn't even planned on mentioning Mary Ann.

"And your *love* life?" she asked.

He gritted his teeth.

"Mr. Fitzgerald?"

"Call me Gabe."

"All right, Gabe. I noticed you referred to a relationship in the past tense in the waiting room."

Shit. Where was his brain? "I lived with someone. Two years. She wouldn't accept me staying up all night. She took it personally."

"I can imagine."

"Can you?" He lasered a look into her big brown eyes. He was wide awake now.

She stared right back, pleasant, open, nonjudgmental. Seconds passed. She established silently but firmly that he wasn't about to fluster her on her own turf. Message sent, she riffled through some papers on her desk.

Gabe rubbed his eyes. What the hell was he doing? He

wasn't there to put her on the defensive. He needed help. "Look, when do I get to see the doctor?"

"I am the doctor."

Just his luck. At least she didn't get huffy about his sexist assumption. "Nice to meet you, Doc."

"Nice to meet you. Shana."

"Pardon me?"

"Shana Getz. In case you'd forgotten. Doctorate in psychology from Purdue, primary experience in counseling and behavior modification." She pointed a thumb over her shoulder at a diploma on the wall. "Needless to say, I specialize in sleep disorders."

"Behavior modification. Is that like Pavlov's dogs, some kind of brainwashing?"

"Everyone, and I mean everyone, starts out treating sleep disorders on their own. They go to bed earlier or later; they drink warm milk or tea; they fiddle with the thermostat, the pillows; they watch the clock. Behaviors intended to fix the problem exacerbate it. For example, your running to wear yourself out. Did you know strenuous exercise actually *keeps* you awake?"

"Are you saying twenty years of insomnia is nothing but a bad habit?"

"You don't snore by any chance?"

"No."

"Have any of your sleep partners ever mentioned it?"

"My 'partners' as you call them have never complained."

She took more notes. "Short attention span? Shortness of temper?"

He scowled. "It's been mentioned."

She glanced up.

"I'm snarly. Or so I've been told."

"Snarly." She fought a grin. The pen scratched against the paper.

"Look, I know what the problem is. I have insomnia."

"Including the acute episode you're going through now."

"Yes."

She addressed her next question to her notepad. "These women in your life, they've objected to your not sleeping with them."

"That's what I said."

"And your inability to sleep drove them away?"

"Yes."

"Has it ever occurred to you that you might be using your insomnia to keep women at a distance? As an excuse not to get involved?"

He'd been rocking his chair until the wheels squeaked. The snakelike hiss of the radiator provided the only other sound in the room. Shana tapped her pen against her pad.

"I didn't come here to be psychoanalyzed."

"Sorry. I've been known to goad people. Tell my why you did come."

"I thought you'd know some tricks for helping me sleep."

"I know hundreds. Every one is a Band-Aid. Long-term cases of insomnia don't get solved overnight. So to speak."

"You're saying I'm nuts?"

"I'd never say that."

"That I've got a problem with women?"

"I wouldn't say that either."

He cast a glance at the window in the corner, cross-hatched with chicken wire. "Looks like a loony bin."

"I got the sense you blame yourself for the failure of this last relationship."

"It was my fault. Mary Ann didn't do anything."

She let the words hang in the air, an enigmatic smile on her face. "A woman trying to save a relationship will do a lot of things."

"Then it's my fault she gave up trying."

She set down her pen and leaned back in her chair. For a moment he thought she'd pull a Brice on him, steepling her fingers and pursing her lips. Instead she pulled her knees up sideways onto the chair, her hand loosely gripping her ankles. "You're dead tired yet you refuse to slouch. You haven't relaxed the tension around your eyes since you came in."

The people in his office barely made eye contact. Shana Getz read him like a cheap paperback. "I'm trying to keep them focused. I need sleep. That's all."

"You need to know why you put yourself through this."

"Because I can't sleep," he snapped.

Shana uncoiled her legs, spinning her chair slowly around. Tugging at piles of brochures on a shelf behind her, she glanced at the titles and stuffed half of them back. She soon had a handful in her lap and a mess on the shelf. She'd also given Gabe a moment to pull himself together.

Graciously overlooking his outburst, she delivered a set of instructions. "This is a sleep diary. For the next two weeks I'd like you to keep track of where and when you fall asleep, for how long, how deep, including all catnaps, episodes of dropping off, and microsleep—what you might call 'zoning out.'"

That's exactly what he called it.

"You may be surprised at how many hours you actually accumulate."

"I know how much sleep I get."

"I'm sure you do. After twenty years it's probably an obsession."

"Yes. No." He didn't know what answer to give. "I'm not neurotic if that's what you mean." Shadowy spots floated across her lab coat. His brain felt like a rusty engine, the pistons gritty with used motor oil. He was winding down, his second wind long gone.

She came around the desk and placed her hand on his shoulder. "At the end of two weeks I'd like you to come back. We'll discuss the results and schedule a night in the sleep lab."

"Sure." He lurched to his feet.

She placed her hand on his chest. His heart thudded beneath her palm. Her face had a fringy aura. Her eyes, exaggerated by her glasses, grew wider as he looked into them. Surprised, flattered, he liked that she wanted to be close to him. A lazy heat curled through him, energizing, fortifying. She tipped her chin, her lips parted. He leaned into her.

She shoved him back on his heels.

Gabe shook his head. Something wasn't clicking here. "We'll continue with our interview in two weeks."

"Interview with a vampire."

"Pardon me?"

"They call me the Vampire. Because I'm up all night."

"In that case all I can recommend is that you be home before dawn and keep the coffin closed."

His laugh grated like a wood rasp. He edged his way to the door. The frame tilted. He staggered through it before the whole thing collapsed.

"Gabe?"

The hallway loomed ahead. If only he could make it to the elevator.

Her arm wrapped around his waist. "You don't think for a minute I'm going to let you drive."

Her breasts were full and cushiony against his chest, her upturned face sweet but startled. Did she think he was going to kiss her? He remembered wanting to. He ran a finger tenderly down her cheek. "It's okay, honey. I can drive."

"And I could be sued for negligence. Come with me."

"Where are we going?"

"To bed."

He wished he could be of more help. His legs felt like lead and his brain had all the flexibility of cold oatmeal. Not only was he listing heavily to the left, something troubled him, something to do with beds. "We hardly know each other."

Unimpressed, she huffed. "Here's a room. Take a nap. Take your time. I'll write your next appointment on this brochure."

She seemed nervous, flustered. Maybe it had something to do with how quickly they'd gone from hospital to hotel room. As far as Gabe was concerned, life had stopped making sense hours ago. Caught in a dream, he went with it.

A bed floated on beige carpeting. The nubby bedspread reminded him of one he'd had a long time ago as a child. While Shana folded down the sheets, he sat on the edge, hands between his knees. He noticed a marred maple desk with chipped drawers, a steel sink and mirror. A camera was bolted to a corner of the ceiling. A honeycomb of white plastic covered the buzzing overhead lights. The room fell away as he tumbled backward.

"Timber!" she said.

He chuckled along with her. He liked the sound of her laugh. He liked saying her name. Maybe their going to bed wasn't such a bad idea. "Shana."

An answering "Sh" sounded from somewhere beyond his heavy lids. Someone tugged at his shoes.

He crossed his arms over his chest in a loose hug and rolled onto his side. She'd felt good, Shana had. When she'd put her arm around him she'd felt solid and real. She had none of those scarecrow ribs Mary Ann starved herself to achieve.

She was sturdy, fleshy, *pillowy*. She reminded him of a warm bed, rumpled and softly scented. Somewhere in his murky brain it struck him as funny, the notion of woman as bed. Woman as sleep. Woman as comfort.

Oblivion stole over him like a blanket, warm and woolen. He felt its scratchiness against his chin. A hand caressed his cheek. "Sweet dreams," someone whispered.

The door thudded softly shut.

He was gone.

3

"This building!" Shana sighed. The orderlies probably knew every inch. Maintenance people too. After six months, she still got lost at every turn.

She tried again to find her way through the empty corridors. Maybe she had early onset Alzheimer's.

He'd called her grandma.

Shana swung the gold chain over her head, stuffing her glasses in her pocket. He was beat, Mr. Fitzgerald was. His vision had probably been blurrier than hers. There was no reason, two days later, to obsess over his first impression of her.

Mr. Fitzgerald himself was another issue entirely. His was a complicated case, perfect fodder for her late-afternoon walk. Insomnia of that duration had multiple contributing factors. She could think of a dozen clinical approaches.

She thought of him, his pain, his lonely determination. Lack of sleep had isolated him, ruined relationships.

Ironic, she thought. For her, sleep itself ruined them.

Not many men enjoyed being kicked out of bed by a woman—literally. Her thrashing and nighttime wandering had unnerved more than one lover.

She strode on, her steps softly echoing beneath the vaulted tile ceiling of the fourth floor. Arched dormer windows cast crazy angled shadows on the floor, spilling off abandoned iron bedframes painted white. The unused top floor of Building D was so old Shana imagined Florence Nightingale passing through it with a candle in her hand.

Florence. Her dad had called her that because she wandered the house at night, sound asleep. It wasn't so cute when she grew up.

She turned the corner, resolutely looking on the bright side. So what if the failure of her third and final romance had driven her to Arizona? Flagstaff boasted the best sleep clinic in the country. Even if they hadn't cured her case, at least she'd found her passion in helping others. She knew what people went through, the humiliation, the lack of understanding.

"Why can't you sleep like a normal woman? Hell, Shana, I'm black and blue. How can any man sleep with you?"

She turned down the next corridor, her heart thumping with a pain unrelated to exercise. She forced her thoughts away from Stephen and back to the case at hand.

She'd put groggy patients to bed before. She'd handled the inevitable comments about "sleeping together," about her "bedside manner." She'd never come across a man more in need of help than Gabe. And yet, unlike most patients, he'd been curiously reluctant to spill the whole story. Pride? Male vanity? Shame?

Something else haunted him. Jingling the gold chain in her pocket, she took the next corridor as if chasing the demon down.

Beginning her third lap, she faced the fact that thinking about Gabe's case gave her a convenient excuse to remember the man: lean, striking features, well-honed body, intense ice-blue gaze. She remembered the taut muscles that stretched along his waist, the cant of his shoulders, the tension around his eyes.

A voice murmured up ahead, a distant conversation. Shana titled her head, slowing to a halt. She pictured a maintenance worker's cart with a radio perched on it. But who'd clean a deserted wing? A creeping sensation snuck up her spine.

Merryweather, the sleep clinic's director and resident psychiatrist, had warned her about wandering the deserted upper floors. There'd been an assault in the stairwell, a handful of muggings in the parking garage. Back in the city after three years away, she refused to succumb to urban paranoia.

She slowed to a halt anyway. Head cocked, she picked up two voices: one male, tense and low; the other female, wavering, pleading. Shana inched toward the corner, pressing her cheek close to the wall. She inhaled the musty leaden smell of peeling green paint. She peeked cautiously around the corner. The hairs on her neck prickled.

Sixty feet away, a couple huddled by the elevators. Even without her glasses, Shana could tell the woman was solidly built, of medium height, forty-five maybe fifty. Quality people, her aunt Shayna would say. She noted a dated but expensive winter coat drooping from slumped shoulders, a fur collar clutched in the woman's fist. It was the faces she couldn't make out.

The woman's shaking voice implored. The young man gave her a curt reply.

He was considerably younger. His voice and bearing communicated that. Thin, wiry, he wore a white lab coat that hung on him like a sheet.

A doctor? Shana thought. An intern? Up here? An orderly was more like it. But still . . .

There was something odd about the entire scenario. She fished out her glasses.

Light glinted off the lenses. The young man swung around. For one second Shana got a look at his face. She jerked the glasses off. The reaction was illogical, auto-matic, too late. He'd seen her. Nothing she did could erase the look of rage on his face, the startled beady glare of a snake who'd been stepped on.

A deafening silence filled her ears. Adrenaline shot through her system. She ought to say something, make some move. She stayed rooted. He looked familiar. Or was it the coat?

The older woman had barely registered Shana's pres-ence. Taking advantage of the distraction, she clawed something from the man's half-clenched fist.

Even at this distance, Shana knew a pill bottle when she saw one. She strode toward them. "Hey."

The young man gripped the woman's arm, tugging her toward the elevator as he punched the button.

"Hold on there." Shana broke into a trot. She knew junkies came in all shapes and sizes but, dammit, this was *her* building. This whole wing lived or died on the success of the Sleep Disorders Clinic. She wasn't about to ignore drug dealers in the corridors.

They jumped into the elevator.

"Hey!" Running all out, she skidded to a stop before the closed doors. She thumped on them with the side of her fist, pounding the carved graffiti in pure frustration. They'd gotten away.

"Shoot!" She paced up and down.

Maybe it was for the best, her conscience suggested. "Probably not too wise running after drug dealers," she muttered. It wouldn't be the first time she'd let her pas-sion get the better of her common sense.

In her own defense she noted that the woman had seemed more desperate than dangerous. As for the young man—

Shana cocked her head again. Did he work at the hos-pital? There were so many departments; she'd met so many people in the last six months. Maybe she'd seen him on the street. He could have donned the white coat as a disguise, slipping in a side entrance.

Ding.

She glanced at the elevator arrow. It was coming back.

Her heart slowed to a painful thump. She stepped backward. *Coming back.* The breath she'd been trying to catch froze in her lungs. Maybe they sent it back to disguise which floor they got off on.

Or else he'd decided to come back for her. A witness. A woman alone.

A voice in her head told her to run. She looked left and right. Nothing. Nowhere to go, no one to hear her if she screamed. He could step off the elevator with a gun in his hand, a knife.

She blinked in slow motion, trying to take it all in. This couldn't happen. It was crazy, impossible. The hospital had always been her castle to explore. She backed up one step, two. Her back hit the wall. Her knees locked.

The elevator hummed to a halt. Everything became unreal. The color drained from the walls. Seconds elongated to hours. She imagined the doors opening. He'd step out, his narrowed eyes full of fury, the vicious, cunning squint of a man she was sure she'd seen somewhere before.

In his penthouse apartment across town, Gabe awoke, a clammy film of sweat on his skin, a drumming urgency in his veins. Breath rasped out of his lungs, his chest heaving with fear. Like all the other dreams, he'd woken without realizing it. He stared at the ceiling with no sense of time having passed, no dividing line between dream and reality, sleep and wakefulness.

There was none. His dreams became reality. It was as if some god somewhere delighted in torturing him, handing him glimpses of a future he was helpless to change. If the purpose of this curse was to teach him humility, he'd been damn near drummed into the ground with it.

He sat up, his feet thudding against the carpet, his head in his hands. He couldn't change anything. Of all the dreams he'd had, good or bad, he'd never stopped one from happening. Yet.

Achy and exhausted, he stood up. Shana. He had to go to her.

But why her?

He ran a hand through his hair and kept moving. Staggering to the bathroom, he splashed water on his face and tugged on his jeans. Questioning the futility of his actions was as pointless as questioning their inevitability. He couldn't leave someone in danger—not when visions like the one he'd just had about Shana were handed to him on a platter.

God knew, he'd tried. To avoid dreaming, he'd avoided sleep, deliberately fragmenting the few hours he got, getting by on naps, shocking himself awake with alarms, working all hours. That experiment had failed.

So had the attempt to limit his involvements, short-circuiting relationships because the "real" dreams only involved people he loved.

Again the question prodded him. Why Shana Getz? He barely knew her. He'd spent the last two days trying to decide whether to go back to the hospital.

The thought brought back the dream, the crazy angles of light and shadow on linoleum floors, the scent of stale disinfectant, the gritty texture of green industrial paint, the stuffy unused air of a deserted corridor. The sound of an elevator whining to a stop.

That's where the dream stopped. Yanking a sweatshirt over a turtleneck, Gabe didn't know whether to be sorry or grateful. The dreams usually continued through every gory detail, patient, removed, like a documentary of things to come.

He padded across the penthouse apartment. Five-fifteen. In early January that meant pitch-black outside and bitter cold. She'd probably think he was crazy if he showed up at the hospital with such a way-out story. He wasn't so sure himself.

He called the garage to get his car ready. Waiting in

the hall outside his apartment, he reran the dream. Empty corridors. Light that had faded hours earlier.

The penthouse elevator slowed to a stop. A bell dinged, echoing deep in his mind. In the dream a sense of evil had hung in the air outside the elevator like a foul odor. He smelled fear, panic, a lurking danger ready to pounce. He stood completely still.

The doors parted.

Gabe stalked through Building C. Where the hell was she?

He'd dialed the clinic from his car phone, punching in the numbers as he weaved in and out of traffic. A woman named Fiona informed him Shana was gone for the day.

"Did you see her leave?" he demanded. "Could she be somewhere else in the building? In D not C?"

Fiona purred a few polite phrases about not releasing personal data.

Gabe gritted his teeth and clutched the steering wheel, purposely easing the tension in his voice. He could be as normal as anyone else—if he worked at it. He smiled, hoping she'd hear that. "Look, we've got a date. Our first. I hit traffic, I'm running late. I just want to know where to find her when I get there."

A cautious pause.

"To tell you the truth, my plans for dinner didn't include Shana chewing me out," he added in what he hoped was a casual voice.

The woman chuckled. "Shana? That's hard to imagine."

Hard to imagine her having a date or chewing a man out? he wondered. Gabe remembered leaning into her in her office. She'd put him in his place with smooth self-assurance. She'd also put him to bed. The woman could handle herself.

The dream flashed through his mind. Isolation. Danger.

He slammed the bottom of the telephone against the steering wheel as he swerved around a semi. He apologized into the receiver for the blaring horn. "Sorry."

"Sounds as if you should slow down," the woman replied.

Gabe glanced at the speedometer and gave the gas pedal more pressure.

"Try Maternity," she said at last. "Shana volunteers there on Thursday nights."

"Thanks." He hung up fast, the better to take the exit on two wheels. By the time he merged onto the Kennedy Expressway, he realized he didn't know which floor or building Maternity was in. Did it have long deserted halls? Graffiti carved into its elevator doors?

He slammed on the brakes, tires squealing to a halt inches from a Nissan's bumper. A leaden winter's darkness had covered the city. He waited with everyone else as an ambulance screeched past the line of cars, its beacons splashing blood red light on the snow.

Shana rocked softly back and forth. The chair squeaked. The room was tiny, airless, and sterile. She felt safe there. It was an eight-by-eight cell off the main maternity ward where volunteers rocked premature and abandoned babies. Beyond the blinds of its plate-glass window were the banks of bassinets in the main ward. Beyond them the faces of parents and grandparents filled the larger window on the hall. An orderly walked by, his white shirt wrinkled.

Waves of fear shuddered through her. A sick dread lurched through her stomach. She fought it down. Nothing happened, she reminded herself fiercely. The elevator doors had opened on an empty interior. An eerie silence had filled the space, vacant and malevolent.

Since then her heartbeat had almost slowed down. She hoped its erratic thump didn't communicate itself to the baby she held to her breast.

She rocked slower, comparing the man she remembered to the one who'd just walked by. This one wore a shirt, not a lab coat. This one had a round face, stocky build, darker complexion. The man on four had resembled a whippet, rangy, wiry, with pale skin and poor posture. Hunched, skulking, angry. He'd hated the woman who'd taken the drugs from him. He hated Shana for seeing it. Lucky for her he'd done nothing about it but run.

How many times had she promised herself to be more cautious, diplomatic, restrained in the future? How many times had she failed?

"About the same number of times your quick mouth and carved-in-stone convictions got you in trouble, kiddo."

She huddled over the child in her arms, doing her best imitation of her uncle Karl confronting his customers at the counter of the family bakery. "Tell me what you want here. You want short? Long? Sesame seed?"

The child's face puckered for another scream.

Shana traced her fingertips over its tiny lips. "Shh," she whispered, reminding them both they were safe. "It's okay. You want fairy tales? News reports? How about 'Drug Dealers on Four. Film at Eleven'?"

The baby needed her there, not back on four reliving a close call.

"Fairy tales it is. Once upon a time there was this princess." That was as good a start as any. "And she was quite beautiful—as princesses generally are. When she was born the king invited all the fairies in the kingdom to her christening. But one fairy was mistakenly left out. Furious, she cursed the child. She declared the girl would prick her finger on a spindle and die before her sixteenth birthday. Although they loved her very much, the child's fairy godmothers couldn't undo the spell. So they changed her curse of death to a sleep that would last a hundred years.

"And so Sleeping Beauty grew up with this curse hanging over her. The king ordered every spindle in the kingdom burned. But on the day before her sixteenth birthday, bored and maybe a little too curious for her own good, she wandered into a remote part of the castle. There she found an old woman spinning. Never having seen a spinning wheel or its sharp pointed spindle, Sleeping Beauty came closer—"

Shana slowed her rocker to a halt as her stomach tightened. "It was a really stupid thing to do."

Touching spindles or chasing drug dealers? her conscience asked. That man could have had a knife or a gun, even an infected syringe.

Shana turned her attention to the baby. "Moral of the story, kiddo, never share infected spindles."

She caught sight of a dark shape out of the corner of her eye. A frisson of fear snaked up her spine. A man had just passed the plate-glass window of the main maternity ward. There was something vaguely familiar about him, something urgent in his posture. He was searching for someone.

Every muscle in her body tensed. She held her breath until he came into view again. "Gabe."

The womb room had been soundproofed against the babies' crying. The glass tinted the harsh ward lights to a soft amber. That didn't stop Gabe from looking up when she spoke his name. His gaze connected with hers. A shivery heat caressed her skin.

4

She met him in the hall, beaming a thoroughly unwarranted smile. "I was hoping you'd come back."

"Were you?" He scoured her face for a sign.

He saw her steel herself. He knew the intensity he was capable of. To keep himself awake he focused every ounce of concentration on the person he was with. Looking at her upturned face, he knew there was more to it than that.

The moment he'd appeared she'd handed the baby to a nurse and come outside to meet him. "Thinking of having one?" she joked weakly, tilting her head toward the rows of infants on the other side of the glass.

His mouth tipped in a smile. Barely. His eyes remained fixed on hers. "I didn't know they did that anymore."

"Display them in new baby showrooms?"

They gazed at the delicatessen of children, brown, tan, raging pink. Half of them slept, their faces puffed with doughy smoothness. The other half clutched tiny fists to their chests, their wrinkled faces crumpled into silent cries.

A nurse entered the room to pick up a tightly wrapped bundle and bring it to the glass. A pair of doting grandparents gurgled. Gabe scowled. He watched the baby's squinched eyes. He'd felt like that, jerked around, badgered, woken from a sound sleep to be dragged places he didn't know, searching for a woman he shouldn't have been thinking about, much less dreaming about.

Let the baby sleep, he wanted to snarl. Can't you see he's tired?

The irritation was unreasonable and wholly familiar. He needed sleep. He couldn't have it. Not without the dreams.

He caught sight of his reflection. His drawn cheeks and sunken eyes made him look like a vampire in a blood bank. No wonder the nurse subtly drew the baby away from the window. The only person who didn't find his presence there odd was Shana.

She smiled up at him. She touched his arm. "I really am glad you came back."

He told himself not to care. He knew better than to trust his emotions when he was so tired. "Why?"

"I got the impression you weren't too happy to be here the last time."

"Is anyone?"

"Finding someone who can help can be a wonderful experience."

She was talking about sleep. He thought of her. He'd found her. She wasn't dead. She wasn't molested. She seemed perfectly fine. What a fool he'd been.

He ran a hand over his face, pacing the corridor he'd nearly taken at a run five minutes earlier. The real dreams had never proved false before. What the hell was going on here? he wondered.

First off, it wasn't *here* he'd dreamed of. These halls were painted jolly white, striped with baby-boy blue and little-girl pink. A mural of balloons and teddy bears greeted visitors as they stepped off the elevator. He'd vaulted out of it. Storming in, he'd demanded to see Shana Getz. The nurse behind the console probably thought he was nuts. He couldn't say he wasn't. Neither could he deny the rush of emotion that had careened through his system when he'd glimpsed her beyond that window, safe, unharmed.

She indicated her hospital gown, cap, and mask. "The babies are very susceptible to germs. I'm surprised you recognized me."

It had taken him only one look. Beneath the mask, tendrils of coiled blond hair had snuck out to frame her face. Above it, freckles dotted her broad cheeks. Brown eyes met his, warm as melting chocolate. Seconds before she'd been holding a baby as tenderly as any new mother would.

She could be one. What did he really know about her except that he'd imagined her in danger and come running? "I must have been a real asshole."

"Pardon me?"

He winced and apologized for his language. He covered expertly. No one knew about the dreams. No one alive. "I don't remember what I said or did at our last meeting. Except you putting me to bed."

There it was again, a weird connection, a subterranean kind of pull. Did he imagine that too?

Her eyes quickly sought the floor. She raised her arms to fiddle with the face mask's knot at the back of her neck. Despairing of ever figuring it out, she twisted it around to the front. "I wasn't sure whether our next appointment would work for you. I know I wrote something down."

"Next Friday at four."

"Good. Then you can make it?"

"I'll be in San Francisco."

"Oh." She'd begun strolling as they spoke. He remembered her restlessness last time, how she'd sent a wash of words over him, willing him to wakefulness.

Tonight she was more circumspect. Peering into a fire-extinguisher case, she used the glass as a mirror while she worried that knot. His reflection caught her by surprise as he came up behind her. "This darn knot," she said with a chuckle.

He rested his hands on her shoulders. "Let me."

"I can manage."

"Didn't you just say something about how good it is to find someone who can help?"

"This someone's all thumbs." Her deprecating smile was a vain attempt to hide the apprehension in her eyes. She'd been ducking him since he'd arrived, using every evasive tactic she could to pretend the attraction wasn't there.

He'd seen her in a dream. He wondered how she saw him.

He molded her collarbone with his fingers. Tension flared between her shoulder blades. Had something happened to her today? He couldn't tell. He sure as hell couldn't ask.

He tugged her imperceptibly closer. One pluck and the knot unraveled. "Better?"

"Great." She shoved the scrap of fabric in the breast pocket of her gown. "Thanks."

He slid her cap off, his open palm caressing her hair in the same motion. Ash-blond tresses tumbled around her face. Confusion clouded her features.

She rapidly finger-combed her hair into place, ringless fingers catching in the tangles. "About your next appointment—"

"About us. Something's happening here, Shana." Like a lot of things in his life, he couldn't explain it but he couldn't deny it either.

Perversely, his revelation relaxed her. She adopted a tolerant, indulgent smile, one that implied patients got crushes on their counselors all the time. "We need to talk about your sleep habits."

"Want to start with this afternoon?"

"What happened?"

"I had to make sure you were okay."

"Why would you—" Alertness darted through her eyes. Just as quickly, it disappeared. "I'm fine."

"Not in my dream you weren't."

"I don't know what you're talking about. Pardon me, I think I do. When starting something new, anxiety dreams are common. You've struggled with insomnia for twenty years." Striding down the hall, she put a quick distance between them. "Lifestyle changes, even good ones, can be threatening."

"What about elevators?"

She turned slowly on her heel.

"Are elevators frightening, or is it what comes out of them?" he asked.

She edged away, giving him a wary sidelong glance. "It wasn't you. I'd have recognized you."

He narrowed the gap instantly, backing her into the corner. "Who was he? What happened?"

"Nothing," she whispered.

"Being scared half out of your mind isn't 'nothing.' "

"How would you know?"

I was there. He'd dreamed it—but nothing beyond the elevator opening. The dream had stopped because the danger had ceased.

Relief settled in his stomach. He touched her face, the freckles on her cheeks. He barely knew her. He never dreamed of strangers. Then again, he never would've dreamed he'd do what he did next.

Kissing her seemed inevitable, preordained. Frigid cold, posted speed limits, a maze of hospital corridors—none of them could have stopped him from coming to her. The startled look on her face couldn't stop him from taking her in his arms.

His lips brushed hers. He felt the delicate radiating heat of her cheeks flushing pink. Her lips parted as she drew an unsteady breath. Her back tensed beneath his hands. He pulled her closer. "You're safe."

The words unlocked something in her, a yearning sur-render, a vulnerable, fledgling trust. Her mouth softened under his. Her body shivered.

"It's all right." He found himself trying to convince them both. Perhaps the spell had been broken; perhaps the dreams had lost their potency.

What began as inexplicable relief soon grew into a ba-sic man-and-woman need. She clung to him. He savored her taste, coffee and mints. A hint of perfume sifted through her hair. A part of her opened to him.

A part of him closed off. He didn't want her getting too close, becoming too important. He'd never been able to protect anyone he loved.

Who said anything about love? He broke off the kiss.

Trembling faintly, she stepped out of his arms. "What was that for?"

He had no business getting involved. What did he have to offer a woman besides crazy hours and unbeliev-able dreams? There was only one way out. He pulled her roughly against his body. "Cure me."

"I'll try everything I know. But Gabe—"

"Good evening, Shana."

She wrenched out of his grasp. "Dr. Payne."

A balding man stood behind them by the elevators. His body had the shape of a hard-boiled egg, his head a shiny oval. His eyes peered at them like blue stones under rippling water. Extremely cold clear water. "How are you, Dr. Getz?" He placed an insinuating emphasis on her title before stepping onto the elevator. "There's room for two more."

Shana shook her head. "Thanks, but we need to set up an appointment."

He glanced from Shana to Gabe. "I see."

Gabe's fists clenched.

"See you at the meeting?" The doors closed.

"Colleague?" Gabe asked.

Shana rolled her eyes. "He's the head of the commit-tee overseeing the sleep clinic's budget." As if realizing where they were, she stepped briskly onto the next open elevator.

Silent, they stared at the scratched graffiti. It looked as if someone had tried to claw their way out. The elevator began to rise.

"I can't believe we just did that," she declared.

"I believe in a lot of things."

"It isn't going to happen again. Not if you want me to help you."

They rose one floor. He followed her down a corridor to a crosswalk. They tramped through an unheated Plexiglas tunnel spanning the distance between Building C and Building D. So far Gabe hadn't seen anything that resembled the dream. Dingy walls lit by overhead lights turned amber with age and grime proved to be the familiar hue of the Sleep Disorders Clinic.

Fishing her office keys from her pants pocket, Shana unlocked her door and hurried to her desk. Neatly blocking him from entering, she returned with her weekly planner. "According to my book I can see you at ten A.M. Monday morning, if you prefer not to wait two weeks to discuss your problem."

"Fine."

He wasn't leaving this woman until he knew why she, of all people, had played a part in his dreams. He'd gotten three hours sleep—no wonder he wasn't thinking clearly. He should probably apologize for that kiss.

A short-haired brunette with catlike green eyes sauntered up beside them. "Hi, I'm Fiona. How's your date going?"

"Date?" Shana asked.

"Aren't you two going out?"

"I had to find you," Gabe explained.

Shana's eyes flashed daggers. "I bet you did." She slammed the door in his face. The sound echoed down the hall.

"Guess you didn't find her in time," Fiona said with a laugh.

He'd found her just in time. He just didn't know what on earth he was going to do with her.

"Okay, who is he?"

Wide-eyed, Shana glanced at the staff members gathered around the conference table. Flora Dava Coleman and Fiona Riordan sipped their morning tea, each one gazing in rapt attention at the television monitor.

It was Fiona who'd made the friendly accusation. She dunked a tea bag in her Star Trek mug. "I got here at nine last Tuesday night, flipped on the monitors, and what did I find? Sleeping Beauty in room two."

Shana gaped at the television set on the end of the table. The VCR hummed nearby. A grainy black and white picture showed a nondescript bedroom with a double bed. On top of the covers a half-naked man tossed and turned.

She'd watched hundreds of clinic tapes, but never one like this. Gabriel Fitzgerald wore one sock, the other was a black blot on the floor. His slacks were unzipped, his belt discarded. Above his waist whorls of black hair covered his chest, sweeping in a dozen different directions. The brush marks of an artist in a hurry, she thought. An artist who knew the male form very, very well.

But who knew the mind? More to the point, who really knew what went on during sleep? He'd claimed he dreamed of her in danger. How could he have known? She returned her troubled gaze to the screen.

On tape, he shifted. The open zipper on his slacks gaped. Shana clutched her can of diet soda. She knew the gap would reveal nothing but dark-colored boxers; she'd been *extremely* careful unzipping those slacks.

She'd been less cautious the previous night. Her body had brushed against his, her breasts skimming his chest with a light, indelible touch. Her nipples pebbled at the memory.

"Well?" Both staff members turned her way.

"I was trying to make him comfortable," she explained.

"Who's *him?*"

She moved smoothly around the table to her usual seat, shrugging inside her lab coat. "He's a patient."

"We can see that," Fiona and Flora said in unison. They squared off, arms folded across their chests, eyes boring in on her.

Apart from their similar poses, her two colleagues couldn't have been more different. Fiona Riordan was a raven-haired beauty with sparkling green eyes and pearly white skin. A graduate student at the University of Chicago and a confirmed night owl, she manned the sleep lab, monitoring patients all night while working on her master's thesis.

Flora Dava Coleman was another story. A stout black woman in her mid-fifties, she had the seen-everything air of a life-long nurse and mother of four sons. She'd gone back to school five years before to become a respiratory therapist. She specialized in sleep apnea. She swore she'd heard every kind of snore from fluttering whispers to roaring freight trains.

She also swore she'd see Shana married before she retired. She had ten years to work on it.

Setting out her folders in three lopsided piles, Shana pretended to ignore them both.

"Fess up, girl," Flora demanded. "Who is he? Did you pick him up off the street?"

"Is he one of your charity cases?" Fiona asked.

Shana's mouth fell open. "Does he look like a charity case?"

All three women stared at the screen. The man was no derelict.

"My, my, my." Flora shook her head in pure admiration. Her hair moved with the motion, heavily sprayed and straightened into a shoulder-length Jackie Kennedy sweep.

Her necklace, a strand of chunky gold links, matched her earrings exactly. Her collarless red suit complemented the rosy tones in her medium-brown skin. Her nylons matched her shoes. Flora was fashionably flawless.

Shana, on the other hand, covered whatever garments she'd grabbed from her closet with her no-fail lab coat. Her idea of makeup was a dab of concealer for the circles under her eyes and a swipe of blush for her pale cheeks—two swipes, if she went out for the evening.

She briefly wondered when she had last needed a new blusher. She'd never need it again if she kept thinking of Gabe's lips brushing hers. He'd been possessive and tender, a seductive combination. "He's just a patient."

"Do I have his file?" Dr. Merryweather strolled in, a cup of black coffee halfway to his lips.

Shana sighed in relief. Their chief of staff was a boyish forty-year-old gay psychiatrist, shrewd, soft-spoken, even-tempered. Although every staff meeting involved some good-natured teasing, he'd soon get them down to business and off the subject of Shana's new patient.

Merryweather paused to watch the TV screen. Adept at handling the politics of a big-city hospital, he was as territorial as a Rottweiler when it came to securing funds for his department, and as tolerant as a doting uncle when it came to supporting his staff. "Okay, Shana, if he's a patient, why isn't he hooked up?"

"Because we weren't supposed to tape him."

"That is one of our rooms."

"He needed a place to sleep."

"Shana—"

"Chronic insomnia compounded by severe sleep deprivation. I wanted to make sure he had some rest before he got in his car and drove straight into the headlines; 'Busload of Children Killed by Man Asleep at the Wheel.'"

Everyone nodded. They knew a sleepy driver was as dangerous as a drunk.

"He was so groggy, I insisted he sleep it off."

"Now there's a cure for insomnia," Merryweather drawled. " 'Sleep it off.' " He took his place at the head of the table. "So what's your game plan regarding our mystery guest? Offer him bed and board? Tuck him in?"

He had no way of knowing she'd done that. Especially since the near-naked Mr. Fitzgerald had kicked off all his covers. "He contacted me yesterday regarding a follow-up consultation." She didn't specify the kind of contact. "My game plan is to evaluate his sleep diary and continue from there."

"Fine." Merryweather leaned back in his chair, pulling a pipe from his coat pocket.

As the meeting officially started with this customary signal, the staff reviewed the cases they'd brought for discussion. While Merryweather made up an informal agenda, Shana's gaze strayed to the screen. Even asleep, there was something disturbing about Gabe, something that extended beyond sinewy good looks. Twenty years of insomnia had forged a tough and unyielding man. Even in his sleep he kept his guard up. He was hard on himself, that was clear.

And strangely gentle with her.

On screen his taut skin shone with a light film of sweat, his slumber disturbed by the onset of unknowable dreams. A frisson of physical awareness skittered beneath Shana's skin. He'd dreamed about her.

Coincidence, she assured herself. It was something instinctive, like deciding to kiss her when she was at her most vulnerable and shaken.

Merryweather tapped his pipe onto a napkin. He proceeded to scrape out the insides in a complicated ritual involving pen knives and pipe cleaners. Satisfied with the mound of ash he eventually produced, he glanced at his staff. "Didn't you have someone scheduled last night, Flora?"

"Another apnea case."

"Are we done with this?" Fiona fast-forwarded Gabe's tape. The numbers in the bottom corner raced toward midnight.

Half listening to Flora's case, Shana watched Gabe's

every move. He awoke. He swung his legs over the edge of the bed, hunched his shoulders, and gripped the edge. He reminded her of a boxer who'd fought a tough bout the night before and was paying the price the next day.

"She's a goner."

"I'll say."

Her gaze rocketed to Fiona and Flora. Both women watched her with undisguised pleasure.

"Told you she liked him," Fiona teased.

"Who wouldn't?" Flora answered.

"So I sympathize with a patient," Shana snapped.

"Is that what it's called?" Flora inquired archly.

"How would you feel if you'd gone forty hours without sleep followed by a twelve-hour knockout punch?"

"Knockout is right." Fiona sighed. "The man's gorgeous."

"He is *not* gorgeous," Shana stated emphatically.

"Speak for yourself," Merryweather murmured, an appreciative smile curving his lips. He watched Gabe shrug into his shirt, splash his face with water, and leave the evaluation room. "Straight or gay?"

"Straight," Shana replied, making it clear it was nobody's business either way. "He said something about losing a girlfriend."

Merryweather tsked, tapping his pipe stem against his lower teeth. "Too bad."

"The majority of married people meet on the job," Flora reminded her for the umpteenth time.

"Those are co-workers. Doctors don't date patients." Shana looked to Merryweather for confirmation.

He stuck his thumb in the bowl of his pipe.

"Nonsense, child," Flora said. "In the real world people cross the line all the time. Take 'em where you can find 'em, I say."

Shana closed her eyes and took a deep breath. "You people amaze me. It's like having a trio of fairy godmothers hovering over me."

Merryweather pursed his lips. "Watch who you're calling a fairy, dear."

She gave in and laughed with the others. Honestly, their matchmaking would have been funny if she didn't get the same thing from her family every Saturday morning. "Marriage isn't for me."

"So live in sin," Flora said.

"Live dangerously," Fiona agreed.

"Live a *little*," Merryweather murmured.

"I'm single and single I'll stay. Get used to it." She yanked on the chain that held her glasses. Flora called them schoolmarmish. She called them convenient. At least she didn't lose them twice a day the way she used to.

She read from Gabe's form in a testy voice. "Thirty-four, employed, college-educated. Not overweight, doesn't smoke, no drinking or drug problem that we know of. From our brief interview I deduced his chronic insomnia is exacerbated by poor sleep habits. In other words, a good case for me."

"Here, here."

"I'll second that."

"He's for you, all right."

Shana shot them all a quelling look. "His sleep is disrupted and brief. We didn't get into dreaming states."

"The man's a walking dream" Fiona said.

"I'd like to live in *his* state," Flora added.

Shana rolled her eyes. "Those are the behavioral aspects. There's also the possibility of depression as an underlying cause—due to the collapse of that previous relationship."

Merryweather perked right up. "Depression would be my territory. Thinking of sending him my way?"

"I can manage." Could she? She remembered Gabe's responses to her questions about his last relationship. He'd seemed on the verge of giving up—the way she had. She wouldn't let him. Her sleepwalking might be incurable, but his insomnia wasn't. She wasn't about to give him up.

Give up on *him,* she corrected herself silently. "Could we *please* move on to other business?" she pleaded.

Merryweather scooted forward in his chair. "This Fitzgerald wouldn't be the financier, by any chance?"

Shana raised both brows over the rims of her glasses as she scanned the form. "Under Employment he wrote 'stocks and commodities.' "

"Bingo! We've hit the lottery."

The staff traded looks.

"He's a major player." Merryweather reeled off the names of half a dozen investment newsletters that had featured Gabriel Fitzgerald. "He manages money for some of the world's top investors."

"Venture capital?"

Merryweather gave Shana the charitable but patronizing look he reserved for someone who thought an IRA was a major investment. "Considerably more than that. Cure him and he might be very grateful. The hospital board is always impressed by massive endowments and generous one-time gifts."

Shana knew her boss wasn't entirely joking. "Now I'm after him for his money *and* his body?"

Merryweather's grin made him look ten years younger. "You could do worse."

Flora tapped the top folder on her stack. "Can we get back to my case?"

Merryweather blinked. "Flora. Excuse me. I was temporarily blinded by the dollar signs."

"You can't be that desperate."

"If you'd heard the hard time Payne gave me the last time I reported to his committee, you'd be scrounging for outside sources of income too."

"We've been here a year," Flora argued. "They can't pull the rug on us that fast."

"Are we in trouble?" Shana asked.

"We're fine." Merryweather smoothly avoided her glance. "Flora, your case."

Flora settled her tortoiseshell glasses on her nose. "I've

got a woman who's been in three times for sleep problems. She has only one: her husband. The man snores so bad he sounds like a spoon caught in a garbage disposal. Naturally he denies everything."

"Not that he'd be awake to know," Merryweather said.

"The only sleep she gets is three nights a week when he's away."

"Second family? Hidden mistress?"

"If he has one, she's deaf."

"Have you tried the tape-recorder trick?" Shana asked.

"We loaned the wife one last week. From the sound of it he not only snores, he stops breathing every few minutes."

"Classic apnea," Fiona stated.

"You've got it," Flora agreed.

"Your approach?" Merryweather asked.

"I've asked the wife to come to one of your group sessions, Shana. She'll have him drive her and ask him to sit in."

"A setup."

"It's the only way we'll get him in."

"How about Wednesday?"

"Perfect."

Shana patted her pockets for a notepad and ended up jotting the information on a scrap torn from an old report. An unusual approach for a sleep clinic, her group sessions had caught on.

"You might add Mr. Fitzgerald to your list," Merryweather murmured.

She'd been wrestling with the thought. After that kiss, group encounters might be safer. "I will if you promise not to hit him up for money."

"Done." Merryweather added a couple of candidates from his own list. "Aurora Bennett, Doris Cain. Both need psychiatric care, but immediate behavioral changes should improve their sleep."

"Looks as if we'll have a full class. Flora, what was your husband-and-wife team?"

"Shirlee and DeVon Johnson. He's an engineer at the rail yards."

"Tell me what trains he runs and I'll take another route home," Merryweather joked.

Flora nodded. "You just might. He's self-medicating with alcohol."

Shana rolled her eyes. "Alcohol makes people sleepy then disrupts their sleep the rest of the night."

"Tell *him* that."

"I will."

The staff traded smiles while Shana wrote. When she felt strongly about something she wasn't shy about expressing it.

Interfering bitch. About time she left the conference room. The others had left five minutes ago. Not Shana Getz. Poking her nose where she didn't belong. Asking questions. Snooping. She probably called it "concern."

The sneer felt good, a rictus reflected in the window of the staircase door at the end of the hall.

Not that she'd notice, plodding down the hall absorbed in her do-good theories. Clothes never right. Hair never combed. Could be beautiful. Was without half trying. Slut. Next time she interfered she'd find out the consequences.

Hate felt even better, invigorating, head-clearing. Better than fear. Anything was better than the clawing, barbed-wire sensation, like a thousand insects screaming to get out, or the clamminess of nerves that came when someone like her was on the verge of finding out.

Then again, that was half the excitement, wasn't it? She wanted people to sleep. Maybe she should try it, a real sleep, the kind you didn't wake up from.

5

Juggling files in both arms, Shana glanced at her watch. An hour and fifteen minutes; not bad for a staff meeting. She fumbled a key into the lock on her office door.

"Shana?"

She jumped and whirled.

"Sorry to scare you." Merryweather grinned, slipping his pipe back into his pocket. "Just wanted to mention something."

Crossing warily to her desk, she set her folders atop a pile of paperwork and sank into her swivel chair. Merryweather only dropped by when there was trouble. "What did I do now?"

He perched on the desk's edge, the veritable image of a pipe-smoking gentleman in a book-lined library. "I talked to Payne yesterday."

"An apter name was never bestowed."

"He's in charge of our budget."

"Slashing and burning it."

"He saw you in Maternity."

"I volunteer there."

"And pester the nurses to turn down the lights?"

"Preemies can be hypersensitive to light. They need a peaceful sleep environment."

"Doctors need to read their charts."

"Are we here to help the patients or the providers?"

"We're here not to piss off the people who pay our salaries."

She took a deep breath. "I'm rocking the boat, I know, but—"

"But nothing. Every time you raise a fuss I have to unruffle the feathers. I'd appreciate you steering clear of Payne."

Shana bit her tongue. "He has to care about babies."

"He cares about power. And I care about this department. You're making an enemy we don't need. Point taken?"

Shana nodded.

Merryweather rose to exit. "Be careful, okay?"

Unfortunately, being more careful was one of her New Year's resolutions, not one of her talents. She excelled at passionate engagement with causes, not tactful compromise.

"Shoot!" She rushed after him into the hall. "Michael?"

He turned.

"My report, the one about the people I saw on the fourth floor. What did Security say?"

"I didn't show it to them."

Her mouth dropped open.

He closed the distance between them, lowering his voice to a harsh rasp. "You want me to hand Payne an excuse to raze the entire building? I'll talk to Security myself. *You* keep your mouth shut."

He saw the shock on her face. Rubbing a thumb across the lines in his forehead, he looked suddenly older. "I'm sorry, Shana. I've been under a lot of pressure lately. Payne is not a man I enjoy going up against."

"I'm sorry if I put you in that position."

"It's not just you. No hard feelings?"

"None."

She closed her office door, her empty stomach churning. Merryweather *was* under a great deal of pressure. They were all doing their best to make this clinic a success.

She noticed the videotape on her desk. Hospital politics aside, she had a more pressing problem. She had a patient whose compelling intensity drew her like a magnet. Who, it turned out, was worth millions. Whom they'd taped without his permission.

Not that he needed to know. She could tape over it, toss it. Take it home and watch it. Repeatedly.

She laughed at her audacity. Actually, they could sell tickets. Probably make a fortune.

The message light flashed on her phone. Come Monday she'd have to sit across this desk from a man nicknamed the Vampire and tell him what had happened. Did she have a knack for finding trouble or did it find her?

She could erase the tape. Stonewall. Cover it up. Where had she heard that combination before? "Does the name Watergate mean anything?"

She sighed. There was only one ethical choice. Tell him. And hope he didn't sue.

Gabe sat across from her, his long legs crossed, one arm crooked over the back of a chair he'd set gently rocking. Gone was the tension that coiled around his eyes when he'd seen her in the maternity ward. It had been replaced with a lazy relaxation, a seductive repose that made the distance between them seem even smaller. He looked considerably better.

Apparently he liked the way she looked. His gaze traveled up and down her body. It rested briefly on her name tag, the breast beneath it.

He smiled.

Shana gulped. Her chest felt tight. She hadn't realized how difficult this second official meeting would be. She fiddled with a loose button on her lab coat. Maybe she should mention that kiss, just to get it out of the way.

He smiled wider.

She couldn't. She'd have to trust she'd laid that issue to rest in the maternity-ward elevator. She began with the obvious. "You look much better."

"I feel better."

"How have you been sleeping?"

"Deeply." He pulled his ankle up onto his knee. The fabric of his slacks stretched taut across his crotch.

Shana dove into a pile of paperwork. "Let's get down to business, then."

She ignored his softly murmured, "Let's."

With the sincere remorse of the hopelessly disorganized, she searched desperately through the stacks on her desk. She should have had his folder there and ready to open. Towers of paperwork teetered and swayed. Like a nightmare, they seemed to grow as she rummaged through them. "Aha. Here you are."

"Here we are," Gabe repeated.

Teenage girls working the drive-through at Burger King probably went weak at the knees at the sound of a voice like that, Shana thought. Of course, a man like Gabriel Fitzgerald ordering meals at Burger King was probably as uncommon as her having a crush on a patient.

This is crazy, she thought frantically. If only she hadn't seen him in bed, tossing and turning, his body glistening—

"You wanted to see me?"

She'd seen plenty. She'd also kissed him back. "I wanted to continue where we left off last time. I mean, your first appointment."

"This time I hope I'm awake enough to appreciate what's really going on here."

She sincerely hoped not. "Mr. Fitzgerald—"

"Gabriel. Don't tell me you forgot."

How could she forget the name of the archangel? Especially when he gave her the most devilish looks?

He knew, she thought. He saw through her nervous gestures and total lack of eye contact and he *knew* how much she'd put into that kiss.

The radiator worked overtime. Her chair squeaked each time she moved. Perspiration tickled her skin inside her clothes, making her incredibly aware of her body. She longed to take off her coat. She remembered her T-shirt, a gift from a patient who'd overcome particularly poor sleep habits. "Good in Bed" it said.

She came clean. "Gabe, I simply must apologize. I have something I'm sorry to tell you."

"You're married."

She croaked a laugh. "Ha, ha. No." Her flippant wave fooled no one. She wasn't good with men. Actually, she wasn't bad. She'd had relationships. Some of them had proceeded all the way to bed and *then* they'd fallen apart. "We taped you."

"You what?"

She swung around in her chair and retrieved the black plastic box. When she swung back he was still smiling. This time a cautious glint lurked in his blue eyes.

"The night tech on duty in the sleep lab the evening you were here filmed you sleeping. It's common practice, we do it all the time."

"Do you?"

"I'm apologizing because we didn't have your permission."

"Ah." He took the tape from her, his tapering fingers touching hers. Their gazes met and held. "Did you watch it?"

Where were those stacks of folders when she needed a place to hide? "A little. You seemed to have slept well."

"Like the dead." One side of his mouth curved up.

She'd never noticed the way his brows arched, like Gothic windows in a gloomy cathedral. He had an air of the fallen angel about him, the devilish rogue, the lost soul. He'd referred to himself as something of the sort, though she couldn't remember exactly how.

She felt light-headed. The atmosphere was too close. She'd been lost in his eyes too long. She needed air. She could handle this. She rose, her legs shaking, and edged her way around her desk. From there to the window seemed like miles.

He turned his head, following her with his eyes. His body seemed unnaturally still. Hers seemed unbearably energized. Her pulse skittered through her veins. Her breath skimmed in and out of her lungs.

"So you've been sleeping better," she said, making conversation, gripping the window frame. The wood was ancient, the paint peeling and dry. She shoved. The frame didn't budge. Pressing her wrists against the chilly glass, she tried again. Her breath frosted the pane. She inhaled the musty odor of rotting wood.

Gabe reached around her from behind. She froze, her breath trapped in her lungs. He rested his thumbs on her knuckles, splaying his hands on either side of hers. In one sharp move he thrust the window upward. The wood screeched like an angry bird.

In the ensuing silence, traffic noise rose from the street below. Cold air flooded the room, slithering into the gaps of her coat, shocking her with its icy fingers. She turned with great effort. Sagging against the sill, she gripped the splintery wood on either side of her thighs.

Gabe rested his hands on her shoulders. "Shana."

She'd heard that whisper before. It echoed in her memory. Once before she'd seen the curve of his mouth as he murmured her name. He'd been so groggy when she'd put him to bed a week earlier. So harmless.

When he'd kissed her in the maternity ward, he'd been completely different, powerful, protective.

His grogginess was long gone. A feral alertness sharpened his features. He lingered over her name like a starving man after a gourmet meal. His lids lowered. He concentrated on her lips. She longed to taste his.

She fought for air, for sense. She couldn't do this. Whirling in the tight circle of his arms, she flattened her palms against the glass. They instantly formed a misty outline, ten fingers clutching thin air.

His fingers closed over her wrists like talons capturing her hammering pulse. His thumbs curled into her damp palms. Mingled breaths frosted the pane, blotting out the world outside.

"Please," she panted. She was slipping, her will ebbing with every weak breath. This wasn't right. She pressed her cheek to the window, letting the mind-clearing reality of bitter cold bite into it. The chill penetrated her clothing, pebbling her breasts. The hard line of the sill pressed across her thighs.

An eerie, incongruous warmth whispered across her face. His breath. He lifted her hair off her neck. She tried to protest. Her lips barely parted. "I can't believe we're doing this again."

"Believe."

"We can't."

"We can."

He kissed her, a gentle sweep across her cheekbone, a dry rasp from her ear to her jaw to her neck. She held her breath until her lungs ached. Her body felt heavy and numb, every nerve concentrated along the undefended corridor of her bared throat. Blood pounded thick and restless through her limbs.

His lips paused on her throat. His hot tongue laved her dry skin. A cry rose in her, halted by the sudden sharp drag of his teeth against her flesh. He traced a line downward, downward, exquisitely painful, unbearably precise.

She turned her head from side to side, futilely resisting. Her lips smeared the glass in a silent scream. Her head lolled back. She was terrified. She was ready. The penetration was sweeter than anything she'd ever known.

The rumble of a far-off train invaded her cloudy mind. Her eyelids flickered. It took all her will to open them. A line of light, narrow as a razor, sliced through them. She shut them tight. From now on everything would be darkness and Gabriel.

The rumble grew louder. She'd never realized an elevated train ran past the hospital on this side. She tried desperately to lift her hand, to wave to the oblivious riders, to cry out. But would her cry be one of fear or ecstasy?

With exquisite patience he drained her of blood, breath, the will to fight. He suckled at her neck like a baby then he wrapped her in his arms like a man. One hand spread upon her abdomen as he urged her closer, his body molded to hers from behind. Flames licked at her, consuming her. She knew if she surrendered she'd be his for eternity.

The roar intensified. The train—The people—She had to fight, to struggle, to cry out—

"Wake up, Chicagoans! It's another sunny day!" The blaring voice of a morning deejay jolted her eyes open.

Shana smacked the snooze control, burying her face in her pillow. "No," she moaned.

A train grumbled inches away. Glaring through squinted lids, she fixed a look at the fifteen-pound tabby cat crouched on the pillow beside her. His green eyes stared back indifferently, his motor in high gear.

Six A.M. Breakfast time. "Romper, please."

She'd kicked off the covers. Her nightgown was wound around her waist. A breeze from the open window slithered across her bare behind.

She rolled onto her back and clamped both hands to her face. The next time she used the phrase "in my wildest dreams" she'd know exactly which one she meant.

Romper whined, pawing at her hair as it snaked out over the pillow. She scruffed his head. He hated that. Giving his ears a violent shake, he scooted off the end of the bed. Tail high, he tossed her a baleful look and headed for the kitchen.

She padded after him, automatically gauging the state of the living room, the kitchen, the entryway. If she'd tried sleepwalking out the main door, she'd have set off the alarm and woken herself. As it was, the apartment seemed undisturbed by any nighttime wandering.

She viewed it as a good omen, a bright antidote following a wretched week. Putting the dream out of her mind, she reviewed her schedule: two appointments, a short meeting with Merryweather—

It still astonished her that he'd lost his cool. Granted, Payne was a man one didn't want on one's bad side, but if the cause was worth fighting for, like babies trying to sleep despite glaring overhead lights . . .

She gave the bathroom mirror a wry look. "Lecturing *me* now?"

What she had to remember, for the hundredth time, was that her passions got the better of her. She could've gotten herself killed chasing that drug dealer on the fourth floor. She'd butted heads with the man in charge of their budget—more than once. She didn't want to alienate the man who'd hired her.

"Tact," she chanted like a mantra. "Diplomacy. Prudence. Circumspection." Those rare and cherished qualities would come in handy when she dealt with her other little problem, Gabe Fitzgerald and the unauthorized videotape. They had an appointment at ten.

Applying just a hint of blush, she glanced in the mirror, remembered the dream, and turned bright red. Mondays didn't come any worse.

A cab nearly clipped him. The horn blared on the empty street.

Gabe didn't blame the guy. The gray light of a grim January morning outlined the buildings in blurry shadows. He'd been running for nearly an hour, ignoring the lights, treating the streets as his own. No one else wanted them.

The bitter cold galvanized his lungs. He'd gone looking for this kind of loneliness. No matter how many miles he ran, he couldn't erase the dream.

Thankfully the dream hadn't been a real one. It had

lacked the unearthly clarity, the sense of real time unfolding. That didn't mean it had lacked punch. It had been a no-holds-barred, red-blooded, body-throbbing wet dream. He hadn't had one in years.

Glancing left and right, he darted across another intersection. He squinted into the frigid breeze off Lake Michigan. The dry version of a cold shower did no good. The dream stayed with him, like perfume on a woman's skin, red wine clinging to the palate.

The images had evolved in slow motion, languid, beguiling. A shadowy room, a satiny bed. Filmy fabric draped a woman's luscious contours. He'd drawn it down, tracing his fingertips over milky skin, a peach fuzz as fine and delicate as her indrawn breath. She'd wanted him. He saw it in her eyes, Shana's deep brown willing eyes.

He'd covered her soft body with his sinewy one. They fit perfectly. He'd moved from heated flesh to moist core, his mouth zeroing in on her ripe breasts as he entered her. Taking her at his own pace, he'd driven into her until their groans entwined like limbs, farther, hotter, faster. She'd begged him—

In the predicting dreams he stood by, a paralyzed witness to events beyond his control. Until the elevator dream, those events had always involved someone he loved. He'd limited that circle. Then Shana had entered his dreams.

The question still nagged him. Why? He'd gone to her because he wanted to change. Maybe the dreams were changing, their scope widening to include people who were important to him for other reasons. Shana was important because she could cure his sleeplessness, as a doctor not a lover.

The good doctor couldn't cure his aching body. A sharp inhale brought icy shards of air into his lungs. His sweatshirt chafed against his chest, a prickle of sweat crawling down his back.

Brice had once compared him to a scalpel, slicing straight to the point. He needed Shana to break the cycle, the sleeplessness, the sense of being an eternal outsider. Once she cured his insomnia, he'd handle the dreams himself. He always had.

As for last night's X-rated fantasy, that was between him and the bedsheets. He had other issues to settle.

He staggered to a lamppost, bracing an outstretched arm against it. His apartment building towered in the distance, the lights of the empty penthouse glowing. The lines of a poem his grandmother used to recite flowed through his mind. *For I have promises to keep. And miles to go before I sleep.*

6

At ten forty-five Monday morning, Gabe's folder lay open on Shana's desk. Notepad at the ready, she'd cleared away her case histories and made a dozen nearly neat piles along the wall. No hiding behind nightmare towers for her. She was armed and ready.

He was late.

She cupped her hand over her telephone's message light. Shielded from the bright morning light flooding in the window, it refused to flash.

She reviewed her list of questions regarding his sleep history. Other questions badgered their way to the top of the list—such as why he'd kissed her. She was no Sleeping Beauty. After a long day of work and an hour in the womb room, she couldn't have looked very enticing. After her encounter on four, she'd probably looked completely frazzled.

The strength of her curiosity served as a warning to avoid the subject. She was there to counsel him on methods to improve his sleep efficiency. Case closed, lips sealed.

So where was he?

She tapped the plastic box holding her paper clips, maneuvering it into line with her telephone pad, her pen holder, her unopened address book. The only time she organized objects—or cleaned house, her mother claimed—was when she was nervous.

When she slept she *disorganized* things. Dishes got taken down from cupboards, furniture was rearranged, clothes were strewn from closets as if in preparation for a trip. Wandering, her father had called it. Or searching.

For what? What could a woman spend her life searching for? What dreams did she long to act out?

"Good morning." Gabe leaned in the doorway, arms crossed over his chest, one long leg crossed over the other. The overbright window cast a diagonal shadow across his face.

Shana popped out of her chair like burned toast from a toaster. "Mr. Fitzgerald. Please. Do come in. Have a seat. I'm afraid you caught me daydreaming."

"Those can be the best kind."

It wasn't anything compared to the dream she'd had the previous night.

He took a seat.

She smiled. Silly, really. His eyebrows weren't arched like Gothic windows, they just had a certain slant to them. His eyes were a very standard blue, his face softened by a surprisingly charming smile. "I brought the sleep diary even though it's been only a week."

"Thanks." She reached for the slim form. Before his fingertips got within six inches of hers, she yanked it out of his hand. "Thanks."

"I'll be curious to see what you think."

As long as he didn't ask what she dreamed.

She shoved her glasses onto her nose, the gold chain swaying rhythmically as she bent over the form. She comprehended about twenty-five percent of it. She had to get this tape business out of the way. She took a deep breath.

Gabe sat across from her, one arm crooked over the back of the chair he'd set rocking. "Well?" He pulled his ankle up onto his knee. His slacks stretched taut across his crotch.

Shana tugged at her turtleneck. In her stuffy overheated office, the collar choked her. His eyes lingered on her throat. She snatched her fingers away.

His gaze slid slowly downward, resting briefly on her name tag and the breast beneath it. He frowned.

"Is there some reason you're staring at my chest?" she blurted out.

Startled, he apologized. "Correct me if I was hallucinating but I remember you wore funny T-shirts. 'Madam Sandman.' You've got your coat buttoned so high I couldn't tell if you had one on or not."

"I don't."

The conversation faltered. Tracing the edge of the worn-out carpet, Gabe darted a glance at the books piled helter-skelter in her bookcase. He looked embarrassed, angry, a man used to being in control. "About my first visit. I've gone a lot longer than forty hours without sleep and handled it better."

"With the little sleep you get, you don't have the reserves most people have."

"What excuse do I have for what happened in the maternity ward?"

A hot flash darted through her. "No explanations necessary."

"I told you a little about my dream."

She'd had more than enough of dreams. She reached into her drawer. "Before we go any further, I'm afraid there's something I have to tell you. We taped you."

"I beg your pardon?"

"It's I who must beg yours."

Good Lord. She sounded like something from *Forever Amber*. She cleared her throat. "We taped you sleeping.

Inadvertently. The night tech didn't know you weren't a patient. Yet. If you'd been one, we'd have hooked you up to electrodes, a heart monitor, measured your oxygen levels, eye movement, leg movement, et cetera." She was babbling. She peered beseechingly at him over the rim of her glasses. "You won't sue, will you?"

He barked a startled laugh. "How bad was it?"

"It's not bad at all."

"I didn't talk in my sleep, did I?"

"Not at all."

"Walk around?"

As if that were the worst thing a person could do. "For the record, you slept twelve hours straight, got up, got dressed, and went home."

"If that's all . . ." He extended his hand.

Their fingers touched as she handed him the tape. A jolt of electricity arced up her veins.

Gabe read the writing on the label. After a long moment he glanced up. "Was that a shock?"

"Seeing you on tape? Yes. No. I mean, not really. We watch people sleep all the time. It's what we do. There's nothing personal about it."

His grin crooked at the corners. "I meant the electric shock between us."

He'd felt it too. She plucked at her turtleneck. "Dry in here."

"Is it?" His brows rose in a definitely devilish manner. She smiled wanly. "Stuffy."

"Then open a window." He might as well have suggested they fly out it.

"We can't."

"Why not?"

"It's stuck."

"I could help you with it."

She wasn't doing anything to make that dream come true no matter how innocent he looked—which wasn't very. "I don't think so."

"Let me give it a try." He was halfway out of his chair.

She was all the way out of hers, and desperate to change the course of events. "You haven't seen the sleep lab."

"I slept in it."

"I didn't give you the tour."

"You were too busy putting me to bed. To tell you the truth, that's what I remember most about our first meeting. As for our second—"

The doorknob swiveled three times in her damp palm before she hauled it open. "Follow me."

He scowled at her retreating back all the way down the hall. He'd blown it. The one woman who might have helped him ran at the sight of him. He'd been nuts to show up demanding to see her, lying to her colleagues about dates, kissing her in the middle of corridors.

They passed a closed door with the name Merryweather on it and an open one with the name F. D. Coleman. Out of the corner of his eye he glimpsed a smartly dressed woman; her head shot up as they tore by.

Shana snagged his arm and tugged him into an unmarked room. "The lab," she announced.

His gaze strafed the line of television monitors hanging from the ceiling. VCRs were stacked beneath them on metal shelving. A large boxlike machine on casters had been rolled off to the side, its paper surface covered with the inky peaks and valleys of a polygraph.

"The poly*somno*graph," Shana said. "For measuring sleep."

Could they measure dreams? How deep they hit? How true they became?

A striking woman with short black hair swiveled on a stool. She pointed a remote control at a television and clicked it off.

"This is Fiona," Shana said.

She extended her hand. "We talked on the phone."

Shana turned to Gabe. "Fiona asked that I bring you in and show you off. I mean around."

"I see."

"She's working on her graduate degree. She works all night and goes home in the morning." Shana glanced pointedly at her watch.

"Just rewinding the last of last night's tapes," Fiona purred. "I saw a bit of yours."

Gabe hefted the plastic case. "Not too much, I hope."

"Enough."

Flirting could be fun, especially with a woman whose cool green eyes made it perfectly clear she wasn't the least bit interested. That minor point seemed lost on Shana. She dragged him toward a side hall. He went.

"And this is one of our sleeping rooms."

"I see."

She was on the warpath, pointing out cameras, pulling out drawers full of little gray buttons attached to a variety of colored wires, determined to show him everything while guaranteeing he never once met her gaze.

"These are the electrodes. We attach them like so." She went to work on the back of his hand, scuffing the skin with something called emery tape, peeling the paper backing off a plastic circle, sticking it on the back of his hand, and shoving a jumble of wires into his palm. They formed a multicolored bird's nest.

"See? Very lightweight. In a matter of minutes you'll be so used to them, you won't notice they're there. We attach them to your chest, your temples, your pulse. Twenty-four places in all."

"Do 'we' attach or do you attach?" He leaned an elbow on the countertop. "Speaking of which, are you attached?"

"I was just demonstrating." She yanked the electrode from his hand, taking a few hairs with it. "Leave that here."

He took the stinging sensation with him.

She showed him another bedroom, exactly the same. He told himself he didn't mind. If she was meant to play a role in his life it began there, in the clinic.

.   .   .

They ended up in the cafeteria instead, a cavernous windowless room where night was indistinguishable from day. A counter of harvest-gold Formica ran the length of the room. Shana slid her tray along it.

Clumps of tired doctors, harried nurses, and anguished loved ones slumped at the tables. As he followed Shana, Gabe noticed a tall, youngish man with curly brown hair by the far wall. Mulling something over, the man pulled a pipe from his pocket and clamped it between his teeth. Shana changed directions faster than a windsock in a gale.

She settled on a spot behind a pillar. They sat.

She tore open her sugar, spilling half. "Such a slob. Excuse me." She wet her fingertip with her tongue, collecting granules. Rubbing her thumb and forefinger together, she sprinkled them in her coffee. "Sorry, I didn't get much sleep last night."

"Neither did I." He wouldn't get any tonight, not when he remembered the way she sucked her fingertip before daintily dabbing it on a napkin.

She gave him an innocent look. "You say you didn't sleep well?"

"Insomniacs don't as a rule."

She smiled, aimlessly tapping her stirrer in time to the piped-in music. "You say it's lasted twenty years."

"Yes."

"So tell me about it. The story of your life."

He huffed a dry laugh, fingering the chipped rim of his cup. "Put that way, it sounds easy."

"Is it difficult?" Her gaze rested on him, brown eyes asking without prying. It was the questions that came fully loaded.

He couldn't tell her about the dreams, not yet. Not after the way she'd looked at him in the maternity-ward hall. He stared into his cup. The first dream happened when he was nine. "The insomnia started when I was fourteen," he began in mid-thought. "I suddenly found I couldn't sleep."

"Adolescents often go through a period of sleep adjustment. Something to do with hormones."

"They usually grow out of it too."

"Unless they make it a way of life."

He'd done that all right, it just wasn't much of a life. "Think this is all a question of bad habits?"

"They don't help."

He sipped the brutal sludge they called coffee. "So where do I start?"

"At the beginning."

He shrugged, narrating the movie in his head, keeping to the facts. "My parents died when I was nine. I lived with my grandmother for five years. When she died, I moved in with Uncle Jim. That's when the insomnia started."

"I'm sorry, Gabe."

"Run it all together and it sounds like one tragedy after another. Five years is a long time for a child."

"You adapted each time."

"I didn't have much choice."

"It's made you very strong. It has. Determined too. And apparently very successful."

"Except for my sleep habits."

She reached for a plastic thimble of cream and picked, picked, picked at the paper cover with her thumbnail. "This all began when you moved in with your uncle."

"Pretty soon thereafter. I'd wander around the apartment at night."

Her eyes widened slightly. "In your sleep?"

"Wide awake." He wasn't sure why that disappointed her. "Bedroom floors, living room couch, bathtub—I'd sleep anywhere. A regular Prince Bolkonsky."

"Who?"

"An old man in *War and Peace* who ordered his bed moved to a different room of his palace every night, looking for a place to sleep."

"I'm afraid I never read it."

"One of the advantages of staying up late."

She grinned.

"When I started reading *Playboy* for the articles, Uncle Jim knew I was *really* mixed up."

Shana laughed with him, slyly watching his tension ebb. He'd begun the story as if it were a shameful episode. "Do you have trouble talking about this?" she asked.

"I don't like burdening people with my problems."

She understood. Even with love, a child who'd lost those closest to him might learn to play life close to the vest. "And after *Playboy?*" she prompted.

"Uncle Jim took me to a shrink. He said the insomnia was 'temporary displacement owing to my unsettled childhood.' Said I'd grow out of it."

"The treatment of sleep disorders is fairly recent."

"Think I need another shrink?"

She knew a psychiatrist who'd love to meet him. Merryweather could wait. "What happened next?"

"One night, middle of the night, Jim caught me playing with his computer. He gave me a manual, figuring it would bore me to sleep. I became fascinated. He worked at the Chicago Board of Trade. To me the commodities, the price listings, the sales represented real things, corn, cabbage, livestock, family fortunes. One storm in Nebraska could send prices tumbling. It was like watching a movie with money attached. I was hooked."

Shana smiled. Surprised at the power of the memory, Gabe did too.

"Uncle Jim got me online with the Japanese stock exchange so I could watch trading at night. At breakfast he'd ask me how they did. I tracked prices and trends for him; he gave me a thousand dollars of play money."

"And?"

"I parlayed it into ten thousand. For that he gave me a real stake. It paid my way through college. Notre Dame."

Shana whistled low. She was a terrible whistler; it sounded like someone blowing through a straw.

Gabe laughed and shook his head. "It's been a long time since I impressed a woman with that story."

"That would impress anyone."

"Most of the women I know got Porsches for graduating from high school and Mercedeses for making it through college."

In other words, he'd just deftly informed her she wasn't his type. Shana knew that. She hadn't even thought of him that way—outside her dreams. She swept the table clean with the side of her palm. "Were there any years you slept better than others?"

"College."

"You slept through the night?"

"No, but nobody noticed when I didn't. It took some of the pressure off."

"Did you feel pressured because of your insomnia?"

He thought a moment. "I knew Uncle Jim worried. Until I started enjoying myself, that is. Following the markets was exciting."

"Instead of shameful or problematic."

He didn't flinch. "Yes."

"And you're still in this line of work?"

"I deal exclusively with markets on the other side of the world. I need to keep their hours to keep my edge."

"Meaning you're up all night."

"You snooze, you lose."

"In my profession, you snooze, you win."

He smiled grimly. "Do you think I should change jobs?"

"It appears you've found a way to turn sleeplessness to your advantage. Which leads to the inevitable question, Why change?"

Because life was passing him by and being alone wasn't a life. Because, having dreamed about her, he couldn't let her go, not until he was sure she was safe. "I need to know why. Why I struggle against something I want more than anything in the world."

"We can start with your habits."

"Name one."

"Don't engage in strenuous exercise shortly before sleep."

"Done."

"No caffeine."

He glanced at his empty cup. "Check."

"Naps are to an insomniac what snacks are to a dieter. No more fragmented sleep."

"What about women?"

"I beg your pardon?"

"What's your position on sleeping with someone?"

She found a world of fascination inside her coffee cup. "My opinions aren't really relevant."

"I want to sleep," he insisted. "That means someday with somebody. You can help."

"As long as we both understand this doesn't include me sleeping with you."

"Point taken." Except that she'd gotten mixed up in his sleep the minute she'd appeared in his dreams.

"Oh no." Shana rested her head in her hand.

"What is it?"

"Flora."

Bound and determined to make Gabe's acquaintance, Flora sashayed her way through the crooked tables and parked herself beside them.

"We're in the middle of an appointment," Shana murmured politely.

She stuck out her hand, gold rings flashing. "Flora Dava Coleman. Mrs."

"Gabriel Fitzgerald."

"A pleasure to meet you." She gave him a keen, assessing gaze, as warm as hot tar, as calculating as a tax collector. Or a prospective mother-in-law.

By the time she finished shaking his hand, he figured she'd evaluated the dryness of his palm, the force of his grip, the length of his fingers, and that tiny break in his lifeline.

"I must say after one visit he looks much better."

"He looks wonderful," Shana muttered. "Now if you'll excuse us."

Flora wasn't prepared to do anything of the kind. "I'm the respiratory therapist here, Gabriel. Has Shana spoken to you about apnea?"

"I'm not sure. I wasn't too swift my first visit." He omitted the second.

"Obstructive sleep apnea involves excessive snoring and cessation of breathing during sleep. It's a killer."

"I'm afraid that's not my problem."

"I didn't think so."

"You saw the tape," he guessed.

She gave him a conspiratorial wink. "You hang on to that, child. When your grandchildren snicker at your gray hair and droopy cheeks, you show 'em that. That'll open their eyes."

He threw his head back and laughed. "I never thought of it that way."

"That day'll be here before you know it. You're going to want someone around who knew you when and can testify. Our Shana here—"

Shana swallowed her coffee with an audible gulp.

"—she has very high hopes for you. We all do."

"I see."

"I hope not," Shana muttered.

"I take it you'll be joining us at the group session Wednesday?"

"Session?"

"We haven't had a chance to discuss it yet," Shana said with a growl. "Good morning, Flora."

Mrs. Coleman patted him on the shoulder. One hundred percent wool suit, fine tailoring, the thinnest of shoulder pads, and a body toned by regular workouts. She nodded in approval. "We'll see you then, Gabriel."

"Friend of yours?" he asked when she was gone.

"Colleague and part-time fairy godmother." Shana's head turned as she followed her friend's exit. She swung back, hurriedly sipping the last of her coffee.

"What now?"

"Payne."

Gabe lurched forward and grasped her wrist. "Where does it hurt? Are you okay?"

She burst out laughing. Hair whispered around her face as she shook her head. "*Dr.* Payne. Remember him? Outside the elevator."

Gabe remembered. The portly man stood in the cafeteria entrance. His beady eyes rested on them briefly before moving on. Gabe released his grip a second too late. "What does he do, follow you around?"

"Feels like it." She sighed.

"I didn't get you in trouble, did I?"

A deeper shade of pink inflamed her cheeks.

"I'm capable of getting in trouble with that man all by myself, thank you. If you'll excuse me, I have to get back to my office."

"When will I see you again?"

"Wednesday at eight, if you care to join our group sessions."

"Collective whining?"

"Behavior modification. I teach relaxation, meditation, sleep hygiene."

"Hygiene?"

"Come to the session and find out."

7

From the hallway Shana scanned the assorted patients gathered on the sagging sofas in the clinic lounge. Secondhand lamps on scarred corner tables replaced the clinical overhead lights with a warm golden glow. Or tried to. She and Fiona had done their best to make the lounge a relaxing setting. So far not so good.

None of the patients looked happy. Aurora, an ash blond who suffered from night terrors, jabbed at her cuticles with a stiff stick of gum. Doris, an obsessive whose list of things to do before bedtime kept her up all hours, plucked imaginary lint from her navy skirt. One of Shana's patients, an elderly woman named Marie, complained of prickling in her legs. Lucille Hawkins was a bus driver recently reassigned to an early morning shift. At present she was deep in a slumbering haze. Shana almost hated to wake her up.

On the other hand, it would be a pleasure breaking up the tense standoff on the right-hand side of the room. DeVon and Shirlee Johnson, the snoring husband and his

sleepless wife, sat side by side in perfectly matched, resolutely unyielding poses. A birdlike woman with graying
hair and ebony skin, Shirlee sat bolt upright, knees together, hands folded over her patent-leather purse. Her
plain high-collared wool dress was unadorned by accesso-
ries, her hat perfect for an evening church service.

The husband was another species. A belligerent
middle-aged man, DeVon Johnson dwarfed his tiny wife.
Noting his hefty shoulders, sagging jowls, and mean eyes,
Shana secretly admired Mrs. Johnson's resolve. Talking
her husband into accompanying her to this session
couldn't have been easy.

For Shirlee's sake, Shana would give it everything she
had.

That left her troubled and troubling patient, Gabe
Fitzgerald. He'd pulled an orange plastic chair between
two sofas. He viewed the others through narrowed eyes,
impatient, restless. Yoke-straight shoulders bore up under
invisible burdens. Tension charged the air around him.
"Determined" was a word that came to Shana's mind. Also
"intimidating," "alone," and "bone-tired." She wondered if
he'd slept at all since their conversation on Monday.

What drove him? He'd had a number of family trage-
dies. Depression or displacement could have started his
battle with insomnia. What kept it going? She wanted to
talk to him again. And dream about him less.

The dry humor she'd glimpsed in their last interview
intrigued her still. So did his charm. His undisguised interest in her put her every nerve on alert. Careful, she
thought. Or better yet, care less. She was beginning to feel
for Gabe Fitzgerald on a deeply personal level.

"Evening, Shana." Merryweather unfolded his six-foot-
four frame. "I think we're all here." He sent a meaningful
glance Gabe's way.

She sent him a pained one. Gabe was a person, not a
checkbook.

Drawing his pipe from his pocket, the psychiatrist addressed the group with his usual laconic delivery. "As

Shana will explain much better than I could, behavior is
a component of almost every sleep disorder."

While he explained the short history of St. James'
Sleep Disorders Clinic, Shana considered her predica-
ment. Gabe's treatment would take more than a few visits.
If she intended to survive them with any kind of self-
composure, the skittering heat that flushed her cheeks
each time she saw him would have to disappear. She was
a professional and a damned good one. Merryweather was
in the midst of saying so.

"Her innovative group sessions have been not only entertaining and edifying for hundreds of patients in the
half-year since she joined us, but beneficial as well. Dy-
namic and dedicated, Dr. Getz has a talent for speaking
directly to the heart of the matter without resorting to jargon or acronyms."

By the time he finished they'd expect her to turn cart-
wheels down the halls and heal the sick by the laying on
of hands.

"I give you Dr. Shana Getz." Merryweather concluded
and sat down.

"You do this to me every week," Shana muttered out
of the side of her mouth.

"We all need challenges. You'll rise to yours."

Her challenges were rising faster than a rain-swollen
creek. She stepped briskly into the middle of the circle
and unbuttoned her lab coat. "Thank you for that wonderful introduction, Dr. Merryweather."

Hands in the pockets of her favorite jeans, she let her
audience get a good look. What the outfit cost her in au-
thority, she made up for in relaxed camaraderie. Perfectly
at home, she wanted them to feel the same. Even if her
heart was pumping a gallon a minute.

Her T-shirt read "Welcome to the Land of Nod."
"What do you think?"

Aurora smirked. DeVon humphed. Awakened by the
noise, Lucille blinked and got her bearings. Gabe canted
his head to the side and studied her. She sensed that.

Whether it was peripheral vision or extrasensory perception, his gaze touched her like a feather flitting down her skin.

The Vampire was back, his body as still as a velvety night. His gaze focused on her like a moonbeam through a tower window. Unwavering blue eyes captured hers every time she glanced his way. She didn't fold her arms, button her coat, or blink without feeling that gaze on her like a cool hand. An answering rush of warmth heated her skin. She told herself unnerving stillness was a part of him. It was nothing personal.

The way her body reacted was too personal for words.

Taking a deep breath, she planted her feet on the all-purpose carpet. She extended her arms straight out, waggling her fingers toward the far walls, arching her back. Eyes shut tight, she opened her mouth for the best face-stretching, nose-wrinkling, jaw-unhinging, shoulder-blade-scrunching yawn of the day. "Ahhh. That felt good!" Her arms dropped to her sides. She grinned at her bewildered audience.

"I wasn't *that* boring," Merryweather muttered.

The ice broke. People laughed. Lunging forward, Shana pointed a finger at her first victim. "Lucille Hawkins! Don't tell me you didn't want to do the exact same thing. Don't be shy," she cried, glancing at each one. "You're all stuck here for an hour and a half. The air is stuffy, the couches are soft, not to mention sagging, and Dr. Merryweather's short introduction wasn't exactly an Oscar acceptance speech. This white coat says I work here. So what? The important thing is *I can help you sleep.* Now, Lucille, give me a yawn."

The routine was embarrassingly simple and fiendishly calculated. Yawning was more contagious than chicken pox. Sensing a lump in every throat, Shana caught the blond daintily covering her mouth. "Aurora, right? That's it. Everybody, go ahead. Who's next? Marie? Gabe."

She always picked on her own patients first. She was determined this time would be no different. That didn't stop her from questioning the wisdom of picking on a man who resisted sleep at every turn. She hoped his sense of humor hadn't evaporated since their last meeting.

Sliding comfortably lower on his plastic chair, hands sunk in the pockets of a crisp pair of khakis, Gabe stretched out his legs, crossed them grandly at the ankles, puffed out his chest, and yawned until the gold caps on his back molars glinted.

"A flycatcher!" Shana led a round of applause. "Who's next?"

Doris discreetly covered her mouth, her cheeks swelling behind her manicured hand.

"Good. Mrs. Johnson?"

What began as a demure inhale turned into a vocal sigh Shana dubbed "the groaning ghost." "Doesn't that just make you want to curl up with a pillow?" Apparently not, if one judged by the frown on Mr. Johnson's face.

Shana sidestepped the inevitable confrontation by turning to the group. "Don't you just hate it when you have a sore throat and you want to yawn but it gets stuck halfway?" That nifty bit of reverse psychology provoked even more yawns. "Human beings crave oxygen and relaxation. We crave sleep. That's why you're here."

"Not me," DeVon Johnson grumbled. Arms folded across his sizable belly, he thrust his chin forward in a prove-it-to-me pose. "Better off sittin' in front of the TV gettin' a good nap than puttin' up with this stuff."

"Is that where you get most of your sleep? In front of the TV?" She whirled back to the group. "Mr. Johnson has hit it on the head. We start with the basics here. Where do you sleep best? When do you sleep? How do you sleep? Not well, obviously, or you wouldn't be here."

Disconcerted by her enthusiastic response, Johnson retreated behind his sullen glare.

Shana breezed on. "All of you are seeing specialists who will help pinpoint the *cause* of your sleep disturbances. We've brought you here tonight because every sleep problem has a *behavioral* element. Sleep is a habit.

Any disruptions in our sleeping patterns can upset the entire process. So let's start at the beginning. What do you need to go to sleep?"

"A bed?" Aurora guessed.

"Before that." Blank looks. "You need to be sleepy. To be sleepy, you need to be relaxed. Tonight I'll teach you techniques for relaxation—"

Another grumble. This one sounded like "hocus-pocus."

A tiny voice reminded Shana of her resolution regarding tact and prudence. However, if she didn't challenge Johnson directly, he'd disrupt the entire session. She turned toward him. "You said you'd rather be asleep? Fiona, get this man a pillow!"

Primed, Fiona pulled an airline pillow from a stack hidden behind the sofa. She tossed it to Shana who handed it to DeVon. When he yanked at it, she held on to the other end. It was like playing tug-of-war with a caged bear. "First, tell the group your name."

"DeVon Johnson." A railroad man, his voice rumbled like a train coming through a tunnel.

"Welcome, DeVon."

"I'm only here for the wife."

"Shirlee, is it? Would *you* like a pillow?"

The birdlike Mrs. Johnson gave a quick nod.

Shana handed her a pillow, offering the next to the group at large. "Don't be shy, people. We're here to talk about what you do in bed."

Nervous laughter. In a well-practiced fireman's drill, Fiona tossed while Shana caught, handing out pillows one by one. The drooping Lucille raised a hand. The blond flicked her spiky red nails in the air.

"Who have I missed?"

Squirming on the couch's aged fabric, Doris stuffed her pillow between the greasy sofa arm and her pristine suit. Gabe slung his over his shoulder, wedging it between his back and the sharp upper edge of the chair. The elderly Marie hugged hers to her chest. Lucille was already doz-

ing, her cheek mashed into the white softness. Mrs. Johnson set hers atop her patent-leather purse, hands folded
primly over it.

"Is this it?" her husband demanded. "We sit here with
pillows?"

Shana smiled wider. Yawns weren't the only contagious gestures; laughter was catching too. "What was it
you said the other day, Dr. Merryweather? The best cure
for insomnia is to go home and sleep it off?"

People chuckled.

Merryweather tapped his empty pipe against his palm.
"Actually, I believe that was your line," he drawled. "If I
remember correctly, we were discussing Mr. Fitzgerald's
case."

"Ah, yes. Thank you. So much." Lancing an indignant
stare his way, she sensed Gabe's sudden interest. She con-
fronted that next. "My first helpful hint of the evening:
naps are to sleep what snacks are to dinner. Gabe knows
this one. If you nap during the day, you'll find yourself
awake longer at night. Make sense?"

Gabe nodded.

"Lucille?"

Marie elbowed the softly snoring woman to her left.
Lucille awoke with a start. "Next stop Union Station."

Shana grinned and leaned over her. "I just love it
when I put people to sleep. It makes me look good."

More laughter.

"I've got another helpful hint," she announced.

"What is this, a test?" DeVon again.

Shana reminded herself that there were patients and
there was patience.

Mrs. Johnson put her hand on her husband's arm. He
shrugged it off. People who lacked sleep were often short-
tempered. In Shana's opinion DeVon Johnson could give
a pit bull lessons. All the more reason to tiptoe around
him.

She charged right in. "When sleep is disrupted, we not

only feel draggy and slow, we find ourselves easily aggravated, snappish, testy. Can I see a show of hands?"

"I've been told I can be a real bastard." Gabe's low voice drew looks from every quarter. The longest from Shana. "I get irritated, short with people. I can't concentrate."

Understanding smiles lit the faces around him. The other members of the group joined in one by one. "I can't remember where I put things," Aurora said.

"I've fallen asleep sitting at a bus stop waiting for passengers to board," Lucille added.

"I get confused," Marie said.

Gabe had gotten people involved by revealing his problems first. He'd also shifted the focus from DeVon's anger. Shana thanked him with a smile.

"If I got more sleep, I'd be more relaxed," he concluded.

"By the same token," she added softly, "if you were more relaxed, you'd get more sleep."

"Is it a vicious cycle?"

"It doesn't have to be."

Their gaze held a long moment. Her words seemed to hang in the air. *You don't have to fight this alone.* "Sleep isn't something you need to wrestle with. It means relaxing, giving in." As with love, sometimes one had to surrender. She imagined surrendering to Gabe Fitzgerald.

The radiator clacked like a rimshot. Shana cleared her throat. "After I get done filling your heads with tips and advice, Fiona will show two short films on sleep problems. Say hello, Fiona."

"Hello."

"Flora Dava Coleman is our respiratory therapist. She'll talk about sleep apnea. We'll conclude with a couple of relaxation techniques then I'll give you your homework assignments." She waited for the requisite groans. "We'll meet two more times after this to chart our progress and discuss other techniques. Are there any questions?"

"What kind of homework?" Aurora asked.

Shana chuckled. "There's decaf coffee and tea on the table over there. There's also a pop machine at the end of the hall. I've marked which brands are caffeine free. See you in fifteen minutes."

Fifteen minutes to make up his mind. Pushing his chair back with his heels, Gabe brooded. His head felt banded by a vise. His neck creaked and his shoulder blades felt as if someone had plunged a knife between them. He was tired. Tired of fearing sleep, avoiding it, defying it. This obsession had already robbed him of too much life.

The previous night was no exception. He'd worked through until dawn. Nothing unusual about that—except the struggle, the extra effort it required. The markets had been dead: national holiday in Japan, stagnant trading in Hong Kong. The brokers in Bombay couldn't stop talking about a one-hundred-part serial debuting on Indian television the night before.

He'd stared out the floor-to-ceiling windows for hours. It wasn't like him to get distracted. Sitting in the clinic lounge, he scrunched his shoulders, made a couple fists, and released them. He thought of what Shana had just said, that we got the most restorative, dream-filled sleep in long stretches.

At least he'd been on the right track. He'd tried limiting his dreams by limiting his sleep. The side effect had been constant exhaustion. At first he'd figured anything was better than glimpsing the future. Until wakefulness taunted him with memories of the past.

He prowled over to the coffee cart, catching sight of his reflection in the window. In the black January sky a small plane circled. Its lights blinked like faraway stars. They could wink out at any moment, lost on the radar screen of the sky.

His gaze raked the room. He'd told Shana about his

insomnia. If he wanted to be cured, he'd have to tell her the rest of it.

He paced, clutching a black cup of coffee he didn't even remember pouring. If he wanted to be more than a puzzle to her, he'd have to give her the rest of the pieces. That meant talking about his parents, the plane crash. His dreams. His failure to act.

If Shana had hoped for a brief respite from Gabe's intense presence in the lounge, she wasn't getting it from her friends on the staff. Fiona, Flora, and Merryweather joined her in a friendly coven around the pop machine at the end of the hall.

"Whew, is he gorgeous," Flora declared.

"And so helpful," Fiona purred.

"Quite nice," Merryweather drawled.

Shana rolled her eyes. "I'm sure he'd hate being called 'nice.'"

"Then what word would you use?"

She slugged quarters into the machine.

"Yummy?" Fiona offered.

"Sexy?" Flora suggested.

"Will you *please*," Shana hissed. "He might hear you."

A murmur of voices rumbled from the lounge. They were alone in the hall.

Flora lowered her voice all the same. "With insomnia you never have to worry about a man rolling over and going to sleep after sex."

"That man gives new meaning to the phrase 'up all night.'"

Shana nearly dented the can clutched in her fist. "I'm conducting a class not a dating service."

Flora clucked in agreement. "We can't all be Naomi Campbell, but child, you've got to do the best with what you've got. Look at this hair, falling in your face."

Shana silently agreed. She'd fidgeted with it from the start of class. She'd run her hands through it, tossed it over her shoulder, and generally reduced it to what her mother called "yellow seaweed."

What else was new? She'd never be elusive and alluring like Fiona, warm and earthy like Flora, suave and composed like Merryweather. She was passably pretty and made no effort to go beyond that designation.

"Don't you own an iron, girl?" Flora asked.

"I'm fine the way I am."

"You hide yourself."

"By standing in front of a group of people?"

"By hiding behind a curtain of hair."

"I must've combed it off my face ten times."

"Without once using a real comb. Get these bangs thinned. And tell that woman to shape it around your face more."

"In case you haven't noticed, I have a career here. One from which I get immense satisfaction."

"You have to advertise your assets."

"My asset is big enough as it is."

"I noticed those jeans," Fiona put in. "Any chance that was intentional?"

Shana groaned. "Every time I wash them they shrink two sizes and every time I stop by the bakery I grow one."

"Men like that filled-out look."

"I don't."

"Temper, temper," Merryweather said.

"You'd think she'd been up all night," Fiona murmured as the staff withdrew. They strolled down the hall, heads bent in whispers.

Shana grimaced and fed another quarter to the machine. She'd been up all right. At four A.M. she'd gotten out of bed for a glass of water. She'd gotten as far as the kitchen. Her heart plummeted just remembering it.

Bowls, plates, and silverware were piled on the stove. Tumblers and juice glasses lined the windowsill. The counter was covered with beaters and spatulas and sieves. Eggs sat shattered and seeping in a bowl. Flour dusted the canisters. She'd groaned and raised her hand to her mouth; a floury film coated it. She'd been baking in her sleep.

The cat hopped on the counter and commenced licking the bowl. Shana scooted him away and feverishly wiped up. Why sleepwalk then? And why cook? She wetted a paper towel.

Perhaps cooking represented fitting in with her family. She sniffed at the weird concoction in the bowl. On the other hand, perhaps cooking badly meant she wanted to escape her family. Love them as she did, she'd grown up longing to flee the bakery. The nonstop blend of work, home, and family life could be smothering and claustrophobic. Especially to someone who messed up instant pudding—the kind that came right out of the can.

By four-fifteen she'd finished cleaning. When she doused the lights she noticed the glow from the living room.

She stepped cautiously around the corner. Lit candles dripped red wax on her white lace tablecloth. A bottle of dusty wine sat ready, its cork ruined by her clumsy attempts to open it in her sleep.

Romper twitched his tail near the candle flame. Shooing him frantically, she hustled the candles off the table as fast as she could. If she dispensed with them quickly enough, she might avoid the obvious conclusion: she'd dreamed of cooking for Gabe. "Donna Reed meet Sigmund Freud."

He'd invaded every part of her subconscious, from wish fulfillment to erotic dreams to sleepwalking episodes.

Sipping her soda outside the lounge, she insisted all this had a reasonable explanation. The little he'd told her about his childhood had aroused her sympathies. The exceptional way he'd adapted provoked her admiration and respect. The things he *didn't* say made him a mystery. The way he kissed—

She stopped that thought in its tracks. They had no hope of a relationship. She imagined her fantasies coming true: he'd spend the night, they'd make love, he'd wake to find her acting out some weird homemaking ritual.

She shuddered at the thought and walked back toward the lounge.

She was a counselor not a consort. No matter what spell her subconscious wove at night, her conscious mind knew better. Like in all her other relationships, she wouldn't indulge the dream only to see it evaporate in the light of day.

She had a group of people who were desperate for help to focus on now—and that called for desperate measures. She hoped at least one of them learned something tonight.

A bare light bulb on a frayed cord hung suspended from the ceiling of the cement-block room. In a corner, water dripped in a discolored sink.

The unshaven young man trembled in the wooden chair, his T-shirt torn and drenched with sweat. Hoarse, panicked, he pleaded for mercy. Two burly men in military uniforms approached. Gripping him under the armpits, they dragged him toward the sink. He screamed, kicking and wrenching with every step. With a vicious thrust, they forced his head under water. Ten seconds elapsed, twenty. His body bucked. They let him up, impassively waiting as he retched the water he'd inhaled. They shoved him under again. Finally, with more disgust than mercy, they threw him to the floor.

One soldier prodded the boy with his toe. Stepping to the sink, he soaked a shapeless piece of cloth until the fabric was heavy with water. He roughly tugged the suffocating hood over the boy's face. The fabric collapsed on his gaping mouth each time he struggled to breathe through it.

"Are we ready to talk?" Shana hit Stop on the VCR remote control.

After a long pause, Gabe spoke. "This is what you'll do to us if we don't do our homework?"

After the laughter died down, Shana hit the lights.

She indicated the screen. "What we've just seen would be considered torture in any country in the world. And yet, this is a perfect metaphor for sleep apnea."

She felt DeVon Johnson's furious glower like a blast of heat. He recognized the phrase—and the fact this whole show had been put on for him.

Shana had known he was the kind of man who'd never recognize himself in the video featuring the pleasant retired couple discussing the husband's snoring. "Actors," he'd say. "Bullshit," he'd say. "Just trying to sell me some damn machine to strap on my face so oxygen can blow at me."

He'd needed shock therapy. She'd obliged.

"In cases of obstructive sleep apnea, snoring is the struggle to breathe past soft tissue in the throat. The obstruction can be like trying to breathe through a wet cloth. In extreme cases, your breathing can stop completely."

Having rewound the video, she clicked it back on, muting the audio. The men forced their victim's head under water. "Starved of oxygen, apnea patients gasp for air, waking themselves up so they can breathe again. They may not even be aware of it. But imagine undergoing this three or four hundred times a night."

She listened to the quiet as the patients held their breath along with the submerged boy. The suspense stretched. The boy fought his way to the surface, choking and sputtering.

DeVon lurched to his feet. "I'm getting outta here."

Shana held her ground. "Is it any wonder men with apnea wake up exhausted? Is it any wonder they die in their sleep?"

"You ain't talkin' me into this." Muttering obscenities, he staggered to the door. "You coming?"

His wife sat, her purse clutched on her lap, her shoes tight together, pointed as straight as her chin. "I'm staying."

"Then you'll be walkin.'" He spat a curse and slammed

the door open. Changing his mind, he marched into the circle, shaking a finger inches from Shana's face. "Don't you be jerkin' me around, bitch. I don't got a problem, and I don't need some doctor tellin' me how to fuckin' sleep!"

The door slammed so hard, Shana expected glass to tinkle to the ground. The window held. So did the silence.

Her knees shaking, she crossed to the blackboard, trying to buy some time. She'd taken a chance, hoping to shock him into awareness of a potentially fatal problem. The whole thing had backfired.

She pointed the chalk at the next topic, underlining it with a jittery line of white. It broke. She palmed the stub in her clammy hand. "Apnea is one of the physical causes of sleep disorders. Can you think of any mental causes?"

Alternately watching the door and Mrs. Johnson's statue-still profile, no one dared venture a word.

"Stress?" Fiona suggested at last.

Grimaces substituted for grins.

Shana tried to whip up some enthusiasm. "Stress. Okay. Family problems? A guilty conscience? All those good things that keep you awake late at night? Any others?"

"Nightmares."

She thanked Aurora. "Nightmares." Her second piece of chalk broke as she underlined that one. She tossed the remaining sliver in the metal tray, wiping her hands hastily on her jeans. Grimacing at the marks that made, she glanced around the group.

"How about dreams?" Gabe's grainy voice made her pause.

"I think we covered that with 'nightmares.' "

"I'm talking about the kind that come true."

The entire group turned to him. The radiator crackled and hissed. Shirlee Johnson leaned forward slowly. "You mean visions?"

"Maybe."

The silence grew. Shana didn't want to get into this. She'd already lost one patient. How could she accept the idea that dreams came true?

Gabe answered that question for her. "When I was nine I dreamed my parents died in a plane crash. They did. The next day."

A band of pain wound around her chest. She saw where this was leading. "That doesn't mean your dream caused the crash."

"No, but I could have prevented it."

"Guilt can produce sleeplessness."

"Twenty years' worth?"

"You told me your insomnia didn't begin until five years later."

"True. The dreams began earlier." He hunched forward. Elbows on his knees, he rubbed his hands together. He reached for the coffee he'd set beside his chair. He never got around to drinking it. The liquid sloshed gently in the Styrofoam, a muddy brown tide from which he scavenged memories.

"I was nine, staying with my grandmother for the summer. My dad leased a plane so he and Mom could fly in and pick me up for Labor Day. I had a dream the night before; I watched the plane go down. When I woke up screaming, my grandmother calmed me down by promising to take me to the airport the next night. I went. It made no difference."

Gabe shook his head. "It was a little plane. It looked like a bonfire on the other side of the airfield. My grandmother held me while people rushed through the terminal. The lights of the fire engines were like red fireflies, too small to do any good." He grew silent, watching the scene in his mind.

"It couldn't have been your fault," Shana said softly.

"I could have yelled louder, caused more of a fuss. I should have *made* someone listen."

A nine-year-old boy making adults believe he'd seen the future? "Anything could have gone wrong, Gabe. Pilot error. Equipment malfunction. Maybe your father had a heart attack at the controls."

"Yeah, and maybe he fell asleep." The cutting words fell like rocks in a pond. No one moved until Gabe broke the spell. He raked a hand through his hair and downed the coffee with a grimace. "Shit, maybe you're right. You snooze, you lose, huh?"

"Could that be it?" Shana asked, zeroing in. "Perhaps you don't want to sleep for fear you'll lose the people closest to you."

Nice theory. Neat. It had one drawback. "I don't want to sleep because my dreams come true."

8

ꙮ Shana took a step into the clammy cement-walled parking garage and stopped. Stale exhaust-scented air greeted her. Nevertheless, she welcomed the change of scene. A tight-lipped debate with Dr. Payne's committee had her empty stomach in knots. In the two days following the group session and Gabe's revelations, she'd barely been able to concentrate. Successive sleepless nights hadn't helped.

She kept imagining a fourteen-year-old—a nine-year-old—carrying the responsibility of his parents' death. No wonder he'd been hounded by insomnia for twenty years. Either he was punishing himself with unwarranted guilt or he restricted his sleep out of fear.

She recalled the rest of the group session. They'd gone over relaxation techniques, meditation, general tips for improving sleep efficiency. It was all anticlimactic after Gabe had told his story. He didn't really believe he saw the future, did he?

A tiny thrill coursed through her each time she considered the thorny twists his case had taken. She loved going up against a challenge, ferreting out motives, gauging responses, getting results. Sleep was her passion. If she could cure him of this unfounded belief, she could cure his insomnia.

Unfortunately, the purely intellectual rewards of curing Gabe Fitzgerald tended to get mixed up with other sensations. At the drop of an eyelid, she dreamed of him. Her subconscious pestered her with questions of its own; what kind of lover would he be, how would he take her in his arms? She already knew how he kissed. That didn't stop her wanting to kiss him again.

"Fantasies," she told herself, stalking through the parking garage. She'd breezed right by the Staff Only section; reserved spaces always went first. She never remembered where she'd parked. "I know I'm here somewhere."

She passed three Toyotas, a Cherokee, and a Saturn, filing that information away in case she needed it again. If she concentrated, she could keep her mind off Gabe. Case in point, she'd managed to prepare a coherent report for tonight's committee meeting. She'd spent the afternoon working herself up to deliver it.

She might as well not have bothered. Her ideas concerning lighting levels in the neonatal ward had elicited only glimmers of interest.

Glimmers, she thought, an ironic twist to her mouth. Didn't people see that that was precisely what those tiny infants needed? Soft, glowing light instead of the harsh glare of hospital whites. The cycle of night and day. No human being, no matter how small, slept well in constant bright light.

Payne had argued that doctors couldn't read babies' charts in the dark.

"Are we here to help the patients or the physicians?" she'd retorted. "Who comes first?"

"Monitoring devices don't glow in the dark."

"And babies don't sleep well in the light." She'd nearly smacked her palm on the table. One quelling glance from Merryweather had lowered her voice and brought her presentation to a stumbling halt. "I hope you'll accept my proposal," she'd concluded lamely.

She winced recalling it. Arguing wasn't easy when your superior refused to back you up. Merryweather claimed she got carried away. If the issue was important enough, well—hell, yes, she'd get carried away. To tell the truth, it had been the only issue compelling enough to distract her from thoughts of Gabe.

Sighing, she turned and glanced behind her. The structure was built like a series of flattened zees with each level divided into two slants. Could she have tromped right past her car without noticing? She reached the end of level three and turned again. A movement caught her eye. Standing very still, she peered at a van halfway down the row. She reached for her glasses, which she'd buttoned up tight inside her coat.

She held her breath, eventually dismissing her worries as paranoia. Walking down the center of level four, she toted up the week's highs and lows. First stop, her massive miscalculation regarding DeVon Johnson. If she hadn't been so busy thinking about Gabe, she might have predicted his reaction. Flora hadn't heard from Mr. or Mrs. since the session.

Between DeVon, Gabe, and tonight's meeting with Payne's committee, it was no wonder she'd barely slept. Or that tired minds played tricks on people.

Putting the tough week farther behind her with every step, she reached the top level. She recognized the tick of high heels a couple levels below and breathed a sigh of relief—people. But no one nearby. On this level cars crouched between faded yellow lines, hulking, cold, unfamiliar. The Exit sign glowed at the end of the slanting roadway. A metal door thudded shut somewhere below. Silence bounced off the walls. She was alone.

She slogged down the slope again, her steps sturdy and purposeful, half a beat out of synch with the ones following her. A door slammed. She jumped. Her nerves were getting the better of her. On these canted levels, sound ricocheted in weird ways. She sped up anyway, trotting toward the elevator at the end of the row just in case she needed a way out. When she was ten feet from it, its gaping doors slid shut, summoned to a lower floor.

After her meeting with Payne she'd been too damn exhausted to wait for an escort from the security guard. Besides, it was embarrassing having some man follow her around while she tried to find her car. Better than having a stranger follow you, she thought.

She spun around. No one. Just the gray seeping walls of the garage and the sickly gleam of cars under sodium lights. She clutched her purse to her side, digging surreptitiously for her pepper gas. If all else failed she could always slap a Porsche; the car alarm going off would be louder than any scream she could utter.

"Hello."

Her shriek pierced the air. She lashed out with her purse, pepper gas flying.

Gabe lifted his hands in a gesture of surrender. "Sorry."

"You scared the—the blank out of me!"

He tried to smile. The customary tension between his eyes ruined the effect. "Jumpy today?"

She'd been jumpy all week. "The last time I saw you someone was calling me a bitch and walking out of my class."

He did her the honor of glancing around. "You don't think he's still mad at you?"

"He could be."

"What was his name?"

"Johnson, DeVon."

"You think he's dangerous?"

"Or do I just get panic attacks in parking garages?"

"That was my next question."

She marched ten steps, shaking her head. The rest of her shook just fine on its own. "I hate these places. I also hate the horror stories women are told to keep them scared out of their minds and locked in their houses."

"Need an escort?"

"The security guard was AWOL."

He fell in step beside her. "Where's your car?"

"Equally AWOL. Every level in this place looks exactly the same, especially after a twelve-hour day."

"We can take mine."

"Yours?"

"To dinner."

To her surprise, Shana felt her tension evaporate. She closed her eyes and sighed. "That's the most romantic two-word invitation I've ever heard."

"I like getting to the point."

"So I've noticed." Her pulse still skittered and her limbs quaked. She'd skipped dinner for the presentation to Payne's committee. Her stomach was in knots and all her appeals to common sense couldn't shake her conviction that someone was watching them.

She peered the length of the next level. She could have sworn a shadow lurked between a windowless van and a truck. A moving shadow.

"What is it?"

She rapidly unbuttoned her coat and fished her glasses out. When her search turned up nothing, she sheepishly looked up at Gabe. "Nothing."

"This place has you spooked."

"Exhaustion is playing tricks with my eyes."

"Tell me about it." His eyes were sunken and shadowed from lack of sleep. The ugly lighting made him look leaner, paler.

"Maybe dinner's a good idea." It would give her a chance to lay down the rules. She wanted desperately to help him. She had no intention of becoming emotionally involved.

Suddenly he turned his head, his eyes raking the shadows between the cars.

"Apparently paranoia is contagious," Shana observed. "Do you know where your car is?"

He nodded.

"Lucky you. Let's go."

The BMW purred out of its parking space. Leather seats filled the interior with a scent almost as enticing as a bakery laden with fresh bread. Shana inhaled and sat back.

"I dreamed about you this afternoon."

She bit her tongue. What could she say? "That's nice?" Or worse, "Me, too"?

They pulled into the street.

"You don't believe me," Gabe said flatly.

"That dreams can predict the future? I believe that you believe them."

"Is that as condescending as it sounds?"

She laughed and reached across the gear shift to touch his arm. "It's the belief that's causing the insomnia, not the dreams."

He squinted at a red light, as impatient and intense as the engine he gunned. "What if I could prove it?"

It wasn't a careless dare. "How?"

"First tell me where you want to eat."

Tired as she was, she needed a breather before she took him on. Gabe could be as difficult as he was fascinating. "You choose. Wake me when we get there."

Gabe sensed her relax, deliberately, purposefully. He assumed she was using one of her relaxation techniques to clear her mind. He'd tried a few himself the last couple days. Unfortunately, all he thought about was her.

The dream he'd had that afternoon had clinched it. She wasn't in any danger, not unless loving him was dangerous. He was almost tempted to let the dream unfold as predicted, except he was so used to fighting them, trying in vain to prevent what he foresaw. And failing every time.

That's why he'd come to her. Let *her* break the pattern. All she had to do was to refuse to play along.

He pulled into a parking spot across from Leonardo's fifteen minutes later. Patting the envelope in his pocket, he leaned over. She looked exhausted. A wave of tenderness washed through him, seeping through a crack in the wall he'd spent so many years erecting. He kissed her. "Hey, Sleeping Beauty. Wake up."

Her lashes fluttered on her cheeks. She looked up at him, dreamy, dewy-eyed. Brown embers sparkled in her eyes, remnants of a subterranean heat. "Where are we?"

In trouble, he almost replied. He didn't want to love her. He'd kept love at bay all his life. "Dinner," he responded tersely. He nodded toward the burgundy awning with the flowing white script on the side. "I thought you'd like Italian."

She scooted up in her seat, wriggling to get the wrinkles out of her skirt. "If it's food, I'll like it. I bite anything that doesn't bite back."

Gabe laughed. The soft huff of breath wafted across her cheek. She gave him a curious look, as if surprised at how close they were, how close he stayed.

He drew in a lungful of her faint perfume. Spidery lash-shadows fanned across her cheeks. Wariness warred with expectancy as her eyes widened.

"Are you hungry?" he asked. Low, suggestive, the words didn't emerge the way he'd intended.

Breathy, whispery, her reply echoed his. "Yes. I am."

Good. Dream or no dream, he couldn't have prevented himself from kissing her if he'd wanted.

He touched her first, his driving glove's soft suede tan against her suddenly pale skin. He traced her cheekbone back toward her hair, her jawline to the shell of her ear. The wool of her coat gave off hints of the brittle cold it had absorbed, mingling with the pungent scent of jasmine shampoo.

The power of scent and memory combined, a one-two

punch melding the knife-sharp world of his predicting dreams with the erotic haze of his nocturnal fantasies.

"Gabe?"

"Shana." He wanted her to say his name again, that half-moan that said she wasn't sure what she was doing either.

With a passion that took both by surprise, their mouths mingled. The taste flooded Gabe's body with sensations old and new. The dream he'd had earlier might have made his body ache; it had nothing on the woman in his arms.

Her tongue darted toward his. He cradled it in his mouth, stroking the velvety underside.

"We shouldn't do this," she whispered.

"Are you as hungry as I am?"

She looked at his lips. "More."

He dragged her into his arms. Their legs bumped the dash, their arms thudded against the door. A car drove by, its lights sweeping the interior. It barely distracted them. A grumble the size of a snowplow intervened. Aghast, Shana met Gabe's startled look. She patted her stomach. "I guess I am hungry."

"I guess you are." He leaned back, a smile creasing his face. He'd hoped she'd prove his dream wrong. He wasn't making it easy.

She rested her hand on the door handle. "Think we should go in?"

"Before we do something crazy? Good idea." He yanked his own door handle. A blast of cold air stung his face, tumbling a lock of hair down his forehead. He walked around the car, fast, his topcoat wrapped over the throbbing remainder of their kiss. He opened her door. "After you."

She sat a moment, abashed, apologetic. Any minute now she'd be hemming and hawing, talking a mile a minute to explain away what they'd just done. She stepped onto the slippery sidewalk. "Gabe, you know we shouldn't—"

He touched his leather glove to her lips. "Let's wait until we're inside."

"If you insist," she said primly. But prim women didn't have their hair in tangles or their cheeks the color of a bordello's satin sheets. The two of them got as far as the short flight of cement steps leading down to the restaurant. "We have to talk about this, Gabe. It can't keep happening."

If his dream didn't come true, the curse would shatter, he was sure of it. All Shana had to do was turn him down. He should be happy; if a simple kiss unnerved her, she'd never agree to the rest of his dream. "This whole evening is up to you. Everything that happens from here on out is your choice."

"Then I suggest we keep this as businesslike as possible."

"Fine. Let's get a table and we'll talk."

The tables were filled. As in his dream, Gabe stood aside while Giuseppe guided them to a booth near the back, a burgundy banquette with red velvet curtains and all the romantic privacy a couple might wish. A candle guttered in a Chianti bottle.

Coincidence, he insisted. It didn't mean the dream was coming true. To prove it, he left the wine up to Shana. She ordered diet soda. Gabe smiled. Giuseppe paled visibly. Undeterred, the waiter brought soda as requested. Unasked, he brought a bottle of Gabe's favorite—a vintage red.

Shana allowed Giuseppe to pour her a glass. She toasted Gabe. "To your continued progress."

He drank. Progress, according to his Webster's, didn't involve the sensation of sinking backward into a pit. He knew from his dream that their next kiss would mingle the tastes of red wine and garlic.

"Is there something wrong with the wine?" she asked.

He shook his head. His whole life was one long fight. If he wasn't struggling against sleep, he was wrestling with the idea of being yoked to a future he saw but couldn't change.

He left the ordering up to her, working out his strategy. He wanted her to stop what was about to happen, to refuse to participate in events he'd already lived in his dreams. He also wanted her to believe him.

By the time the night was over she'd either believe—fat chance—or she'd run screaming into the night, convinced he was crazy.

The wine went down hard; he'd considered that last possibility more than once.

The waiter slipped a loaf of Italian bread onto the table. Pouring a shot of olive oil onto a plate, he crushed a clove of garlic on the rim. "Enjoy."

Two glummer people never shared a table.

With a quick sigh, Shana set down her menu and began the conversation Gabe knew was coming. "I should apologize for my behavior in the car. Heck, I should throw myself in front of the nearest salt truck. From an ethical point of view, what we just did was thoroughly unforgivable on my part."

And completely predictable on his.

"So!" She balanced her elbows on the table and folded her hands. "With that behind us, what shall we talk about next?"

"Kissing?"

She choked on her soda. "How about your treatment?" She dabbed at her lips with a red cloth napkin.

He crushed his in his fist. He set it on the table like a gauntlet; this better work. "All right then. You asked me the first time we met if I use my insomnia to keep women at a distance."

"Mm-hm."

"You're right. I've always avoided getting involved."

"And why do you think that is?"

Her counselor tone. Who was he to sneer? His bad habits were worse.

He paused while she searched through her purse, coming up with a pen but no notepad. She grabbed a stiff "How Was Our Service" flyer and took notes. "Please. Go ahead."

"I avoid relationships because I only dream about the people I'm close to. I'm afraid if I allow a woman in my life, something will happen—something I've foreseen but can do nothing about." How was that for nuts?

Eyes lowered, she sketched something on her paper. "Just because you dreamed about your parents and it came true, Gabe, doesn't mean that one event has to rule your life."

"I haven't told you all of it."

"I understand. You feel guilty, responsible."

He laughed, a harsh, ugly sound. "Apparently I didn't fell responsible enough to stop it."

"You were nine years old. Dream or no dream, what on earth could you have done that would have made any difference?"

"I could have stayed awake."

Silence descended like a curtain. Shana stared at him, her breath caught in her lungs.

Gabe reached for the wine. His fist gripped and regripped the neck. "I threw such a tantrum after the nightmare that my grandmother promised to take me to the airport the next night. An hour after we got there, I fell asleep on a sofa. I knew that plane was going down and I slept through it. Even the sound of the crash didn't wake me." He poured the wine like watery blood. "Mom always did say I slept like the dead."

Shana winced. "You'd worn yourself out arguing. You were nine."

"True." All the excuse-filled explanations were true in their own way.

"What did your grandmother say about it?"

"About the dream?"

"Did she blame you in any way, imply it was your fault?"

"We never talked about it." It became their shameful

secret. "I grew up believing it was all one big nightmare. Until the next one came along."

Tingles of anticipation started beneath Shana's skin. The warmth of the wine couldn't dispel the chill in her veins. "You had another dream?"

"I was fourteen, living with my grandmother. I dreamed I was walking through our apartment. Moving boxes filled every room. I read my uncle's address on the shipping labels. When I woke up, I knew it was another dream, the 'real' kind. If it came true, that would mean the one I'd had when I was nine had been real too. I demanded that my grandmother tell me if we were moving. She denied it."

"Then?"

"She had a massive stroke a week later. A few days after the funeral everything was boxed up. I walked through the apartment reading the shipping labels. After that I moved in with Uncle Jim. After that I didn't sleep much."

Shana sat in silence. Giuseppe set their plates down. She absently stuck a fork in her fettuccine and began twirling, unraveling the possibilities. "Maybe you sensed something, overheard a conversation with her doctor. She could have been having a series of small strokes, things only someone who lived with her would notice—"

He cut her off. "That doesn't explain the others."

Shana's fork clanged against the rim of her plate. She sat back. "How many?"

To her surprise, his face relaxed in a reassuring smile. For the life of her she couldn't fathom how a man could smile under the burden he carried. True or not, he believed these dreams. "How often do you have them?"

He reached for her hand. She let him take it—they both needed the contact. "One, maybe two a year. I've gone as long as three years, buried in work, living alone. Then—"

"Then?" she croaked.

"The closer I am to people, the more likely I am to see things."

She looked around the restaurant. Diners chatted and ate, a strolling violinist filled the air with the theme from *The Godfather*.

She tugged her hand back, the better to twist her napkin in her lap. Focusing on her plate of pasta, she deliberately reached for the pepper mill and twisted a healthy sprinkle across her fettucine Alfredo. Next she powdered it with parmesan. They'd barely made a dent in the bread. She tore off a chunk and dipped it in the white sauce.

"Your food is getting cold."

"You don't take me seriously."

"I take *you* very seriously."

"But not my dreams."

"There are probably a hundred explanations." She munched for a few moments, noting the bread's crisp crust and tender center. Butter, it needed butter.

"It's like a horoscope," she said at last, slathering butter across her bread with the swipe of a knife. "Most people read their horoscope over breakfast then forget it by the end of the day. They only remember it when it comes true. Then they say, 'Aha, these things work.' One too many coincidences, and they begin shaping their lives around the predictions."

She stared at her plate. He stared at her. "I've organized my life around my dreams, is that what you're saying?"

"I'm saying that because you're always on the lookout for coincidences, you notice them more than most people."

"These aren't normal dreams, Shana. I can tell the difference. I can smell it, taste it. It's as if I'm there, living it."

She looked patiently at the bruised shadows beneath his eyes, the drained lines etched into his cheeks. His suffering was real. "How many hours of sleep have you gotten in the last two days?"

He rubbed his neck. "Counting this afternoon? Four, maybe five."

She let the information sink in. "I know this will sound like a lecture, but sleep deprivation means dream deprivation as well."

"So?"

"When you finally sleep, your brain catches up. Dreams kick in faster; they're more intense, crammed with more information."

"More reality."

She evaded his dogged insistence. "On those rare occasions when a dream comes true, it reinforces your belief that you're seeing the future."

"I am."

"Will you at least consider the possibility?"

"That it's all coincidence?"

"That there might be other explanations."

He read her earnest supportive expression. She wanted to help him. He wanted to believe her. There was just one problem. According to his dream, the next time she reached for that olive oil she was going to knock over her diet soda.

"Oh, my gosh. What a slob. I'm so sorry." Her red napkin darted across the table, dabbing and sopping.

He caught her wrist. Slowly prying open her fingers, he replaced her napkin with his. "Use mine. Marco will get the rest." No sooner had he said it than the young son of the owner rushed over to blot the stain.

Shana flushed. "I get so wrapped up in things, I don't watch what I'm doing."

"No problem." Gabe sat back, suddenly exhausted. He'd told her the worst parts, and she hadn't believed him. He'd almost convinced himself he didn't care. No one had ever believed and no dream had ever been prevented. What made him think he'd talk her out of the kiss he knew was coming?

Hell, he might as well eat.

"I don't mean to lecture," she apologized again. "But these beliefs are interfering with your sleep, your life."

He speared a meatball.

"It's tormented you for years."

And it would go on tormenting him. His only consolation was that the dreams weren't all bad. Like what he and Shana would be doing in approximately an hour and a half. He tore off a large chunk of bread.

"That's better, eat. Nana always said food was the stuff strength is made of."

"Shakespeare," he murmured.

"Pardon me?"

"A paraphrase of Shakespeare. 'We are such stuff as dreams are made on.' More of my teenage reading list." Grim but determined, Gabe finished off his entree. His eyes were flinty with lack of sleep, his shoulder blades aching from sitting before a computer.

Realizing that Giuseppe was in no hurry to refill Shana's diet soda, Gabe poured her another glass of wine. To her credit, she didn't play coy. She'd said nothing about two being her limit, or fettuccine being too rich for her diet.

It struck him that up to now they'd played none of the first-date games. Maybe it was time he learned more about this woman who inhabited his dreams. "While I was busy with all that reading what did you do as a teenager?"

She offered him the last piece of bread.

He declined.

"It's good stuff."

"I believe it's homemade."

She pursed her lips as if savoring a tasty morsel of gossip. "That may be, but this isn't the home it's made in."

"Don't let Giuseppe hear you say that."

The waiter scurried over on cue. "Would madam care for another soda?"

"The wine is fine. Oh, and Giuseppe?" She saluted him with a chunk of bread. "Uncle Karl sends his best."

The waiter straightened abruptly. Tossing a napkin over his arm, he swept the empty basket off the table with a flourish. "The next loaf, she is on the house."

"Thanks." Shana grinned.

"You know them here?" Gabe asked.

"I'd know Uncle Karl's garlic bread anywhere. I've been sampling it since they put me on solid food."

"You were raised in a bakery." He'd never imagined her as a child. "Why is that so funny?"

"Raised? Like bread dough? Get it? Growing up over a bakery you hear them all. In school I was the girl with cute buns and lots of dough."

He laughed. It felt good. A simple getting-to-know-you conversation was all too rare. "Tell me more."

She shrugged, her eyes lit by candlelight, her cheeks warmed by the wine. "When you live above a bakery the business is home and home is the business. When we went to visit relatives we visited their bakeries. Aunt Shayna, Uncle Karl, Nana Sofia—that's my grandmother on my mother's side."

"They all had bakeries?"

"Did you grow up in Chicago?"

He nodded. She signaled the strolling violinist and whispered in his ear. He lifted his instrument and swung into a catchy jingle.

" 'Pascewski bakeries bake the best,' " Gabe declared, repeating the final words to the song.

Shana grinned despite herself. "Our radio jingle for twenty-five years. Only a native Chicagoan would know it."

"I grew up on it."

"So did I," she agreed ruefully.

"You don't like it?"

"It was like growing up with the name Oscar Meyer! The song follows you around."

He hummed a few more bars.

She took his teasing in stride. "I stop by to help out when I can. I walk in the door, and they put me to work behind the counter."

"You don't bake?"

"Not a cake, not a cookie. The family theory is that

my mother was frightened by a frozen dinner when she was pregnant."

Gabe grinned. "I doubt that."

"I'm serious. My favorite theory, which I love because I love fairy tales, is that my aunt Shayna read me 'Hansel and Gretel' when I was too young. I've been afraid of large ovens ever since. Although it never stopped me from getting fattened up—à la Hansel."

"Or leaving breadcrumbs as clues?"

She swatted a few off the table. "What kind of clues?"

"To your personality. I'm enjoying this."

For some reason Uncle Karl's bread tasted dry. Shana gulped some wine, avoiding Gabe's trenchant gaze. They'd moved this discussion to the level of casual flirting. She should be relieved. Except that there was nothing casual about Gabe.

She gave a comical shrug. "Around the bakery everyone pulled their weight. I gained mine."

"I think you look just fine."

Her smile faded. "I appreciate the compliment, but I'm not into dating patients. You're very attractive. *Very*. I'm sure you've sensed I'm not immune. But, and I mean this very seriously, I do not want to get involved. I don't get involved."

"You already are."

"I've had a few relationships, nothing at present."

"I meant with me. I had a dream."

"So did Martin Luther King."

He'd thought he wanted her scoffing. He found himself reaching for her hand instead. "It was one of the real ones. That makes two with you in them."

She graced him with an indulgent smile and a pat on the hand that set his teeth on edge. "You can't base your actions on dreams."

He canted his head toward a waiter balancing a tray on his shoulder. "Watch this."

The waiter's tray tipped. Swiftly overbalancing it to

compensate, a bottle of wine tottered then crashed to the floor. It shattered on the terra-cotta flagstones.

"I knew that would happen," Gabe said simply.

Resolutely unimpressed, Shana gave him a deadpan expression. "You dream about waiters dropping things. Very significant."

"I told you, I dream about people close to me."

"We've hardly met."

"That's why I need to know why you're part of it."

She took custody of her hand again. "Parlor tricks."

Gabe indicated the waiter mopping up the spilled wine. "What if I tell you he's going to cut his hand on that glass?"

"My mother would say exactly the same. Then she'd predict he was going to catch cold if he went outside without a sweater—"

A gasp, a curse, and a stream of Italian. The waiter rushed by, holding his hand in a bloody napkin.

Gabe never took his eyes off her.

"Lucky guess." She dearly hoped the snappy retort would hide her wariness. This was getting too strange. Sleep was a mysterious and strange process, but dreams were like fairy tales, they did not come true.

As a counselor, she strove to maintain her objectivity. Gabe would be an easy man to fall for—self-assured, intelligent, sensitive. He had a dozen admirable qualities. And a sleep problem she identified with more than he knew. "I know *you* believe your dreams—"

"I dreamed you were running down a hallway," he said, narrating the scene in a flat tone that brooked no comment. "This was a week ago, the evening I came rushing to the maternity ward."

She held very still. He'd hinted at something at the time. She hadn't listened, too shocked by his kiss.

"You were in a corridor, alone, late afternoon. There was a man, a woman, their faces too blurry to make out. They disappeared into an elevator. You ran after them, running toward danger when you should have run from it."

"I wasn't in danger," she repeated, the words bubbling up from memory. "Nothing happened."

He clenched her fingers until they hurt, refusing to let her pull away. " The elevator returned. You were terrified."

She was going to be sick. She ripped her hand from his and stood. Curious diners looked on.

"How did you know?" she demanded.

"I dreamed it. Because I saw it I had to be there, to try to prevent it if I could."

"But nothing happened."

He eased her back into the booth. "You're right. That's as far as the dream got."

She searched for a logical explanation. "Okay, maybe I came across some guy selling drugs. It's a big hospital, a big city. Dream about drug deals in Chicago, and if you're in the right place at the right time, you'll see one."

"Has he been around since?"

"No." She would've sounded more certain if she'd been able to keep the tremble out of her voice. "I reported it to Dr. Merryweather. Everything's under control."

On the contrary. As far as Gabe was concerned, everything rode on a very fine line. He stepped across it. "That was the first dream about you. Today I had another."

She shook her head, her hair obscuring her face as she twisted around for her coat. "I think that's just about enough."

Gabe tossed a couple of twenties on the table and followed her into the frigid night air. It calmed them both briefly. "You didn't let me finish."

"I'm finished listening."

"I don't want the dream I had today to come true."

"Am I in more danger? You didn't seem too concerned when you met me in the garage."

"The dream started there." He didn't say where it led.

"I'm calling a cab."

"Go ahead." He stepped back. "But take this with you." He handed her the envelope from his coat pocket.

Shana read the raised black script in the corner, "Grier/Fitzerald." "Your company?"

"My dream. I wrote it down. When tonight's over, I want you to read it."

She bounced it against her fingertips. "I've seen magicians do this. Do I pick a number from one to ten now?"

Sarcasm didn't faze him.

She eyed him with a cautious squint, reviewing their evening. "You were waiting for me in the parking garage. You drove us here so you knew where we'd be going. You probably knew we'd kiss in the car."

"I was hoping."

She jabbed him with a pointed finger. "How do I know you didn't pay off that waiter? If this is some kind of sick set-up—"

"That's why I'm letting you call the shots from here on out. You say what we do and where we go."

Straight to the loony bin, Shana thought. She sized up the icy sidewalks and the BMW parked across the street. Behind it wispy snowdrifts piled against the granite base of a skyscraper. Her gaze rose to the tenth floor, the twentieth, the fiftieth. "I say what we do and where we go."

"Right."

"And then I read this to see if you were right?"

"Mm-hm."

She thought of demanding he take her back to her car in the parking garage. Entirely too predictable. "Up there."

"The Sears Tower?"

She folded the envelope in two and shoved it in her purse. "All the way to the top."

It was supposed to be impossible. At this hour they'd never be allowed into the Sears Tower. Then a harried yuppie with a bulging briefcase held the door open as he exited and they slipped inside. The same thing happened with the elevator. Shana began to wonder if Gabe had contacts everywhere.

She glowered at him suspiciously.

The elevator waited as his finger hovered over the buttons. "Your call."

She pulled out a coin and flipped it. Tails. Rats. "All the way up," she announced. "I want to see stars."

The night outside was heavy with snow-laden clouds. He mentioned that.

"Guess your dream won't come true."

He pushed the button and stepped closer. "Are the stars my dream or yours?"

Her stomach dropped as the elevator rose. "This isn't my fantasy."

"You can make it mine." His lips brushed hers.

The whole world slowed. Her feet lifted slightly off the floor. Her hands rose to his sides. She could push him away or hold on tight. Before she decided the doors hushed open on the thirtieth floor.

A tiny woman in a cleaning uniform grinned from ear to ear. "Lovers shouldn't be here," she chided in a heavy accent, wagging her finger at them. She rolled her cleaning cart on board.

Shana and Gabe took up positions on either side of it.

"We really shouldn't be here," Shana apologized, recovering her common sense. "We'll leave quietly. I'm sorry if we caused any trouble."

Completely impassive, Gabe pointed to the ground-floor button. "Anything you say."

"Wait!" Damn him. It would be entirely too predictable for her to chicken out now. She ran her fingers over the raised lettering on the envelope. She'd foil his arrogant predictions yet. If only she knew what they were. "To the top," she repeated.

"I don't know if this elevator goes all the way."

"You want to be on top?" The cleaning woman winked at Gabe and nudged him aside. Finding a key on her immense key ring, she inserted it in the elevator panel. "Lovers, they like this. Stars for men. Moon for woman. You go."

In seconds they'd reached the top. The doors parted on a vista that took Shana's breath away. Beyond the glass the black sky glittered, diamond-strewn. A white scything moon hung like a hook, catching wisps of clouds on its barbed tip. Beneath them denser clouds floated, pillowy and mysterious, shielding them from the city that had surrounded them moments before. It was as if the world had been blanketed in a spell.

She turned. Like a sorceress in a fairy tale, the old woman was gone. She'd transported them someplace magical then disappeared.

"You couldn't have planned this," Shana said.

"A man can dream, can't he?"

She tried to laugh. She tried to be frightened. She didn't want to believe the things he told her. She wanted more than anything for him to take her into his arms. "Things like this don't happen."

"Don't they?"

They could have been talking about something besides dreams, something nebulous and untrustworthy such as love.

"It's up to you," he murmured.

Maddened by his nonchalance, wild to read that envelope, she gripped his lapels and tugged him closer. "I am not the woman who's going to make your dreams come true."

He nodded.

"I mean it."

"I know."

They were in an incredibly romantic place. She was a woman who did not get involved. This mesmerizing man seemed unaccountably attracted to her. More fairy tales. She was an ugly duckling. She wasn't a princess waiting to be rescued; she rescued others.

Gabe waited for her to prove him wrong. If she cured

his belief in his dreams, she might cure the insomnia that plagued him.

Very well. She thought of the most unpredictable, unlikely, un-Shana thing she could do. She kicked off her snow-soaked pumps, dropped her coat, and threw her arms around his neck. The man wouldn't know what hit him.

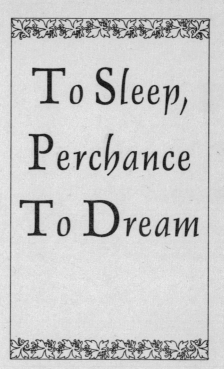

BOOK TWO

To Sleep, Perchance To Dream

9

"Lie back." She placed her hands on his chest and gently pushed.

Gabe obeyed. The room was another anonymous bedroom in the sleep clinic. The woman wasn't the one he wanted.

Fiona checked the attachment of electrodes on his chest, her fingers threading through the wires leading from his temples. Fine, brightly colored filament sprouted from Gabe's wrists, measuring a pulse that was erratic at best. "Your machines probably go wild every time you tell a man that."

"You mean 'lie down'?" Fiona tucked a strand of short hair behind her ear. "I've heard every line from 'Only if you join me,' to 'Ladies first.'"

"In other words, I can't compete?"

She did him the honor of looking him up and down. "Oh, I wouldn't say that." Her gaze drifted from his hairline to the plastic button stuck to his forehead, professionally noting the ones taped to his temple, his earlobe, and his neck.

"Where is she?"

"Shana? Probably in her office." Her indifference was supremely irritating.

Like numbers that didn't add up, or deals that lost him money, Gabe used the aggravation to keep his edge. If he didn't, the memories would flood back in.

Shana had kissed him Friday night on top of the Sears Tower. She'd thrown her arms around his neck, her mouth meeting his in a parody of wild passion that quickly became passionate fact.

In the maternity ward he'd kissed her with relief. In the car he'd kissed her out of tenderness, curiosity. On top of the Sears Tower he'd kissed her back.

Their mouths had broken apart after untold minutes. Tangled in each other's arms, they tasted each other's wine, the sultry liquid of tongues and teeth and astonishingly hungry mouths.

She'd staggered back, snatching up her shoes, her coat, the envelope falling out of her purse. "I didn't mean that."

He'd pulled her up to face him. "I can't stop this."

For a second, she looked seriously scared. He'd hated that. He might be helpless before his dreams but one word from her, one no, and he'd stop no matter what demons drove him.

She didn't say it.

He touched her cheek, running his thumb across kiss-swollen lips. "Shana."

"She may be in later," Fiona replied.

He'd spoken aloud. His eyes snapped open.

Fiona leaned across him, giving one more electrode a nudge into place.

"What happens next?" He longed to ask another woman that same question. But wavering concentration was a sign of sleeplessness, weakness. He made himself pay attention as Fiona explained the process at hand.

"This is an MSL, Multiple Sleep Latency test. Shana didn't explain it?"

"No." Shana had talked to him once since Friday, a terse phone call to schedule this test.

"You'll take four naps. We judge how sleep-deprived you are by how quickly you fall asleep."

"And how often I dream?"

"You've been reading up."

He'd read anything when he couldn't sleep. "And if I'm too wired to sleep?"

Fiona hefted the bundle of wires and winked. "You'll get used to them."

Gabe groaned and lay back. How could he sleep? For three days he'd wrestled with the possibility Shana wasn't meant to be his doctor, she was meant to be his lover. "When does the test start?"

"As soon as I turn out the light." Fiona headed for the door, pausing to plug in a red bulb.

"I don't need a night-light." A lifetime of sleeplessness had left him used to the dark.

"This allows us to tape you. It accomplishes the same thing as an infrared camera only it's cheaper. One of Shana's innovations. Smart, huh?"

The door closed. Gabe breathed a curse and stared at the red-tinged shadows. He'd never stop thinking about her now.

"He's in two," Fiona announced over the intercom.

Shana mentally rehearsed her answer. A light "That's fine." A brusque "Thank you, Fiona." A cool "I'll look in in a few minutes." Although she doubted she'd have the nerve.

"Shana? Are you there? Is this phone system messed up again?"

Shana hit the button. "I'm here, Fiona."

"So's Gabe Fitzgerald. I just put him to bed."

Shana bit her tongue. "Fine. That's great. I'll be in in a minute. To look in, I mean. Check things out."

Fiona signed off with a chuckle, saving her from further babbling.

Shana hung her head in her hands. She stared at the letter lying on her desk. She could see Gabe was a successful businessman. The letter was flawlessly typed, the language clear and precise. He'd even used bullets to indicate the main points.

. We meet in the garage. I drive to Leonardo's.

So far, explainable. He described their dinner, the wine, the waiter and his tray, Shana spilling her drink. She was a klutz. Any perceptive man would have picked up on that. If he made her nervous enough, she was bound to knock something over.

. We go to the top of the Sears Tower. We kiss.

She'd kissed. She'd kissed him until her lips burned and her toes ached from standing tall. She'd kissed him until he bent to her, holding her hungrily in his arms, pressing her ardently to his chest. She'd kissed him until her lipstick was gone and her common sense a thing of the past.

She'd have bet Nana's pierogi recipe on her ability to keep men at a distance. She'd succeeded just fine for three years.

It was all her fault. She'd kept telling herself she was proving his arrogant, unspecified predictions wrong. Except there wasn't an arrogant bone in Gabe's body. The arrogance was all hers for thinking she could outwit her feelings. She'd kissed him because part of her longed for contact, romance, a man who looked at her with undisguised passion. She'd taken one look at those stars and that moon and wanted all of it.

She got it.

Shana flattened the letter with her palm as if putting out a fire. How could she? How dare he write it down?

. She takes my shirt off.

"She didn't." Shana moaned.

She did. Her last coherent, defensible action had been bending to pick up her shoes. She'd been about to flee.

He'd drawn her up. "I can't stop this," he'd warned her.

A frisson of fear had rippled through her. She'd died inside when she saw the shame on his face. It wasn't him she feared, it was her unchained desires, pent-up longings coming unleashed.

She'd tried teasing him as she stuffed the envelope back in her purse. "You probably have ten of these, each one describing a different scenario."

Wordlessly he opened his suit coat, spreading it wide for her inspection.

She gingerly dipped her fingers in the inside pocket, feeling the warmth of his chest, sensing the unsteady pounding of his heart. Her hand strayed to his shirt pocket. Unforgivably, it stayed. Her fingers splayed on the cotton as she inhaled his scent, expensive, elusive, all male.

In minutes she discovered the muscles defining his rib cage, a shirt radiating body heat, a tie that needed loosening, and buttons that urgently required undoing.

He shrugged out of his coat. She'd helped. The shirt went when she tugged it from his waistband. His chest looked as if it were shaped by a sculptor's chisel. Black swirls surrounded taut nipples, dusky brown.

If she'd been paying attention to something besides the way his skin rippled at her touch, she'd have noticed he was tugging her blouse free, flicking the buttons from their holes, unsnapping the clasp of her bra. Her eyes fluttered shut when his mouth raked her neck, sinking to her left breast.

"Gabe." She made sounds she'd never heard, a gasp then a moan that shuddered up from her soul. Looking down, she watched his mouth mold around her. Matched to the sensation, the sight nearly buckled her knees. She clawed her hands through his hair, kissing the top of his head tenderly, reverently. No man had ever made her feel that naked, that desired.

She held his face away from her. "I can't believe this."

He looked up. Eyes unfathomably dark, he slowly rose. He rubbed his body along hers in an erotic dance. Something inside her melted like hot wax down a candle.

"Believe *me*," he whispered. He coaxed her leg around his waist, wrapping his arm around her back. Carrying her to the window, he pressed her bare skin to the piercing cold of the glass.

She cried out, the shock filling her with an awareness so acute it was almost painful. No cold could compete with the heat coursing through her. She drew him closer, her legs high around his waist, her body yearning to be joined to his.

"She's either sleeping, reading, or having an out-of-body experience."

Her head jerked up. "Flora."

The respiratory therapist folded her arms across her ample bosom and stared down her nose. Fiona stood beside her, shaking her head. "I vote for the out-of-body experience."

Shana's body felt as if a thousand candles had been lit inside it, half of them melted, the other half still sizzling. "Guys. Hi."

Flora and Fiona traded glances. "I'll take over," Flora said.

"Good luck," Fiona replied. "When she's conscious tell her her patient isn't."

"He's asleep already?" Shana called, scurrying around her desk to catch Fiona as she strolled back to the sleep lab.

"Entered REM after three minutes," Fiona called over her shoulder.

"Looks like he isn't the only one dreaming," Flora added tartly. "Where was your mind, child?"

"At the top of the Sears Tower." Knowing the reference would make no sense to Flora, Shana sighed and gestured to a chair. "Care to sit down?"

Her colleague eyed her for a moment then accepted. "I have two words for you. DeVon Johnson."

A name designed to get Shana's attention. She swept the letter into her drawer and sank into her squeaking leather chair. "Any sign of him?"

"He's coming to your group session next week."

"Is he bringing a gun?"

"Not funny."

"Who said I was being funny? The man hates me."

"Luckily for us he listens to his wife."

"Could've fooled me."

"Let me amend that. He listens to his wife's tape recorder. She taped him sleeping the other night."

"I thought she did that before."

"That time she was trying to prove he snored. This time she got him to listen to the spaces in between."

"When he wasn't snoring, you mean."

"Or breathing. That's why he's coming back. He's got apnea and he knows it." Flora paused. "Smile, sugar. We won one. You scared him straight. He's willing to listen. Which is more than you're doing."

Shana peered at her colleague. "Flora?"

"What?"

"How do you know which blush to use? I mean, with your skin tones, how do you know whether ruby red or cranberry surprise will work better?"

"You're asking me for makeup tips?"

"Just curious."

Flora eased her way out of the chair, making no sudden moves as she backed toward the door. "Sure you are, honey. And I'm Whitney Houston."

.   .   .

"Is she in her office?" Gabe strode past Fiona, his shirt barely buttoned. Test one was done, naptime over.

The night tech whirled on her stool beneath the banks of television screens. "You can leave the lab between tests but it'll mean reattaching some of the electrodes."

Fine, he didn't want what was about to happen showing up on any graph. He strode down the hall. Twenty minutes of sleep had given him a much-needed respite from the turmoil of the last few days. He took full advantage of the moment of clearheadedness. He'd wanted to do this for days.

"Hello." He stood in the doorway to her office.

Shana looked up.

She looked wonderful. Tired. Pale. Mussed. Glasses perched on her nose. She had on a T-shirt with a wild design beneath her white lab coat. A folder lay open on her desk, bits and pieces of paper strewn everywhere. He recognized the satisfaction survey from Leonardo's covered in her loopy shorthand. She'd been reading up on him.

He didn't need notes to recall Friday's encounter.

He'd been dreaming about her. Not a "real" dream. All the same, he wondered how their charts would graph that. He let the slow pounding of his heart guide him. Stepping inside, he quietly but firmly shut the door.

"Ah. Gabe. Good to see you." She shuffled bits of paper into some kind of order. "What we'll be doing today is measuring your level of sleep deprivation."

"Fiona explained."

Shana talked to his admitting form. "As I believe I mentioned, four or five hours of sleep per day may be normal for you. Your problem may be nothing more than these extended sleepless states." She hid behind jargon when she was nervous. He remembered that.

"What you think of as twenty years of insomnia may in fact be a natural state for you."

"Like wanting a woman?"

She stumbled to a halt.

The corner of his mouth turned up in a grin.

"I'm not saying your problems aren't real or chronic."

"We're the problem, Shana."

She tossed him a glance as she slid her glasses a little farther down her nose. "There's no we and there never will be."

"There already is, and I didn't come here to play word games."

"How about mind games?" She pulled open her drawer, slipped his letter out, and shoved it in among the papers in his file.

He stood behind the swivel chair, his fingers denting its back. So that's the way it was going to be; noted and filed away. "You can't hide it, Shana. We can't pretend it didn't happen."

"How have you been sleeping?"

"Not well." The last thing he wanted was her treating him like a patient. He ran through the routine to get it over with. "A few hours here and there."

"And your first nap today?"

"Twenty minutes. I fell asleep almost instantly. Remarkable, considering I was thinking about you. Some memories keep a man wide awake. Take my word for it."

She believed him. From what he saw she'd suffered the same fate. He gauged the lines around her eyes, the glazed eyes that didn't focus on anything long.

"I've been doing a lot of reading," she explained.

"Always my favorite method."

"I'm not an insomniac. I—" She seemed to change her mind in mid-sentence.

He thought for a moment she was going to say something more revealing than a lame "I'm fine."

A buzz of aggravation droned in his head. Dancing around the point wasted what little time they had. "You don't look fine."

"Thank you for the compliment."

He snorted at her icy response. "You read the letter."

She jumped up from her chair, pulling books from the shelves. "I've uncovered a number of theories that might explain your dreams."

He glanced at the ragged stacks, surprised he hadn't seen that one coming. He was bone-tired, muscle-tired. Anger and surliness lurked just beneath the surface. "You've been trying to explain it all away, is that it?"

"There are theories."

"Don't you think I've read them?"

She picked up a yellow notepad, her head tilting as she followed her handwriting around the margins. "Freud theorized that dreams were wish fulfillment, a way for the subconscious to deal with urges the conscious preferred not to face."

"Does that explain your urge to kiss me?"

"In a sense. A woman my age, single so long. It might have been predictable."

"Bullshit."

Prepared for that, she breezed on. "A more modern theory states that the subconscious uses dreams the way a computer does. It sorts and stores data gained during the day and dumps what it doesn't need."

"Are you dumping me?"

"Theory three: dreams may be no more than random neurons firing in the cortex. We create narratives around these images so they make sense."

"Conclusion: in and of themselves my dreams mean nothing."

"They have whatever meaning you give them."

He leaned across her desk, tapping the corner of his letter. "Then this means I wanted you. Your kissing me back meant you wanted me just as badly. Explain that, Dr. Getz."

"It may not mean exactly that—"

"It still doesn't explain how I could have predicted it. Right down to you wrapping your legs around my waist—"

"There are only so many basic positions—"

"And we barely scratched the surface."

She swallowed. Apparently she'd forgotten the part about scratching his back.

Remembering her wild abandon made him ache elsewhere. He eased into the chair, his ankle balanced on his opposite knee. "I want to see where this is going, Shana, not make it go away."

"That's very flattering but—"

"Dammit! Don't patronize me by pretending you don't care. We both have the scars to prove it."

She touched the tiny bite on her neck. "We got carried away. It happens."

"And I knew it would."

"We need to stick with reality here."

He spit out a curse. Launching himself out of the chair, he paced to the window and back, clenching his fists at his sides. "The letter means nothing?"

"It was amazing but—"

"Something on the order of bending spoons or magically repairing broken watches."

"I'm sure there's an explanation."

"So what's *your* excuse?"

She stood, her trembling hands flattened on her desk. "I hate to think I'm that—that transparent. But it happened. We'll deal with it and move on."

"An open-and-shut case."

She raised her chin. "I am truly sorry, Gabe. I don't know what came over me. It won't happen again."

"And if I want it to?"

"That's my decision."

He rubbed his gritty eyes. This was all his fault. He'd thrown too much at her. He didn't want her ashamed or embarrassed *or* defensive. As for expecting her to believe his dreams—*Dream on.*

"Look, don't believe me. No one else ever has, including the shrink I saw at fourteen. He thought they were manifestations of guilt, some garbage like that."

"They might be."

"Why would any man feel guilty for wanting you?"

She ducked the compliment, flustered, flattered, regretful.

His voice rasped. "I still need to sleep."

Relieved, she relaxed her shoulders. "I can help you with that. As long as we keep this relationship business-like."

The woman never guessed she was dealing with a negotiating expert. Gabe instantly altered the terms. "I'll stick with the program. I'll do your relaxation exercises. I'll follow every sleeping tip you give me. But I won't pretend we never happened." He reached for her, his hand filling with soft curls. "I want to keep seeing you. In real life, not in dreams."

Her eyes grew wide, soft, sorry. "I don't date patients. Amend that. I don't date. Period."

"I find that hard to believe."

"Didn't you notice that nervous Nellie sitting across from you in the restaurant, knocking things over, chattering away?"

"I noticed she was funny, charming, intelligent, sexy. Her eyes glowed in the candlelight, her lips were wet with red wine." His fingers skimmed her cheek. "You're a beautiful, passionate woman. Don't tell me no man's ever seen it."

"Maybe they saw another side of me."

He snorted. "You've got a body like Venus, only warmer. A face like a madonna, only sexier. A mouth like wet velvet, and a neck—" He traced his fingers down her neck, watching her swift intake of breath. "Is the rest of you this sensitive?"

He should know. He'd kissed her breasts.

He grinned at the way their unspoken memories combined. He closed the gap between them. She didn't want to kiss him. She was frightened, unsure. It was the sadness that stopped him, the longing he saw in her eyes. She looked at him as if he were a distant ship on the horizon, a jewel behind Plexiglas, a star in the sky.

"Give us a chance," he urged.

"It won't work. It never does."

She'd been hurt, bad. He'd find out about it someday. Doubt like that called for promises, assurances, pretty words he couldn't say. The more he let her into his life the more she'd enter into his dreams. She'd be hurt, and he'd be helpless to stop it.

He dropped his arms to his sides, walking silently to the window, fighting his feelings all the way. The day he staggered into this clinic he'd vowed to change. He would not let these dreams rule his life.

He turned and sat on the windowsill, hands clutching the dry wood. "I want to see you. It's that simple. Dates, dinner, theater, whatever you like. Think we can manage that?"

She hesitated. His sudden shift in mood hadn't gone unnoticed. "Dates."

"I'm not talking deep involvement. Neither one of us is ready for that. I've got my problems, you've got your reservations."

"It isn't you, Gabe."

He held up his palm. "No problem. My ego's intact. I haven't found a woman yet who could put up with my sleeping habits. I just want someone to talk to."

She didn't believe it.

"Friends?" He held the reassuring smile a second longer, then stuck out his hand. "I think we could both use one."

She shook his hand limply, her eyes narrowing. "What's the catch?"

"Mr. Fitzgerald?" Fiona rapped on the door. "Time for your second nap."

Gabe opened the door. They had nothing to hide. He told Fiona he'd be there in a minute. Then he stepped up to Shana, their bodies a breath apart. Her breasts barely rose or fell. Her lips barely parted when she darted her tongue between them.

"You call all the shots, Shana. I won't kiss you or

touch you. Not unless you want me to." Hands raised in a gesture of surrender, he backed out the door and into the hall. "Promise."

Anyone passing would have thought she had a gun on him. Anyone passing would have had no idea how her face fell when he left without kissing her good-bye. The words "not unless you want me to" hung in the air.

She wanted all of it, kissing, caressing, making love, sleeping with a man and waking up beside him.

Which is where every relationship inevitably came to a screeching halt. When it came to love she was the perfect sleepwalker, stumbling around in the dark.

He wanted to see her.

She didn't want him seeing her that way, not ever.

10

Gabe shoved through the swinging door leading to the emergency room. A mixture of relief and dread settled in his veins. Déjà vu. It was like reentering a world he'd just escaped.

The dream clung to him like camphor or smelling salts; a car hitting ice, swerving across traffic, slamming into a concrete retaining wall. Highway exit signs flashed by as an ambulance raced beneath them. The generic tiled walls of a hospital swam into view.

Awaking in the sleep clinic midway through his third nap, he'd leapt out of bed, stripping off electrodes like a deep-sea diver clearing off seaweed. The lab was deserted. Commandeering Fiona's telephone, he'd punched the number to his office. "Is Brice there?"

Shelly answered with her usual aplomb. "Mr. Grier left for a downtown luncheon."

Gabe dialed Brice's cellular phone. His finger paused over the last digit. What if answering the car phone caused Brice to take his eyes off the road? What if the warning itself caused the accident? He slammed down the receiver. Why was he cursed with this foresight then damned with the inability to do anything about it?

It was an age-old question; one he didn't have time to answer. His gaze had darted to the clock over Fiona's desk. Three-ten. He headed for ER.

At least he got the location right. Maybe all emergency rooms smelled like the one in St. James', disinfectant and blood, the scent of fear clinging to skin like sweat. He checked off the details from his dream: posters in Spanish regarding AIDS, warnings about blood and bodily fluids, the sounds of crying children. A clump of relatives huddled at the admitting desk meekly requesting information. Harried interns shouted medical jargon at nurses and aides. Gurney wheels squeaked. A curtain screeched as a nurse pulled it back. Gabe waited.

The clock over the entrance read three-fifteen. The ambulance was already on its way. At three-twenty they'd wheel Brice through the automatic doors. All Gabe could do was sit there and count the minutes until he found out whether his best friend was dead or alive.

She couldn't sit. Two patients had come and gone, their progress encouraging but curiously unrewarding. Shana refiled their folders, deliberately ignoring Gabe's. No matter how many times she tried putting it away, it ended up smack in the middle of her desk. One more glance, she told herself, one more read-through.

She'd spent the weekend researching dreams, trying to explain his eerie predictions. In the end what had it gotten her? He'd agreed to focus more on her sleep tips and less on his dreams. And he'd asked for a date.

She should be ecstatic. At the very least encouraged.

A small voice whispered in her ear. He hadn't kissed her good-bye.

She huffed and rubbed her forehead. She was acting like a desperate female. She'd diverted the attentions of plenty of men these last three years. Although she'd failed miserably Friday night, there was no reason to dread flinging herself into Gabe's arms the next time they met. Especially when he promised not to touch you, she thought.

She wished it had been a little harder for him. He'd traipsed out of her office without a backward glance. After his second nap he'd hung around the lab until his third. She'd been with a patient, she shouldn't have minded.

She didn't. So why did she feel at loose ends? Her next appointment had canceled. She pushed the intercom button. "Fiona, I'm taking a coffee break." She didn't wait for an answer.

Determined to walk off her nagging frustration, she headed for the elevator. Pacing before the scratched doors, she waited all of two minutes then headed for the stairs.

The steel fire door clanged shut behind her, reverberating up and down the stairwell like a jail door in an old prison movie. Since the incident on the fourth floor, she'd begun walking the halls surrounding the basement cafeteria. Heading downward, she stalked ten steps to the landing, turned, then stalked another ten to the first floor. One more flight to the basement.

She paused at the foot of the stairs, her hand on the old doorknob with its faded brass finish, her mind brimming with theories. *What if dreams did come true?* Even if they were random images generated by the brain, the meaning people assigned those images revealed a great deal about them.

Gabe's dreams suggested he wanted her. That he'd predicted her response to that desire was no more than coincidence or crackerjack intuition.

"And *your* excuse?" He wanted to date her. What did she want?

She remembered the relationships she'd ruined with her nocturnal thrashing. There was no point subjecting another man to the unnerving business of waking up to find her glassy-eyed and semicoherent, baking inedible concoctions in her kitchen or packing for imaginary jour-

neys. She had too much self-respect to subject herself to
that humiliation again.

But why deny herself friendship? Companionship?
Dates, for heaven's sake. "You're a grown woman. You can
handle this." She'd accept his offer. In the meantime she'd
stop pining for lost kisses.

She turned on her heel, determined to march right
back upstairs and talk to him. His third nap should be just
about over.

A door shut somewhere above her, a heavy hollow
echo bouncing off the cement-block walls. Shana trudged
on. Gradually, imperceptibly, the silence caught her attention. No footsteps followed the sound of the door closing.

The hair rose on the back of her neck. Up above, out
of sight, someone had to be waiting. For what? She swallowed, recalling the drug dealer.

She leaned over the rail, craning her neck to see. She
glimpsed a brown pant leg, a long dark coat hanging to
the shin. Her heart flipflopped in her chest. "Who's
there?"

He backed up.

She backed down. Her foot tapped the air behind her,
searching for the step below. Her hand slid on the rusty
handrail. Four steps and she reached the first-floor door.
She felt behind her for the knob. What if it was locked?

Her heart burst into a staccato rhythm, her stomach
lurching. She was almost afraid to turn it.

She twisted it, barely daring to breathe. It clicked. She
heaved a sigh and opened it a crack. Arm outstretched,
she leaned back toward the rail. "I can leave anytime, you
know."

No answer. She peeked up as far as she could manage.
Whoever it was was trying very hard not to be seen. Suddenly crafty, she let the door clang shut. Maybe it would
draw him out of hiding. No sign of him.

Maybe he'd already left. If he'd slunk out onto the second floor someone would see him, Fiona, Flora, even
Merryweather.

She shoved open the first-floor door and hailed a passing orderly. "Hold this open!" She bolted up the stairs to the second floor. Chest heaving, she yanked open the door.

Fiona stood in the familiar hallway. "Where have you been? Merryweather was just looking for you."

"Did you see anyone come this way?"

"I heard someone yelling in the stairwell. Kids probably."

"That was me. There was someone else there. He wouldn't answer."

Fiona shrugged. "Why should he? I never talk to people on the staircase. It gives me the creeps."

Shana strode down the hall, jiggling the locked doorknobs of vacant offices. Hands on hips, she stood in the center of the corridor, eyes darting left and right. "He couldn't have simply disappeared."

Fiona hummed the theme from *Twilight Zone*.

"Very funny."

"You want funny? Come into the lab, I've got something you ought to see."

"Weird science, huh?"

Shana stared at the peaks and valleys of the polysomnograph. Silent after a frenzy of recording, the needles rested along the left margin. She lifted the scrolled paper out of the basket, following the bizarre scribblings.

"Ever see an REM like that?" Fiona asked. "Look at the brain waves."

"It's like a trance."

"Weirder."

"This line is typical stage five sleep—"

"Yeah, but how does anyone fall into the deepest stage of sleep during a ten-minute nap?"

Shana shook her head, pointing to another series of jagged lines. "And how does anyone dream in stage five?

Look at the rapid eye movement. Technically they're incompatible."

Fiona imitated a hammy actor's voice. "My God, Doctor, I've never seen anything like it!"

Shana rolled her eyes. "When was this taken?"

"Nap three. He fell asleep within four minutes, this started a couple minutes later. That's when I came looking for you—"

Shana clamped her hand over the hairs on the back of her neck. They were dancing again, on tiptoe. "Him?"

"Gabe Fitzgerald. This is his test."

Shana tried to breathe evenly. There had to be an explanation. "When did he wake up?"

Fiona tapped her fingernails against her coffee cup. "Um, I'm not exactly sure. I'd have to check the readout—"

"You what?"

"The minute I saw what these waves were doing I ran down to your office. You were gone."

"Where is he?" Shana began flicking on television monitors. "Which room?"

Fiona released a short sigh. "When I got back from looking for you, he was gone. I'm sure he'll be back for test four."

Shana dropped the readout and headed for the door. "Did you check the stairs?"

"I was heading that way when you came running out. Oh, and Merryweather really wanted to see—"

"Oh!" Shana bumped into Merryweather as she opened the door. "I'm sorry."

"No problem." The lanky doctor wiped pipe ash from his suit coat. "Going somewhere?"

"We've got a missing patient."

"Sleepwalking?"

Shana's gaze rocketed to his. The day he'd hired her she'd confided the reason she'd gotten into sleep research in the first place. Now she wasn't sure whether his benign smile was a smirk or something more innocuous. "We're doing an MSL," she explained. "It's almost time for his fourth nap."

"Then he's in no danger."

"None." She wished she could say the same about herself. Lack of sleep was playing havoc with her imagination. Gabe's dream come true, the lurker on the stairs, shades of the drug dealer on four—she was having a hell of a day.

"Perhaps you could spare me a few minutes," Merryweather said. "In my office?"

At least it would get them out of the lab. She wanted to think about that printout before showing it to him.

Fiona drew the scroll to his attention. "Before you go, Doctor, what do you think of this?"

Merryweather sucked on his pipe stem, poring over the pattern. "It's either incredibly deep REM or stage five involving eye and brain activity. Neither of which is supposed to happen. Shana, what do you think of him?"

She thought that was a very strange way of putting it. They hadn't said who the patient was. "I think we need to find him for his next test."

"Good idea. By all means." Merryweather tapped his pipe bowl with his index finger. "Fiona, why don't you call down to the cafeteria. He might be lost in the maze somewhere. Meanwhile Shana and I have some things to discuss."

"But I'd like to help."

"I need you first. This way." Merryweather escorted her down the hall, one hand on the back of her arm in his proprietary, gentlemanly way.

Shana liked Michael. Hiring her from Arizona, he'd given her the chance to test her innovative approaches in a brand-new setting. She was sincerely grateful, even if the term "new" was relative. The hospital was aging, the halls decrepit, the clinic equipment cobbled together. Nevertheless, it had been the chance of a lifetime.

Unfortunately, her bullheaded go-for-it style meshed with Merryweather's laid-back calm like oil and churning sea water. Every time he tried to take her under his wing, mentorlike, she charged head-on into some thorny problem.

He unlocked his office door. "Coming?" He'd caught her staring down the hall.

"Fiona said you were looking for me. You didn't use the stairs by any chance?"

He barked a laugh. "Me? I never walk when I can ride." As if to prove the point, he crossed the room to an imposing leather chair. Sinking into it with a sigh, he crossed his legs.

"Brown pants," Shana murmured.

Merryweather raised the toe of a highly polished shoe topped by the cuffed hem of a brown pair of slacks. "Been in style since Reagan was in office. I have charcoal if you prefer."

Shana smiled weakly. How could she have suspected him? And of what? Stepping into the stairwell for a moment's peace?

Her tension eased. She unclenched her fists and sat in the nearest chair. Merryweather calmly watched her think, the psychiatrist in him measuring her mood.

"The shoes are fine." She sighed. "The suit's fine. Your taste is simply—spiffy."

"Not the word I'd use," he replied dryly, "but I'll accept the compliment."

Shana reined in her wandering thoughts. The quicker they got through this, the quicker she could search for Gabe. "Michael, I know I raised my voice in Friday's committee meeting. I didn't intend to irritate Dr. Payne."

"You irritate Payne by breathing."

"I feel very strongly about those babies in neonatal."

"So do we all."

"They need an advocate."

"The research on this is inconclusive."

"Let's turn the lights down and see for ourselves."

"This jump-first attitude is one of the reasons Payne has such a hard time listening to you."

"And the other twenty-five?"

He chuckled. "You're the only woman I know who fishes for criticism."

"I want to do the best I can here, Michael—"

"Whoa, Shana. The job interview was months ago. I just wanted to warn you about Payne."

"Again."

"Don't ever forget how much I care about this clinic. It's my baby. Probably the only one I'll ever have, considering."

Shana chuckled with him. "Warning received loud and clear."

"Good." Languidly shoving off from his desk, Merryweather rolled his chair to the window. With a wink, he opened it. Pipe in one hand, match in the other, he gave her a sheepish smile. "You won't narc on me, will you?"

"You know I love the smell of pipe smoke."

"You know I don't mind bending rules any more than you do." He aimed a stream of smoke through the drafty opening, dousing his match on a pile of snow on the windowsill. "If you were to get the nurses' cooperation, it might make an interesting study."

A new form of adrenaline kicked in, the kind that raced through Shana when she was onto a fresh approach. "You'll let me do it?"

"I'm authorizing nothing. In fact, I know absolutely nothing about it." That wide-eyed look was completely convincing. "Any official change in procedure would be up to Maternity. As for unofficial changes, lights get left off sometimes."

The chance to help those babies outweighed any risks. "Thank you, Michael."

"Just stay out of Payne's way."

"I promise."

He blew a smoke ring in the air over his head, hastily dissipating it when he heard steps in the hallway.

"Speaking of narcs," Shana said, "whatever happened to my memo regarding the drug dealer?"

Merryweather examined his ashes. "Why do you ask?"

"You wouldn't have mentioned it to anyone, would you?" There might be a totally reasonable explanation for Gabe's knowing about her encounter on four. "Could someone have overheard you discussing it?"

"I haven't mentioned it to anyone."

"Not even Security?" The words were out before she could stop them.

He fixed her with the same innocent look he used a moment earlier. "I asked Security to keep strangers from prowling our building. I thought that was enough."

"Ah." Shana hoped her smile didn't look as forced as it felt. If Security had been warned, they'd done a poor job of it. That person on the stairs could have been a mugger, a rapist. Then again, Security's funds were stretched as short as the clinic's. Building D wasn't the priority A and C were.

Merryweather tapped his pipe against an ashtray. "Just one more thing. About the ball."

"The what? Oh, no." Shana made a move to rise. "I'd better get back to my patient."

Merryweather jabbed at her chair with his pipe stem. "Sit. Every man, woman, and clinician in this department is going to cheerfully, nay, gleefully participate in the annual fund-raiser. A united front says we're part of this hospital and we plan to stick around."

"A medieval theme complete with roaring hearth and serving wenches?"

"A Valentine's Day gala. It will be a veritable feast for those who enjoy making catty comments about fashion, food, and fellow employees. Dish, darling. What could be more fun?"

"Root canals? Parking tickets."

Merryweather happily set out his pipe-cleaning instruments. "I'm sure you'll be there with bells on."

"Alarm bells." Her arguments were useless. The Festival Ball was the major fund-raiser of the year, the last touch of glamour associated with their tired old hospital. "I have nothing to wear. We're talking ball gowns here."

"So? Borrow one of mine."

Shana snorted. "Now that I'd pay to see."

They were back on familiar ground, teasing, talking hospital politics. Merryweather saw her to the door, his lanky frame towering over her. "David and I are having our tuxedos pressed. He's attending as a friend."

She understood. She'd never set eyes on Michael's companion. He practiced such complete discretion concerning his private life she sometimes wondered if there *was* a David. Nevertheless, she felt a pang of sympathy. It had to be hard loving someone while keeping them at arms' length in public.

For some reason she thought of Gabe. "I really do need to find that patient."

"Good luck. And remember the ball. I'm sure whatever ensemble you choose will be simply spiffy."

Ten feet outside Michael's office, she broke into a run. She took the corner into the sleep lab. "Have you found him?"

Fiona shook her head, wearily hefting a hospital directory. "I've talked to every department. His fourth nap was scheduled for fifteen minutes ago."

"Any other patients coming in?"

"None scheduled."

"You go that way, I'll go this." She strode toward the elevator while Fiona headed for Building C. Pushing the Down button, she listened to the creaking cables. A thought occurred to her. She turned toward the stairwell.

What if Gabe had been the one waiting? She tried to remember what he'd been wearing when he'd come to her office. All she remembered was his partially unbuttoned shirt. "Shameless hussy."

With one arm outstretched behind her, she held the

door open while she peered over the banister and down the well. Unable to see more than one floor down, she gave the door a shove then scooted back to the rail. Was that a shadow? She leaned farther.

The door clanged shut with a deafening slam. She nearly jumped over the rail. "Dammit!" She whirled and gave the knob a crank. Her palm squeaked across it. Locked.

"Oh, no." Rising on tiptoe, she peered through the steel mesh of the tiny rectangular window only to see Fiona disappear around the corner at the other end of the corridor.

"Shit! This is what happens to exceedingly stupid women in bad horror movies." She swallowed her pride and pounded on the door. Merryweather would come loping down the hall. She'd have to endure that benign smirk of his. "Michael!"

His door was firmly shut; probably smoking like a chimney.

A sound behind her stopped her fist in midair. A very small sound, a scurrying mouse, a skulking rat, a man's shoe scuffing the cement stairs.

She listened with every fiber in her body. The blood rushing in her ears swallowed every other sound.

II

"Some accident."

Brice's chubby grin was minus a couple teeth. His puffy left cheek made him look like a lopsided chipmunk. "You should've been there."

"Thanks a lot," Gabe said.

"In my dreams, huh?"

"More like mine." Gabe's comment went right over Brice's bruised head.

Left arm in a sling, ribs bandaged, he motioned for the remote with his good arm.

"TV, already?" Gabe said. "I think you can go a day without Oprah."

"Fuck you."

"So pleasant when you're sick."

"What would you know about it?"

Besides watching it happen in slow motion? In a sense, Brice was right. Thanks to his dreams Gabe was always on the outside looking in. He'd built his life around that role, deliberately keeping people at bay. He'd thought Brice was outside that circle.

"What are friends for?" Gabe asked.

From the moment Brice had woken up he'd done what he could—which wasn't much. "I called Peg."

Brice winced. "She's gonna hate me."

"For Christ's sake, why?"

"I wrecked the Rover."

"She won't mind."

Brice's eyes popped open. He tried to sit up, the painkillers making him oblivious to the broken ribs. "You mean it's okay?"

Gabe shoved him back against the pillows. According to the dream there wasn't an undented panel on their brand-new Range Rover. "It's totaled, but take it from me, Peg won't give a damn."

Brice groaned. "Tissue."

"What?"

"Get toilet paper. Lots of it."

Gabe scowled. He hadn't thought of this kind of emergency. "You want me to help you out of bed?"

"Bring a couple rolls. We'll just unwind it as she cries."

Gabe grinned at the image. "I think Peg's sturdier than that."

"You don't know her like I do."

He'd called her from the ER.

"Brice has been in an accident. You'd better get down here."

"How is he?" she'd asked, voice shaking but under control.

"I don't know." How could he? They hadn't even wheeled him through the doors when Gabe called. "Just get down here, okay?"

Brice fussed and fidgeted as if a neatly folded sheet would fool his wife into overlooking his injuries. "She's great, isn't she?"

"Yeah."

"I never apologized."

"For what?"

"That I married her and you didn't."

He stared at the blank wall over Brice's head. This wasn't a subject he wanted to discuss. He was foggy from his nap, wound up from his dream. He'd lost so much sleep this weekend, he didn't think he'd ever get the ache out from behind his eyes. One other thing he knew for sure—"Peg didn't love me."

The neck brace prevented Brice from wagging his head back and forth on the pillow. "You never gave her a chance."

"She fell in love with you."

"After you broke it off with her."

"There wasn't anything to break off. I wouldn't commit. Standard-issue male excuse. Besides, she's crazy about you. Still is."

His friend blinked back a watery glow. "She's great, isn't she?"

"You married the right woman." He wondered if he'd ever be able to say the same.

He wanted to talk to Shana. He didn't care whether she believed him; telling her was all that mattered. He found himself wanting to explain what Brice meant to him, how long they'd been friends, how Brice's family was as close as Gabe had ever gotten to having one of his own.

He pinched the bridge of his nose, his drowsy mind drifting to Friday's dream. Using Shana's tips, he'd gotten a full six hours' sleep that afternoon. In return he'd dreamed of her. Typing the dream out, he'd sensed it was more than a slice of the near future. It might be a glimpse of the rest of his life, what it could be if she stuck by him.

He shut his eyes tight, resting his forehead on his splayed fingers. God, he wanted to see her anyway. Just hold her, not even explain.

The door swung open with a whoosh. Peg Grier stormed in. "What the hell are you doing here?"

A woozy Brice tried to sit up. "Honey—"

She stopped at the foot of his bed, the better to assault him with questions. "What the hell did you think you were doing, driving on a day like this! There's ice everywhere."

"It's January, hon."

She snorted, dragging the sleeve of her winter coat across her damp cheek. She'd drawn her red hair back in a severe ponytail, strangling it with a ribbon. It flared out behind her like the tail of a stallion galloping through a storm.

Gabe scanned the room for a place to hide. Peg in a temper was nothing to take lightly. He tried a comforting smile.

"What are you smiling at?"

Gabe took her shoulders in his hands and kissed her on each cheek. "He's fine. I was here when they brought him in."

His soothing tone did little to abate her fury. She hung on to it for dear life. "What did they do, call the office first?"

He didn't answer that. "I came as soon as I heard."

The neck brace gave Brice a double chin, which he enthusiastically bobbed up and down. "I'm fine, honey. Painkillers up the wazoo."

Gabe touched Peg's arm. "He will be all right."

"All right?" Her eyes brimmed. She stripped off her black gloves, waving them at her husband. "This looks like all right to you?"

"Bruised ribs, busted arm, sprained ankle." The sheet tented as Brice enthusiastically raised his cast. "Must've been stomping on the brakes when that bridge abutment came along."

Peg sniffed as she stalked around the side of the bed to get a closer look. "You were probably thinking about that Super Mario game you lost to Billy last night." She lifted his lids to glare into his eyes.

"Did you bring the kids?" he asked.

"They're in school. They don't even know their daddy almost—" She clamped her lips shut.

"Ouch."

"Hold still." Apparently when a nurse took time off to raise her children the bedside manner was the first thing to go.

Gabe watched while she prodded Brice's blue cheek. "He'll have the best care, Peg. Everything's okay."

"It is not!" Tears burst forth. "He's hurt. He's got contusions, abrasions, broken bones—"

Gabe pulled her into his arms. "Shh."

"I hate this! I'm terrible at it."

"Watching your husband in pain? How could any wife be good at that?"

"I should be better, consoling, comforting."

"You mean well."

"Feelin' no pain," their patient crowed happily.

Peg dabbed her nose with a fistful of tissue Gabe had wadded into her hand. Her redhead's pale skin was flaming pink, her blue eyes red-rimmed and swollen. And suspicious. "Even if they called you first, how did you get here before me?"

"Faster car," he lied.

She shook her head, fat tears rolling freely. "Nothing could have been faster than me."

"I know the way. I've been coming to the sleep clinic."

"It's about time you got help with your sleep. You can be a zombie sometimes."

"And a remote, unfeeling, short-tempered bastard the rest."

She remembered. "That was a long time ago. I think you hurt my ego more than anything else."

"The best man won. He's waving, by the way."

They turned back to Brice. Gingerly reclaiming what she'd come so close to losing, Peg avoided the neck brace and cupped his cheek in her hand. Calmer now, she tapped her fingers around the purple swelling like a mother inspecting a child's playground scars. She combed his thinning hair back. Her expression shifted from cool-eyed evaluation to remembered fear. "Don't you ever pull a stunt like this again," she whispered.

"Promise."

She tugged on his forelock. "Promise."

"I did."

She kissed him fiercely, ignoring his grunt of pain.

Gabe backed toward the door to give them some privacy.

Shana shoved it open. It swatted him on the behind. "May I ask what in God's name you're doing here? I've been looking everywhere!"

Brice grinned from ear to bruised ear. "Marry that woman! They only yell when they care. Right, honey?"

Gabe gave Shana an apologetic shrug. "Don't mind him, he's on drugs."

"And what's your excuse?" She folded her arms across her chest, chin tilted for battle. "You had an appointment."

He nodded toward the bed. "These are my best friends. Brice Grier, my business partner. His wife, Peg."

"Hi." Never one to let an acquaintance get away without becoming a friend, Brice tried to sit up and shake hands.

Shana rushed to his bedside, reassuring him the sitting up part wasn't necessary. She reached across him to shake Peg's hand.

"This is Dr. Getz," Gabe said.

"Shana," she amended. "Look, I'm sorry to barge in but we had an appointment."

"Don't let us stop you," Peg said, a curious gaze slanted Gabe's way.

"Go ahead," Brice said. "About time you got a good night's sleep, Gabe."

"Yes it is," Peg murmured, looking at Shana. "Take good care of him."

"I will."

·   ·   ·   ·   ·

She trudged down the hall toward the crosswalk to Building D, Gabe in close pursuit. "You can visit all you want after your fourth test."

"I had to come. I dreamed it."

She was afraid he was going to say that. "I know."

"How could you?"

"We got it on tape."

She had every intention of taking the crosswalk. Gabe gripped her arm and sidestepped her into the staircase. "Not again." She moaned, glaring at the cement walls. She'd been locked in the stairwell off her own office corridor for all of five minutes—until she'd worked up the courage to storm down to the first floor. She'd met no attackers, no vengeful drug dealers. Her temper was all the worse for having been scared by nothing.

"How?" Gabe demanded, wrenching her attention back to him. "How could you tape it?"

"We recorded the effects of it on the polysomnograph. Brain waves like that don't happen every day."

"Then you believe me?"

She stared into his eyes. From unusual brain waves to seeing the future was a big step. "Tell me what happened."

He raked a hand through his hair. He turned left then right on the narrow landing. "Any car can go into a skid on the highway in the middle of January. This was Brice's car. I saw it."

"As if it were in slow motion?"

"No. It's always real time, real smells, real sounds, everything. I saw them bringing him into the emergency room. I took a chance it was this one."

"And kissing me?" she asked softly. "You saw that clearly too?"

"Yes."

"I don't know what it all means."

He wrapped her in his arms. "You think I do?"

She rested her cheek to his chest. "Don't run out on me again like that, okay?"

"I won't."

She sighed, safe in his arms. It didn't seem possible that they could be so close so soon. All her other relationships had blossomed from long-standing friendships. It was the endings that had happened fast. "We barely know each other."

"I dreamed about you, and that means I care."

"Ah. Then everything will be okay."

He traced her face with his fingertips. "My dreams led me to you. Don't ask me why. I have to find that out for myself."

A sound shuffled somewhere above them. Shana looked up. She stepped out of his arms, suddenly uncomfortable. "I'm bushed. You don't look much better."

"Thanks."

"I'd like you to try one more nap. Do you think you can?"

"I'll try. Shana?"

She turned on the bottom step. His gaze flitted over her lips. "If you'll even consider the dreams, that's more than most people have."

"I'd like us to set up an appointment for early next week. We'll talk about it then."

He stepped up beside her, his smile erasing years from his face. "Do I need an appointment for this?"

He'd kissed her. Why that should surprise her anymore was a mystery. His kiss confirmed what she'd sensed minutes earlier in his embrace. He held her to him as if she were infinitely precious, necessary. The word "love" flitted into her head.

She stood up from her desk and marched across her office, shutting her door as if showing the unwelcome thought the way out. It was way too soon to be thinking fairy-tail endings, dreams come true.

She needed to think. She drifted toward her office window. Gabe had gone directly to the lab for his final test. Fiona was under strict instructions not to let him out of her sight. If he had another dream—

Shana shivered and wrapped her arms across her chest. He'd said the episodes only involved people he cared about. It was obvious the people he'd introduced her to in Emergency had been close friends.

It brought home the fact that, except for their one date, she'd never seen him outside the hospital. Perhaps a few dates wouldn't be such a bad idea.

"Just keep your mouth to yourself," she muttered. In the late afternoon light the east wing's shadow fell across her window. She studied her faint reflection, her hand straying to her lips. What did he see in them? They were completely unremarkable. Her hair was a mess, no news there. Her eyes were brown, not chestnut, not charcoal, just brown. He looked at them as if they held all the answers.

A knock on the door startled her. She checked her watch as she crossed to open it. "That was a short nap. Gabe, I—oh."

"I don't have an appointment." The middle-aged woman slipped inside the door as if hiding from suspicious eyes.

People often found sleep problems shameful, embarrassed that something that came so easily to others eluded them. Shana gestured toward her desk. "Come in."

Having come this far the woman seemed afraid to go further.

Shana took a few mental notes. Round face, sagging cheeks, dated red lipstick. Her curly hair was a combination of slate-gray streaked with white. She'd probably been lovely once, before her eyes were bloodshot and her cheeks veined with thin blue lines. In the unforgiving afternoon light fine wrinkles covered her skin, as if someone had crumpled a piece of paper then flattened it out again.

"I need your help," she whispered. Rocking slightly, she hunched forward as if bowing into a strong wind. She clutched the collar of her wool coat as if she were used to fur collars, Shana thought.

Suddenly she knew who her visitor was. Her heart rocketed into double time. The last time she'd seen this woman, she'd been leaning forward in the same way, desperately clawing a bottle of pills out of a man's hand on the fourth floor.

Shana's nearsightedness had prevented her from keying in on the man. She hadn't needed to focus to remember the woman. Her posture communicated itself loud and clear, conveying an air of desperation, supplication.

"What kind of help do you need?" Shana asked, subtly slipping her glasses onto her nose. The better to study her guest. She hoped they made her look more kindly, more professional.

Silently considering her course of action, the woman shook off her first decision with a jerk of her head.

"I'll need some information before we can get started. Please, sit down."

The woman scanned the room for the chair right in front of her. Vague, furtive, she sat.

Shana noted her nervousness, the dry lips, the inability to settle down, the scattered concentration.

"My husband would kill me if he knew."

Exaggeration? Paranoia? "You're perfectly safe here. What's your name?"

"Call me Hazel. Nothing else."

"Hazel it is."

The woman crossed her legs. She wore brown slacks. Shana was so tired, she almost laughed. Had this terrified woman been lurking in the stairwell half the afternoon working up the courage to come in to see her?

Shana bit back a sigh. For once in her career she reached into her drawer and found a notepad the first time out. Uncapping a pen, she spoke as if continuing a perfectly innocuous conversation. "And what drugs are you taking, Hazel?"

"He gives me pills."

Shana's pulse jumped. They'd gotten directly to the man on the fourth floor. "And what is his name?"

The question struck her visitor as odd. "He's my husband."

"And what is his name?" Shana prodded gently.

Hazel shook her head. "He's—powerful."

She frowned. The man she remembered hadn't given the impression of physical strength. Wiry, yes, sinewy, perhaps. "Let me make sure I understand this; your husband supplies your pills."

"He—he gives them to me. To make me sleep."

"You need help sleeping."

"No." Her agitation grew, her voice shrill. "I don't need them. I don't need anything."

Schizophrenic personalities often claimed they were being poisoned by their medications. Shana made a note.

The woman grabbed the edges of her coat in both fists, closing it over her knees. Her knuckles were red and abraded. Shana's stomach lurched when she saw the blue and yellow bruises on her wrists. Maybe she was telling the simple truth about her husband.

She waited until she had Hazel's complete attention. "Our first step will be to get you off the drugs."

"I don't want to take them! I never have." She nearly sobbed.

"That's good. But I don't want you to completely stop. That could be dangerous. These drugs have what we call a half-life; they build up in the body—"

"Then you'll give me something."

Her pen skimming across the intake form, Shana paused. "Pardon me?"

"You'll give me pills."

"I thought you wanted off them."

"I don't want to sleep. He makes me sleep. Bad things happen when I sleep, horrible things."

"You have nightmares?"

"No, they're real," she practically shouted. "He makes

me sleep. Don't you understand?" She ground her fists into her thighs, rocking herself into a frenzy, her breath wheezing out of her lungs. "He *makes* me. That's why I need the others, the ones that keep me awake."

"Using amphetamines to combat sleeping pills is incredibly dangerous."

Hazel jumped to her feet. "You don't know anything!"

"I—"

"You've never been where I've been. You don't know what goes on when you're half asleep. When you can't wake up, no matter what kind of nightmare you're dreaming. I *have* to be *awake*. Don't you understand?"

"Hazel, I want to help. I need to know."

She slapped her palm on Shana's desk. "Give me something."

"I can't."

"Bullshit."

The unexpected vulgarity pushed Shana back in her chair. "I don't prescribe."

"You've got a medical doctor on staff, that Merryweather. Make him give me something!"

So she knew about their clinic. Shana inched up out of her chair and tried to reach the door. If this woman was delusional, a psychiatrist could make a better diagnosis. "Let me introduce you to Dr. Merryweather. Maybe he can help you."

"No!" Hazel cowered near the door. "Don't open it. I can't let him see me."

"Who, Michael?" In one short meeting Shana had no hope of separating drug-induced paranoia from mental illness. It had been a horrendously long day. She forced herself to go slowly. She reached for Hazel's hands.

The woman flinched at the contact, her eyes darting everywhere. Shana held her ice-cold hands until Hazel calmed down. "I want to check you in. You'll be safe here."

"No. Not here."

"Then where? You need sleep."

The woman shut her eyes. The rocking began again. "I have to stay awake. Have to."

"You need rest. Sleeping problems can create all kinds of emotional problems. We don't make decisions as well. It can be hard to think, to trust our feelings."

The woman's mouth was trembling, her face contorted through a host of emotions. "I have to stay awake," she mewed pitifully. "He won't let me."

"Hazel, help me. I need you to fill out an admitting form. That's all we need to get started. Can you do that for me?"

The woman seemed trapped in some world inside her head. She peeked out into the hall, shutting the door and sagging against it. "He has eyes. He'll know I'm here."

Shana scooted behind her desk, flipping through the stack on her credenza. Pulling out the form she needed, the entire stack slid off the shelf. Papers fluttered across the floor. She hissed a curse under her breath and stooped to pick them up. "Excuse me a minute."

Reaching under her desk, she kept up a steady stream of reassuring words. "You're going to be okay. We'll observe you while you sleep. If your dreams are threatening, we'll be there to wake you up. If it's a person threatening you, we'll protect you from him too. No matter what, we've got to get you some sleep. To do that—" She peeked over her desk.

Hazel was gone.

For a crazy moment she thought the woman might have passed out on the other side of the desk. Nothing but carpet. She raced into the hall. A distant door slammed. Running footsteps echoed down the stairwell.

Her shoulders slumped. She'd lost one.

Merryweather opened his door a crack as she walked by. "Patient still missing?"

Shana gave him a tired smile. "I found the first. You didn't happen to see a—"

Merryweather lowered his pipe as if the answer were

obvious. When he smoked he never set foot outside his office.

"Never mind." Shana nodded. "It's been one of those days."

He shut his door tight. For a weird moment Shana thought she heard voices on the other side of it, a radio maybe.

She stopped at the lab. "Is Gabe—"

"Gone home," Fiona replied. "He said you were with a patient."

He'd checked on her before he left. The idea gave her a much-needed boost. She tried not to read anything into it. "See you tomorrow, then."

"Wait. Thought you'd like to see for yourself." Fiona nodded toward a monitor. DeVon Johnson was being fitted for a CPAP device in room three. He glowered as Flora slid a strap over his head. The face mask and attached tube would blow a steady stream of oxygen down his throat, keeping him breathing all night long.

"He came in under his own power?" Shana asked doubtfully.

"Yep. We're betting it won't last. According to the latest pool, Flora thinks he'll yank it off within a half hour, I bet ten minutes, and Merryweather picked fifteen. Loser buys donuts. What're you in for?"

Shana stared at the burly man on the small screen. She'd had too many close calls in one day already. She remembered his fury in the group session. "I think I'll pass."

"Long day?"

"Interminable."

Tomorrow would be even worse; she'd agreed to help out in Maternity again. Guilt tweaked her conscience. She'd been looking forward to talking to the nurses, encouraging them to secretly implement her plan and turn down the lights on a regular schedule so the babies could sleep better.

At the moment, all she wanted was a good night's sleep of her own.

12

Shana balanced the small bundle on one arm. The drone of her voice had put the baby to sleep. She wanted to hug it to her chest and rock it. Instead she held it away and kept talking. Sleep was the most precious gift she could give it.

"Where were we? Sleeping Beauty, right? The bad fairy had put a spell on Beauty. Or Beaut, as we call her for short. But the good fairies fashioned spells too. They put the entire kingdom to sleep with her. While everyone dozed Beauty existed in her own little dream world. Until the day a prince from another kingdom came along."

Her chest rose and fell with her breathing, her body moving gently back and forth. She felt as if she'd been asleep her whole life, in a self-induced spell she'd endured for years. Gabe had woken her to desires and needs long unmet. What could she offer him? Alarms on bedroom doors? Nighttime pummelings?

Her cheeks flushed. So many reasons to avoid a replay.

"But she missed kissing," she said aloud, narrating the

story in her mind to the baby in her arms. "Beauty may have lain there peacefully slumbering but she wasn't really alive. She didn't age, she didn't fade, but she didn't really *live*. Until he woke her up."

He'd said it before. *You're a beautiful woman. I don't believe no man's ever seen it.*

They had. It was the brittle light of day that changed their opinions. Gabe's would change, too, if she ever made the dreadful mistake of sleeping with him.

"That awful spell didn't mean they couldn't have a relationship," she told the baby. They could date, touch, caress, and kiss. They could make love if it came to that. "She just couldn't sleep over."

The baby fussed. "You're right," Shana reassured him. "I'm getting ahead of myself."

Gabe would return. When he did, they'd have more to talk about than dating. There were the dreams, the one that had come so stunningly true the previous weekend at the top of the Sears Tower and the one he'd dreamed in the lab. How could he have known his friend would be in an accident?

She'd called down to Admitting to find out more about this Brice Grier. She hefted the baby closer to her face, raising her brows in a "gee whiz" look. "What's more surprising, kid? That Gabe has dreams that come true or that he has friends?" Cheeky but true. She knew so little about him. "And here I sit planning how far we can go sexually. That's almost as premature as you are, sweetie."

A soft tap on the door brought her head up. The baby jolted awake. "Oh, no," Shana wailed.

The baby scrunched up its face, summoning the energy to scream. Bundled tightly, it bounced its tiny fists together as it let out a shriek.

"Come in," Shana called. She hoped her low-pitched timbre carried beneath the baby's high-pitched wail without adding to its distress.

The door opened. Her breath caught. She'd expected Marilyn, the head nurse, or another volunteer.

"Am I interrupting?" Gabe lifted the mask around his chin before he stepped inside. A green hospital gown hung to his knees. The cap covered his raven-black hair.

She'd have recognized him anywhere. His blue eyes focused on her and nothing else. Her heart thrummed with a steady elevated beat from anticipation, excitement. She'd gone a whole day without seeing him. She hadn't gone ten minutes without thinking of him.

"The prince found Sleeping Beauty in her tower," she muttered to the squalling baby.

"Story time?" Gabe asked.

"Mm. Isn't going over very well."

The baby's scream ricocheted around the tiny soundproofed room.

Gabe took the rocker along the side wall, at an angle to Shana's. Leaning forward, he balanced his elbows on his knees.

She kept her eyes on the baby, trying to communicate a calming presence as Gabe studied her. She felt his gaze fix intently on her face. If she was given to fancies, she'd have thought he wanted nothing more than to see her, to remind himself she was real and not a dream.

This was no fairy tale. Far from Sleeping Beauty's castle tower, the womb room sounded more like a torture chamber. The baby screeched at the utmost capacity of its tiny lungs, a nails-on-blackboard keening that raised the hairs on the back of her neck. And *she* was used to it.

"I've heard car alarms less piercing," Gabe said.

Behind her mask, a wry smile lifted her cheeks. She never took her eyes off the baby. She crooned without stopping. She whispered. She rocked. She urged the baby's head against the mound of her breast. "For the heartbeat," she explained softly.

Hers was beating a mite too fast for this remedy. Gabe's unblinking consideration made her acutely aware of her eyes, her lashes, the heat flooding her cheeks. Thank God for masks.

The baby bucked its tiny body against her breast. Gabe

had kissed those breasts. She'd cried out in delight when he'd suckled her, her boby aflame, her senses begging for release, fulfillment. "Slow down," she urged the infant.

"He'll tire out eventually," Gabe replied.

She tossed him an apologetic glance. "I hope you don't mind."

"I was in the neighborhood. Visiting Brice."

"Oh. Of course." Her conscience chided her for thinking he'd come all the way there just to see her.

Another shriek. Judging from the twitch in his mask, Gabe gritted his teeth. "Are you recording this?" He indicated the tape player in the corner.

"Ocean sounds." The penetrating screams had all but drowned out the wash of waves with its undercurrent of a human heartbeat. "Womb sounds."

"Ah." He held on another few minutes, fingers linked tightly between his knees. "How long can he keep this up?"

"Until he exhausts himself to sleep."

"Let's hope he doesn't have insomnia."

She grinned. In the dim lighting his eyes seemed incredibly deep, like night rimmed by the blue-gray of dawn.

The glimmer faded. His gaze dropped from her eyes to her mask, from there to her breasts, her lap. The voluminous green gown should have made her feel dowdy. She felt naked inside it.

She shoved a few strands of loose hair under her cap, exasperated by her failure to calm the child. For all of ten minutes he'd been peaceful. It wasn't Gabe's fault. "Crack," she said tiredly.

He leaned closer, peering up into her face as she bent over the baby. "Pardon me?" He'd intuitively figured out how to talk under the baby's cries instead of shouting over them.

"Crack cocaine," Shana explained. "Or heroin. Their mothers ingest it, and they're born addicted. That's why they cry this way."

His eyes grew as flinty as his voice. "That kid's no bigger than my fist."

"Withdrawal makes them incredibly sensitive to light, sounds, any sensory input."

"What about touch?"

"Touch too." Nevertheless, she cuddled the baby closer to her breast. "Even difficult babies need love."

"That's a tough form of love."

"I know. Sometimes it feels like you're hurting them while trying to help them."

The baby screamed as if to prove her point. Gabe worked his hands together until his knuckles turned white. "You volunteer for this?"

"They need people."

She didn't specify whether she meant the babies or the staff. Gabe didn't suppose it mattered. He watched expressions flicker in her eyes like clouds crossing over the moon. Encouraging, caring, soothing. All of them directed at a baby too young to make out her face.

It hiccuped and paused for breath. Shana's brows arched high on her forehead. "That's it, sweetie. That's it. Rest now." Like a seer sensing an aura, she passed her fingertips over the baby's face so it could sense her nearness without having to feel her touch.

Love, Gabe thought. The woman had more love than this hospital had rooms. Or the city had drug-addicted mothers.

Eventually the baby's cries diminished into the ragged irregular pants of a kitten. Shana's rocking subsided to a slow pulse. The tape recorder's ocean sounds blanketed the room in a rhythmic pulse.

Without intending to, Gabe reached out. He tucked one lost curl gently into Shana's cap, tracing the wet trail of a tear to the spot where her mask soaked it up. "Shh," he whispered. "It's okay."

She blinked hard, her lashes clumped together. "Don't tell. We're not supposed to get too attached."

Gabe silently scoffed. Shana aloof? Impossible. As for

the wisdom of not getting attached, he'd lived his life according to that weak rule. It wasn't worth a trunkload of junk bonds.

Maybe that was why the idea of falling in love with her, in that room at that precise moment, hit him like a punch to the chest. He had to follow up on it. It wasn't a question of sticking around to figure out why he dreamed of her. He had to be near her, to touch her, taste her, to see those cinnamon freckles and inhale that subtle scent. He could have sat there for hours.

"Did you want to see me?"

How about every day for the rest of my life?

He sat back slowly, his abdominal muscles tight. He told himself he didn't want to startle the kid. Nevertheless, the force of his emotions shocked the hell out of him. "What's his name?"

"The nurses call him Martin."

Gabe grunted. "Think Martin'll mind if we talk?"

They both studied the baby's face, the web of veins beneath the translucent skin, the furrowed brow. Even in sleep he guarded himself against intrusions, his oversensitive nerves always on alert. "Keep it low," Shana murmured.

Gabe nodded. Feet firmly on the sound-deadening carpet, he eased back into the rocker. In minutes the familiar ache of tiredness crept through his muscles. Like a blanket, it muffled the wired tension he'd been riding since yesterday. "I've been thinking about that dream."

"It's amazing you can think of anything else. If they come true, that is."

"The maddening part is that I can't do anything about them."

"You don't want them coming true?"

"I was talking about Brice. Not us."

The tiny word hung in the air. Gabe gave her some credit for not arguing the point. They were linked. It was only a matter of time before they found out how deeply. "I want a life. I won't live it around sleeping or waking, dreaming or not dreaming. If the dreams come, fine. There's nothing I can do about them."

"I get the feeling you're not as resigned as you sound."

"You haven't stood by and waited while your friend's car skidded out of control."

"You can't blame yourself for Brice's accident."

"I couldn't warn him. I couldn't *not* warn him." His voice rose, grating in the confined space. The baby fussed.

They both held their breath.

Gabe purposely relaxed, forcing his shoulders back against the chair. He managed his short temper the way he managed his tiredness, with iron control and sheer force of will. He hated the snappishness that lurked so close to the surface. Time was too damn short for pettiness. And he was too damn proud to sink to it. Awake, aware, and totally focused—that was the image he strove to present. The alternative was to be seen for what he was, exhausted, vulnerable, struggling.

He looked at Shana. She'd seen that side of him. For some crazy reason, he didn't mind. Around her he said things he hardly dared think around anyone else.

"Have you looked at yesterday's test?"

Without moving or jarring the baby, she sat back. In the soft whispers they'd confined themselves to, the conversation took on an unusual intimacy, like two people talking in bed.

"We went over the readout in staff today. It's an unusual series." She tucked the blanket around the baby's chin. "I've never seen peaks and valleys like the ones from your third dream. No one else has ever seen the onset of stage five sleep come that quickly."

"What is that?"

"It's the deepest sleep. Restorative. Normally people need hours to reach that stage."

"And me?"

"About four minutes."

"What does that tell you?"

She managed a discreet shrug. "You're an unusual case."

He smiled coldly. "What else is new?"

"Add to that the fact that your dreams seem to come true."

"Did you mention that in your staff meeting?" He barely took a breath.

She evaded the question. "I need more information before I write it up. How is he, by the way?"

"Brice? Bruised, banged up. In more pain today than yesterday."

"He's healing, then."

"And giving Peg a hell of a time."

"She seemed nice. They both did."

"Why are we making small talk?" Subtle as a panther, he'd leaned forward. He wasn't about to jostle the baby, or let Shana play remote.

"There's not a lot we can say here."

"We can say anything. I told you about Brice after the fact. That makes for a poor prediction. Is that why you didn't mention it to the staff?"

"I need time to think about it."

"Or is it because if you told them about the dreams, you'd have to tell them about the one I had Friday. As predictions go, that was a beaut."

Her head shot up. He assumed he'd hit a sore spot. He didn't spare his own. "Or is it because, if you told them I claimed to dream about the future, they'd think I was nuts?"

Shana shook her head. "I have to assimilate it before I can put it down on paper."

"Is that what we're waiting for?"

She gave him a level look. "I wouldn't call seeing you two days in a row 'waiting.'"

She had him there. Visiting Brice wasn't much of an excuse. "I wanted to see you. I want to go on seeing you."

"I've been thinking about that."

"Say yes."

"Yes."

His brows rose. "That was fast."

"As I said, I've been thinking about it. I'd like to go out with you."

And he'd like to take her in his arms and kiss her until that flush flamed out across her chest the way it had Friday. He swallowed the knot in his throat. "So where do we start?"

"I thought small talk was fine."

Her gentle chiding made him feel like a thundering dolt. "Are you married?"

The question startled them both.

"I know it's obvious but I never asked."

"It's about time you did." She laughed softly. "And no, I've never been married. You?"

"Thought about it."

She glanced up.

"That's as far as it got."

She gave the baby a smile and a quiet coo. A thought furrowed her brow.

"Are we bothering the baby?"

"No. I was thinking of yesterday. A patient came in. I was so tired I lost her."

Shana smiled at his shocked look. If she'd had a free hand, she'd have rested it on his arm. "Not that kind of losing. My patients generally don't die on me. I meant I lost the chance to help her. I worry that if we get too involved, I might miss something important about your case."

"That's ironic."

"Why?"

"I worry I'll see exactly what's coming."

She looked away. "The future's always uncertain. In one way or another."

Gabe traced his fingers over the back of her hand where she cradled the baby's body. He touched each knuckle, dipping his finger in the spaces in between. She remained as still as silence.

Getting down on one knee, he kissed the back of her hand, his tongue dipping in the same sensitive spaces his fingers had.

It was all Shana could do to keep her breath controlled. A groan would surely wake the baby. "Gabe."

She reached for him with her other hand. His late afternoon stubble chafed like a whisper inside the mask. The moist heat of his breath transferred itself through the fabric to her skin. He clasped her palm to his cheek.

Suddenly the hot liquid press of his tongue seared her flesh. She gasped at the unexpected sensation.

He'd lowered the mask just enough to kiss her. "Will it hurt the baby?"

She shook her head. "It's a rule—"

The hell with rules. Gabe placed another suggestive, treasuring kiss in her palm.

She drew a breath from deep inside, like water raised from a well. Gabe's tongue darted between her fingers, crude, concise, unbearably erotic.

He raised his mask when he raised his head. He tracked his thumb across the hidden outline of her lips. "I want to kiss you without all this covering up."

The knock on the door was no more than a thumping heartbeat. Gabe heard it and stood. Shana tried to slow her heartbeat, convinced its heavy thud had drawn Marilyn.

"Shana?" The head nurse spoke quietly but unmistakably on the other side of the door.

Her knees knocked as she stood. "We need to take this slow," she told him.

He reached for the doorknob. "We'll take it wherever it takes us."

Marilyn stood on the threshold, arms outstretched. Shana handed the baby over. Jostled, it screeched itself awake, flailing inside its bundle of specially laundered cloth. Both women sighed.

The minute they were in the hall, Shana pulled off her mask and cap. The bustle of Maternity was quiet compared to Martin. "Do you think you can get Maintenance to install a dimmer switch in the next week, Marilyn?"

A streak of rebellious mischief lit her eyes. "We'll see," she replied. A plump woman, she looked like an uncooked loaf of bread in her white uniform. "Personally, I think it's a great idea. Politically, if Payne finds out, we're dead."

"You're exaggerating."

"You're an optimist."

Shana waved good-bye as she and Gabe walked down the hall. Jabbing the elevator button for the second floor, she rubbed her shaking hands together. It astonished her how moist they were. Then she remembered Gabe's kiss. "Close call."

"Not close enough."

The elevator was half the size of the womb room. Shana filled it with chatter. "I need to stop by my office. I hope you don't mind."

"It'd be a good place to continue our discussion."

Discussing wasn't what they'd been doing. The sleep clinic would be deserted. As far as she knew, there were no sleepovers scheduled. They'd be alone.

The elevator doors opened. She stepped across the threshold. The grooves lay between them like a dividing line.

"I have to warn you, Gabe, I can only get so involved."

He tried to step out. She held him back, her palm on his chest. He inhaled, the muscles sinewy and firm.

She withdrew her hand, clamping it in the other. "I know this sounds blunt. It's definitely presumptuous, but I think you should know. I have a line I draw for all relationships. I won't, I can't, sleep with you."

There, she'd said it.

He showed no reaction.

Her sinking heart told her that that in itself was a reaction. "If you can't deal with that, if you don't want to, I'll understand."

"We've had one date, and you're already planning the grim conclusion?"

Nowhere near as grim as waking up beside him after a night of thrashing.

"If it's for moral reasons," he began.

"Oh, no. It's not as if I'm a virgin." She couldn't believe she'd blurted that out.

The elevator doors began to close. Shana thanked them, and God, that she'd been spared the spectacle of standing there turning beet-red.

Gabe stopped their glide with one hand.

For one thrilling, galling moment, Shana was sure he'd step into the hall. He'd take her in his arms and kiss her until her doubts dissolved.

All he said was, "See you tomorrow."

13

She didn't want to sleep with him. Fine. He could handle that. Hell, he had enough sleep problems. He'd told her how left out the women in his life felt when he snuck out of bed. Naturally, she'd given him notice she wouldn't be one of them.

He jingled the change in his pocket. It wasn't as if he'd proposed marriage. He'd just thought the way she came into his arms, the way her lips became so pliable, so kissable whenever he leaned into her—

"Evening, class."

Forget it. Self-pity wasn't part of his emotional portfolio. She didn't want to sleep with him. He was a man. He could handle it.

He tossed back the last of the bitter decaf coffee and watched her greet the other patients one by one. When he walked into the offices of Grier/Fitzgerald the seas parted. When he phoned Asian prime ministers, secretaries put him straight through. When Shana Getz entered a room, he waited his turn.

Parked beside the coffeepot, he poured himself another cup, loading it with sugar. He tore the second packet with unexpected force. He swiped crystals off the table, half of them clinging to the side of his palm. He recalled the same thing happening to Shana in the cafeteria. Since then he'd opened up to her in ways he'd never opened up to anyone. No wonder she backed him off.

Standing on the far side of the lounge, he caught her eye. He darted his tongue along the side of his hand, tasting sweetness, remembering.

She remembered too. Her tongue flicked across her lips. She pulled a pile of file folders closer to her breasts.

She wasn't immune. He knew it. She just wouldn't sleep with him.

She took it on herself to break the spell. "Lucille," he heard her say, "how are you? Are you sleeping better?"

Lucille filled her in on how well she'd adjusted to her morning shift. All of it thanks to Shana, the Shana who loved everyone, who gave so unselfishly of herself, who kissed a man as if she'd been waiting for him all her life. Who wouldn't sleep with him.

Hey, he was the one who'd claimed he wanted to know her better, take this slow, go on dates. What business did he have wanting to stride across the room, haul her into his arms, and kiss her hello? The openmouthed, soul-baring, delving kind of kiss that held nothing back.

His feet remained planted. She settled everyone down, casting a nervous glance his way. He wandered over to his place on the loveseat.

Session convened, she made a few announcements. Never looking too sure where the next piece of paper was coming from, improvising as she went, she won everyone over with her spirit, her passion, her absolute interest in their lives. "Let's go around the room with our progress reports. Doris?"

The clean freak, far left. Gabe half listened as Doris recounted her nightly rituals. They'd doubled since the first session. He sent Shana a wry smile; never give an obsessive more things to obsess about.

To his surprise, her smiled flickered in response. His body heated slightly, his mouth firming up at the romantic notion of two people communicating across a room with a look, a glance. Just like a real couple.

"Shirlee, how are you?" Shana asked next.

Gabe turned his attention to Shirlee Johnson, the primly dressed wife of the man who'd stormed out the week before. The rest of the group sat up a little straighter, jazzed by the possibility of real-life drama. Shirlee wasn't supplying.

"I think we're making progress," she said diplomatically. "Flora Dava Coleman, your respiratory therapist, is working with us."

"She couldn't be here tonight but will join us next week," Shana explained to the group.

Shirlee folded her neatly gloved hands over the purse on her lap. "My husband came along."

"Did he?"

"He worked a late shift so he hasn't had dinner. I believe he's in the cafeteria."

"Maybe we'll see him next time."

Gabe presumed that was relief relaxing Shana's smile as she finished with Shirlee.

"Who's next?"

Marie, the old woman to Gabe's left, told them about the prickling pains that continued to plague her at night.

"Okay. Gabe?"

He'd been waiting.

"How have you been sleeping?"

Without you.

While he tested how much a look could convey, Shana stuck with body language. She presented him with that concerned body-forward pose she used with everyone. He was probably the only one who sensed how stiff it suddenly had become.

"You have been sleeping," she said.

"Some."

"The insomnia isn't quite as severe?"

"It's worse when I think about things." His gaze slipped downward.

Shana had worn a skirt for a change. She tugged the hem over her knee. "Have you tried the meditation?"

"My mind wanders."

"That's fairly common at first." She flipped through some files, opened what he assumed was his, and tipped a page sideways so she could jot in the margins. "Perhaps the imagery you're using isn't restful enough."

"I think of you."

Her pen stopped. Everything in the room stopped except the clacking of the radiator pouring out dry heat from the corner. Sofa springs squeaked. Eyes shifted.

Shana cleared her throat, her gaze glued to her paperwork. "Because I've guided all of you through these relaxation exercises, you may find yourselves associating my voice with your imagery. Beaches, floating clouds, wave sounds—"

"Water beds?"

Her smile crooked by a couple degrees. "I beg your pardon?"

He didn't need to raise his voice. An intimate growl carried just fine. "Last year I decided a new bed might help me sleep. I got a water bed. I lie there, meditating, and there you are beside me."

She laughed weakly. "I bet that puts you straight to sleep."

"Just the opposite. I'm up for hours."

Shana swore she could have heard a jaw drop. The temperature in the room crawled up a notch.

"Am I late?"

Twenty minutes past eight, Aurora was right on time. Shana leapt up to greet her. "Aurora! You're very welcome. Please, have a seat. We were just catching up."

The leggy blond made her way across the lounge, the leather fringe on her jacket swaying with each step of her stiletto heels. She slung her backpack alongside the sofa and settled her miniskirted rear end onto the cushion Shana had indicated, right beside Gabe.

He barely spared her a glance.

Aurora crossed her arms over her chest, crossed her even longer legs, and tapped her dangling foot in time to her gum chewing. "Did I miss much?"

"We were talking about sleeping alone," Gabe said.

Aurora smirked. "Must be going around."

"Care to tell us about it?" Gabe turned his laser-blue eyes on the twenty-two-year old.

Shana interjected with something closer to their purpose. "How are the nightmares?"

"Scary," Aurora replied, completely without irony. "I had another last night. Lotta screaming. I'm surprised the landlord doesn't kick me out." She relayed the information as if it were no more frustrating than freeway construction.

"Care to tell us more?" Shana urged gently.

Shrugging, Aurora recounted a dream about turning into a mannequin in a shopping mall, her monotone spiced by a southern Indiana twang.

"So you felt on display," Shana asked.

"All dressed up, nowhere to go."

It seemed Freudian enough. Feeling more prized for her looks than her substance, she'd dreamed of being a plaster object.

"When the dresser tried to detach my arms that's when I woke up screaming."

"Does the fear of dreaming keep you awake?"

"Not really, it's just—I dunno. They're dumb. Even my boyfriend says they're dumb. I don't even think they're scary once they're over."

Shana frowned at Marie, who'd begun humming faintly to herself. Doris fidgeted. It wasn't easy keeping the group interested in a subject even the sufferer didn't take seriously.

"They're just nightmares. You know. It's just, at the time, some of them seem so real—"

Shana watched Aurora shrug and withdraw. She was about to question her further when she noticed Gabe. While the group's concentration drifted, his never yielded. He hung on every word Aurora said.

"They're real?" he asked.

Eyes downcast, she worked her gum to the other side of her jaw. "Some of 'em seem like it. I tried writing 'em down once."

"Good idea," he retorted.

"I asked Dr. Merryweather about it."

"Did *he* believe you?" Gabe demanded.

Aurora cast a wary glance from Shana to Gabe. She resorted to a defensive shrug that said no one really cared. "He says I've got issues to work on."

Gabe snorted at the psychiatric double-talk.

Shana stood up for her colleague. "I'm sure you can talk to him anytime you need to, Aurora."

"I suppose," she allowed. "It's just, he's a doctor. He doesn't want to be woken up with stuff even my boyfriend thinks is dumb." Aurora rearranged her crossed legs and ran her finger along the collar of her ribbed turtleneck. She glanced sideways at Gabe. "It'd be nice, though, if I had somebody to call, when I first wake up? That's when talking helps. But, you know, it's the middle of the night. I don't know anyone who'd appreciate being called then."

Shana knew of someone. She tried to remember whether Gabe had mentioned his hours to the group. She shouldn't have worried. Instead of picking up the hint, he seemed lost in thought. He strafed the carpet with his gaze, his thumbnails gouging half-moons in the Styrofoam cup.

He suddenly fixed Shana with a glance that made her blood run cold. What if he wasn't the only one? What if other people dreamed the future?

She shut her folders and cleared her throat. "I think that covers everyone's progress so far. Let's take a ten-minute break while I get some supplies for our next exercise."

It wasn't the most graceful exit in the world. Nothing had prepared her for Aurora's revelation—or Gabe's reaction to it.

Correction, she thought, rifling through her desk for notepads, you weren't prepared for the attention Gabe paid *her*.

It shouldn't have surprised her. She'd told Gabe she wouldn't sleep with him, and he'd lost interest. Typical male reaction.

But so fast? her heart asked. She could have sworn Gabe wasn't that kind of man. He committed to things heart and soul, whether he was determined to stay awake or cure his insomnia. He didn't give up easily. Nor did he flit from one woman to the next.

Do you know that for sure? asked her conscience, the voice of cynicism. If you won't sleep with him—he'll find someone who will. Some men are like that. She knew of two.

Leaving her office empty-handed, she stopped at the soda machine. Absently checking her reflection, she wished Flora had been there to comment on her makeup. Had she overdone the eyes? Or was it too little too late?

The red and white plastic of the machine wavered with a faraway reflection. Shana turned. At the other end of the hall, the stairwell door stood closed. The elevators sat silent. Every office but hers was locked for the night.

Was someone coming back from the ladies' room around the corner? She doubted it. When she'd left the lounge most of the patients looked as if they planned to mill around there until she came back. The idea that Hazel might have come back intrigued her. She almost gave chase.

Then she glanced at her watch. The break was halfway over. After her hasty exit she couldn't come back empty-handed.

Fiona was organized. She'd have some notepads in the lab.

A dry whistle, a breath between chapped lips smeared with Vaseline. The tune: "Here Comes the Bride." The words rearranged.

Here comes the whore. Who could ask for more. Put her on the bed then—

Not funny. But evocative in its way.

They'd left the lab unlocked while the whiners talked in the lounge. The halls had been deserted, easy. The electrodes lay in a drawer in the first bedroom. Wonderful place for them—a bedroom. Fine thin wires in festive colors. Vein-thin. Skin-tight. Wrap one around a wrist, watch the skin bunch, pale on both sides. Pale as death, the red marks as livid as fresh scars.

Quiet, here she comes. Out of the lounge to her office, from there to the soda machine. Pretty today, aren't we? Pretty slutty. Is that makeup? Are you advertising it or asking for it?

Whore. Come in here. They'd never notice she was missing, not for a while. Could tie her with her own wires. Tape her mouth with this gauze. Film it on their videotape. Watch it sometimes . . .

Voices from the lounge. She turned. No one venturing out. Not even the black-haired one who works in there. Fiona. Snooty, superior, studying all the time. Another bitch.

Like to put her to sleep. Put 'em all to sleep. Like pets. Parents.

The image came back. A coffin. Momma's head on a pillow, her hands on her chest. She's sleeping. That's what they said. A long wooden bed with a lid on it.

"She's sleeping." Smelling like soap, like Sundays, Grandmother's skeletal hands clutched at tiny shoulders. "Go to her now. Say good-bye."

The child was lifted even with the lid, the pale face. "Make her wake up."

"You want to say good-bye, don't you?"

"No! Don't close it. She can't breathe. Make her wake up! Momma! Momma!"

Wait. Listen. She's coming this way. The interfering bitch can't leave him alone. Hide down the hall, in the back, the bedroom with the wires. Wait for her.

Shana searched through her drawers, scattering pens and pencils. "These little things?" She hefted a fistful of multicolored stick 'em pads. They'd have to do.

Grabbing her soda, she flicked off the lights on the way out. A red glow from one of the bedrooms caught her eye.

She sighed. A night-light. When sleepovers ended and the overheads came on, the small red bulbs were easy to overlook.

"You only see them in the dark." She headed down the hall to switch it off.

She is in the main lab. Shuffling through drawers. Muttering.

Wrapped around both hands, the wires creaked when pulled taut. So taut a line of blood was drawn. It looked like black ink in the red light. Careless; it might show later. But it was winter. *Wear your gloves, Momma would say.*

A click, a jab of electricity. She'd just turned out the light. The darkness grew, seeping into every corner, the afterimage of the bedroom fading seconds later, like a photographic negative dissolving in acid. *In a minute she'll be back in the lounge. It'll be safe to head downstairs, wait in the garage with its clammy cement walls. Like a multistory grave.*

Slowly, like blood seeping from a wound, objects began to loom in the red shadows. *The light! Turn it off!*

The footsteps came closer. *She'll see. She'll know.*
She'll scream.
Hide. Behind the bed. Breathe shallow. Let the wires crawl
and wriggle in your hands, like veins writhing beneath the skin,
muscles twitching and jumping when pain is applied. Pleasure
and pain, mixed, indistinguishable. Cries of ecstasy so like cries
of pain.

And yet, picturing her scream was nothing compared
to her silence. The wires would hold her, unconscious, un-
moving. A few involuntary twitches—
Here she comes. Don't move. Hold your breath. Let the
excitement build as the lungs beg for release. Lack of oxygen is
supposed to add to the sensation. Like a hand over the mouth.
Or a pillow over the face.

Shana came around the door and yanked the red bulb
from the socket. The room plunged into darkness. "Shit."

She edged to her right, patting the wall for the regular
light switch. She should have thought of that before she
turned off the only source of—

Something moved behind her.

"Shana?" Gabe's low voice rumbled down the hall
from the lab.

She flicked the switch. "Back here," she called, scanning the room as she blinked at the bright light. The
drawer caught her attention. She frowned at the unchar-
acteristic way Fiona had left it wide open. "A person could
walk in here and whack their hip." She did it at home all
the time, especially when she'd been opening things in
her sleep. She slid the drawer shut, making a mental note
to tell Fiona they were getting short on electrodes. The
drawer was almost empty.

Something shuffled in the corner. If it was a mouse,
she'd just die.

"There you are."

She whirled.

Gabe stood in the doorway. "I wanted to talk to you."

Escape...
into Romance and embrace special savings.
Get 4 New Loveswept® Romances
for just $1.99 !
Plus FREE shipping and handling!
Get swept away by 4 New Loveswept Romances. Preview them risk-free—with no obligation and nothing to buy!
Keep them and Save $12.00! That's...
85% Off the cover price!
Get a FREE Gift!
To get your FREE personal lighted make-up case, peel off and affix this sticker inside!

Save 85% Off the Cover Price on 4 New *Loveswept* Romances—

and Get a Free Gift just for Previewing them for 15 Days Risk-Free!

Imagine two lovers wrapped in each other's arms—a twilight of loneliness giving way to a sunlit union. Imagine a world of whispered kisses and windswept nights, where hearts beat as one until dawn. If romance beats in your heart and a yearning stirs in your soul, then seize this moment and embrace *Loveswept!*

Let us introduce you to 4 new, breathtaking romances—**yours to preview and to lose yourself in for 15 days Risk-Free**. If you decide you don't want them, simply return the shipment and owe nothing. **Keep your introductory shipment and pay our low introductory price of just $1.99! You'll save $12.00—a sweeping 85% off the cover price! Plus no shipping and handling charges!** Now that's an introduction to get passionate about!

Then, about once a month, you'll get 4 thrilling Loveswept romances hot off the presses—*before they're in the bookstores*—and, from time to time, special editions of select *Loveswept* Romances. Each shipment will be billed at our low regular price, currently only $2.50* per book—a **savings of 29% off** the current cover price of $3.50. You'll always have 15 days to decide whether to keep any shipment at our low regular price—but **you are never obligated to keep any shipment**. You may cancel at any time by writing "cancel" across our invoice and returning the shipment to us, at our expense. So you see there is **no risk** and **no obligation** to buy anything, *ever!*

Treat Yourself with an Elegant Lighted Make-up Case—Yours Absolutely Free!

You'll always be ready for your next romantic rendezvous with our elegant Lighted Make-up Case—a lovely piece including an assortment of brushes for eye shadow, blush, and lip color. And with the lighted make-up mirror *you* can make sure he'll always see the passion in your eyes!

Keep the Lighted Make-up Case—yours absolutely FREE, whether or not you decide to keep your introductory shipment! So, to get your FREE Gift and your 15-Day Risk-Free preview, just peel off the Free Gift sticker on the front panel, affix it to the Order Form, and mail it today!

*(Plus shipping and handling, and sales tax in New York, and GST in Canada. Prices slightly higher in Canada.)

Save 85% off the Cover Price on
4 *Loveswept* Romances with this
Introductory Offer and Get
a Free Gift too!
no risk • no obligation • nothing to buy!

Get 4 Loveswept Romances for the
Introductory Low Price of just $1.99!

Plus no shipping and handling charges!

Please check:

❑ **YES!** Please send me my **introductory shipment of 4 Loveswept books,** and enter my subscription to Loveswept Romances. If I keep my introductory shipment I will pay **just $1.99—a savings of $12.00—that's 85% off the cover price, plus no shipping and handling charges!** Also, please send me my **Free Lighted Make-up Case** just for previewing my introductory shipment for 15 days risk-free. I understand I'll receive additional shipments of 4 new Loveswept books about once a month on a <u>fully returnable</u> 15-day risk-free examination basis for the low regular price, currently just $2.50 per book—**a savings of 29% off the current cover price** (plus shipping and handling, and sales tax in New York, and GST in Canada). There is no minimum number of shipments to buy, and I may cancel at any time. My **FREE Lighted Make-up Case** is mine to keep no matter what I decide.

PLEASE PRINT CLEARLY   20800   4B106

NAME_____

ADDRESS_____

CITY_____APT.# _____

STATE_____ZIP _____

SEND NO MONEY!

Affix
Your
FREE GIFT
Sticker

Prices subject to change. Orders subject to approval.
Prices slightly higher in Canada.

**Get 4 Loveswept books for the
Introductory Low Price of just $1.99!
And no shipping and handling charges!**

Plus get a FREE Lighted Make-up Case!
You risk nothing—so act now!

"We don't have much time."

"Our ten minutes are up?" He made it sound as if their relationship hadn't been meant to last any longer.

Maybe it hadn't. That didn't mean she'd give up so easily. Pride, and a leggy blond rival, could do a lot for a woman's nerve. "What did you want to ask me?" She leaned her hip semiseductively against the counter. She flicked a strand of hair over her shoulder. She blinked her long lashes slowly, hoping none of the mascara flaked off onto her cheeks.

She shouldn't have worried. Gabe fixed her with his usual laser stare, his mouth grim, his body taut. "What about dinner Saturday?"

From his demeanor she'd half expected him to announce his car was being towed and he had to leave.

"Dinner?" she repeated.

"Saturday."

Relief buzzed through her like the hum from the overhead light. She tried not to beam. "Oh, uh, I thought— uh, yeah, sure. I mean, no, I can't. You said Saturday?"

A smile flickered across his thin lips. He leaned a hand on the counter, canting his shoulders at an angle.

She almost thought his relief matched hers.

"Care to try that again?" he asked.

Apparently, he hadn't minded what she'd said the previous day. Everything wasn't over. But— "Saturday won't work for me. I have to go to the bakery."

"It takes all night to buy bread?"

"It does to bake it."

"Ah, your family."

"Paczki season."

He squinted. "I know whatever they are they probably don't grow on trees."

"They're doughnuts," Shana replied.

"There's a season for doughnuts?"

She reached around the corner for the hall light switch. Gabe leaned back, giving her just enough room to brush past his body. When she'd turned on that light, she flicked off the bedroom light. They walked toward the lab and out into the main hall.

"Paczkis are a Polish tradition. We make thousands every Lent."

"That's a few weeks away."

"You're Catholic."

"With a name like Gabriel Fitzgerald?"

Her laugh echoed up and down the hall. "I'm sorry. I wasn't thinking. Easter season is to Polish bakeries what April is to accountants. We're swamped. We add extra people, we put in hundreds of hours—"

"You cook?"

He'd remembered.

"Fortunately we're not *that* desperate. I told Uncle Karl I'd do inventory before the rush starts. I'll be there all day this Saturday and most of the night."

"So no date."

"I don't want you to think I'm putting you off."

He held up a hand. "No. I understand. You made it clear."

"I'm afraid I didn't."

They paused just outside the lounge. She lowered her voice. "When I said that part about not sleeping with you, what I meant was—Oh, DeVon. Hello."

DeVon Johnson stood a dozen feet away, his hulking presence surprisingly silent.

"I didn't know you'd be joining us." Shana said it as pleasantly as she could manage.

"Joining the wife," he explained tersely.

"Please. The session's just about to start." Shana backed away from the door and let him pass. She reserved her parting words for Gabe. "If you can stay a minute, I'd like to talk to you afterward about—about what I said."

"I'd like to do more than talk."

Her cheeks flushed. "Sit," she hissed.

He mastered a perfectly arrogant, insufferably male smirk. "Anything you say, Doc."

• • •

The session reconvened, this time with DeVon Johnson sitting glumly beside his wife. He listened to everything Shana said. He played along with her games. He didn't argue, challenge, or provoke. Shana counted her blessings, handing out the colored notepads and pens. "I call this a cultural exercise."

"We think of famous authors until we fall asleep." Fiona's quip earned a laugh.

"It's about how our culture views sleep," she explained. "I want you to write down all the phrases you know regarding sleep. You've got ten minutes."

Or about the same length of time it had taken Gabe Fitzgerald to turn her world upside down. He was back. Not that he'd ever dropped her. Not that her self-esteem rode on what any man thought of her. It did feel good, however, to have someone show an interest, someone who wasn't scared away by the limits she imposed.

When time was up, she collected the pads. " 'Early to bed, early to rise, makes a man healthy, wealthy, and wise.' 'A well-earned rest.' 'How can you sleep?' All these phrases suggest that if we can't sleep, there must be something wrong with *us*. This blaming attitude prevents a lot of people from seeking help."

She thought of DeVon and his reluctance to admit his problem. At least his presence was a step in the right direction. And Hazel? She thought of her troubled patient. A few minutes earlier she'd found herself picturing her so strongly, she'd half expected Hazel to slink into their session.

Gabe brought her attention back to the present by offering another quote. " 'Miles to go before I sleep.' "

She nodded. "Another one about earning the right to sleep."

"It could also mean we have a long way to go."

Oh no, he wasn't starting that again. Shana recognized

that intimate rasp in his voice. She turned to the rest of the group. "Any others?"

They tossed out phrases. " 'Asleep at the wheel.' "

" 'Don't fall asleep on the job.' "

" 'Now I lay me down to sleep.' "

" 'Putting a pet to sleep.' "

" 'Rest in peace.' "

"Rip Van Winkle."

Now they were rolling. "Rip Van Winkle's a good one," Shana noted. "He fell asleep and the world passed him by."

"Sleeping Beauty?" Doris suggested timidly.

"Another one whose life is passing her by."

Shirlee raised her gloved hand. "The apostles who fell asleep while Jesus prayed."

"What about them?"

Shirlee related the story like the long-time Sunday school teacher she was. "Jesus asked his apostles to keep watch while he prayed but they couldn't stay awake. They failed him."

Gabe shifted in his seat. Fists loosely clenched around his third cup of coffee, he stared at the floor.

Shana guessed what he was thinking. As a child he'd been expected to stay awake watching for his parents' plane. Whether the dream had been true or not, he still carried the guilt. "I'm sure Jesus forgave his apostles," she said.

Gabe glanced up, a grim smile on his lips. "Actually, I think he yelled at them."

Shirlee gently corrected him. "It showed they were only human."

"They screwed up. They knew something was about to happen, and they didn't stop it."

"No one can stop God's plan."

He went back to staring at his coffee. "Maybe not."

In the ensuing pause, Aurora's little-girl whisper surprised everyone. " 'To sleep, perchance to dream.' *Hamlet*, Act Three."

Shana gaped.

Aurora shrugged. "I can't just lie there. When I can't sleep I read."

"Welcome to the club," Gabe said. "How does the rest of it go? 'And in that sleep of death, what dreams may come must give us pause.' "

Aurora lifted her gaze very slowly. "You know it."

That wasn't all he knew. Their eyes met and locked. The profound connection blocked out everyone else in the room.

Shana wondered where all the air had gone. "How do you interpret that, Aurora?"

The blond averted her gaze, a guilty flush beneath her carefully applied makeup. With studied nonchalance she petted her leather coat, smoothing the grain away from her. "I guess it means dreams can be scary."

"Is that all?"

"You're the expert. You tell me."

Shana didn't feel like an expert. She had no idea how to handle the situation. Complicating matters was the surge of jealousy twisting through her like a corkscrew whenever Gabe's eyes locked with Aurora's.

Aurora. Even her name was pretty.

Shana summed things up shortly before ten. She handed out a list of foods known to keep people awake, then led the group in a final meditation exercise.

She took a deep breath as the patients filed out. She'd taken so many deep breaths during their relaxation segment, she felt light-headed. Nevertheless, she filled her lungs one more time, exhaling to a count of ten as she walked over to Gabe. She intended to speak to him about what she'd really meant when she'd declared she wouldn't sleep with him.

He stood as she neared the sofa. So did Aurora. Slinging her backpack over her shoulder, she nearly sideswiped Shana. Her ash-blond hair cascaded down her back as she looked up at Gabe with innocent fawn eyes. "Could you do me a favor, Gabe?"

He glanced at Shana. "If I can."

"Can you walk me to my car? That garage is sooo gloomy."

Gabe glanced around the room. DeVon Johnson had already escorted his wife out the door.

Marie tottered over, jabbing the carpet with her cane. "Are you the only gentleman left to us? I wouldn't mind an arm myself."

Gabe immediately extended his. "It would be my pleasure." That left the other arm for Aurora. He gave Shana a meaningful look. "Maybe later?"

"Sure. Give me a call, we'll set something up." She managed a tight smile. That didn't mean she didn't want to tear Aurora's arm right out of its socket. Kind of like the mannequin dresser in Aurora's last nightmare, Shana mused. Maybe there was something to these predictions.

"Until next week then," Gabe said.

She held the smile until the threesome was out the door. Had he forgotten the weekend? She'd thought they were going on a date.

He offered. You turned him down. Remember?

"Only for Saturday." She bustled around the clinic, arguing with her conscience while straightening chairs and picking up coffee cups. "There's still Sunday afternoon, Friday night—"

Fiona came back in. " 'Ooh, that garage is soooo gloomy.' "

Shana shot her friend a dirty look. "It isn't funny."

"Green is so becoming on you."

"Does it show?"

"You dust that table any harder, and you're going to rub off the varnish."

She shoved a curl off her forehead. "I guess the place is clean enough."

"You organize things when you're nervous, right?"

And disorganize them in her sleep. Which was a perfectly valid reason to avoid sleeping with Gabe. That didn't mean she had to ditch her entire social life. They could make a relationship work as long as he was willing to let her have her limits.

As long as he didn't run off with Aurora.

"Who knows?" she said aloud. "Aurora might be the woman of his dreams."

"And you can be the fairy godmother who brought them together."

Once upon a time, she'd have been happy with the role. At the moment she'd had it with helping others. Selfish or not, she wanted more. She wanted Gabe, and she meant to have him.

14

By Saturday her surge of confidence had evaporated like an uncorked bottle of cooking sherry. "Maybe it's for the best," Shana told herself. She marked the number of star-shaped cookie cutters on the shelf in the storage closet at her uncle Karl's bakery. Tin towers clinked and tottered as she separated out nine pine trees and eight reindeer. "Where are the hearts?"

Aunt Shayna wiped a chestnut curl off her forehead with the back of her flour-coated wrist. "What day is it?"

As far back as Shana remembered her aunt had tried to teach her to think for herself by answering questions with questions. At times Shana longed for a simple answer, something along the lines of, "It's January fourteenth."

"And what's a month from now?"

"Valentine's Day."

Aunt Shayna slapped a woodblock table with a cudgel of bread dough. Kneading with gusto, she put her whole weight behind it, all five feet two inches and one-hundred-and-fifty pounds of her. An eager smile made her round face even rounder. Her cheeks rose like dough, her eyes uncannily similar to the chocolate dots they used to make eyes on gingerbread boys. "So, you have plans?"

"For Valentine's Day?" Shana winced. Now she was doing it.

"No nice boy asking you out?"

"He's not nice and he's not a boy," Shana muttered. "As it stands, I have no idea if he's ever going to ask me out again."

"What was that?" Shana's mother scraped the contents of a cake bowl into the large mixer and flipped the switch.

"The hearts have been set out for Valentine's cookies," Shana shouted above the whine of the mixer. She made a note in the margins of her form to count them when she found them. Crossing to the second storage closet, she pulled the string attached to the bare bulb. All three Pascewski bakeries had identical supplies. None of them shared a similar layout. Uncle Karl's, her inventory location this weekend, was honeycombed with nooks and pantries. Each nook was lined with shelves, each shelf filled with bowls, mixing attachments, and utensils. "I wonder how old these wooden spoons are?"

"Older than you," her mother chided, bustling past to reach an icing bag. Her mother specialized in cake decorating. With utmost delicacy she placed brides and grooms atop wedding cakes. Her hints concerning Shana's single status were as subtle as Aunt Shayna's slapping of those loaves against the table. "Those spoons have fed whole families. Generations have eaten from those."

"Only if they survived on cake and babka."

"Don't be smart." Her mother waved a batter-covered spoon under her nose.

Shana licked it.

"Bah! Are you here to work or torment?" Her mother tossed the spoon in a soap-filled sink and hustled over to her sister. "Shayna, how is Esther's asthma? Marie told me she had an attack at church last week."

Shana snuck up beside them, filching a bite of fresh dough while her aunt discussed "female" troubles. As far as Aunt Shayna and Ma were concerned, everything from bunions to backaches were classified as female troubles. And yet, every conclusion they reached held a kernel of psychological truth.

"I think I see where I got my talent for counseling," Shana observed. "It took me four years of college and graduate school to learn as much about people as you two."

Her mother scoffed. "You see, she leaves out the doctorate. Our advice is equivalent to a master's?"

"Bachelor's," Shana teased, giving her mother a hug.

Her mother pushed her away with an indignant shove. "Get out of here with that hair. You wanna get us shut down by the health inspector?"

"I don't see how he could object." The low male voice froze all three women in place. "She has beautiful hair."

Shana felt every strand of it stand up on the back of her neck. With her back to the intruder, she looked across the table to Aunt Shayna for confirmation.

Giving her loaves a pat, her aunt tossed a towel over them, wiped her hands on her apron front, and checked if her hairnet was in place. Her fingers left white flour patches on her cheeks. "You've come to inspect our premises or our dumplings?"

Shana flashed her an indignant look before turning. "Gabe. Hi."

"Hello."

"Don't let them intimidate you."

"Us?" Her mother swatted her with a dishtowel. "Someone you know, Shana?"

Without his permission, she couldn't reveal he was a patient. "He's a friend of mine. Ma, this is Gabriel Fitzgerald. Gabe, this is my mother, Sylvie Getz, and my aunt Shayna."

Gabe shook Mrs. Getz's hand. He looked for a place to

set the topcoat thrown over his arm. Every surface was covered in flour.

"No, no," the older woman blurted out, hustling him into the main showroom. "You put that there, you'll never get it clean. Shana. Come on out. Show him where he can put his coat."

"He can put it upstairs where any gentleman caller would wait for his girl." Uncle Karl marched importantly out from around the counter, his apron spotless and perfectly pressed. The women took up sides on either side of their adored youngest brother. With thumb and forefinger, Uncle Karl narrowed his goatee to a vee and twisted the end of his mustache into a sharp point. All three eyed the young man approvingly.

"She could do worse for herself," Uncle Karl announced.

"If I'd known you were coming, I'd have warned you," Shana muttered out of the side of her mouth. "Welcome to Pascewski's."

"It smells wonderful." He said it without taking his eyes off her, in the tone a man usually reserved for a woman's perfume.

Their audience traded looks.

Shana sent them a stiff smile. "Why do I feel like my prom date just arrived?"

Gabe laughed low. "Is there somewhere I can hang my coat?"

Vainly attempting to hide the thrill of this surprise, she swallowed. "Did you plan on staying?"

"I've got an hour or so. Before bedtime." He turned to her mother and aunt. "She's got me going to bed at noon."

Brows raised. "Does she?"

"Therapy," Shana replied flatly.

Her mother sprang into action, shooing them with both hands. "Therapy, shmerapy. Be a hostess. Take him upstairs. The table's clean. There's food in the refrigerator. Make him feel at home."

"Maybe we would be safer upstairs," she murmured, leading him toward the stairs.

"Make him lunch," her aunt called.

"Thank you, I had a bite on the way here."

"So polite," Aunt Shayna staged-whispered when they were still in earshot.

"Makes a living," Uncle Karl deduced. He pinched his apron to indicate Gale's wool sweater. "Imported."

Shana sighed. These stairs had never seemed so steep, nor the light from the oval window so filled with motes of dust. The wallpaper curled in places. The paint on the apartment door was covered with a web of fine cracks, like old china. She pushed it open. "Welcome to the nineteen fifties. A typical ethnic living room/dining room combination. I don't think he's changed it since Aunt Miriam died."

Gabe slanted her a smile. "Norman Rockwell would have loved it. I bet you do too."

Shana ran her hand along the edge of the oval walnut table with the lace tablecloth her late aunt Miriam, God rest her soul, had brought directly from Poland for her wedding. Nana's wax fruit centerpiece held the place of honor. The chairs were Duncan Phyfe, as her grandmother never failed to point out.

"We used to come here every Sunday for dinner. This place brimmed with cousins, noise, food set out everywhere. It's an old man's apartment now."

"Your uncle can still set a gentleman caller back on his heels."

"Did he?" She laughed at her uncle's gruff image. "I tell him he's like a day-old paczki—crusty on the outside, full of jelly on the inside. He's a sweetheart when you get to know him. I've grown closer to him ever since my father died."

"I'd like to get to know him."

That implied a future. Shana glanced in the mirror over the heavily carved buffet. The only powder she wore was powdered sugar on her chin and a dab of flour on her nose. "I'm a mess."

"You look wonderful." He closed the distance between them, kissing her lightly. "It's good to see you."

It was heaven seeing him. "You said you ate. I could offer you a cookie, a roll, anything in the display cases. Baked fresh."

"You know what I'd really like a taste of."

She shouldn't give in to him. No sensible woman should wilt at the very idea of a man taking her in his arms. Instead of an argument she gave him another kiss. He tasted of strong coffee. She probably tasted of sugar. They blended well.

Downstairs a bell rang; a customer entered the shop. "We shouldn't."

He spared the room a glance. "You don't neck above your uncle's bakery?"

She eased out of his embrace, gesturing at the dated room. "Are you kidding? By the time I was fourteen I was desperate to get out of here."

"They seem like very loving people."

"They are, every last one of them. It can be a bit suffocating, living where you work, working where you live. The showroom downstairs was as much my living room as this." Her fingers squeaked on the layers of heavy, dark furniture polish on Nana's chairs.

"You lived here?"

"Above the store on Casimir. Same place, different address."

"I tried that one. Your cousin Stephen said I'd find you here."

He'd been looking for her. She'd been dreaming of a man like him all her life. She shook off the romantic notion. "I'm surprised word of your arrival didn't precede you. They pound the bottoms of copper pots, like jungle drums. I call it the Polish telegraph. Word travels fast when I've got a date. Not that this is a date."

"Do you want it to be?" He lifted her hand to his lips, licking flour off her little finger. "Good enough to eat."

She wiped the kiss on her sweatshirt. "I'm a mess. Give me a minute, will you? I really should wash up."

He caught her chin between his thumb and forefinger, rubbing off the powdered sugar. "I'll wait."

He wasn't good at waiting. Seconds after she'd headed down the short hall, he paced the apartment. He studied the family photos crowding the buffet, a wedding in the old country, a young man with a Kaiser Wilhelm beard and his two doting sisters, the sisters' weddings.

He picked up an advertising still. "I remember this," he called, "Roly Poly, Pascewski's Fresh Kid."

Shana rejoined him, her face washed, her lashes clumped into spiky stars. Without so much as a glance, she took the photo and wedged it behind the others. "Our mascot. He was a cross between the Michelin Man and the Pillsbury Doughboy."

"His picture was on the dinner rolls my grandmother bought. He was as famous as the song."

"They played it wherever he went."

"You didn't like him?"

She gritted her teeth, steeling herself for his reaction. "I was him."

"You what?"

She shrugged as if it hardly mattered. "I couldn't cook. I dropped spoons in mixers. I never, ever learned to break an egg with one hand—although I broke them every other way known to man. I was a baking klutz."

"So you became the family mascot?" He picked up the picture again, eyeing the toothpick legs that stuck out beneath a costume constructed to resemble two giant dinner rolls and a muffin head.

"I had no brothers or sisters to take my place, so they took me around to old folks' homes, grocery-store openings, home ec classes. I walked in the St. Patrick's Day Parade once."

"Was it that bad?"

She laughed at her own defensiveness. "My father used to say, 'In this family, we all have our "roll" to play.' "

Gabe groaned.

"It was mortifying, humiliating, and the costume was hot as hell, but child abuse it wasn't. However, it did point up my need to find a line of work besides baking."

Slipping his arm around her shoulders, Gabe looked over the rest of the photos. All of them featured the bakeries or apartments similar to her uncle's. The lone exception was a brightly colored snapshot of Shana beneath a saguaro cactus. "Where was this taken?"

"Arizona. I lived there for three years."

"A long way to go to escape a bakery."

"In one way or another I've been walking away from it all my life."

"You seem very loyal. You're here, aren't you?"

She faced him, her brown eyes caramel and gold, her cinnamon freckles washed free of makeup and flour. He couldn't resist touching them.

She closed her eyes, reveling in that tender concern. "I was safe here. Safe down there." She indicated the bakery below. "My family would have protected me forever."

"From what?"

Needing distance, she strolled to the other end of the room. She stood silhouetted in the bay window that fronted the street, wrapping her arms across her waist. "They couldn't stop me from walking out on them. I'd been doing it since I was six. In my sleep."

"You sleepwalk?"

"Regularly."

"That's it?" His jaw clenched the minute he heard his own disbelieving tone. Who was he to make light of someone else's sleeping problem?

She welcomed the chance to downplay it. "It's a common childhood disorder. Most kids outgrow it."

"Like insomnia."

She nodded, awarding him a point for making the connection. "Hang around here long enough, and you'll hear all the stories. The one about my father finding me in the bakery breaking eggs one night, dozens of them. The time they heard me downstairs pushing the No Change button on the cash register to hear it ring. I must've just seen *It's a Wonderful Life.* I'm telling you, I was a handful when I was asleep."

"I bet you were a great kid."

She shook her head, a faraway smile on her face. "I never fitted in. Even in costume. I was the Ugly Duckling."

"You're not ugly by any stretch of the imagination."

"I wasn't fishing."

"I know."

She crossed the room to a low bookshelf. From the worn covers, Gabe guessed the children's books had entertained a couple of generations of readers.

"I love fairy tales," she said. "I think it's one of the reasons I went into psychology. They're full of subtext, all primal conflicts and archetypes."

He crouched beside her. "If you say so."

She grinned at her own jargon. "They're also great stories."

"Like the Ugly Duckling?"

She faced him head-on. "How would you feel if you lived in a bakery and were a disaster around food? My family understood—to a certain extent. They helped me with college. I planned to pay them back by majoring in accounting; I'd help out with the books. I walked out after three weeks."

"Accounting wasn't for you?"

"I literally walked out. One night I sleepwalked right out of the dorm. We decided I'd be safer at home."

"Oh."

"But I couldn't hide here forever. After a year I went back, this time to study psychology. I was sure there was a deep-seated reason for all this nocturnal searching. One doctor told me I wanted to escape the bakeries."

"A brilliant deduction. So you moved to Arizona?"

"Nope. I stayed on and got my degree, then my master's, then went for my doctorate. I counseled troubled teens for a few years. Good work. Meaningful."

"Any meaningful relationships?"

She took a deep breath. "Over time, three. I walked out on them too."

"Sleepwalked."

"I also thrash in my sleep. It's called parasomnia. Aren't you glad I'm telling you this up front?"

"So I'll know why you won't sleep with me."

At that moment she wouldn't look at him either. She ran her hand over the book. "Most men don't adjust well to being kicked out of bed. Not that I'm blaming them."

"Mind if I do?"

She grinned, her gaze on the illustrations as she idly fanned the pages. "Nana would say it served me right; they shouldn't have been in my bed in the first place."

"I agree. Especially if they didn't love you enough to stay."

"That's very chivalrous of you. But why would any man put up with it?"

"Love?"

"Someday my prince will come, and he'll accept me exactly as I am. If you believe that, there's a bridge in Arizona I could sell you."

He took the book out of her hand, the pages yellowed on the edges, brittle to the touch. "Desert air doesn't cure sleeping problems any more than it heals broken hearts."

"Arizona has one of the best sleep disorders clinics in the country. They can even cure sleepwalking, with the right drugs."

"Then why—"

"No drug works in all cases." She shoved the book back in the case, letting him lend her a hand as they got to their feet. "That's why I drew the line with you. I like you. I'd like to keep seeing you. We can even—well, if things get more involved, I wouldn't mind sleeping with you."

"As long as we don't actually sleep."

She flushed and grinned at the same time, squinting up at him. "Yes."

He was a man who got to the point. He didn't waste time because the times when his mind was unclouded by sleepiness were brief. Besides, that hopeful/hopeless look on her face was killing him. "You forget one thing, angel. I'm a man who doesn't sleep. What if it turns out we're the perfect pair?"

She tilted her head to the side, the better to get a bead on him. "Like Jack Sprat who ate no fat and his wife who ate no lean?"

He tipped her chin up again, his thumb straying across her full lips. "I haven't had a woman fall asleep on me yet."

Gabe walked out of the bakery loaded down with bags of brown bread, black bread, rye, sourdough, tarts, petit fours, a half dozen bagels, a pie, and two unwieldy stalks of French. An aromatic blend of yeast, flour, and marzipan filled his car. Shana's relatives stood at the window and waved. She'd retreated to the back rooms to finish her inventory, leaving him to run the gauntlet of her uncle's showroom, a culinary death march punctuated with the phrase "just taste this."

Loosening his belt a notch, he started the car, waved one more time, then steered into traffic.

Shana's kiss till burned on his lips. A lifetime of raisin bread couldn't dull that sweetness. Opening her heart to him, she'd offered him a glimpse of her soul. He slapped the steering wheel with his palm. He'd *known* she understood him on a level deeper than any textbook. Sleep problems had haunted her relationships too.

Did that mean they were doomed? He could promise to accept her wandering nights. But he knew how flimsy promises could be. How many women had told him they didn't mind him working all hours? Sitting at his computer, Shana's thrashing wouldn't bother him a bit. But how long would it be before his insomnia wrecked them both? Before she saw his distance as emotional as well as physical?

One of them had to find a way out. If drugs couldn't cure her problem, maybe a new lead would solve his.

"Thanks for stopping by," he said.

The young blonde flung her backpack onto the restaurant booth. She wriggled her jeans-clad rear end along the leather seat. "This isn't like a date, is it?"

Gabe sipped his coffee and looked into Aurora's pale gray eyes. She was flattered and suspicious, as beautiful girls often were.

"I've been thinking about what you said in the group session," he said. "About dreams."

She glanced at the ceiling, squirming in her seat to check out the other noontime diners. Turning back to him, she flattened her hand on the table, her red nails spread. "Let me make one thing clear, okay? You're a nice-looking guy."

"That's not why I asked you here."

"Good, 'cause I just don't get into older men. Okay?"

Gabe gulped. He'd known Aurora might misinterpret his interest but *older*?

Her head bobbed in time to a tune in her head. "You're a runner, right?"

"A few miles a day."

"You look like a runner. Personally, I prefer volleyball players. They don't have that 'lean and hungry look' like you runners."

Us "old" runners, you mean, Gabe thought. He pinned

down the quote. "*Julius Caesar.* Cassius's lean hungry look."

She was flattered. "A lot of people don't think I'd know Shakespeare."

"I was more surprised at what you said about dreams."

"Yeah, well. Can we get a coffee or something?"

"I asked the waitress to bring another."

"No milk. Dieting." She patted her tiny waist.

"You can talk about it, you know."

A warning flashed in her eyes. "I don't know what you mean."

"The dreams, Aurora. The real ones. The ones no one else believes."

She gave her hair an arrogant toss. "You mean she doesn't believe you either?"

"Shana?"

"She's your counselor, right? Mine? Merryweather? He thinks the dreams *mean* something. Like I'm screwed up. Like I care about any of these people. I just dream them."

"What do you mean?" His sharp demand brought a flare of rebellion to her eyes. He worked his jaw until a vein beat in his cheek. He usually left diplomacy to Brice. He lowered his voice. "How can you not care when you dream about people?"

She shrugged. "They're nothing to me."

The waitress brought him another coffee. By the time Aurora had decided on a decaf mocha, he'd broken two stirrers and spilled a sugar. "Are you saying you dream about strangers?"

"Sure." She dumped in a packet of artificial sweetener and stirred up a whirlpool. "Don't you?"

"Never."

"Huh."

That was it? Huh? Gabe downed half his coffee in one gulp. He knew what he'd heard. "They seem real, you said."

"Totally. Like the bus thing."

"You saw one crash?"

"Boy, have you got a melodramatic streak. I saw one pull out, from the aquarium, you know? School field trip. But this kid got left behind. He curled up and slept by the shark tank. I saw that."

Gabe had seen something about it too. "On TV, you mean?"

She gave him a "you should know better than that" look. "I saw it in a dream. I called them. I told them this kid was sleeping with the fishes. They laughed at me. So I go, 'Check it out.' I just wanted to help. They found him okay the next morning."

She tapped her spoon against her cup, satisfied with the ringing sound. "That's it. Lost wallets. Kids in malls wandering away from their parents. I call and pretend I was shopping there and saw where the kid went. It's easier that way."

Gabe scowled into his coffee. This wasn't helping. He'd expected someone who shared his fears, his dilemmas, his frustration.

"What about you?" she asked pleasantly.

What about him? he thought. Two nights later he stared out his window, waiting for the blinking light on his computer to tell him Singapore had received his transaction.

He couldn't shrug off his dreams the way Aurora did, not when they featured the people he loved. He'd told her that, describing the urgency, the sense of futility. These were people he knew. For God's sake, he had to *try*. Otherwise what were the dreams for?

She'd popped a stick of gum in her mouth. "To prepare you?"

"For what?"

"Whatever. Most people don't get any warning. When they lose someone they never see it coming. Maybe your dreams are a gift."

His neck ached, his head thrummed. Back at his computer, the conversation revolved in his mind. All his life he'd dreaded his dreams. He'd avoided sleep, relationships. And then, when he finally found someone who shared his curse, she refused to see it as one.

"You know, it could be kinda nice," she'd said.

"Nice?" He'd practically spit out his coffee.

"Even if you couldn't change what was about to happen, you'd be ready."

For what? He'd dreamed of kissing Shana atop the Sears Tower. What could have prepared him for that?

He jabbed at his keyboard. The cursor on his screen blinked twice, like an airplane's lights detaching themselves from the surrounding stars, circling to land, going back to the beginning.

He remembered his first dream. He'd tried warning his parents about the crash, his grandmother, anyone who'd listen. But what if the dream hadn't been intended for them? What if it had been sent to prepare *him*?

It was a stretch. A total reversal. He'd always seen his dreams as a trap, a burden imposed by cynical gods who jeered his pitiful attempts to change the unchangeable. But what if he was wrong? What if the dreams were a gift, an opportunity?

The question still applied. Why him? Why had God singled him out?

Apparently the notion had never bothered Aurora. "Who knows?" she'd said.

He conjured up another dream; Brice's crash. Gabe had gotten on the phone to Peg. He'd been there in Emergency when they brought Brice in. He'd done what he could. The dream had given him a head start. Maybe that's all they could do.

Looking at them that way, he'd never need to fear his dreams again.

Maybe Aurora was right. Like sleep, like love, the dreams could be a blessing or a curse. The approach was up to him. If he accepted them, he could live with them. He could sleep. He could love a woman.

He smiled grimly at his reflection in the glass. "Prepare yourself." For the second time in two months, he was about to change his life.

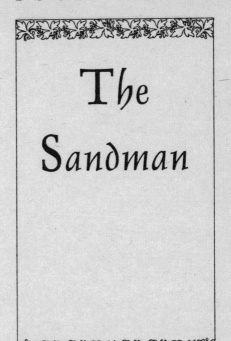

BOOK THREE

The
Sandman

15

Ten minutes past two A.M. Gabe picked up the telephone, his gaze focused on the tickertape running across the top of his computer screen. "Fitzgerald."

"It's Aurora. I had another dream."

He swung around in his chair. He'd asked her to call. In exchange for being there to talk her down after a nightmare, she'd promised to fill him in anytime she had a "real" dream. She'd had two in the last three weeks—both involving lost children. Each ended happily, even prosaically. No biggie, according to Aurora.

Gabe hung on every detail. He needed to know the dreams they shared didn't have to spell disaster. They could be a blessing; like his new, normal life.

It had started simply, dates with Shana, meeting more of her family, cooking her dinner. It astounded him how happy he could be, how easy it could be without the threat of dreams hanging over his head. He hadn't had so much as a hint of a prediction in weeks, despite the fact he was sleeping up to five hours per day.

On the other end of the line, Aurora concluded her tale about a gloomy parking garage, a damp spring night, a man with a pipe. She was fuzzy on the details.

"Then it wasn't a 'real' dream," Gabe concluded.

"It was and it wasn't. It wasn't my usual kind of nightmare. I don't know. There was something about it." The girl could be maddeningly vague.

Gabe squinted at his screen. A stock he'd been waiting for had dropped a quarter point in the last twenty minutes. He typed in a purchase bid, keeping the keyclicks to a minimum. "It's not hard telling the difference between a regular dream and a real one."

"I know. The real ones are so—real. But I've never had one that was scary."

Speak for yourself, Gabe thought.

"Anyway, I've got to get back to bed. Eddie's here. If he found me talking to some guy in the middle of the night—"

Gabe's mouth quirked up at the corner. "Tell me about it." He'd had women get jealous over him dealing with Tokyo in the middle of the night. "Have a good one. And Aurora, thanks for the call."

He wanted to keep them coming. The concept of the visions as gifts was as new to him as talking to a woman in the middle of the night. He wondered if Shana would object to him talking to one of her patients. As far as he was concerned, it was a version of the buddy system. Like Alcoholics Anonymous, only someone who'd been there could understand. Aurora understood—to a point.

The clinic staff, on the other hand, remained stumped by his mysterious MSL readout. They'd invited him for two more sleepovers. The nighttime visit had been a total washout. He'd brought work and spent the wee hours writing a proposal for a Samoan bond issue. The next sleepover took place in the afternoon. He'd had an erotic dream featuring Shana, him, and a hammock. His temperature, heart rate, respiration, and pulse had zoomed. His brain waves remained normal.

He'd cornered Shana in her office afterward. She'd been scowling at his printout. "Don't tell me I disappointed you in bed already."

She'd fixed him with a glare. "You slept four solid hours. That's wonderful. I'm proud of you."

"You mean I snooze, I win?"

"You're improving every day."

"Like fine wine?" He'd sat on the corner of her desk, running a finger along her cheek.

"With all this sleep it's no wonder you look so good."

He'd preened shamelessly, slicking his hair back on both sides with his palms. "Really?"

"Seriously. Even if we never find an explanation for your dreams, your insomnia seems to be lessening. You're on the verge of being cured."

He stacked his hands on his thigh. "You didn't tell them about my dream, did you?"

Shamefaced, she traced a jagged line along the printout. "I told the staff I didn't understand your wave activity any more than they did."

"Are we sweeping the dream-thing under the rug?"

She'd returned his look with a steady one of her own, her intuition zeroing in on the truth. "They don't seem to haunt you the way they used to."

"I'm learning to accept them." The way he'd accepted a woman in his life. He combed a strand of hair off her cheek. "Of course, the whole theory could fall apart the next time I dream."

"Maybe you won't."

He tipped her chin toward him. "I'm dreaming right now."

She'd swatted him off her desk with the readout. "Tell me another one."

"Hey! I didn't know you were into spanking."

She shooed him out the door. "Peddle it elsewhere, Romeo, I've got work to do."

He backpedaled into the hall, grinning as he went.

He'd rather see her put him off with teasing than see her frightened by the doubts shadowing her eyes. "Friday?"

"Maybe."

No maybe about it. They'd gone out six times in the last three weeks. She'd stuck to her rule about not sleeping with him—in either sense. But they were getting closer, in every sense, on every date.

He tracked it back to that morning at the bakery. Alone in her uncle's apartment, charmed by what she'd told him of her family, challenged by her revelation of her own sleep problems, attracted to her passion for life, he'd stolen a kiss. Then another. Without removing one strip of clothing or unbuttoning a button, they'd driven each other to the edge. Her mouth had opened for him, her breasts pressed to his chest. She'd ridden his thigh with a pulsating abandon that still sent a throb of heat to his loins. The ringing bell of a customer entering the bakery had stopped them just in time, along with the belated realization that a shop full of chaperons awaited them downstairs.

He still chuckled at the way his legs had shaken as he'd descended that long flight of stairs. He'd refused to let go of her waist until they reached the bottom. There he'd brazenly slid his hand downward, cupping her luscious rear end. She'd swatted him away that time too.

Watching a rented movie at her place a week later, they'd been considerably less prudent. His Shana had a weakness for neck kisses. She practically sizzled when he touched her there. Just thinking of her enthusiastic, uninhibited responses made his body hard. She threw herself body and soul into anything that excited her. Apparently, his touch did.

A light blinked rapidly in the corner of his screen. The computer demanded his attention. He hunched forward, ready to get back to work. But first he slicked his hair back on both sides. A smirk grinned back at him from the screen. This falling-in-love business wasn't half bad.

. . .

"Look, I'm going to hang up if you don't say who you are."

A woman cried softly on the other end of the line, struggling for breath.

"Who is this?" Shana reached for the alarm clock. Three-twenty A.M. "That does it."

"Wait. Please."

She set the clock back down. Her heart had rocketed into her throat when the ringing dragged her out of a sound sleep. Her first thought was family emergency. Her second, obscene phone call. Her third was to listen. A dry sob, like the pant of a terrified, exhausted animal set her nerves on alert. "Who is this?"

"He did it again. It's been almost a month." An older woman. Her trembling voice threatened to break once more into ragged gasps.

Shana pictured her rocking back and forth as she spoke. "Hazel?"

"He came home with the pills. He knows I try not to swallow them. He figured that out months ago. He—he sticks his fingers in my mouth to make sure."

Shana swallowed by reflex. "Is he there now?"

"He's taking a bath."

The homey scene almost shocked her into nervous laughter. She controlled her reaction. In the last few weeks Hazel had called twice, both times at the office. Shana would answer and Hazel's excited, rambling voice would drop hints about coming in, begging for a means to stay awake while her body and mind demanded sleep. "If he's abusing you, Hazel, if your husband is dangerous, we can help you."

"If?" Her voice grew sharp.

"You have to check into the hospital. It's the only way we can help you."

"I got my help. I guessed the mood he was in. I took

the other pills; I got ready. No matter how many sleeping pills he made me take, I'd be awake."

"Buy why? Why does he do this?"

"He likes it. He can do anything he wants. I used to let him, when we were first married. I used to think I was being a good wife. I couldn't help it if I cried, sometimes it hurt. I told him I'd try better next time. Then he started bringing home the pills. He said the scarves and the ropes weren't enough to hold me still."

Shana's skin crawled. Sitting up in bed, she grasped at the covers, tucking them in all around her. She switched on the light, the better to banish shadows. She even hauled the cat over. "Hazel, I can't help you on the phone. If he's getting sleeping pills illegally, we can stop him. We can help."

She'd stopped listening. The sobs dried up. Her voice, unnaturally calm, narrated the rest like a repulsive bedtime story. "He calls himself the Sandman. He wants me to sleep. At first he said they'd calm me, make it easier. But then he'd wait—until I was completely under, unconscious. I'd wake up the next day groggy, not even sure until I felt it in my body, on my skin. Sometimes there were signs, bruises, bites—"

Shana covered her mouth with her hand.

"That's why I couldn't sleep, couldn't let him put me to sleep. I never knew what I'd find when I woke up. If I woke up. So I take my other pills when I think he's in that kind of mood. He gives me his pills and I pretend to fall asleep while he lays out his things—the scarves, the cut-up strips of cloth. He was picking out the color he wanted while I pretended to fall asleep."

Shana shuddered. "Hazel, tell me where you are."

"It isn't as bad that way. At least I know what he's doing. There isn't that sense of drowning, of being swallowed up by drowsiness, smothered."

"Come in now. Come to the hospital tonight. I'll meet you there."

Her urgency didn't register. "He wants to increase the

dosage, he says they're weakening. I think he's guessed. It was my fault—"

"None of this is your fault."

"When he got the cord, I flinched—Now he knows." Shana rested her forehead on her hand. "Hazel, please."

"Please what, dear?"

Her sudden politeness struck Shana as something her mother might say. She remembered her sense that Hazel came from a moneyed background. Then again, abuse happened in the best of families. "Hazel, I know someone at the hospital has been supplying you with uppers. Combining them with sleeping pills is incredibly dangerous. If you can't come in tonight, come in tomorrow, after your husband leaves the house. I'll meet you at the door. Your husband will never know."

"He'd find out. He's powerful. No one knows him the way I do; no one suspects. Looking at him, you'd never guess—"

Although Shana deplored bribery, she extended a carrot. "We can prescribe pills for you. Legal ones. They can ease you off the combinations you're on."

"I can't."

"You can't function much longer the way you're going. You're nervous, irritable, unable to focus on things for long."

"That's what my husband says."

Shana winced.

"He says if I slept more I'd handle things better."

"Let me be the sleep expert here, okay?"

"Oh, he knows what he's talking about. He's studied."

Researching ways to shove pills down his wife's throat? Shana thought angrily.

"He's a very intelligent man," Hazel said, a wistful remembered pride in her voice. "It was months before I realized. I'd wake up and feel as if something had happened to me while I slept. He said it was my imagination."

The last part made Shana pause. She was getting carried away. This *could* be Hazel's imagination, a delusional or paranoid fantasy brought on by mental illness *or* the pills she'd been taking. Either way, if she was admitted to St. James for sleep disorders Shana could get her examined for other problems.

She was forced to repeat herself. "Please, let us help you."

Hazel's voice dripped with contempt, her moods shifting faster than Shana could react. "He'd find out. He'd punish us all. You know what he's like."

Shana knew what she'd been told. "No one is that powerful. There are shelters—"

The receiver slammed down.

Shana sighed. Dealing with the lightning-quick personality changes of the sleep-deprived was never easy. The dial tone's buzzing drone reminded her of a heart monitor flatlining. "Lost her again."

She hauled Romper into her lap and rocked him until he purred. Eventually she lay back. Images of a man putting a woman to sleep wormed their way into her mind. Just imagining being trapped in something as comforting as sleep, unable to move, to react while someone touched her, manipulated her—

She reached for the telephone.

Gabe automatically calculated the time in Tokyo as he reached for the ringing receiver. The embassy would tell him the new tariffs. If they were under the limit he'd set for investment—

"Uh, sorry, wrong number," a woman said.

"Shana?" He sat forward so fast, he knocked a stock offering askew. "Is that you?"

"Gabe. What did you just say?"

"Hello in Japanese. I was expecting Tokyo."

"Good. I mean, I'm not waking you up, then."

"At this hour? It's the middle of my workday, kid."

"Do you have a minute?"

"I think I could free one up." Sloping back in his chair, he caught sight of his reflection in the window. He had an ear-to-ear grin on his face, a hey-baby cant to his shoulders, and an ankle propped high on his desk. He could have bought and sold the entire Pacific Rim. For his entire working life he'd prided himself on iron-willed concentration. One sound of Shana's voice and he chucked the whole thing. "What's up?"

"I am," she moaned miserably. "Are you busy?"

"Just doing some horse trading."

"This third world country for that one?"

"You flatter me. What can I do for you?"

"I wanted to thank you for dinner last week. Oh, and the tickets to the Bulls game. Uncle Karl and cousin Steve were thrilled. Although my kindly cousin almost refused to take his son."

"Bobby?"

"He wanted Bobby to wear the Roly Poly suit. Steve's into free publicity."

"Bobby said no."

"He lost his head. Literally. I used to do the same thing. Ma said I'd lose my own head if it wasn't sewn on. It's been attached with snaps ever since. The costume's head, I mean."

"I got that part. Did you take Bobby's side?"

"Of course. Wouldn't you?"

"Hey, your family's been keeping me in bagels for a month. I know which side my French bread's buttered on."

"Very funny."

He hitched one leg over the other. His voice lowered a notch. "Are you in bed?"

"Yes."

"You don't sound happy about it. Of course, being there alone, I can understand."

"It would be nice if you were here."

His heart thumped. "Say the word."

She let the silence speak for her. Not yet, it said.

"What are you wearing?"

That earned him a laugh. "I didn't know I was dialing a nine hundred number."

"Phone sex. Maybe we should try it."

"Down, boy."

He laughed along with her. "You didn't call at this hour to thank me for last week's dinner."

"I've thought about it. We never did get around to the standard things like 'thank you' and 'good night.'"

They'd very nearly gotten to her bedroom, though. Gabe recalled the white-hot kiss they'd shared at her apartment door. She'd invited him in, drinks only, showing him the Southwestern decor she'd transplanted from Arizona. Oranges, pinks, and teal blues warmed up the third floor she rented in an old Victorian mansion in Evanston. Her cat served as official greeter.

"How's Romper?" he asked.

"Fine. He's on my pillow purring."

"Does he always sleep there?"

"Wouldn't you like to know."

He let her win that round. Not that he minded the cat. The first time he'd met him, Romper had collapsed at his feet. Paws in the air, the furball had rolled onto his back for a stomach rub. After five minutes on the sofa, Gabe found himself wearing the animal like a boa. He'd had to peel it off before he strolled into the kitchen to offer his assistance. Rattling a coffee cup into a seldom-used saucer, Shana had shooed him out. "I know how to make coffee," she'd claimed, breaking the seal on a fresh jar of instant. When he'd traipsed toward the bedroom, Shana had bolted out of the kitchen as if propelled. "Don't go in there! It's filthy." "So's my mind," he'd quipped.

"Gabe?" Her late-night voice broke into his reverie.

He shifted the receiver on his shoulder. "I was remembering the first time I saw your apartment."

"That traumatic?"

"I still can't picture you in bed. You've never let me get that far."

Shana hesitated. "I'm having some rewiring done."

"So you said."

"I know you think the sleepwalking is something we can work around—"

"On the contrary. I'm beginning to think it's more serious. I wonder if you've got Roly Poly in there, stuffed à la *Psycho*. Maybe you do weird voodoo rituals, like slathering him with butter and popping him in ovens."

She tried to laugh.

"What's wrong?" His feet hit the carpet. Stupid of him not to pay more heed; she'd never called so late. He swung his chair away from his screen, the better to concentrate on everything she said. "Shana, what is it?"

"I don't know where to begin. I can't really begin anywhere; it involves a patient. It's confidential."

"And bothering you. Aren't you the one who told us not to think of work in bed?"

"This one came looking for me."

"A patient at your house? Are you okay?"

"It was a phone call."

"Obscene?"

"Yes and no." Shana's smile faded, her fingers twining in the kinked telephone cord. It was sweet of him to be so protective. Not like Hazel's husband—

"It wasn't that DeVon Johnson."

"Oh no. He doesn't scare me anymore. Actually, he's working with Flora. She says it's a struggle but they're making progress. No, this was a woman. That's about all I can say. Imagine Sleeping Beauty under her spell, only the prince is some kind of sex pervert who likes it that way."

"I can see why you're still awake."

She curled on her side, the cat by her knees, the receiver between her and the pillow. "I knew you'd understand." Staring across the bed, she imagined Gabe's profile on the other pillow, how nice it would be to talk to him late at night, to turn to him, hold him.

"Am I losing you?" he asked softly.

"Just dreaming."

"A good dream, I hope."

She wanted it to be a reality. The thought sobered her; she shouldn't want what she couldn't have.

But things were going so well between them. He'd eased into her life so well she couldn't imagine a day without him. An apartment she'd always seen as a refuge felt vaguely empty each time she came home alone. On evenings when she expected him, she wore a path in the carpet pacing to the window, waiting for his car to pull in, the crunch of tires on snow, his voice on the intercom.

If she dragged herself out of bed right now, she could go into the living room and sniff his cologne on the sofa pillows. She could look at the spot beside the door where he kicked off his shoes. He'd made himself at home in her life. Her family loved him.

So did she.

But could she risk giving him that love? Could she risk sleeping with him?

"I knew you couldn't do it," he murmured.

"Do what?"

"Stay awake at this hour. You conk out at eleven."

"I don't."

"Just like Cinderella."

"That's midnight."

"It's after three."

"Oh, right. I guess I should let you go."

"I'm not going anywhere. Tokyo's playing tough. They loathe the idea of a Westerner putting this deal together. I can make 'em wait another ten minutes before I make my offer. Talk to me."

She longed to. Just the memory of Hazel's voice made her queasy. She pictured a puppet manipulated by strings, trussed up in them. Is that what turned her husband on? Is that why he tied her up?

She pressed her ear to the pillow, trying to shut out the words. *The Sandman.* "Technically she isn't even a patient yet."

"Then tell me."

"I'm trying to get her to come in."

"If she isn't a patient, how'd she get your home number?"

Shana sat up slowly. It was as if he'd opened a window. A frigid breeze slithered over her bare shoulders.

Gabe sensed her instant tension. "I'll come over."

"No, I—Thanks, I'm fine. I never thought of that."

"Are you in the book?"

"I've only been in Chicago six months. She—she wanders around the hospital. She must know my routine." Every time she'd called the office she'd caught Shana alone. "Maybe Fiona told her."

"Fiona's not dumb."

"Hazel's obviously disturbed but I don't think she's dangerous. I'll leave that honor to her husband. One of them's sick, that's for sure."

"I don't like the sound of this."

"It was like a dream, the nasty kind you can't shake. I'm not even sure I believe her. She's fighting pills with pills. She could be sleep-deprived, delusional, mentally ill. I'm sorry I dumped all this on you."

"People call you in the middle of the night with their problems; why shouldn't you have someone to talk to too?"

Why, indeed? She punched her mattress with the side of her fist. "But I can't help her if she won't come in."

"Maybe you help just by listening."

She smiled, her eyes gritty with sleep, her heart full. "So do you." There they were again, the words "I love you" backing up in her throat. They'd sound so natural if she said them then. "Gabe?"

"Yes?"

"I've gotta go. Early day tomorrow. Thanks for being there."

"Hey, if Marti can call Steve at the bakery to bring home a gallon of milk, you can call me at the office anytime."

But they weren't married like Marti and Steve. "Good night."

"Don't forget to set your alarm."

"Right. 'Night." She hung up, sparing a glance at the locked bedroom door. Although he hadn't meant it that way, Shana trudged across the room, opened the door, and glanced at the alarm on the living room door. Its red eye glowed, armed and set.

"It's as if you're locking people in, not out."

After Brice had recovered they'd doubled-dated with Brice and Peg. An electronics freak, Gabe's business partner had hovered around her alarm system for half an hour.

"Don't mind him," Peg had said with a laugh. "Our house gets a new alarm every two years."

"Gotta keep one step ahead of the bad guys. The way your sensors are set, a burglar would have to be on his way out for this thing to ring."

In that moment, Shana had been the burglar. She had done everything she could to lure him away from the door.

Peg laughed again. "The kids and I can't keep up with every new gadget. I'm constantly setting off our alarm."

"So am I," Shana admitted grudgingly. But not for the reasons Peg assumed.

She'd glanced over at Gabe. She'd been too embarrassed to tell him why she had the alarm. Every time the issue of her sleepwalking came up he insisted it wasn't a problem. And the kicking? The lashing out? How accepting would he be in bed?

Brice had poked at the wires until they protested with a piercing wail. "This thing'd wake the dead."

"Kind of the idea," she'd grumbled. Pinching his sling between her thumb and forefinger, she'd yanked him bodily away from the door.

"Enough with the toys," Gabe had said. "The movie starts in an hour."

And the relationship ends the first night we sleep together. Sitting on the sofa's arm, the light from a street lamp filtering in, Shana felt like a total coward. The more she loved Gabe the less she wanted to risk making love with him. What if she fell asleep?

She headed for the kitchen. Romper came running the moment the refrigerator opened. She knew midnight snacks were no way to combat insomnia. It was a quarter to four. "Consider this a very early breakfast." At least she'd be conscious while cooking it.

16

Shana stepped out of the limo and took a deep
breath. The red satin stretched across her bosom in
horizontal pleats. It dipped in the center before flowing
gracefully, lusciously, to the ground. Sleeveless, backless,
strapless, it held her so tightly in place, she barely dared to
exhale.

Like the fabric, she'd stretched her paycheck to the
breaking limit buying it. The least she could do was look
happy. Not an easy task when appearing in public with
Gabe Fitzgerald and some of Chicago's most famous bene-
factors and philanthropists at St. James' Hospital's Festival
Ball.

Wearing such a dress required more than money. It demanded confidence, courage, a womanly savoir faire. It reminded her of Ava Gardner, Jayne Mansfield, any other
Hollywood goddess known for cleavage. Ever since Shana
had "filled out," to use her mother's phrase, she'd tended
to minimize her chest. At work, a lab coat sufficed. For
the festival Ball, she'd gone all out.

Bending to exit the limo, she did her damnedest to keep it all in.

Straightening as she stepped onto the sidewalk, she heard the limo door shut behind her. Gabe thanked the driver and came up beside her. "Ready?" He draped the mink cape over her shoulders.

Its sumptuous weight swayed against her calves. "You know, I can't really approve of killing animals for their coats."

"You aren't going to throw ink on it, are you?"

"It's just that it used to be someone else's."

"She left it at my apartment. She accused me of buying her things as a substitute for affection. She was right."

"Actually, I was thinking of the animals who owned it first. I just imagine some tiny armed robber, an armadillo maybe, cornering a mink in an alley saying, 'Your coat or your life.'"

"You have a bizarre imagination, you know that?"

She hugged the sinfully soft coat around her. "I'd feel less guilty if it didn't feel so wonderful."

"It looks even better. On you." He took her hand.

Shana watched the couple approach in the hotel's mirrored glass doors. His black hair combed back, his features hawk-lean, his stride purposeful and compact, the sinewy financier kept pace with the elegant woman at his side. Any minute she'd awake from this dream. She deliberately refused. From the moment her mother had tsked over the price of the dress, to the moment she had handed over her charge card for the matching shoes and purse and had made the call to the hairdresser, Shana had relished the unreality of it. Every fairy tale ended. Before this one did, she'd cherish every minute of it.

The doors parted with a hush. The vision vanished. Shana clung to reality in the form of Gabe's solid arm.

"Nervous?"

She tossed her head. "Why should I be? No one on earth will ever recognize me."

"You look incredible."

It wasn't the first time he'd said so. He'd barely touched her in the limo. He hadn't needed to. The looks he'd raked across her bare shoulders and creamy flesh had carried the force of a caress, lingering, blatant, smoldering.

In the middle of the lobby, he did it again, sliding the fur off her shoulders. The satin lining glided across her bare skin. She trembled deep inside.

"Cold?" he asked.

A whisper of heat curled through her. The idea that he'd sensed her reaction made her knees quiver. Just because he insisted on leaning forward and whispering in her ear, his lips inches from her neck, didn't mean he knew every time she trembled. Or did it? Did he guess the power he had over her?

He planted a kiss on her cheek. Suavely, he turned and handed the fur to a coat-check clerk. "Take care of her for me."

Furs, Shana reminded herself, required special handling. A grown woman, on the other hand, should be able to handle any situation with the normal mix of aplomb and sheer terror. This woman, this "knockout" to use Gabe's word when he'd picked her up at her apartment, was another question. Shana didn't know how attractive women behaved. She'd never pretended to be one.

Avoiding any glimpse of herself in the gilded mirrors lining the hall to the ballroom, she made conversation. The coat seemed a safe subject. "So it's not a family heirloom?"

"After you described this dress over the telephone I thought you'd need a wrap."

"Full-length furs are not 'wraps.'"

"Consider it a winter coat."

"Only if I'm planning on going into hibernation." Actually, a coat like that was meant for going out, regularly, highly visibly.

They paused in the crush of people near the ballroom doors.

"I'd like you to have it," he said.

Shana touched her gloved fingers to her powdered chin, the better to prevent her mouth falling open. "I was teasing."

"I'm not." His softly spoken declaration commanded her full attention. "I don't make mistakes twice. I've avoided buying you presents because I didn't want to fall into the trap of giving things instead of feelings. So far I've bought you dinners and that's about it. I thought this—"

She couldn't believe what she was hearing. "Gabe, I've had a wonderful time. Every date we've had, I've enjoyed. It may not seem special to you, but I'm perfectly happy renting a movie and ordering pizza."

He filed that away. "For now, accept the coat."

"I can't, really."

He grimaced. "You think I'm a total boor, don't you? Insensitive, macho, thickheaded."

"For giving me a fur?"

"A former girlfriend's fur."

"That isn't the issue."

"I didn't think you'd take a new one. Too extravagant."

"You're darn right. Even a used—" She noted the ritzy crowd surrounding them. "Even a preowned fur is too extravagant. Flowers. Candy. No, not candy, I'd never fit into this dress again. A couple tickets to a show maybe—"

"Keep it for a week. If you don't want it, you can give it back to me."

Shana sighed in relief. "You really are a tycoon, aren't you?"

"Getting people to say yes is part of the job. Keep it a week."

"You'll see it Saturday."

He leaned closer. "One more thing."

"More negotiations?"

"Don't wear anything under it when you give it back."

Her jaw dropped halfway to her chest.

He shrugged. "It's a fantasy of mine."

An old woman in front of ·them rotated her head on her neck like an owl. She glanced Shana up and down, restricted her second look to Gabe's face, and, with a private smile, tucked her hand in her husband's arm and pulled him a little closer.

"It's crowded enough in here," the old man groused.

"Never you mind," his wife said. She didn't turn around again.

Good thing, Shana thought. Blushing from top to toe, a pink flush glowed deepest across her chest. She felt the zinging heat and smelled the subtle fragrance of the perfume she'd shamelessly dipped between her breasts seconds before Gabe arrived.

"You're beautiful when you blush."

If he breathed on the side of her neck every time he spoke, she'd never stop. She trained her eyes on the man collecting the invitations. "I don't want you thinking I require expensive presents."

"It's Valentine's Day. I had to give you something."

He'd already brought so much into her life, excitement, mystery, a scintillating awareness of her sensuality.

They took the final steps into the ballroom, standing atop a multilevel staircase that flowed downward on three sides like a fountain of pink and white marble. Heads turned. Shana felt like Cinderella, Sleeping Beauty, and Snow White rolled into one. She was hotter than cinders, paler than snow, and more beautiful than sleep—in Gabe's eyes.

Bald old men nursing double bourbons and trophy wives watched them descend. The wives watched Gabe. Protective, possessive, he kept his hand on Shana's arm. The gesture would've been reassuring if he hadn't used it as an excuse to skim his thumb along the soft flesh on the inside of her arm. Butterflies raced through her veins, wings beating like a flurry of fairy dust.

"Point the way," Gabe murmured. "The evening is yours."

She didn't want to move. Looking out over a sea of ball gowns and gold-tinted mirrors, listening to the orchestra play a waltz, sensing Gabe beside her, it was too perfect. If she breathed it would end. "It's like magic."

She was magic, Gabe thought. Her face lit up with wonder and delight, as if she had just seen doves alight from a magician's sleeves or scarves fluttering in an unending chain. She smelled like jasmine.

He should have had flowers waiting in the limo. Diamonds too. Everything he could buy her and all the things he couldn't, like caring, support, warmth, thoughtfulness. Things the women in his life had said he lacked in spades.

All the things he'd declared off limits in former relationships barely got him in on the ground floor of this one. Was it any wonder she kept putting him off? He'd spent his life preventing women from getting too close. In the long afternoons when sleep proved elusive, he gruffly reminded himself that what he knew about putting deals together had little application to building a relationship.

He stepped aside to let another couple descend. Feeling insecure wasn't like him. Neither was being head over heels in love.

They were blocking the stairs. Shana nodded to the left. "Merryweather should be by the food. Let's start there."

Gabe curved his hand around her slender arm. The warm silk of her long white glove had him fantasizing about peeling those gloves off her, unwrapping that dress.

"On second thought."

"What is it?"

"Payne."

Conversations about work had clued him in on Shana's office politics. "He's on all the major committees, right?"

"I'd rather he not spoil my party. Let's try the other side of the room."

"Anything you say." Anytime. Anywhere.

They reached the bottom step and paused. "Once we get in that crush we'll never get out," he muttered.

"Don't lose me."

He gripped her hand. "I won't."

"If it isn't my useless college buddy!" Brice and Peg emerged from the crowd. "No use hiding, we saw you come in."

"I'm surprised we didn't see you." Shana laughed, oohing and ahhing over Brice's jaunty cane and plaid sling.

He pulled his jacket open to reveal a matching plaid cummerbund. "Neat, huh? Buddy, you wouldn't believe the clients we've got here. You picked a great event for your coming-out party."

"Chicago's social elite—" Peg commented.

"—meets Chicago's best-kept secret." Brice whistled low, his gaze drifting lower on Shana's dress. "Where have *you* been all my life?"

Peg yanked on his sling. "Watch it."

"I am. I am."

"I can see that." The humorous tilt of his mouth didn't hide the warning glare in Gabe's eyes.

Brice's free hand rose in the Boy Scout's Oath. "Sorry. Couldn't resist."

"Shana, you look like a million."

"Thanks, Peg. I feel like a very tall fire hydrant."

"Red is your color."

"I knew I'd be surrounded by women who were dolled up, decked out, and relentlessly bejeweled. I had to buy something."

"That's something, all right." Peg laughed with Shana. "Have you ever seen Rita Hayworth in *Gilda*? You could give her a run for her money in that dress."

She was no screen goddess, much less one famous for a striptease. She glanced at Gabe, acutely aware of the tension building in his panther-still body. Eager to inject some humor into the situation, even more eager to deflate the false image the dress created, Shana sang a few bars of the movie's famous song.

"That's it." Peg chuckled.

"I can just imagine me as a vamp." Swaying her hips to and fro, she danced up one step and down again. Humming, she edged one long glove down her biceps. With a sultry pout she nudged it over the bend of her elbow, bunching it near her wrist. For her intimate audience, she let one shoulder drop provocatively. She peeled off each finger of the glove.

Peg clapped appreciatively. Brice put two fingers in his mouth and let out a whistle. "More, more."

"I think we get the picture," Gabe said tightly.

"Needless to say, I can't do it justice."

"Oh, I don't know," Peg said, eyeing her gaping husband.

"You can play it for me when we get home." Gripping her naked arm, Gabe maneuvered her halfway across the ballroom. His eyes were focused dead straight ahead, his scowl thundering disapproval.

"You're squeezing my arm."

"Oh, yeah? It's nothing compared to the bind I'm in."

Shana scampered after him, her dress rustling between chairs and tables, heads turning as they passed, her brand-new shoes sliding on the carpet. "Oh, come on. It's not as if I stretched that glove over my head and flung it to the crowd."

"Wanna bet?"

"Taking one thing off is hardly a striptease. Gabe, for heaven's sake."

"Heaven has nothing to do with it."

To prove it he hauled her to him the moment they hit the dance floor. Her body bumped to a stop against his solid chest. Her thighs lined up with his. Maneuvering his hips forward, he let her feel the throbbing result of her dance.

Shana's cheeks flamed.

Gabe cupped her bare elbow and bumped it upward.

She grudgingly wrapped her arm around his neck. "I didn't mean—"

His flat stare cut her short. Reaching for her other hand, he bent his own arm behind his back, bringing her arm in tight contact with his waist.

His feet moved, their legs glancing against each other as they began to sway, her dress hushing between her thighs and out again.

"I'm sorry," she said. "Really I am." He might have believed her if she'd been able to maintain that sheepish, apologetic look. Unfortunately, a bubble of laughter kept tickling her throat, a surge of outrageous joy that she'd excited a man like Gabe without half trying. The scent of power, her power, was as potent an aphrodisiac as champagne or chocolates or the mirrored ball twirling lazily above their heads. Tonight was different. *She* was different.

The white-suited orchestra swung into a slow Duke Ellington number, saxophones moaning low.

"The next time you want to move your hips like that, give me a few days' notice," he said with a growl.

"I wasn't being provocative."

A look.

"Not deliberately."

"Right." His jaw clenched so hard, a vein beat on the side of his cheek.

Shana was sorely tempted to kiss it. It would serve him right for all those whispery words he'd breathed across her neck in the lobby. He wasn't the only one who could turn someone on completely unintentionally. "I wasn't trying to be a tease."

"Don't you think I know that? That makes it ten times harder to handle." He muttered under his breath. "It makes it damn hard."

Another brushing glance proved it. She batted her lashes and tilted her head to a coquettish angle. "Why, Mr. Fitzgerald, I didn't know you cared."

He gritted his teeth so hard, the enamel creaked. "You're enjoying this."

"Every second. I've never seen you like this."

"And I've never seen *you* like this. You're like some damned siren."

"You don't sound happy about it."

"Should I be? I haven't been forced to hide an erection on the dance floor since high school."

"We could sit the next one out."

"We could leave."

"What? I love this."

His eyes burned a dark blue. "I want to love you. Come home with me."

The music seemed to stop. Her feet shuffled to a halt. He wanted to make love to her. He was daring her to love him back. "Tonight, Shana."

"Flown in fresh or flown in frozen?"

Merryweather sniffed the shrimp before dipping it into the silver sauceboat. "Frozen. Not bad, though."

Fiona crowded beside him at the buffet, picking out a vegetarian plate. "Ask Shana about those caraway-seed muffins. She'll know the bakery."

"Meyer's. I got the scoop from Uncle Karl." Shana popped another miniature muffin her mouth. Any more and the form-fitting top of her dress would pop. Any less and she'd have to acknowledge how hard her hands shook with nothing to occupy them.

"Oops." A seed tumbled down her cleavage. *Smart move, Getz. What next? Sleepwalking out of Gabe's bed or karate-kicking him off the mattress?* She pictured the alternatives if she took him up on his one-word challenge.

"Tonight."

Sensing him coming up behind her, she spun around. She latched onto Merryweather's sleeve. "Michael, this is Gabriel Fitzgerald. Fiona, you two have met, haven't you?"

"More than once. It usually involves beds."

Gabe shook her hand. Caught by the crowd at the table, he managed a curt nod to Merryweather. "You introduced Shana at the first group session I attended."

"Usually do. She's one of our stars."

"So where's your David?" Shana asked in a hushed whisper. "I've been dying to meet him."

"Who?"

"David."

"Oh, um, he's here somewhere." Merryweather scanned the crowd with mild interest. "Friend of mine in real estate," he explained to Gabe. "Always working a crowd."

"Kind of like Fiona's friend." Shana nodded at the insurance salesman Fiona had brought, who was handing out business cards. "It's so interesting to see people's private sides."

Merryweather pursed his lips, his brow furrowed as if thinking of something else. "Some people you'd never picture together. Not in your wildest dreams."

Shana dipped her shrimp in cocktail sauce. Cold on her fingers, the sauce burned spicy hot on her tongue. She licked it off.

Gabe didn't miss a lick. He hadn't taken his eyes off her since the dance floor. "Speaking of wild dreams."

He'd insisted they dance one more. Swaying, barely moving, he'd kissed her neck, a long, loving imprint that sealed his intentions. A dizzying, syrupy desire coursed through her limbs. He'd wrapped both his arms around her, idly reaching up to strum his fingers along the back of her dress. Where flesh met fabric, he found the zipper. His one tug had gone through her. She knew that if that zipper parted, she'd unravel with it, her body spreading, parting for him.

"Tonight," he'd murmured. A prayer. A promise.

At the buffet, she gulped a Bloody Mary. This was all her fault. She should have never teased him. She'd been desperately defiant, fighting her own insecurity, testing her limits. She'd been intoxicated with the idea that in this dress, with this man, anything could happen.

Tonight it might.

She dabbed her lips with a red napkin. Gabe contemplated those lips. She dashed her tongue across them. Wrong move. He turned away, his back rigid, and reached for the nearest wine glass on a passing tray.

"Child, you could stop traffic in that dress."

"Flora!" She practically threw herself in her colleague's arms. At the last moment she caught herself. Bending forward too far would dislodge more than an elusive caraway seed.

"You're a knockout in red. Why don't you wear it more often?"

"It's not really me." She meant that. Gabe didn't know what he was getting into. He'd been temporarily blinded.

Even Flora's husband, a trim professor of African-American Studies, smiled at her in a thoroughly unprofessorial manner. "I'd say that's you all over."

"Too much of me, I'm afraid."

Gabe stood behind her, his breath fanning over her throat. "I'd take every inch," he murmured for her ears only.

Her shoulders rose, tiny thrills of excitement erupting in gooseflesh.

He dusted a kiss across her collarbone as naturally and unaffectedly as if they'd been married for years. In the low-cut dress, Shana couldn't hide her sharp intake of breath.

Switching gears effortlessly, Gabe extended his hand to Flora's husband. "Gabe Fitzgerald."

"This is Richard Coleman," Shana sputtered.

"You can call me Rich," Flora's husband replied.

The gentlemen made small talk. Shana tried to slow her heartbeat down. "How's your problem patient?"

"DeVon? Give him thirty days of the CPAP machine, and we'll know how he's adjusting."

"Fingers crossed."

Shana turned and her eyes widened. She gripped Gabe's arm. "Hazel," she hissed. "I *knew* she'd find a way

to be here. It's as if she's circling the clinic, like a bird trying to land. She won't come down until she knows it's
safe."

"Safety in numbers?"

She peered out over the faces. "Yes, but how'd she get
in? Never mind. I've got to talk to her. Excuse me,
everybody."

Stealthy as a cat, determined as a hunter, she maneuvered through the crowd. Gabe might want her. There
was no doubt she needed him. But Hazel needed her help.

She dodged elbows and drinks. Had Hazel been telling
the truth? She'd said her husband was powerful. Chicago's
most powerful and influential men were at this ball. Or
else her supplier from four had snuck her in. Shana had
assumed he wore the white coat as a disguise. What if he
was a doctor, an intern, an orderly?

She scanned the faces around her. The first possibility
seemed more likely. Any one of these rich men could
abuse his wife with impunity. Social position would shield
him. Meanwhile his wife was slinking through the crowd,
glassy-eyed from exhaustion, intuitively staying one step
away from the woman who longed to help her.

A clump of murmuring guests blocked Shana's progress. She elbowed her way through a knot of socialites and
waiters. Each time she got near, Hazel moved just out of
reach. For Hazel's sake, Shana refrained from calling her
name. Who knew how close her husband might be?

Her frustration rose. "Dammit, Hazel, I want to help
you. Why else are you here?"

Gabe wasn't used to being dumped at the buffet. The
women he'd known had loved claiming him in public,
wrapping their manicured hands around his biceps like
talons.

Shana wasn't like any woman he'd known. She was
dying to help her mystery patient. Without betraying any
confidences, she'd told him what she could. Abused

woman. Possibly dependent on pills. The usual pride and reluctance to get help for a sleeping problem. He should know.

He should help too. Setting his drink down, he started after the most likely suspect, a middle-aged woman with white-streaked gray hair, hollow, sleep-deprived eyes, and a distracted, nervous air.

"Excuse me. Pardon me." There she was, sidling past a woman with a grating laugh then disappearing behind a large man with a bolo tie.

It had to be Hazel. The longer he looked, the more convinced he became. Looking at her was like looking in a mirror, only with Hazel the fear was on full display. She was terrified she wouldn't pass as normal, her careening emotions bobbing and waning like a cork on the ocean, her control fraying with every wave of exhaustion that battered her.

He hoped to God he'd hid his weariness better than she did.

The thought made him ashamed. He pressed on, telling himself it was the harsh truth. He recognized every tic, every evasive move sleepy people used, the phony stilted posture, the stiff smile, the standoffishness necessary to keep people at bay just in case any cracks showed. She wanted the world to think she was managing.

Sleep was winning. He saw it in her eyes. She'd been staring down the night for too many years. She couldn't keep it together much longer.

Gabe circled around. Ten feet away, he spotted Shana on the far side of their prey. If Hazel eluded her one more time, he'd cut the woman off. He could talk to her, tell her what a difference Shana had made in his life.

He knew what endless nights were like. He'd been there.

The two chairmen discussed their boards, their dividends, their golf getaway on Marco Island. Like the recent stock prices, they refused to budge. Shana yearned to squeeze past them. She could just about reach Hazel's arm. It was vital that she touch her. If she tugged on that glove, she'd not only get Hazel's attention but she could subtly pull the sagging fabric a little higher and hide the bruise.

Give her her dignity, Shana thought. The woman's been through enough.

Blocked out, she gave in to frustration and called across the two chairmen. "Hazel?"

"Ms. Getz. Or should I say *Doctor* Getz?" Dr. Payne wedged between her and the chairmen, blocking all sight of her prey.

"Oh, hello, Doctor. Excuse me, I—"

His perfectly bland egg-shaped face lost what little warmth it had. "You can pretend a little more civility than that, *Doctor*."

Shana wondered how he did it. With one carefully wrought sentence he made her feel ten inches high. In Payne's opinion she'd never be educated enough, classy enough, or titled enough for this setting. She wrestled between a desire to prove him wrong and her need to reach Hazel.

"I thought I saw someone I knew," she explained, straightening her shoulders. If that pushed her chest out, tough.

"You certainly look eye-catching in that dress."

She flinched when he touched her bare upper arm with his cool fingers.

"Let me introduce you over here. Although I've noticed you've made it your mission to get involved in all aspects of the hospital, there are probably a *few* people you haven't met."

"Or hounded?" she asked defensively. She craned her neck over her shoulder as he turned her away.

The sea of people parted. Hazel receded further.

"I'd like you to meet Dr. Stanley from the Oncology Department at Reed Medical. Mr. Karstens, Philco Corporation. He's a very generous sponsor of our refinancing program."

"Did I hear someone say you work with people who can't sleep?" Mr. Karstens asked.

Shana smiled. She had no idea why Payne wanted to help her meet people. On the other hand, Merryweather would never forgive her if she passed up the opportunity to put in a plug for their department. "I'm part of the Sleep Disorders Clinic at St. James."

"I didn't know they had one."

"People spend a third of their lives sleeping. If sleep is disrupted, every aspect of one's health can suffer."

"Makes sense to me."

"It's an offshoot of holistic medicine." Payne placed equally derisive emphasis on both words.

"It's good medicine," Shana argued. Gratified by Karstens's interest, she talked on. Half listening to Karstens's replies, she glanced at Payne. His watery blue eyes were scanning the crowd. Maybe she could make her escape.

"Stay a moment." One move and his entire hand had closed over her bare upper arm, his fingers as slick and reptilian as his bald head. "There's someone else I'd like you to meet."

She saw no one new joining their circle. When Mr. Karstens turned to Dr. Stanley, she stole a moment to survey the crowd. She nearly cheered; Gabe had found Hazel. He was leaning forward, murmuring something, introducing himself.

Shana's heart swelled at the trouble he'd gone to for her sake. She saw the gentle way he treated the woman. Resting a hand on her arm, he indicated Shana standing twenty feet away.

Hazel's eyes darted left and right. Sudden panic overtook her. She backed away, frantic. Gabe pursued her. Out of nowhere, Michael Merryweather stepped forward. He tapped Gabe on the shoulder. When Gabe turned, Hazel dissolved into the crowd.

"No, don't let her go," Shana wanted to shout.

"Perhaps high finance bores you, my dear, but it's the lifeblood of this hospital."

Jerked back into the conversation, she glared at Payne. "You were speaking of the city services tax bill. I heard every word."

Mr. Karstens gave her a wink. "I get so bored with this stuff sometimes I feel like checking into a sleep clinic myself."

She gave him a wan smile. "Some people would really benefit."

Gabe met up with Shana beside the organizer's podium. "I couldn't get past Merryweather."

"Payne cut me off."

"She got away?"

"She got away."

"Step up here. We'll get a better look."

"We can't be that obvious."

From the hair piled on her head to the red fabric puddling at her feet, Gabe raked her with a deadpan look. "In that dress you're worried about being conspicuous?"

She huffed at his perfect logic. Grabbing a fistful of skirt, she took two stairs at once. In seconds she gripped Gabe's arm. "There she is! God, I love these contacts. I can see anything."

"What about me?"

"I love you too. Thank you!" She gave him a peck on the lips and dashed back into the crowd.

Gabe chuckled, pulling a glass of wine off a passing tray. Nothing would stop her now. She'd part the Red Sea to help that woman.

17

She said she loved you, his conscience murmured.
"I heard her."

Standing on the podium sipping his wine, he blamed her reaction on high spirits. He blamed his own on low cunning. He meant to make the most of that declaration. Later.

The music stopped. A woman in full socialite regalia swept past him up the stairs. Tapping the screeching microphone with her two-inch nails, she began the list of announcements. "Is everybody ready?"

A sea of faces turned his way. Unwilling to relinquish his vantage point, Gabe frowned right back at them. With the ceremonies under way, movement among the crowd had slowed to a glacial pace. People held their ground, listening with polite boredom as dignitaries announced the amount raised for each hospital department. Shana slipped among them like a red beacon.

"It looks as if your date has deserted you."

He stepped off the bottom stair, not bothering to fake a smile for Payne. "She'll be back."

"She's one of those—lives for her work. Rather have a job than a man."

"You're not pretending you know her, are you?"

"She knows you. Although interviewing patients until one finds what one's looking for in a mate is an unusual tactic even for the nineties. Impersonal. Even a tad unethical."

Gabe saw the trap Payne laid. "I'm not her patient."

"No?" Thin brows rose on his slick forehead. "I've seen you in the clinic."

"You saw us on Shana's coffee break in the cafeteria and one night when I picked her up from the maternity ward. She volunteers there."

"If that's all. I've been meaning to speak to her about what she's doing there. I've heard she bothers people who have better things to do than turn babies' lights off and on."

Gabe spotted Brice's brightly colored sling. He waved him over. "She's doing great work. As a matter of fact, it's the basis of our donation."

"It is?" Brice grinned, sticking his good hand out to shake Payne's, proving to Gabe once and for all that Brice could make friends with anything.

"Brice Grier, Grier/Fitzgerald. Wonderful cause, isn't it? Love this charity stuff. What is the cause, by the way? Cancer? Heart disease? Trauma!" He swung his sling back and forth. "Saw your emergency room. Great facility. Wife wanted me in a hospital closer to home after a couple days, but there's no denying you guys saved my life."

"I'm sure that wasn't Dr. Payne's job," Gabe said dryly.

Aware of the conversation's tense undertones, Peg saw no harm in putting the crisis in perspective. "Nobody dies of a broken arm, dear."

"All the same, I'd be proud to pay them back for their excellent service."

"We're donating to the Sleep Disorders Clinic," Gabe said.

"The sleep clinic. Great idea! Me, I've always slept like a baby."

"You mean you wake up every two hours crying?" Peg's tart retort brought a smile to every face but Payne's.

Payne smirked as he set his glass on a tray. "Give the clinic all the money you wish, Mr. Fitzgerald. I've heard they 'service' their patients very well."

Gabe's jaw clenched.

Brice was too busy reaching inside his sling then his suit pocket to notice. "I knew there was a reason I brought the company checkbook. What's our cut, partner?"

Gabe had a number in mind. He doubled it.

"You what?"

Standing alongside the microphone, peering into the bright lights while the audience gasped and the emcee repeated Grier/Fitzgerald's half-a-million dollar donation, Gabe could have sworn he heard Shana's voice echoing over the crowd.

"You what?"

Just in case he missed it, she repeated it three times at the table and four times in the limo on the way back to his apartment.

"I can't believe you gave them that much money!"

"Them? How about you? Every penny is earmarked for sleep research, sleep programs, sleepwear. Anything you need the hospital hasn't provided. Expect even more; money attracts money. Now that we've brought the clinic to their attention, other people will donate as well."

"Like all those clients of yours?" Shana studied the gray felt roof of the limo. "Merryweather was practically leading a conga line when we left. Flora and her husband were on the dance floor doing the Bump. I didn't even know Richard knew dances like that."

Gabe secretly grinned at her dismay.

"Half a million is serious money," she exclaimed.

"That's because when you have the money people take you seriously. No more scrounging for paper clips or file folders—"

"Or notepads or extra chairs. But—stop that, you're distracting me."

All he'd been doing was sliding her glove off her hand so his palm could press hers. The limo was warm, the driver experienced. He'd slid the smoked glass divider shut the moment they stepped inside. They'd be at Gabe's apartment in minutes. He leaned over to kiss her. "Distracting you wasn't exactly what I had in mind."

"How about driving me to distraction?"

"We're on our way there now."

Pulling the fur out from under her thigh, she wrapped it over her lap with a huff. "You're trying to change the subject. This is serious."

"So am I." Gabe stroked the fur cosseting her neckline. Did she really think anything so soft could serve as armor? He played with a straying wisp of her hair. That up-do was coming undone. "Happy Valentine's Day."

Her eyes sparked with indignation. "That is *not* my present. The only person I'd accept half a million dollars from is Ed McMahon."

"It's for a worthy cause."

"It's nuts."

He traced a finger across her creamy shoulder, her collarbone, the boundary of fur that was no boundary at all, more like a sensual promise, an impromptu bed. "What about this?"

"I'm not accepting this coat either."

"It's chump change compared to our donation."

Her cupped fist brought his chin up so fast his teeth clicked. She fixed him with a furious look. "I am not impressed with money."

"Neither am I. But it can smooth the way with people who are. Payne, for instance?"

The limo pulled up in front of his building.

The mention of Payne gave her something else to worry about. "I don't know what Payne's into. I don't think it's money. I used to think it was power. Whatever it is, he gives me the creeps." She rubbed her upper arm where he'd touched it. "Maybe I'm being mean because we've butted heads so many times. He has this insinuating way of saying things. 'Good evening' is an insult coming from him." She shivered and clutched the fur tighter around her neck. For some reason the gesture reminded her of Hazel.

They cruised to a halt. Shana stepped onto the sidewalk. Gabe waved the driver away, reserving the honor of slamming the car door for himself. "Let's leave Payne here. I want you to myself tonight."

Shana allowed him to escort her to the elevator and from there to the penthouse. She'd been chattering. Keying in on Gabe's outlandish donation was a superb way of avoiding dealing with what was about to happen.

Her stomach dipped as the elevator reached the top and slowed. Caught off guard by the buzz of excitement following Gabe's donation, thrilled by the instant interest generated in her department, she'd had a full evening of talking, drinking, and dancing. All she wanted to do was kick off her shoes, undo the tight zipper, and slink out of her dress. She longed to get naked and curl up between warm sheets.

Unfortunately, Gabe had the same idea.

"After you."

She stepped out of the private elevator and into his penthouse. Despite the fact that she'd made a handful of visits there over the last few weeks, the space never failed to impress. Sixteen-foot ceilings, deep blue carpet, and floor-to-ceiling windows running the length of two walls could do that to a person. At the end of the living room a see-through fireplace cut through to Gabe's bedroom. There the lavish windows let the stars in.

Shana had seen it on her official first-visit tour. She'd never expected to see it again. Except in her dreams.

"I'll fix us a drink."

She smiled after him as he strode toward the kitchen, feeling guilty for feeling so relieved. She was grateful he hadn't taken the time to remove the fur. The sensation of that slinky lining caressing her shoulders would have been more than she could stand. She felt like an exposed nerve. One touch and she'd be begging.

For more or less?

She wandered to the windows, reluctantly letting the fur drape across a chair. The clock on a nearby skyscraper should have been striking midnight instead of one. Her fairy-tale evening was nearly over.

She stared at the falling snow as it kissed the glass. Stars melted into tears. In the kitchen, Gabe whistled tunelessly. At that moment she loved his whistling with all her heart.

Suddenly chilled, she wanted to wrap the fur around her again, comforting, cozy. She memorized every part of the apartment, the photos, the artwork, the low-slung leather sofas. It was so real; holding on to it so impossible.

She couldn't love him, not the way he wanted and not the way he deserved. She'd put him off for weeks, until every good-bye kiss threatened to drag them under, each glancing touch set them on fire. The nights she didn't see him had trudged by like a winter of Februarys, broken only by erotic dreams that left her restless and wanting.

No matter how deeply she longed for him she had to hold back. If she fell asleep after making love to Gabe, who knew what disaster awaited? Was that the kind of love he wanted? Cautious? Preplanned? A woman who made love then left?

A no-strings sexual arrangement had been David's idea of perfection. It wasn't her idea of love.

She frowned at the bowl of flowers Brice and Peg had sent over before the ball. She was making this sound ugly. What Gabe felt for her was anything but. He treated her as if she were a treasure, bragging to his friends, her own family, about how funny she was, how effective as a counselor, how beautiful.

Maybe that's why it hurt so much. She'd always chosen the fairy-godmother role, not the princess role. She told herself it was healthy admitting one's limitations. All the love in the world wouldn't make her sleep soundly.

A wailing teapot drowned out Gabe's dry whistle. "Almost ready."

"What are you dong? Making hot toddies?" Her laugh threatened to break in two. She immediately got control. As his counselor she should be delighted. He'd come to grips with his dreams. He followed her tips. Every day he looked better. Every week he slept more hours. She would not ruin his hard-won sleep with her own flailing.

"Here you go."

Feeling naked without the coat, she crossed her arms over her chest and gave him an apologetic smile. "I think I've had enough to drink tonight. I'm feeling a little light-headed."

"Don't you think I know your drinking habits? Hot chocolate. The perfect nightcap."

Her heart shriveled. How could she leave a man who knew her so well? Who remembered little things as if they mattered? As if she mattered?

"Gabe."

"You've got that look on your face. Let me turn on some music."

Music wouldn't make the chocolate go down any smoother.

He came back, swaying her gently into his arms, careful not to spill the chocolate she cupped between them.

She blew steam off the top, the better to avoid his gaze. "I don't know if I'm ready for this."

He rested his forehead against hers. "Do you think I'd rush you?"

"It isn't you. I don't want to keep you awake."

His lower body brushed hers with a velvet softness. "I don't picture you putting me to sleep."

"You know what I mean."

"And you know what I want." He kissed her cheek, dipping his chin toward the mug. "You're going to get burned here."

"That's exactly what I'm afraid of."

He grinned. "I knew there was a reason I fell in love with an intelligent woman. Never at a loss for a comeback."

Then why did she feel so lost?

"You said something earlier," he murmured. "About loving me too."

It was so like him to get to the point. No evasions, no time to spare. Didn't he see he had all the time in the world now? He could find a woman, a good woman. "You're nearly cured."

"For the time being. I've decided the dreams don't have to be tests I always fail. But until I have another I won't know if that attitude works."

Shana set her cup down. "I know the answer to my problem, Gabe. Drugs that inhibit sleepwalking don't work on me. No ifs about it. I don't want to upset the sleep you've gained."

He cursed under his breath. Having ditched his tuxedo jacket in the kitchen, he snapped off a cufflink. Impatiently rolling up his sleeves, he took a step for every twist of cuff. "I knew it was me."

"How could it be you?"

"It's my problem that's coming between us."

"I didn't say that."

"I still don't sleep at night. You haven't cured me of that."

"You're a night owl. There's nothing wrong with that. Six hours sleep and you're effective, alert, in control—"

"And up all night. You might get me to bed for an hour." He strafed her body with a fierce look. "Make that two. After that, I'd stare at the ceiling. I'd toss and turn. By three I'd be at my computer working, hoping you'd stay asleep and not notice."

She folded her arms. "I wouldn't be asleep."

"Then you'd lie there feeling deserted, hating it as much as any other woman. Yeah, you've cured me; I sleep now. But the sleep I get I get alone. Don't you see? You wouldn't interfere with that. You couldn't."

"And when we're together? I'd lie there scared to death of falling asleep afterward, staring at that same ceiling. That isn't love. It's 'wham, bam, thank you, ma'am' and I'm up and getting dressed. It's you calling me a cab the minute we're finished."

"Are we finished?"

The quiet words barely traveled the distance dividing them. He tore his gaze away, thumping the back of the sofa with his fist. "What happens when we sleep?"

"What do you mean?"

"You should know the answer, Shana. Do two people ever sleep together? The minute our eyes close, we're alone, all of us. Nobody *sleeps* with anyone."

"That's not what I'm talking about."

"It's what I'm talking about." He came around the sofa, gripping both her hands. "I want to make love with you. Just because we don't sleep side by side doesn't mean it's just sex. If we can't sleep together, we won't. Don't let it ruin what we *can* have."

She ached with a pain that tightened around her throat like a claw.

He kissed her palm until her fingers curled. "If I get up or you leave afterward, it won't mean we love each other less."

"And if I want to stay?"

For a moment she thought he was going to pull her into his arms, to kiss her until they forgot their doubts, their faults. He let her go instead, reaching for the hot chocolate. "Drink it before it gets cold."

Watching him over the rim, she sipped. Something slippery touched her lip. He'd added a chocolate drop to it.

"Another Valentine's surprise?" She picked it out with

her fingers, unexpected tears stinging her eyes. Unable to get a grip on the slick surface, she plopped the whole thing in her mouth.

Gabe stepped closer, his hands on her waist, his body swaying in time to the music. "Is it good?"

A syrupy sweetness melted on her tongue. She nodded.

"Give me a taste."

Hesitating, her lips pursed to meet his. He licked the moist sheen off them, prodding her to open wider.

An electric jolt surged through her. Dissatisfied with just a taste, he wanted the whole thing.

She slid the chocolate to him.

Capturing it with his tongue-tip, he tossed his head back. Cheeks drawn in, eyes shut tight, he savored it.

Shana savored him. The lingering richness on her tongue, velvety and dark, was nothing compared to the heat simmering low in her body. She wanted to pull him to her, to take his mouth with hers, to show him and herself she wasn't some fainthearted ninny. She was a woman, with needs and desires and, dammit, she deserved this.

Gabe opened his eyes. He lowered his gaze to her lips. "Want some?"

She'd never longed for anything so much. She stepped up, her body full against his, her head tilted. Their mouths opened. In seconds there was nothing left of the chocolate but a small lozenge that passed back and forth between them. By the time they came up for air neither could remember precisely when it had dissolved.

"You know what I was thinking?" Gabe rasped out.

"What?"

"We're both only children."

"This is childlike?"

"I meant no brothers or sisters. Onlys." His thumb traced her lower lip. "Maybe we're not good at sharing."

"Funny. I didn't get that impression a minute ago." If he'd kiss her again, they wouldn't have to debate it.

"You can prove me wrong."

The way he stroked her throat she'd do just about anything. Her skin sang. Her limbs filled with a rising excitement that made her want to move, and a growing languor that made her want to recline. The carpet looked plusher by the minute. "How?" she dared him.

He dabbed kisses along her neck, her collarbone, the exposed mound of her breast. Caressing her hips, he found her hands and brought them to his waist. He led her to his pants pocket and directed her fingers inside. When he slanted his hip forward, she reached deeper.

The back of her hand stroked his lower abdomen, his muscled upper thigh. His whole body radiated heat. Emboldened, she turned her hand, her fingers splaying inside his pocket, expecting more heat, a shaft of throbbing muscle—

"Find it?"

Her eyes fluttered open. A wry smile tipped her lips. "Found it." With her thumb and forefinger she grasped the paper tag, drawing the foil-covered chocolate out of his pocket. She dangled it under his nose. "I'm going to start calling you the Candy Man."

"Want to open it, little girl?"

She peeled the foil off one side. "Not the kind of foil I was expecting to open."

"You can do that too. Later." He wrapped his arms around her.

She peeled another side of the candy. To her shock, her zipper sizzled downward with each peel. The chocolate wasn't the only thing he wanted undressed. She hesitated.

"Give me that," he murmured.

"It's not ready." The paper tag trembled like a leaf in the wind.

Pinned by his unwavering gaze, she seized on the daring spirit she'd found at the ball. Like a stripper peeling off a glove, she pulled the tag out of the wrapper and cast it over her shoulder.

He unzipped her dress another inch.

She held the chocolate by its wrapper.

"Don't drop it," he warned.

She did just that, letting the chocolate drop between her breasts.

His lips formed a thin line. For a second Shana wondered if she'd gone too far. She was playing. His steely intensity said this was no game.

He tugged the zipper farther.

"Where's *my* treat?" she asked. "We were going to share."

He played by her rules. Dipping his head, he kissed the rounded mounds of her breasts, the perfumed valley between. Her whole body went slack, her legs quivering.

Gabe wrapped both arms around her waist, his face pressed to her flesh, his tongue sweeping up the sweet treasure. She felt his jaw clamp down as he bit into the chocolate. She'd imagined him once biting into her flesh the same way. A shudder reverberated through her. A throaty moan emerged.

His fist bunched at her back. The zipper plunged to her hips. Only the force of his body against hers kept the dress up.

She raked her hands through his hair, roughly tilting his face toward hers. "You forgot to share."

He swallowed the last of the chocolate. "I didn't forget."

He gave her a brief kiss, brusque, unsatisfying. Stepping back, he let the dress fall to her hips.

She tried to cover herself. He caught her hands. With a tug, he urged her to him. One step and the dress collapsed onto the carpet in a pool of red fabric. She wore nothing but smoky nylons, a dusty-rose garter belt, and matching panties.

Gabe hardly noticed. His gaze remained on her face, her cheek cupped in his hand. His look darkened when she planted a kiss on his palm. Shifting his attention, shifting hers, they both followed his hand's course as it curved down her shoulder then filled to overflowing with her breast. His thumb stroked the smooth brown aureole. It shrank at his touch. The rest of her arched toward him.

He weighed the other breast. Desire rippled through her. Shana covered both his hands with hers. He let her dictate the pressure she desired.

"You like that?"

"I love that."

He led her hands lower. Together they explored the slope of her waist, the softly rounded flesh of her abdomen. He reached up under her garter belt, flattening his palm against her softness. His eyes met hers and stayed. "You're beautiful."

His thumb strayed lower, sweeping beneath the elastic, tangling in her hair.

"Can we turn down the lights?"

He glanced over his shoulder toward the bedroom. "They're off."

He lied, she thought when they reached the threshold. A full moon bathed the bed in light, a bluish-white hue smoothing the sheets like a blanket of snow. The windows stretched like black banners. The night outside glittered with icy slivers of stars.

Stars for woman, moon for man. Shana remembered the woman who'd let them onto the top floor of the Sears Tower. There'd been a scything moon then, its tines catching the clouds. Tonight the moon's fullness rivaled the warmth in her belly, the aching fullness that begged for release.

Gabe closed the door. Shana swung around. The light from the living room formed a thin golden slit on the dark blue carpet. Approaching out of darkness, he emerged from the shadows. "Think we can make it the next ten steps?"

They'd kissed and clung, stopping and starting half a dozen times on their way to the bedroom. "How long did it take to get here?" she asked.

"A lifetime."

She wanted to smile. It hurt too much. A lifetime of

waiting loomed behind them both, all those years they'd deprived themselves of contact, of love. Awakened at last, she marveled to find herself there. She curved her arms around his neck. "I don't want it to end."

"We've barely started."

She told herself it was better he didn't understand. She'd go, honest she would. In an hour, maybe two, she'd tell him she had to get home and she'd mean it. No longing looks. No wistful if-onlys. She remembered her New Year's resolutions, all those great words such as "tact," "prudence," "discretion." As long as she didn't let her heart betray her by blurting out how she really felt, she'd be fine.

He kept a tantalizing distance, his finger skimming her cheek. "Afraid?"

"A little."

"I said we'd share."

The chocolate was all gone. He stepped around her, bearing the full brunt of the moonlight. He was clothed in contrasts, cut in half by a white shirt, black cummerbund, and black slacks. The cummerbund dropped first. Next came the shirt, golden studs dropping to the carpet like falling stars.

She touched his hand when he got to his zipper. "My turn."

His hands dropped.

Shana dared. From glancing touches she knew he'd be full and long and hot to the touch. The zipper grated. "Boxers?"

"Yes."

She found the slit. She closed her hand around taut, velvety skin.

His eyes gripped shut, his jaw rigid. He turned his head to the side, as if listening to the far-off thump of his heart, his ragged breath.

She stroked him. His groan reminded her he wasn't the only one there with power. She let him go temporarily, easing her body nearer. She slid his slacks to the floor, boxers included.

He reached for her. She danced out of his arms. The music from the other room was a faint thread of melody, a subterranean beat. She circled back, slinking her abdomen along his shaft. She stroked him from the body side. Rising on tiptoe, she rasped her lacy garter belt across his shiny tip.

Gabe was a dam ready to break. His concentration was nearly palpable. His utter stillness sounded a note of caution deep within her. She had no idea what forces she might unleash in him. She eased her grip. His fists closed around her arms, his eyes resembling black chips of the night sky he'd lived with so long.

They staggered to the bed. Gabe stripped off the top sheet with one violent tug. Shana lay back, his body twined with hers. Surrender had never seemed so sweet, so unlike surrender. This was necessary, a compelling, driving urge to give, to be everything he needed.

He rolled her over him, under him, their bodies writhing in a smoldering dance. The sheet beneath her was crisp cotton, the pillow imbued with his scent. The wrangling ceased as he reached for a drawer and tore open a condom.

Shana watched the muscles of his back moving in the moonlight. She stretched her hands above her head, fingers splaying across the teak headboard. She felt sinfully hedonistic, thoroughly overwhelmed. Her heart slowed to a thump when he turned back to her. The brief respite was over.

He ran his hand along her waist. He removed her garter belt and nylons quickly and expertly. Urging her onto her side, he lay with her, curving his body behind hers. The latex was startling and cool, unbearably intimate against her rear end. Gabe fitted his chest to her back, his hand reaching around to cup her breasts. His chin jutted over her shoulder. He nipped her earlobe then her neck.

She accepted everything, anything. A sizzling satisfaction thrummed beneath her skin. She turned her head, letting him claim her mouth. It was marvelous, delicious. And it wasn't enough. Kisses were only kisses. She wanted him inside her. If he didn't stop caressing her with his fingers, she'd come right out and demand it. "Gabe." She gasped. "Please." She turned onto her back.

Glistening with sweat, he mounted her. She lifted her thighs on either side of his, pressing her lower body unmistakably upward. "Please."

He wouldn't do it, not when she felt the need to ask with her eyes closed. He wanted her looking at him. He made that unmistakably clear.

Her gaze answered his. "Please," she begged.

He parted her lips with his tongue, beginning an erotic rhythm that swallowed every moan, every inarticulate cry. "I need you," she urged.

Balanced on one arm, he kneaded her thigh with his free hand. A bead of sweat trickled from his temple. A lock of black hair fell across his forehead.

Shana hooked her leg around him. The brazenness excited him. He slid his shaft against her, coating it with her creamy moistness. The contact was electric. Shock waves sprang through her, a jolt of pleasure building to a thundering, rolling wave.

It happened so fast. She bucked beneath him, uttering a cry. The room spun, stars dancing.

He held her down, absorbing the tremors that cascaded through her.

"No," she said with a gasp. "Don't stop. Not now."

He pressed himself to her core. Like petals of a honey-drenched flower, she opened to him. With one powerful thrust, he plunged inside.

18

Her ecstatic cry echoed around the room, witnessed by the moon, hushed by the deep-pile carpet. Shana wiped a straggling curl off her forehead. Abashed, amazed, she couldn't believe she'd just done that. "I never—"

"Shh." He stayed inside her. Gradually, the tremors abated.

Her body spasmed around his thickness, forming itself in clenching waves around him. "I didn't mean to—"

"Shh." He closed her mouth with his. A long, languorous kiss told her he wasn't finished with her yet. "Is this okay?" he asked.

"It was wonderful."

"If I move will it be too much?"

She gauged her body's lingering sensitivity. "Maybe if you move right now."

He bent his outstretched arm and lowered himself onto her. Her breasts were tender, his weight unutterably delicious. She wanted to throw her arms around him, to cradle him between her legs.

She was doing that already. Erect, throbbing, he filled her completely. Indulging those sensations sent heat waves cresting through her.

He grunted.

"I'm sorry. I'm making this hard on you, aren't I? Don't answer that."

He gave a ragged chuckle. "Tempt me too much, and I won't be able to stop."

"It wouldn't hurt that much. If you wanted to—"

He stared down at her. "Shana, if you're not ready, I'll wait."

"I guess I was readier than I realized." A heady laziness seeped through her like a narcotic. She combed a lock of hair off his forehead. "Or else it means you're a great lover."

"At least we'll find out how long I can last."

"Is there anything I can do?"

Not a thing. The way she looked up at him, sated, consumed, completely expended, made him feel as if he were the greatest lover in the world.

"Ooh."

He gritted his teeth. He hadn't meant to move like that.

"Gabe."

"Hold still."

She played with her own hair, curling a strand around her finger like a jaded wanton, a thoroughly desired woman. "Maybe I don't want to hold still."

"I'm warning you. We try this now, and it'll be fast and rough. It won't be pretty."

"What if fast is what I want?" She outlined the shell of his ear with her fingernail.

Until that moment Gabe hadn't even noticed Shana had fingernails. Judging from the effect they had on his libido, they were four inches long and painted ruby-red. "I've created a monster." He groaned. He tried to raise up, to prolong the moment.

She rose with him, her abdomen clenching, other parts of her body tightening all around him. "Don't go."

He'd come if she didn't stop. They compromised. He moved. His thrusts were slow and deliberate, his body tightening with the effort. It should have taken seconds. It went on forever, a slick slow climb, all willpower and restraint. Then his hard-earned patience cracked like glass. An animal instinct seized him. Chasing crest after crest, he felt her body tighten around his and he wanted it that way.

She caught her breath, her teeth clamped to her lower lip.

"Again?" he croaked.

She couldn't speak. There was no time, no words. She arched her neck, white, undefended. She was his.

He thrust into her, racing with her to the finish. With a final rending lunge, a hoarse shout of release, he drove home.

"Are you awake?" she asked.

Uncounted minutes had slid by in the dark.

"Are you?" he replied.

"Hard asking the question if I wasn't."

"You could talk in your sleep."

She shifted in his embrace. "No one's ever mentioned it."

He shouldn't have brought it up. He was lying in a minefield of second-guessing and skin-deep emotions. She moved to get up. He held on.

"You said you didn't care if I left."

"I never said I didn't care." He ran a hand over her shoulder. "That's not what I care about."

"Don't split hairs when I'm sleepy." She let out an impressive, somewhat rehearsed yawn. "Believe me, you don't want me falling asleep on you."

"I'd much rather have you awake on me. You can appreciate so much more that way."

"Mm. I might even participate."

"Oh, yeah?" He brought her arm to his mouth and kissed it, the soft part glowing white in the moonlight. "Good enough to eat."

"Just don't compare it to uncooked dough."

They wrestled on the king-sized bed. "We were cooking a minute ago," he said with a growl.

"I'll say. Whew."

His chest constricted at her attempt to play things light. "I love you, Shana."

She looked away. "You don't have to say that."

"I want to. I've never said it to a woman. I've always kept them at a distance. Why else would a single man need a bed this big?"

"You thrash around too?"

"Nice try." He nuzzled her cheek. "I couldn't risk anyone getting close, not if I might dream about them, then fail them. I've never stopped a vision coming true. The funny thing is, when I stopped fighting them, I stopped fearing them. I want a life, Shana. With you in it."

"I can't promise you how this will turn out."

"That's the point. The future will happen no matter what I do or dream. I want you to be part of it, however long it lasts." He added that last part to get the worried look out of her eyes. She wasn't ready for commitments. His were long overdue. He kissed the side of her neck.

She drew a shaky breath.

"Make it come true," he whispered. "Let me love you."

Shana knew from the first possessive stroke how tender love could be with the right man. His finger traced her lips, pulling out her lower lip to dip into moist nectar. His tongue, hot, wet, and intimate, dueled with hers. Love could be gentle and slow; he wanted her to know that. It could also burn like a comet hurtling through the night sky.

She wanted to please him, thank him, thrill him. If she could do for him even half the things he'd done for her . . . Reaching between them, she stroked his growing

shaft. He arced up off her, giving her access. She watched
the play of pale light over his rippling abdomen, the outline of their textures, hers soft, his sculpted. Where their
bodies joined she watched him sink into her. Closing her
eyes, she let her body lead her from there.

Desire ebbed and flowed, a pounding, building force.
She called his name. He rose up, bringing her with him.
Sitting back on his heels, he placed her on his lap. His
thighs were corded and hard. His hands kneaded her softness. He eased her down on him until she mewed with
satisfaction. They moved like water on sand, cresting,
sinking, surging forward, carried on a tide chasing toward
home until they collapsed, spent on the welcoming shore.

Gabe stared at the ceiling.

Shana stroked his damp hair. "Am I keeping you up?"

He gave her a deadpan stare. "After that you have to
ask?"

She laughed in delight, a husky chuckle. "I meant your
work."

He rolled onto his side, his work long forgotten. "You
like laughing in bed?"

"I'm sleeping with you, aren't I?"

"Ow! Right in the ego."

"I couldn't resist." She propped herself on her elbow,
the better to watch him throw himself into a death scene.

"My male vanity shattered, my self-concept reduced to
ashes. I'm melting, melting."

She poked him in the ribs. "I never imagined you being funny in bed."

Snagging a lock of her hair, he lowered his voice to a
velvety rasp. "And how often have you imagined me in
bed?"

His tone reverberated through her like a pealing bell.

He misinterpreted her silence. "Shana, if you want to
go, I won't make you stay."

She died a little inside. *Argue with me,* she wanted to

cry, *fight me on this.* That's what she was doing, deep inside where her insecurities lay. She longed to sleep in his arms, to wake up beside him in the glow of a winter morning, to laugh as if their lying side by side was the most natural thing in the world.

It was. She wasn't. No monograph in the world claimed love cured parasomnia.

She curved onto her side, hands clasped beneath her cheek as she stared at the moon. No, don't argue, she sighed. If he insisted she stay, how long would it be before he began demanding. From there it wouldn't be far to Stephen's resentful accusations; *If you loved me, you'd change. There must be a reason why you do this.*

The reason she'd made love to Gabe was simple; she loved him. She would make love to him tonight, every night, for however long he accepted the little she could give. The first time he objected to her getting up and getting dressed, she'd know it was over. She'd leave like a woman who knew what she was getting into. "I want us going into this with our eyes open."

He leaned over her, branding her mouth with a lingering kiss. "Closed is okay too."

They made love for the third time, teasing, caressing, testing the limits of what they'd discovered. An hour later they lay side by side. Her body was satiated, exhausted, its fire reduced to smoldering embers. His chest heaved with the spent passion of a roller-coaster ride coming to a shuddering conclusion.

Shana glanced around the room, her gaze resting on the computer in the corner, the shelf of financial texts. "You work in your bedroom," she commented.

"I wouldn't call that work."

She gave his thigh a weak backhanded slap. "I meant your computer. It's a bad habit for an insomniac."

"Like an alcoholic living above a bar?"

"It makes it too convenient to get up."

"You told us to get up. If we toss and turn too long, we begin to associate beds with anxiety."

"You've got nothing to worry about there." Sneaking a sideways glance, she caught sight of his feral grin. "Animal."

He growled.

She couldn't help laughing.

Eventually he raised his head until his chin rested on his chest. Briefly contemplating his home office, he let his head flop back onto the pillow. Except the pillow had been knocked to the floor an hour earlier. "The computer's not a problem tonight. The markets don't stay open on my account."

"That's right, it's Saturday."

He raised his head again, every other part of his body dead to the world. "Actually it's Friday in Japan." He rambled something about the international date line. "Doesn't matter. Debts will turn over without me. I can skip a night."

Beneath her strumming skin sleepiness crept up on her. A tranquilizing voice urged her to relax the way he had, to retrieve the tufted quilt they'd kicked off the bed and snuggle inside it until dawn. Just this once. What could it hurt?

She sat up.

"Whoa." Gabe reached for her.

"I need to get going."

"Hold on."

"I can't."

"Give me a minute, I'll drive you home."

She hadn't meant to snap at him. *You said that's what you wanted.*

He got up. Struggling into her nylons, Shana heard the dresser open. He handed her a pair of sweatpants and a sweatshirt. "Here. These might be more comfortable than getting back into that dress."

"Thanks."

"Bathroom's over there."

She went without looking back.

Gabe sat on the corner of the bed. He was trying to be helpful. So why did acting like a gentlemen make him feel like a world-class shit?

She shut the bathroom door before turning on the light. Considerate of her.

He stretched flat on the bed, crooking an arm behind his head. He drew up one leg, rocking it side to side. A half-mast organ rested against his belly.

He rubbed his eyes and stared at the overripe moon. He'd gotten beyond his fears, choosing life, involvement, risk, daring the dreams to take it away from him. He'd changed, dammit.

And immediately fallen in love with a woman who couldn't. Now it was Shana's turn to keep him at a distance, playing it safe, making no promises, making love without speaking it.

"Now you know how Mary Ann felt."

God, he hated irony.

Her husband sat on the edge of the bed. "One more pill."

"No."

"Swallow. I said swallow. Now tell me who you were talking to at the ball."

"No one."

"Mr. Fitzgerald?"

"I don't know any—"

"Darling, I saw you."

So reasonable. So soothing. The pills clicked together like hard-shelled insects in his soft hands. He maneuvered one between his thumb and forefinger. He placed it on her lips. The water glass waited.

"I didn't go near her," she murmured.

"The Getz bitch?"

A hysterical laugh bubbled up, threatening to escape in a scream. Of all the things he did to her, it still shocked her when he used profanity. "You told me to stay away from her."

"You haven't been listening."

"I do everything you want."

He didn't believe her. "How many of the other pills did you take tonight?"

Her skin shriveled. She expected to look down and see it curling back from her fingertips. She dug her fingers into the sheets.

"You're taking other pills. Don't think I don't know. You get them at the hospital. Are they from her?"

"No."

"Now swallow."

"I can't."

"Swallow."

"The last one went down sideways," she said with a whimper. "It hurt."

He offered more water.

She clamped her lips shut, her mouth firm. Her skin was so slack, she felt her cheeks waver when she shook her head. She'd been beautiful as a young woman. People had been shocked when they'd married. They were so different to look at, so unsuited.

He calmly put his hand beneath her neck, lifting her head off the pillow despite her stiff neck. He shoved the pill between her lips, grinding it against her teeth until she was forced to let it through. She gagged when it hit the back of her throat.

Holding the glass to her mouth, he poured until the water dribbled out both sides of her mouth, pooling at the base of her neck. The tears that trickled after were hot and scalding.

His expression never changed, not angry, not malicious, not even there. That farawayness in his eyes as if he didn't see her, hadn't seen her in years. To him she was a body, a fantasy he manipulated any way he wanted. The only time he'd shown a spark of life was when he'd mentioned Shana Getz.

He set her head back down. The wet pillow humiliated her as much as a wet mattress. He knew it would.
She had pride, dignity, that's why he'd married her. That
was why she strove so hard to stay awake. She had to
know. The idea of what he did to her when she was unconscious . . .

The edges of the room blurred. A languid indifference
cushioned her limbs in cotton. She fought to hold on to
the fear, glancing frantically left and right. She should
have taken more pills, the good ones. There'd been no
time; they'd come straight home from the ball. She should
have taken them before.

If she had, she would have never gotten through it.
She would've felt as if she were walking on ice all night,
brittle, breakable. All those people with their screeching
voices and flashing teeth. The men were all her husband,
powerful, preoccupied—except that tall one, the dark lean
man who'd taken her aside. He'd tried to tell her
something—what was it? Something about Shana.

Shh. Mustn't mention her. He might go after her next.
As long as she kept quiet, pretended to let the pills work,
she'd be his only victim. No one else would suffer. She'd
endure. Her mother had taught her that. That's what dignity was.

Across the room, he busied himself. Fastidious. Pre-
cise. Part of her envied him. He never wanted to scream.
He ran everything so smoothly, like a railroad timetable.
She was the hysteric, the one no one believed.

It looked like the ball, all these men in tuxedos striding through her bedroom. Amazing. Unreal. She watched
through slitted lids as her husband stopped by the bed.
The other men vanished, watery illusions.

He unbuttoned his shirt, studying her. She let her lids
close in infinitesimal stages so he wouldn't notice. Pain
cut through her, a line drawn between her breasts. It felt
as if it were cutting to the bone. She stifled a cry. Satisfied
with her silence, he stopped. She peeked when she sensed

him turn away. Standing by the vanity, he wiped the pointed edge of a cufflink with a tissue.

She couldn't raise her head, couldn't see how much blood. The cufflink clinked in a dish. His steps hushed across the carpet. The bed sagged. He began undressing her. He paused with the nylons, stretching them between his hands, calmly considering them for tying purposes. "Are you asleep, my dear?"

She didn't answer. She knew better than that.

"The Sandman's here."

The telephone jangled. Gabe picked it up on the first ring.

"I had the worst dream." Aurora.

He glanced at the bathroom door. Shana would be out any minute. "A real one?"

"Just the usual. I don't know why I call. It's not scary now. It had a boat in it. The *Titanic*, I think. It was on Lake Otsego."

Gabe rolled his eyes. He'd promised he'd hear her out whenever she called. However, the chances of the *Titanic* being raised just to sink again were slight. "Not a real dream, then."

Shana came out of the bathroom. "Japan?" she mouthed silently.

He gestured her closer. Capturing her hand, he held it to his chest. When he was confident it would stay there, he placed his hand over the receiver. "Aurora."

She lifted her palm as if scalded. He clamped it back. "Uh-hum. Mm." The sound rumbled in his chest. He'd shrugged into a black sweatshirt and pants while she was in the bathroom. He directed her hand up under the shirt, letting it rest directly over his heart. "Yeah. Lifeboats. No, that's fine. I was awake."

The moon had moved out of range, dividing the bedroom into diagonal shadows. He couldn't see Shana's expression. He barely heard her leave until the living room light sliced through the bedroom. The music's volume rose. He watched her gather up a red armful of dress.

"Anytime," he said to Aurora. He hung up, squinting into the bright light as he padded into the living room. "She calls me."

"You don't have to explain." Shana poked between sofa cushions. "Have you seen my purse?"

"That tiny thing?"

"I had it when we came in."

"No. I called down for the car."

"Good."

It'd be better if she'd look at him. "She wants someone to talk to after bad dreams. I'm awake; I volunteered."

"I'm sure you did."

"It's like the buddy system. Insomniacs Anonymous. Knowing someone will be there if she has a dream helps her sleep in the first place." The more he tried justifying the situation the guiltier he sounded.

"Did I say I objected?"

"You wouldn't be a woman if you didn't."

"I don't get jealous. We agreed. This has to be—limited."

He suppressed a curse and reached for her. Crushing her to him, he inhaled the familiar fragrance of his sweatshirt mingling with her unique scent. He wondered if she smelled him on her body the same way. "This is a hell of a lot more than 'limited.' We've got a lot in common."

"Common? Us?" She waved her dress toward the black expanse of glass. "I don't live in a penthouse, Gabe. If I call, my car doesn't answer. I don't E-mail people in Hong Kong, and I don't give away half a million dollars as if it were day-old bread."

"Are you still upset about that?"

"Try 'in awe.' We're different."

"We fit."

"I'm too tired to talk about this." Desperate, she looked under the sofa for her missing purse. When she straightened she tossed her hair over her shoulder, unconsciously sexy, unforgivably beautiful. "It's nearly four. I have to be at the bakery tomorrow."

"Which one?"

"My grandmother's on Garfield." Tossing her fur aside, she found her purse at last. "There you are!"

"Mind if I stop by?"

She turned, her lips parted in surprise. He held her stare.

"If you like," she murmured.

"I'd love to."

There was that word again. He almost had her convinced, he saw it in her reluctant, hopeful eyes. He steeled himself against that tremble in her chin. It was late, she was tired.

She got herself under control and backed toward the door. "Maybe tomorrow."

"No maybe about it."

"Are you sure it doesn't bother you, my leaving?"

Her innocent question was as loaded as a tax-free mutual fund. "No problem. Let me get my keys."

The drive back to his place was easier than the trek to Evanston. Holding her hand on the gearshift, he hadn't felt her relax until they were halfway there. They'd kissed good night at her door, his silent promise as tangible as a caress. To him. He wasn't sure how Shana felt.

But that was part of it, ambiguity, doubts. The only time he knew the future was when he dreamed it.

A thought slithered through the car like a draft of cold air. What would happen if he dreamed of losing Shana?

Switching the heater to High, he shook off the idea. It couldn't happen. The dreams had revealed her to him. They wouldn't take her away. They couldn't. She'd signaled a change in his life. That meant a change in the dreams. Maybe, if he was really lucky, the long nightmare was over.

19

Shana opened the door to the staff room. *Bang.*
        "Look out!"

A thump, a curse, and a round of delighted laughter persuaded her out of her hiding spot behind the door. A champagne cork rolled to a stop on the conference table. Merryweather frantically poured foam into paper cups. Flora separated more cups from a stack, setting them out in rows of four.

Michael raised the dripping bottle in Shana's direction. "To our newfound prosperity and the founder of our feast!"

"You're not going to pour that on my head, are you?"

"This Bud's on you," Fiona quipped.

"We're drinking to your health." Flora raised her cup in a toast.

Huffing, Shana set her files on the table. "And I thought we had business to conduct."

"First, a celebration," Michael insisted. "To the end of

ruthless rationing, the cessation of scrounging. No more parsimonious penny-pinching—"

"No more speeches," Fiona muttered under her breath.

Playing host, Merryweather filled Shana's cup to the rim. "Your patient has rewarded us handsomely. For that we thank you from the bottom of our hearts."

"He's not a patient anymore. As of this week I'm letting him go."

"Brava! Another cure, another happy customer. That calls for another drink."

Shana chuckled and sipped.

"I hope you're holding on to Gabe in every other way," Flora commented. "I saw you two on the dance floor. That man held you just about right."

Vertical holds had nothing on horizontal ones, Shana thought. Her nerves still danced. That music she heard was her body humming. Far from washing away the memories, the shower she'd taken that morning had served as a delicious reminder of Gabe's touch. Every inch of her flesh seemed sensually alive. Her body ached sweetly. Even her clothes fit differently.

She wondered if it showed. Gradually she realized everyone was looking at her. She raised her cup, briskly changing the subject. "Since we're saluting successful cures, let's drink to Flora too."

"For?" Merryweather hefted his pipe in one hand and his cup in the other.

"For DeVon Johnson's success with the CPAP machine. Flora's put in a lot of hours getting him used to wearing that gear to bed so he can breathe."

Flora handed Merryweather her cup. "Fill 'er up, boss. That particular patient isn't out of the woods yet."

"What happened?" Shana asked.

"Temporary setback. He got claustrophobic one night. Now he refuses to wear the face mask."

"He hasn't stopped treatment altogether?"

"Sometimes I wish," Flora sighed. She rubbed a heavy pearl earring between her thumb and forefinger. "Why is it the ones who won't admit they have a problem are the first to demand you fix it when they hit a snag? It's like treating a runaway subway train."

"You'll manage," Merryweather assured her. "I have faith in every one of my sterling staff. Fiona, I want you to start reading catalogues. Make lists of lab equipment we can buy, the shinier the better. I want bells, whistles, LED readouts."

"Before we go totally high tech," Shana put in, "why don't you have DeVon come to one of my sessions again, Flora? Relaxation techniques might help him adapt."

"You got him. He'll be there Wednesday."

"Thanks. I think."

"Speaking of dubious gifts, could I talk to you in private, Shana? Enjoy the bubbly, ladies."

Fiona finished hers in one gulp. "My workday's almost done. I'll let you have the rest."

"I'll drink it with lunch," he drawled.

Shana chuckled as they strolled down the hall to his office.

He unlocked the door. "Before the lab acquires its big-ticket items, we need to discuss your portion of this beneficence."

"Let's not spend it all on ten-dollar words."

"Your cut of the pie, then." He settled himself behind his desk, pausing importantly. "You're getting your preemie program."

"I am?" Shana beamed, her eyes sparkling more than the champagne. She wanted to jump up and give someone a high five.

Merryweather raised his palm, halting any overt demonstrations. "It's one of those good-news, bad-news situations, I'm afraid."

"How bad can it be? Now we can actually rewire the fixtures. Lights can be dimmed instead of turned on and off. The flexibility, not to mention the relief for those babies—"

"And the credit for you?"

"I'm not in this for the credit."

"Good. Because that's the bad news."

"I don't understand."

He slid his drawer open and pulled out a pouch of tobacco. He scooped a thumbful into his pipe. "Payne okayed the idea on an experimental basis."

"Meaning he could stop it anytime?"

"Meaning he wants certain controls. He wants the program overseen by an M.D."

Shana gripped the arms of the chair as his meaning sank in. "You?"

"It's still your baby. So to speak. I'll give you full credit in any report." Hearing no objections, he sat back, dusting tobacco off his hands with a satisfied slap.

Shana wasn't so easily brushed off. "That was my idea, Michael."

He heard the quiet steel in her voice.

"It's my innovation."

"I know," he responded. "If you like, you can make a scene. Lecture me on men co-opting their women subordinates' ideas—"

"I know it's not your fault." She rubbed her forehead, peering at the pipe cleaners curving on his desk like woolly worms. "This is typical Payne; giving with one hand and taking away with the other."

"Too true."

She shook off the disappointment. She'd developed innovative approaches before. Her goal was to help people not bask in the glory. "It's the babies who count. If they sleep better, it doesn't matter who came up with the idea."

"Yes it does," Merryweather argued. "The people in this department will know whose idea it was. I hope we count for something."

She gave him a tired smile. She suddenly wanted to get to work. Taking action would alleviate this creeping sensation of having been robbed. "I'll stop over there today and talk to the nurses. We'll put the program in motion as soon as—"

"Don't."

"Pardon me?"

"The less interference—strike that. The less you get involved with implementing this program the less trouble we'll have with Payne."

She sat speechless. "The nurses actually implement the changes. They know how involved I am. We'll need their cooperation as much as we need the dimmers."

"I'll get their cooperation. I'd like you to keep a low profile for a while. You can take satisfaction from the fact things are getting done."

"But I want to be involved."

"I understand."

"No you don't—"

"You've gotten what you wanted. Let's not antagonize Payne in the process, all right?"

She was antagonizing him, she saw it in the rare lines etching his boyish face.

"After your boyfriend's donation, you're high-profile enough, Shana. Not to mention the splash you made in that dress. It's time to fade into the background a bit."

"That's hardly my style."

"Don't I know it? I also know you've saved my clinic. I won't forget it, Shana."

Promises. She wondered how much they were worth and immediately felt guilty for doubting her mentor. Her legs shook as she stood, her stomach churning. She blamed it on drinking champagne at ten A.M. "I'll write up some notes on optimum sleep schedules for premature infants, the effects of cyclic lighting—"

"I'd be happy to see anything you have."

The stale pipe smoke clinging to his office suddenly sickened her. She got halfway to the door.

"Speaking of seeing," he murmured.

"Yes?" She turned.

Lips pursed around his pipe stem, he gave her a steady look. "A question has been raised concerning the propriety of your dating a patient. Not that I'm raising the issue—"

"Of course not. Payne is. As I said in staff, Gabe graduates this week. He'll attend his last group session Wednesday. I'll have a final patient write-up for you Friday."

"Wonderful. That loose end will be tied up."

Merryweather always did like things tied up neatly. Shana stared out her office window wondering how a dream coming true could make her feel as if her career was unraveling. It wasn't just the preemies, although the very thought of having her program taken away tied her stomach in knots.

She took a deep breath and put things in perspective. The babies would benefit. Who cared if it didn't appear on her résumé?

The radiator hissed in the background. Deep breathing did little good if she inhaled nothing but dust and dry air. She wedged her wrists against the glass and shoved the window frame. The aged paint creaked and moaned. She tried again. With a jerk, the window lifted. A sliver of cold air slunk into the room.

She remembered her vampire dream and compared it with the physical reality of loving Gabe Saturday night. He'd moved her beyond her wildest dreams, attentive, forceful, shockingly direct. He'd found depths in her she'd never suspected. He'd made her laugh.

She'd thought she loved him then, though she hadn't found the courage to say so. It wasn't until he'd walked into Nana Sofia's bakery Sunday morning that she was sure. He'd stayed an hour, charming her relatives, munching bagels, burning holes in her self-possession every time she caught him staring hungrily at her.

"Good news, bad news," she muttered to herself, forehead resting against the cold glass. "I love sleeping with him but I can never sleep *with* him."

She sighed and returned to her desk. She slapped a form on top of Gabe's file. The final line read "Conclusions." Terminating Gabe as a patient didn't mean they had to stop seeing each other.

And if this is only a patient/counselor crush? her conscience asked. What if he drifts away once the weekly appointments end?

He'd made a point of seeing her at the bakery, hadn't he?

She picked up the telephone, determined to prove her doubts wrong. They could see each other in the evenings, after work, on weekends. They could do everything but sleep together. As long as he accepted the arrangement, she'd give him all the love she had to give. She might even work up the courage to say it.

And when it ends? her conscience asked.

She'd go on loving him. Like her sleepwalking, there were some things a woman never got over.

"Hello?" He answered on the first ring.

"Good morning."

"Good morning." He'd had that same suggestive rasp when he walked into the bakery Sunday.

It made her skin shiver. A dizzy heat curled through her. "You weren't sleeping, were you?"

"Not for a couple hours yet. Noon to six."

"Six whole hours. That's wonderful."

"That's if I can stop thinking about you."

"Hm."

"You don't sound too happy."

Maybe it was the little things that made her love him, Shana thought, like the way he picked up her signals. His sleeplessness had trained him to notice details, how he came across, how others reacted.

"Is there something you wanted?"

Only you. She played with the telephone cord. Just knowing he was on the other end made her problems fall into place. "This reminds me of last night." She laughed.

He'd called at ten-thirty just to hear her voice. They

talked for over an hour, enjoying the shared silences as much as the conversation.

"Last night wasn't as good as Saturday," he murmured.

"I don't want to keep you up."

"Honey, you lower your voice like that again, and I'll be up all afternoon."

"That's a terrible pun."

"Puns are one of the few things I'm bad at. Besides sleeping."

"But you're sleeping better than ever."

"Thanks to you."

"Thank you," she said, slumping in her chair. "I needed the strokes."

"Having a bad day?"

"It's too complicated to go into. I, uh, I called to let you know I'm letting you go."

The frost in his voice came through loud and clear. "Do you think that's necessary?"

Upsetting him shouldn't please her so. "I'm declaring you cured," she explained. "As of this week's group session, you won't need to come for counseling. Of course, if the insomnia returns, you can always call."

"I plan to. A lot. And not for counseling."

Her heart bounded in her chest. "Of course, that would be fine too."

His knowing chuckle sent shivers through her. "You sound so professional when you call from work. Nothing like you do at home."

Home?

"How you sound in bed is another story altogether."

She cleared her throat. "Uh, Gabe—"

He cleared his. "I'll let you get back to work."

"That might be a good idea."

She leaned forward to hang up.

"Dinner?" he asked at the last moment.

"Sure."

"Hey, Doc. Have a nice day."

She hung up, as breathless as if she'd run a quick lap

around the complex, as shaky as if he'd appeared in her office in a puff of smoke. He wanted to see her, yesterday, today. Tonight.

She groaned and tapped her eraser against her empty head. She hadn't even mentioned her news, how his donation had gone over with the staff, the simultaneous success and derailment of her preemie program. She'd tell him later. All that mattered right then was that she'd given him the opportunity to go—and he'd chosen to stay.

"This is your idea of haute cuisine?"

"You said you liked pizza and a movie. Wait. I left the dessert in the car."

"Hold on." She'd met him at the door with two glasses of wine. She handed one over. "I have my speech all ready. I want to drink a toast."

He slipped inside, setting the pizza on the credenza. Peeling off his driving gloves, he evaded the offered wine and took her in his arms. "Toast me? You can set me on fire anytime." He rubbed his body against hers to prove it. "What's with the wine?"

Her mouth had gone so dry, she sipped some to wet her lips. "You've done wonderfully. Changing your habits, confronting the causes of your insomnia—"

"—even though you don't believe in them."

"How you deal with them is what matters. You've put the dreams in a perspective that works for you. You're better."

He hugged her closer. "I thought I was the best."

"I'm serious. I'm proud of you."

His ambivalent look gave her a queer feeling. He was too used to people complimenting him for the wrong reasons, envying his productivity, his sleepless nights. None of them knew the effort it cost him. They thought his schedule a brilliant coup instead of the cross he bore.

Shana knew otherwise, and she admired him anyway.

"You coped. You excelled. Then you went one better; you found a cure."

Had he? He dropped his hands and stepped back into the hall. "I'll get the dessert."

"Gabe."

He turned in the doorway, his hand braced against the frame. Shana noticed the red light of the alarm system, a warning she should heed. It wasn't the moment to tell him she loved him. "I am proud of you."

"Back in a second."

She strolled to the window, watching him trot to the car, sliding along the icy drive. She should have said it. He'd said it Saturday night. Since then he'd let the issue slide, content to be with her, to let things develop on their own.

The car door thudded shut. Cheeks ruddy, coat radiating the below-zero temperatures, he breezed inside. "Hi, honey, I'm home."

She gave him a big smooch and shooed him toward the sofa. "Hang up your coat and I'll get the paper plates."

An hour later they sat on the couch, the pizza box half empty, the wine almost gone. Romper took up a spot on the VCR, watching them through half-closed cat eyes.

"So Payne's trying to short-circuit your idea," Gabe said.

Shana munched on a piece of pepperoni and told him the rest of the story. She'd dubbed her day "The Good, the Bad, and the Ugly."

Gabe listened carefully. "One of the primary rules of negotiating; it doesn't matter how you get there as long as you get what you want in the end. The babies will sleep better."

"I know. But I wanted more. Is that selfish?"

"Just greedy." He told her about a similar deal he'd been working on for weeks. "I'll know tonight whether it's going to come together."

"So you have to leave early?" She kept her voice carefully neutral. She'd promised she wouldn't cling. If he couldn't deal with their arrangement about not sleeping together, she wouldn't stop him going.

"I'll stay as long as you want me."

"That's a loaded answer."

"Kind of like the pizza?"

She dropped an unwanted green pepper in the box. He dropped an uneaten crust beside her pepper. They sat side by side, avoiding each other's gaze, concentrating on their food.

"You had a tough day." He shrugged. "I can go when the movie's over." He was giving her a way out, offering to play by her rules.

She felt completely dejected. She wanted to be pressured. She wanted him to struggle, to argue, to push for more from her.

She wanted to be the one to say no. She said it to an onion, peeling it off the cheese. She licked her fingers and caught him watching. "I pick at my food."

"I noticed." He popped her discarded green pepper in his mouth. "I hope you're as picky about men."

"I hope you brought a toothbrush."

His brows rose slightly. "Did you want me to?"

She blushed furiously, gathering up napkins and plates. "I meant for the onions."

"Oh. Right."

She schlepped everything to the kitchen, dumping the box in the wastebasket, retreating to the previous subject. "I wish I'd been pickier years ago."

"Some real losers?"

"They didn't seem like it at the time. They weren't. To be fair, I think circumstances got the better of us, that's all."

"Your sleepwalking?"

"Or my kicking."

"They were losers."

She laughed. "You're sweet."

"Is that all?" He leaned back against the counter. Contemplating their easy intimacy, he lazily played with a strand of her hair.

"We should watch that movie. I've got an early day tomorrow."

He trailed her to the sofa. Taking up all the room, he sat and extended his legs. She had nowhere to go unless she reclined alongside him. He patted his chest. She snuggled into him.

All right, she loved it. She didn't have to let him know.

Romper leapt from the VCR to the sofa. Watching Gabe coil Shana's hair around a finger, he pawed at the golden strand. Eventually he realized it wasn't yarn, lost interest, and curled up on the sofa back.

Gabe aimed the remote at the VCR.

"What did you get?" Shana asked.

"Sylvester Stallone."

"Oh, no."

"It was that or some French thing with subtitles. A lot of people must be staying home tonight."

There it was again, the word "home," the one thing Shana could never share with a man. "At least fast-forward through the previews."

"I like to see what's coming."

"Except in your dreams. Give me that." She wriggled in his embrace. He held the remote at arm's length. "It's my remote."

"I've got it."

She glared at him. "You know why men like those things? They're symbols of manhood."

He comically held it with two fingers. "They are?"

"They're remote *and* controlling."

"Ha."

His guard lowered, she snatched the device from his hand and turned down the sound. "At least we'll keep the explosions to a minimum. I have neighbors."

He gave in this time. Shana rested her cheek against

his breastbone. Gabe balanced his chin on the crown of her head. "That okay?"

"That's fine."

He pressed soft kisses to her hair.

Guilt flooded through her. Nobody should feel so happy, so loved and supported, not without returning it fearlessly, wholeheartedly. "This is too much," she murmured.

A car careened through a Hong Kong market, toppling fruit carts and fruit vendors left and right. "Wait'll they get to the good part," Gabe said.

She nestled closer. She was already there.

The chase over, Gabe tore his gaze from the screen. He inhaled the aroma of her shampoo. She wore a baggy ivory sweater and clingy black leggings. The sweater swallowed every curve. It had one good feature, a generous neckline. Subtly, slyly, he bared her shoulder. Craning his neck, he placed a kiss there, then another. Her neck was pale cream. He licked it.

Her breathing remained even. His Shana usually melted for neck-kisses.

Purring in high gear, Romper sniffed at Gabe's cheek. He twitched his whiskers with a disdainful air.

"Shh. Your mistress is sleeping."

The cat knew that. Tucking his paws under his chest, he settled in for the evening.

Gabe had every intention of abiding by Shana's rules about sleep. That didn't mean he couldn't bend them a little. Call it a catnap. Call it a gift. She'd given him days of blessed, restful sleep. The least he could do was be her pillow for one evening.

The group gathered on schedule. Gabe waited. When Shana ran out of excuses for dawdling in the hall, she marched into the lounge. Immediately veering away from her usual place in the center, she strode to the blackboard.

Gabe excused himself from the group standing at the coffee cart. "You're not still angry, are you?"

"I was never angry with you," she responded curtly.

"You can't be angry about doing something that comes naturally."

Marie tottered by. Her brows rose slightly at what she overheard. She planted her cane, waggling the curved handle at Gabe.

He slanted her a look. It was good to know his scowl still had the power to chase people away.

Shana was unimpressed. Fishing a piece of chalk from the tray, she listed tonight's topics. The chalk creaked and screeched over the surface. "We've discussed this. Why don't you take your seat?"

"You fell asleep."

"Exactly." The chalk broke. She cursed.

"Nothing happened, Shana."

"I know. I overreacted and I apologize. It was never your responsibility to keep me awake."

His jaw clenched.

She turned back to her writing. "I was wrong to take it out on you."

"That isn't the issue."

"I promised myself I wouldn't sleep with you—" She lowered her voice. "And I did." Sparing a tight smile for Doris, she went back to her writing.

Doris popped up and started dusting her orange plastic chair with a hanky.

"I could have punched you," Shana muttered at Gabe.

"Why bother when you're doing such a good job of beating yourself up?"

"I mean I could have hit you in my sleep. You don't know what could have happened."

"For once in my life, maybe not. It's a risk I'm willing to take."

"It's my choice, not yours."

"You were fine."

Waking up completely unnerved wasn't her idea of

fine. "What frightens me even more is that you don't take this problem seriously. Respect me on this."

He wasn't a man to respect fear, not in himself, not in others.

She set down the chalk and sighed. The topics slanted dramatically, her letters as shaky and uneven as her voice. "Will you let me do this my way?"

He shoved his hands in his pockets. The group waited.

Shana absorbed his silence like a blow. Biting her lip, she gathered herself before turning to address the group.

"By the way, the CIA did it."

"What?"

Gabe forced a cavalier smile. "The Stallone film. Rogue CIA agents and that sleazy drug guy. You missed it."

She gave him a deadpan stare. "I've been waiting days to hear that."

He hoped his smile would elicit one from her. It didn't. "Let's talk about it after class."

She nodded, mouth grim.

For the first time in a day and a half, the tension eased out of him. Maybe they could work this out.

She presented him with a T-shirt. The words "Miles to Go Before I Sleep" were painted across the front. A cartoon of a worn running shoe flapped below. "To our newest graduate."

The group applauded politely. Gabe sat down. While she covered the night's topics, he directed his attention to the group he was leaving. Aurora had cruised in late and sat beside him; he'd still hear from her. Doris would probably never change, especially since her life revolved around keeping things the same. Lucille, the bus driver, had already returned to "regular" life, adjusting to her schedule with a few hints from Shana. A drug had radically improved Marie's restless-leg syndrome.

And DeVon Johnson? His problems seemed deeper,

and more dangerous than any others. Gabe kept his eye on him. His hackles rose with every sneering comment the railroad man made. He hadn't forgotten the way Johnson had stormed out of that first session.

Shana took the tension in stride. She was in her element, entertaining, educating, inspiring her patients to try less hard and succeed more often. She handled the ebb and flow of group discussion effortlessly. There was no reason for Gabe's protective instincts to go on alert.

"I just don't like the guy."

Walking Shana to her car in the parking garage after the session, Gabe pulled her a little closer. She glanced over her shoulder at the hulking figure half a level behind them. She waved. Johnson kept his hands stuffed in the pockets of his parka.

"DeVon's okay," she said. "He's frustrated. How would you feel if you'd had a taste of how wonderful sleep could be then had it taken away?"

Kind of the way he'd feel if he lost Shana. Just a taste of love made him want a lifetime of it. "So where was his wife tonight?"

"It's his problem, not hers. Accepting that is a big step all by itself."

Thanks to Shana, Gabe accepted his problem, he dealt with it. Why couldn't she accept hers?

"Cold?" She wrapped her mittened hand over his bare one, misinterpreting the reason he held her arm so tight.

"Just want to get you to your car."

"I can't believe you're worried." Her eyes sparkled when she teased him. "If DeVon follows my advice, he should be okay."

Gabe had to admit her approach was clever. She'd concluded the class with a meditation exercise that involved imagining themselves floating underwater. Anxieties darted into their minds and away again like brightly colored fish. They breathed in and out. All except DeVon. For him, Shana provided an imaginary scuba tank. If he awoke feeling panicky because of the mask, she told him, he should imagine it as his lifeline.

"I'm beginning to wonder if 'behavior modification' is just a fancy term for 'attitude adjustments,' " Gabe said.

She chuckled. "If he sees that machine as essential and not some 'effing contraption,' he'll be eager to use it."

"He didn't use the word 'effing.' "

"I know." She grinned, unlocking her car. Straightening, she waved again.

Gabe swung around. "Is he still following us?"

"He's shy. Believe it or not, some men hate asking for help." She rose up on tiptoe and kissed him with a sassy smack. Then she tucked her fanny in the seat. "You wouldn't believe how surly some men can get when they haven't been sleeping right."

Gabe grumbled something unintelligible.

Shana shut her door then rolled down her window. "I'm glad we talked." She meant their discussion before class.

He wondered how much it had solved. He peered across the garage. The sodium lights cast everything in flat shadow. "How about if I follow you home?"

"I'm okay, really."

He braced his hands on the windowsill, the T-shirt clutched in his grip. "I'd like to come over."

Her cheeks flushed pretty pink, even in the yellow light. Gabe took credit for that. "I can't stay late. I've got a deal I'm working on." He wasn't forcing himself on her. He didn't want her thinking he hadn't listened to what she said.

"I'd like that very much."

He forgot the cold, the lights, the damp. He kissed her long and deep, the hell with whoever might be watching. He was cured. She was the one who needed the attention now, all the support he could muster.

Starry-eyed, Shana stared up at him. "See you in a little while?"

Out of the corner of his eye he watched DeVon step

out from between two cars and walk to a van. The engine roared to life in the enclosed space. The van rolled down the ramp, turned the corner, and disappeared.

"I'll follow you," Gabe said.

20

The BMW screeched to a halt on the wet drive of the emergency entrance. "I'll park the car," Gabe shouted.

"See you in a minute." Shana raced across the rock salt and slush. The sliding doors opened. She caught her breath at the entrance desk. "I'm here about a patient—"

The scream cut her off. Halfway down the corridor three orderlies tried to restrain the woman. Average size, beyond middle age, her gray and white hair in disarray, Hazel fought them all off. Her demure two-piece suit was stretched in every direction by the struggle. Her hose were riddled with ladders. She gouged one man with the sturdy heel of a pink pump. Her other foot was bare.

"Let me go! He'll kill me. He's the Sandman. He can kill all of you. You hear me? He's coming! He's coming!"

Shana edged nearer the pandemonium. A blood-curdling scream froze her in place. "Hazel?" she called.

Her voice hardly carried past the orderlies muttering curses and ducking flailing limbs. She flinched as they manhandled Hazel onto a gurney. One man threw himself across her as the other two tied her hands and feet to the rails with restraints.

Shana raised her voice above the din. "Don't do that. Don't you know that's what she's afraid of?"

Rushing from one examining cubicle to the next, a nurse spoke up. "Better stay back, lady. Psycho. Hallucinations, psychotic behavior. Claims the Sandman's coming to get her."

"I'm her counselor. I work here."

The nurse had no time for explanations. "Talk to Paul Wise."

"Who's—"

She darted into a curtained cubicle.

Torn between helping Hazel and getting answers, Shana edged her way between the frustrated orderlies. "Don't tie her like that."

"Then you hold her down," one man said with a grunt.

"I know this woman."

"Bet she doesn't know you," another said. "The lady's freaked."

Shana bent over her. "Hazel. Hazel, it's me, Shana. It's all right."

"Bitch," Hazel shouted. "Slut. You're the one he wants. He says your name. He says it when he touches me." Her voice rose to a shriek. "I told you. I told you what he does to me! He'll do it to you next."

Her blood ran cold. The woman didn't know what she was saying. For some reason she found herself clutching Hazel's discarded shoe. She dropped it at the foot of the bed. "Hazel, you're here now. We can take care of you."

"Get away! Stay away!" Hazel wrenched her wrist sideways in the cloth restraint, gripping Shana's arm with her nails. "Don't let me sleep. I've got to stay awake. Keep me awake."

Staying awake too long had probably caused this breakdown. "When was the last time you slept?"

"Years."

"When, Hazel? It's important. Tell me."

Her glassy eyes rolled back. She pounded her head rhythmically against the pillow. "He wants me to sleep. Forever. He knows I don't. I've got to stay awake. You've got to help me. Keep me awake!" Her voice was a hoarse chant, her skin nearly translucent with exhaustion.

Shana uncurled Hazel's fingers from her arm, marveling at the woman's strength. "He can't hurt you, Hazel, not anymore."

Hazel opened her bloodshot eyes, staring furiously at nothing. Jaw clenched, spittle dotting the corners of her mouth, she bore down on the straps. Saying nothing, she jerked an arm, a leg, silently, desperately fighting for her life.

The cloth creaked against the metal rails. Shana glanced down, disgusted that this late in the twentieth century they couldn't come up with another method of restraining a patient. "These things look positively medieval."

Two of the orderlies had taken a brief rest against the corridor wall. The third waited at the gurney's end for another outburst. It didn't take long. Hazel's eyes widened. Something came at her that only she saw. Her screams clawed the air. She would have torn the restraints from the rails if the orderlies hadn't closed in again.

"Isn't this making her worse?" Shana shouted over the commotion. "She's afraid of being attacked."

"We gotta keep her calm," the burliest orderly shouted.

"I know, but—"

"Are you Shana Getz?"

"Yes."

"Dr. Wise is busy, he asked me to handle this case."

An intern squeezed in beside her. Impervious to the chaos of bodies crammed around the gurney, he callously rested his clipboard against Hazel's thigh.

The screams stopped. An eerie groan began, so deep

and unearthly, Shana wasn't sure where it came from. The bustle of the emergency room slowed; heads turned. The groan rose and rose, an inhuman siren, the strangled wail of a trapped animal. Hazel pulled the restraints so tight, Shana felt the rails bend inward.

"She's got the strength of five men," an orderly said.

"PCP," the intern suggested.

"It's not PCP," Shana spat out. "She's hallucinating. It's sleep deprivation exacerbated by a combination of barbiturates and amphetamines."

"Are you her physician?"

"I'm her counselor." Shana kept her eyes on Hazel at all times, petting back her hair, staying away from those clawlike fingernails.

The intern clacked his clipboard against the rail and read off his observations. His bored tone implied this was just another night in the emergency room. "Hallucinations, rantings, elevated blood pressure. Could be a lot of things."

"If you thought someone was trying to kill you, you'd have elevated blood pressure too. We won't know what she's on until you do a drug screen."

"It's already at the lab. Drawing blood was a treat, I'll tell you. Look, we got a piece of paper from her pocket. Your name and number were on it. If you're not her doctor, who do we call? And what's her last name?"

"I don't know."

"Wonderful."

The indifference people developed in emergency rooms aggravated her. She shot him a look but he'd already turned away, consulting with a nurse about a gun wound in cubicle one.

Easing her hand into Hazel's clenched fist, she allowed her to grip until Shana's fingers turned white. "I'll be back," she promised. She had to call Merryweather. He knew more about sleep-inducing drugs and their side effects than anyone on the staff. Judging from Hazel's fretful, distracted behavior on previous occasions, Shana guessed

amphetamines were involved. Combine them with
benzodiazepines, the most commonly prescribed narcotic,
and the accumulated effect could be disastrous.

She asked the woman at the desk for an outside line.
Leaving a message on Michael's machine, she glanced
around for Gabe. He was still parking the car. She longed
to see him. Just one look and life would make sense again.

A nurse strode past her carrying a large hypodermic
needle. She stopped at Hazel's bedside and rolled up her
sleeve.

Shana dropped the phone. "Wait! What's in that?"

"A tranquilizer," the nurse replied. Puffy-eyed and sullen, she didn't appreciate the interference. "We need to
get her sedated."

"Don't administer that. Not yet."

"The doctor said—"

Shana nearly begged. "Hold off until the test is done."

"Drug screens take hours. She could hurt herself by
then."

"Let me talk to Dr. Wise." The intern had to be in one
of these curtained cubicles. Before she reached the final
one, Gabe rushed through the door.

"How is she?"

"I don't know. I called Merryweather. He'll have a better idea how to treat her than I would. I just know *more*
tranquilizers aren't the answer."

"What about you?"

Shana looked up at him, a sudden weariness stealing
over her. "I love you."

He took her in his arms. "I think I knew that."

Sagging against him, she replenished her strength with
his warmth. "Just for a minute," she whispered.

"As long as you need."

It seemed like hours since they'd gotten the call.
They'd been curled side by side, their feverish lovemaking
a shimmering memory. She'd been postponing the moment when he'd rise to leave her apartment, savoring the
way his skin smelled, how well their bodies fit. For a brief

tempting moment she'd considered asking him to stay. She'd felt cherished and strong. With him beside her she wanted to challenge fate, defy her past.

Then the telephone had jolted them out of their spell.

"I don't even know her last name," Shana murmured.

Gabe stroked her back. Nurses came and went, orderlies stepped around them as if they were a rock dividing a stream.

"What happened?" he asked at last.

"I think she's having hypnagogic hallucinations. That's what happens when a person's been deprived of sleep too long. Thank God it never happened to you."

He smiled grimly. "I wasn't avoiding sleep, just dreams."

She scrunched his sweater in her fist, as if this point were vital. "People need to dream. The brain needs dreams the way the body needs sleep. If it doesn't get them, a person starts dreaming when they're wide awake."

"Is that so bad?"

"It's the next best thing to being psychotic. People hear things, see them, live them. Just like in a dream except you can't wake up."

He indicated the staff gathered around Hazel's gurney. "Maybe you better tell them that."

She hesitated. "I don't want her to suffer more. For all I know the hallucinations may be only a symptom. Fear might be keeping her awake, in which case we need to find her husband. It could be rebound insomnia from the pills stockpiled in her body. It could be an overdose of amphetamines."

Gabe braced a hand on his hip. "It could be anything."

"Or everything combined. Merryweather's on his way. He's an expert."

"At this?"

"On the problems of sleeping pills, he is."

Hazel screamed again. Gabe watched a scruffy intern open a curtained cubicle then step back inside. The man's face was drawn, his cheeks stubbled with beard. Gabe sympathized; another sleep-deprived young doctor working the graveyard shift.

The place sounded worse than when he'd sat here waiting for Brice. It was one in the morning. Somebody moaned. Someone else cried softly. A telephone purred continually behind the desk. Near the door an hysterical woman badgered a policeman about a no-good girlfriend who'd shot her man. Down the corridor, Hazel screamed about the Sandman.

Shana reluctantly pulled away. "I've got to find the intern in charge."

Gabe was there to help. "Try that one."

She strode to the final cubicle. Gabe pulled the curtain on the one beside it.

He wasn't sure what he'd expected: nurses cutting off blood-soaked clothes, doctors shouting orders, patients' chests being pounded back to life. Instead he saw a half-clothed man lying tethered to monitors and breathing machines. Tubes ran up his nose. Bandages circled his chest. Beside him the young doctor leaned against the wall, snatching a few minutes' peace. Ignoring the patient, he rubbed his eyes, stretching his jaw in a weary yawn. Stripping off a latex glove, he covered his mouth with his hand. He turned to pick up a clipboard.

"Excuse me," Shana said, stepping out from behind Gabe. "I need to speak to you about a patient."

"Yeah, right."

Her tone grew icy. "Now, if you've got a moment." She stepped into the corridor, too hyped up to stand still. The moment the intern joined them she launched into her speech. "Until the drug screen comes back I don't want you prescribing any tranquilizers for the patient known as Hazel Doe. We don't know what she's on. You don't know what—" She stopped dead, her eyes growing round. "It's you."

The intern's eyes widened too. He fumbled with the clipboard, flipping the pages as if he could hide between them. It was a pitiful attempt. Gabe nearly heard the wheels grind in the man's head.

Shana shook her finger under his nose. "You're the one who's been selling her drugs!"

"I have not."

"Drugs!" Gabe stepped forward. Splaying his fingers on the man's bony chest, he shoved him back a step. "What are you talking about?"

Shana inched forward. She didn't want to be protected from this guy, she wanted to get in his face. "I saw you. You're the one who sold her pills on the fourth floor!"

"I wasn't selling anything," he snapped. He turned on a nurse vying for his attention. "What is it now?" he shouted.

"Bay three. Cardiac arrest."

"Can't you see I've got enough going on? Get someone else!" He brushed by both women, striding down the hall.

"Stop him," Shana called.

The nurse acted as if this were a nightly occurrence. She turned on her rubber-soled heel and went about her business. The orderlies glanced up. Gabe held Shana back before she could give chase. "What do you mean selling?"

"He's Hazel's supplier. He's the reason she's in this state."

Gabe was three strides ahead of her as they stormed down the hall.

"Stop him," Shana called to the orderlies. "He's a dealer. He's illegally prescribing—"

One orderly wearily launched himself off the wall. Another stepped calmly into the center of the hall, arms folded.

Trapped, the intern whirled on Shana. "Fuck you, lady. I don't know you. I've never seen either one of you. Get out of my emergency room."

"Watch your mouth," Gabe said.

The intern shrank, his beady eyes irate. "You, too, buddy. I don't know what your girlfriend's going on about, but she's as fucked up as this old bag here."

Shana edged around Gabe, shaking a schoolmarmish finger in the weasel's face. "You are not treating this patient."

"And you are? See if I give a shit. It's one less thing on my plate." He tossed the clipboard on the gurney and stalked back toward the cubicles.

"Call security," Shana commanded. "Don't let him get away."

"What about him?" Gabe nodded at the policeman standing by the entrance.

The potbellied veteran rocked back on his heels as he took notes on the shooting victim in bay one. The high-strung woman repeated the garbled details for the third time.

Shana strode up to them, shoulders back, chin high. "Officer, there's a drug dealer on the premises."

"One felony at a time, okay?"

Taken aback, she stared at the policeman in amazement.

"She shotgunned my man," the woman wailed. "That no-good bitch. I saw her. She shot him. Leaned her fat and flappy arms out the side of that car window and shot him right there on the porch! I saw her! I'll kill her! The bitch tried to take my man!"

The policeman tiredly reached out. Yanking the woman back from her mission of revenge, he held his ground while she swayed to a halt. "You're staying right here, ma'am."

"But there's a drug dealer in that cubicle," Shana insisted. "He's a doctor."

"Report him to the AMA. I can only handle one crime at a time. What are you glaring at?"

Gabe stared him down. "The lady's trying to tell you something."

"Is anybody dead?"

"Not yet."

The woman moaned and folded her arms across her stomach. "Henry. She shot my Henry."

Merryweather raced through the automatic doors. "What's happening, Shana?"

"At last, somebody who cares!" Shana stormed away from the policeman. Gabe followed.

"Michael, Hazel's gone off the deep end. Remember the patient I told you about? I couldn't get her to come in? She's hallucinating, psychotic. Either it's a combination of too many drugs or not enough sleep."

"I thought you said it was drugs," the policeman said with a smirk. "No law against losing sleep."

She whirled. "Drugs, sleeplessness, or *both*."

"What room is she in?" Merryweather asked.

"She's in the corridor. Right there. She's quieted down a little. When we got here she was hallucinating."

Merryweather started down the corridor, gripping Shana's arm as they went. The closer they got to the gurney the slower he walked. He finally stopped altogether, as if he'd reconsidered on the way. "Why don't you go home?"

"What?"

"I'll see she gets proper care. I assume Gabe brought you. You can drive her, can't you?"

"Michael, they're talking about tranquilizing her. With the drugs already coursing through her system—" Shana pulled him aside, casting a furious look at the policeman planted in the entrance. "The intern who's treating her is the drug dealer I saw on four. He's been supplying her with God knows what. His name's Wise, Paul Wise."

Merryweather didn't seem to be listening. "I'll handle it."

"What?"

"Shana, I said I'll take over."

The curtain to cubicle three screeched back. Paul Wise stepped out. "Dr. Merryweather."

"Paul."

Shana gaped. "You know each other?"

"I know a lot of people in this hospital, Shana. Mr. Fitzgerald, why don't you take Shana home?"

Too late. She'd sidestepped Merryweather and Gabe, drawn by Hazel's unearthly stillness. "What have you done to her? What did you give her?"

The intern justified himself to Merryweather. "She was hysterical, delusional. I ordered a tranquilizer."

"But she could be swimming in sedatives," Shana cried. "We don't know what narcotics her husband's been feeding her."

"Narcotics?" the policeman called.

"Sleeping pills," Shana responded.

"Oh." He went back to his notes, completely uninterested.

"We only have her word for that," Merryweather said. "The woman could be a mental case. There's no proof her husband's done anything."

"And no drug screen to verify it one way or the other," she retorted.

"We'll have the results in a few hours," the intern protested as if this were entirely academic.

"Until then you shouldn't have given her anything!" Shana insisted.

Evading the commotion, the puffy-eyed nurse stepped to the head of the gurney. Shining a penlight in Hazel's eyes, her one-word diagnosis got everyone's attention. "Coma."

"Shit."

Shana glared at the intern. A sudden calm descended on her. "That would be consistent with an overdose, wouldn't it?"

"It's consistent with a lot of things," Merryweather replied. He pushed up the sleeve of Hazel's frayed wool suit, grimacing at the green and blue bruises on her wrists. Placing his thumb on her pulse, he looked at his watch and counted the seconds. "Get her to intensive care."

Orderlies appeared from all directions. They rolled the gurney toward the elevators at a run.

Merryweather turned to the nurse. "We need that drug screen, stat."

The nurse rushed into a small office.

Shana cornered the intern. "What did you sell her? What is she on?"

"The tests will tell us," Merryweather said.

"A sedative was warranted," the intern insisted.

"I already told you she was on sleeping pills," Shana retorted. "An extra dose, administered as a sedative, and you've got an OD on your hands."

Merryweather interrupted her onslaught. "He couldn't know how many pills her husband gave her."

"I thought you didn't believe in the husband."

Merryweather looked over her head, straightening to his full six feet four. "Dr. Payne."

"What are you doing here?" Shana blurted out.

"Is my schedule your business?" he asked coldly.

Not for the first time in her life she wished she knew how to keep her mouth shut. It didn't matter; this was an emergency.

Payne strolled forward to join them, his egg-smooth head gleaming in the fluorescent light. "I see where Dr. Getz goes Mr. Fitzgerald is sure to follow."

Gabe stepped nearer, taking Shana's hand in his.

"I need to talk to you," Merryweather said to Payne. His usual deferential drawl was gone. He sounded almost forceful. "Thanks for the call, Shana. You can go home now."

"With Mr. Fitzgerald?" Payne asked, one pale brow arching.

Shana felt Gabe's tension. She warned him off with a look. "I'd like to stay. I want to know how serious Hazel's coma is."

Payne's chin turned ever so slightly, like a dog hearing a distant whistle. "Dr. Merryweather?"

"Yes, sir?"

"Is there somewhere we can talk?"

Another gurney rolled into Hazel's vacated space. They all edged toward the small office the nurse had retreated to. Shana heard the sharp words, "What do you mean you didn't get it?" The puffy-eyed nurse whisked by them and down the hall.

Payne entered her office as if he owned it. "Doctor?" Merryweather obediently followed.

So did Shana. "Michael, this is my patient. I insist on being involved in any consultation."

He blocked the door. "She isn't yours."

"She came to me for help."

"I'm afraid I allowed that."

"You what?"

"I've been treating her for months. I was surprised when you said she'd contacted you. It isn't unusual for a patient to prefer a counselor of the same sex. It also isn't unusual for a patient to peddle the same old stories to a new, more sympathetic counselor."

"Why didn't you tell me?"

"I would have."

"But what about the intern?"

"He'll be taken care of."

"But Michael—"

Merryweather shut the door in her face. The last image she saw was of Payne poking through the nurse's paperwork with his lily-white hands. She turned to Gabe, her mouth hanging open. "Am I dreaming this?"

"Is he always like that?"

"Michael? Never." Frowning, she paced the length of the corridor. "We get sleeping-pill dependencies now and then. Usually they go to drug counseling. If they come to us, they go to Michael."

"Then it makes sense he'd see Hazel."

"But he never mentioned her. Not in staff meetings, not to me when I told him about her. This—this is not just a woman overindulging in sleeping pills. There's more going on here."

"I believe you."

She looked at him as if he were an oasis after days in the desert. She opened her arms for a hug. "It doesn't make sense."

"Come home with me."

The puffy-eyed nurse interrupted their embrace. Holding up a vial of blood, she grimaced at Shana. "I'm sending it for the screen now."

Shana looked at her blankly. "Wise said it went down an hour ago."

The nurse snorted. "It was sitting on his desk. Don't worry. It'll get there this time."

Shana called after her. "Whatever you do, don't let him get near Hazel."

"She's in intensive care. She's out of his hands."

21

Shana's thoughts revolved like a spinning tire on an overturned race car. She paced the living room of Gabe's apartment. The tall black windows acted as mirrors without providing any new perspectives. "Something isn't right. No, that's not it. So many things are wrong I can't sort out what matters most."

Gabe handed her a hot chocolate. She set it on a side table and kept walking.

"You're exhausted," he said.

"It's nothing compared to Hazel. Either she's been fighting off the pills her husband gives her or she's so convinced of her delusions, she's driven herself to a complete breakdown."

"You don't believe in the Sandman?"

Shana held her hair back with both hands, covering her ears against remembered screams. "I don't know. I would have never believed Merryweather would keep something like this secret. She was his patient yet she contacted me. I told him about it. He never even hinted—"

"Does the staff discuss every patient?"

She sipped her chocolate, though she couldn't concentrate on it long. "I never mentioned your dreams, though that printout caused a lot of comment."

"I wasn't worried about me."

She studied him a moment. That line between his brows didn't look like confidence. "I'm sorry, I can't think straight. These are your hours. You're wide awake, clearheaded. Me, I don't know what I am."

"You're winding down." They'd been home two hours. She hadn't stopped turning over events in her mind. Every time he'd tried to sit them on the sofa she'd popped up to illustrate some point, to rage at the inconsistencies.

"How could Merryweather ignore Paul Wise like that? To give a woman in Hazel's condition *more* drugs."

"He was beat."

"What excuse is that?"

"I know him."

She collapsed on the sofa. "You what?"

"I know the type. I am the type," Gabe said. "He hasn't slept in more than a day. He's exhausted, irritable. He wants things over quickly so he doesn't have to sustain any ideas. He jumps to conclusions and hopes he's right because it's easier that way."

Shana nodded. Gabe would know exactly how a sleep-deprived doctor would act.

"As an intern he'd be there all hours," Gabe suggested. "Including the afternoon you saw him on four."

"He'd know four was deserted."

"If this woman was pestering him for something to keep her awake, he might have prescribed it just to keep her out of his hair."

"No doctor would do that."

"He would if it meant fifteen minutes peace. It's amazing what you'll do to snag even a minute of sleep. What's his schedule?"

"First-year interns work the same shift, thirty-six hours on, thirty-six off. It's terrible; the body never adjusts to that kind of cycle."

"Forgetting to send the blood sample to the lab would be typical."

"Working the emergency room, he'd be pulled in ten different directions at once."

"A healthy person would have problems dealing with it."

"A sleepy one would make mistakes."

"We saw him make one tonight."

She clenched her fists at her sides. "I can't believe I was so blind. He was right there all along, working at St. James'. I could have spotted him. I could have prevented this."

"And I could have held on to Hazel at the fund-raiser ball. It isn't your fault."

She put a hand to her forehead. "Merryweather should have told me. Why didn't he tell me he treated her? Together we might have—"

Gabe took her in his arms. "We're going in circles, hon."

She let him lead her to the bedroom. "I can't sleep now."

"Try." He pulled an old pair of silk pajamas from beneath a pile of shirts. "Put these on. You can crash here."

She thought twice.

"Do you think you'd sleep if I took you home?"

Her shoulders slumped. "I don't think I'll unwind for a week."

"Then keep me company."

She accepted the pajamas. "I never pictured you as the plaid type."

"Christmas gift."

"What's that beeping noise?"

"My fax."

"All this commotion's kept you away from your work. I'm sorry."

"It's no big deal."

She glanced over his shoulder at the sheet unscrolling from the fax and gulped. "Big deal? I haven't seen that many zeros outside the national debt."

He kissed her on the cheek, lingering longer over her mouth. "I'll call them back while you change."

He pulled out his chair, simultaneously flicking on his desk light and computer. Shana paused in the bathroom door. "Gabe? Thanks for coming with me tonight."

"Sorry I couldn't be more help."

He'd helped more than she could say. She'd never forget how he looked striding through that door, how much she'd needed to be held in his arms for that one moment. "You were wonderful."

He typed in a command and waited for a reply. "So were you, and not just at the hospital." His dark gaze reminded her they'd started the evening in a much different mood. "Did you mean it?"

He meant earlier, when she'd said she loved him. Their bodies entwined in her bed, her heart filled to overflowing, she'd dared say the words that backed up in her throat every time they kissed. "I meant every word."

Minutes later she padded back to his computer from the bathroom. Without tearing his rapt gaze from the screen, he patted the chair beside the desk. "Have a seat."

She tugged a quilt off the bed and snuggled into the leather wing chair. "Got a notepad?"

He pulled open a drawer and handed her a legal pad and pen without breaking his concentration.

"You're good at that," she murmured.

"Years of practice."

She should have known he'd be organized. They were opposites in so many ways. She scratched her head with the pen, clicking it against her skull distractedly as she stared at the blank pad. Where to begin? She wanted to document everything that had happened in Emergency.

After filling two pages, the lines blurred. She focused her eyes with effort. Three headings topped page 3: Hazel,

Merryweather, and Wise. Questions dogged her about each. *Was* Hazel really married? Why hadn't Merryweather mentioned her? Had Wise purposely neglected the drug screen?

Instead of keying in on them, her hand strayed to the margin. She wrote the name Payne then crossed it out as irrelevant. The only question about him was what he'd been doing there. Who'd called him?

Shifting in the chair, her gaze drifted to Gabe. He was deep in thought, staring down at his facts and figures. She silently thanked him for the insight regarding Wise's sleep deprivation. But sleep-deprived interns were nothing new. What if Wise had a less sympathetic excuse?

"He was selling," she murmured, writing hastily, resorting to shorthand to capture it all. "One of his customers came in suffering an adverse reaction to the drugs he'd illegally supplied."

Gabe glanced up.

"To prevent her fingering him, he ordered a sedative—a perfectly justified treatment under most circumstances. However, in this instance, he wanted to silence the patient forever."

"He tried to kill her?"

"It'd be a great way to avoid exposure."

Gabe and Shana looked at each other a long moment. The cursor blinked impatiently. Instead of answering it, Gabe sat back in his chair. "Is that enough motive? We're talking about murder."

The loose ends were coming together faster than Shana could tie them. Suddenly her blood slowed to a chilly rope in her veins. She pulled the quilt closer around her. "What if he's the Sandman?"

"Him? How could he be Hazel's husband?"

"We don't even know she has one, not for sure. She screamed every time he came near her. She said the Sandman was there. Wise could be behind all of it."

"How?"

Shana tapped a staccato beat on the pad. "Even if he

wasn't her husband, he could have been selling her sleeping pills *and* amphetamines. They exaggerated delusions she already had, elevating her paranoia."

"Why risk selling pills to someone who's already unbalanced?"

"Same reason anyone pushes drugs: money, twelve years of med-school loans." She snapped her fingers. "The ball."

"What about it?"

Throwing off the quilt, she paced to the bed and back. "I thought Hazel was there because her husband was as influential as she said, a patron of the hospital. But even then the thought crossed my mind she might be there to meet her supplier. What better cover? *Wise* could have gotten her in. They could have been making a deal."

Gabe summed up. "So he supplies her addiction until she goes over the edge. Then he orders her sedated so she can't tell."

"Right."

"Premeditated cold-blooded murder."

Cautiously, deliberately, Shana nodded.

"And the bruises on her arms? Who did that?"

He didn't miss a thing. Shana shuddered and rubbed her own wrist. "I don't know. I need to think. It doesn't make sense yet but it's coming together."

Gabe extended his hand. She placed her palm in his. His thumb caressed her knuckles as he raised them to his lips. "Let me know when you've got the next piece."

"I feel so responsible. If I'd seen him around the hospital sooner . . ."

"How often does the sleep clinic do business with the emergency room?"

"Not often."

"You're not even in the same building."

"I know, I know. It's just—if I'd seen him, just once, in the cafeteria, anywhere, this could have been avoided."

Gabe's expression hardened. "What if he'd seen you?

What if he'd recognized *you* when he saw you on the fourth floor? He could have come after you."

She shook her head, the idea too enormous to contemplate. "Now you're going to give me nightmares." Kaleidoscopic images buffeted her, that night she'd thought someone was following her in the parking garage, the mysterious person on the staircase. She remembered Wise's fury when their eyes had met on four. She'd seen that same hate tonight.

Gabe spanned her waist with his hands, hauling her against him. "You're staying here."

She plucked at the pajama top. "I'm not going anywhere like this."

"I mean for a few days. Until he's locked up."

Her ego rebelled at Gabe's blunt command. Her body succumbed, too tired to argue, too wrought up to relax. He led her back to the chair. Facing him while he faced his computer, she attacked her notes with renewed determination. "Don't worry about Dr. Wise. After I present this report tomorrow, he'll be long gone."

Tomorrow came at seven-fifteen. Gabe looked out at the dirty gray clouds blanketing Chicago. Snow was on the way. Shana was still there, sleeping soundly in his bed.

He could call the hospital and tell them she'd be late. What would he tell *her*? When she woke she'd know. She'd notice the pillows, the sheets tucked around her. She'd guess.

"Fuck." The word matched his black mood. Shana wasn't the only who'd had a tough night.

She'd nodded off around four, the pad slanting on her lap, the pen rolling to the floor. Her cheek was mashed to the wing of the chair. A napping princess from one of her storybooks couldn't have looked more beautiful.

Gabe let her sleep; he had work to do. But when her

chin drooped to her chest he knew she'd object to him watching her drool. He lifted her chin. Her head tilted back so fast, it thudded against the wall. "Ouch."

She'd slept right through it.

He worked on. Every few minutes he caught himself staring at her. Watching over her gave his nights purpose they'd never had. It was as if he'd been waiting for this all his life.

An energized hum pulsed through his veins as he fired off a final bid, put the closing touches on the deal. He faxed Brice the particulars to read in the morning. It was nearly five.

Shana muttered something, sat up, grabbed the pad, and stormed into the living room. Gabe chuckled to himself. She wasn't letting a single detail get away or a question go unanswered. She was persistent, passionate. When something was important to her she didn't give up.

She wouldn't give up on them either. He knew that. The sensation had grown from a hope to a certainty. Before they'd been called to the hospital, she'd lain in his arms and said she loved him. There she was spending the night at his place, awake, yes, pacing the living room, maybe, but there. The next time it would be even easier and the time after that.

She slammed a kitchen cupboard.

"I'll show you where the cocoa is," he called. He pored over a screen full of numbers. If these people didn't like the terms of the rollover they could—

Crash.

"What are you looking for?"

Her muttered reply made no sense. Squinting at the screen, irritated by the commotion, he told Singapore to back off while he reconsidered.

He found her pulling food from the refrigerator. There wasn't much. "The milk's old. You'd better smell it first."

She didn't even see it. She was sound asleep.

"Shana?"

She walked around him, pulling out eggs, orange juice, piling everything on the counter while he stood there like a tree planted in the middle of a highway.

"I never said you had to make me breakfast," he said lightly. Not much point joking with someone who didn't even register his presence. She'd told him she sleepwalked; she'd never told him what to do about it.

"Shana, I know you didn't want me seeing this, but what do you want me to do?"

She grabbed a bottle of ketchup. Gabe put the orange juice back. The ketchup thudded on the counter. He returned it while she went for the mayo. They could play this game all night.

A strangely familiar hum started behind him. He whirled to see eggs rolling along the counter. One wobbled over the edge and slammed to the floor. He caught the second in midair.

Shana headed for the refrigerator.

"Stop!" He jerked her out of the way before her bare foot landed on the jagged shell. He asked himself whether an eggshell was that dangerous. Was it worth startling a sleepwalker? He held his breath, staring into her glazed eyes. "Shana? Are you okay?"

No reply. In a queer way her silence relieved him. Bending to pluck the shell out of the goo, he ducked a mixing bowl on his way back up. She was into the pots and pans.

"Hold on a minute while I clean this up. You could slip on this."

"I have to watch *Kojak*."

"Huh?"

"*Kojak*."

"Honey, that hasn't been on for years."

She looked him right in the eye. "It's the best show on TV."

"Believe me, I've seen every rerun there is."

"I have to watch."

He gestured toward the living room. Not much trouble she could get into there. It'd give him a chance to clean up.

Except she wasn't going. She opened a cupboard, pulling down a handful of plates.

Gabe ran interference. She got agitated when she couldn't find what she wanted. Was she confused about her new surroundings or was she always so out of it? "She's asleep, dummy."

She turned her head, listening.

He touched her arm. "*Kojak's* in here."

The perishables were put away. He could leave the rest. He gently persuaded her to the bedroom. "Did I ever tell you you look adorable in pj's? Plaid is your color."

She stopped at the foot of the bed, suspicion clouding her features. "I need a teaspoon. Where's the rug? We need a rug."

"Sounds delicious. Now lie down."

She did as he ordered.

"It's okay, babe. You're safe with me."

Light struggled through the clouds. Gabe heard her turn over. The sheets wrapped around her like a Greek statue's body-hugging drapery. He stood with his back to the window so she had to squint to make him out. Lifting her head, she craned her neck for an alarm clock. "What time is it?"

"Seven."

"I'll be late." The sheet fell to her lap as she sat up. Her pajama top was a mass of wrinkles. Bracing her arms behind her, she slumped as limp as a Raggedy Ann doll.

"You were up half the night."

"I've got to take a shower," she said with a groan. "Where're my clothes?"

"When we got the call about Hazel you threw on whatever was handy. I'll take you back to your place so you can change for work."

She combed a handful of bedraggled curls off her forehead, made eye contact with the pillow, and slithered back under the covers. "Just five more minutes."

"Sure." He turned to the window. "I'll call for the car."

"Gabe?"

One word. He didn't have to turn to pick up the tension.

"How'd I get in bed?"

His shrug had a hitch to it. His jaw was set in iron. "You slept there."

"I thought—"

"The chair looked uncomfortable. I put you there a couple hours ago."

"I didn't do anything, did I?" Most women would worry about how a man might have taken advantage of the situation. Shana acted as if she were the one who couldn't be trusted.

He picked up the telephone on his desk. The garage answered. "Fitzgerald. Have my car ready in twenty minutes. Thanks." He shuffled some files into a drawer, avoiding her silence.

"Gabe."

"You were fine."

"Then why aren't you looking at me?"

It wouldn't be easy loving a psychologist. The woman had instincts the way ants had antennae.

"I did it." She couldn't have looked more abashed if he'd told her *she'd* ordered Hazel's drug overdose. "I sleepwalked, didn't I?"

"You were fine." His voice grated like sandpaper. "You got up for a snack, that's all."

She crawled over the covers, heading straight to the door. Before he could block her, she'd run past. She stopped dead in the tiny kitchen. It was spotless. "You cleaned up," she accused him.

"I put some things away."

"How bad was it?"

Nothing to justify the ashen look on her face. "You wanted to cook; I wanted to put you to bed." He grasped her silk lapel between his fingers. "It seemed like a good idea at the time."

She slapped his hand away, seductive tones be damned. "I could have done anything."

"It wasn't bad."

"It could have been!"

"I put you to bed. It was fine." God, he hated raising his voice so early in the day. What was he yelling at her for? "You muttered a few things. None of it made sense. It doesn't matter."

"It does to me."

"Shana."

"I have to go."

"Not until we talk."

"I need to get to work. I've got to see how Hazel's doing."

"I called the hospital. She's stabilized." He followed her into the bedroom as she collected her jeans and socks. He kicked her loafers out from under the chair. "You were under stress. It's understandable."

"If stress caused it, I could accept it."

"Look at me, dammit. I'm not freaked out. I'm not upset. It was nothing."

"You don't know what it's like, going to sleep, never knowing what you might do."

"Or what I might dream?"

"At least you remember when you wake up."

Too humiliated to look him in the eyes, she unbuttoned the pajama top, her hand shaking. "Are you going to leave?" She meant while she dressed.

He refused.

She pulled on her jeans in spite of him, tugging them right over the pajamas. She tossed her baggy sweater over her head as if the plaid silk were some kind of funky chemise. "I'll return them later."

In a box, no doubt. U.S. Mail. She'd never show her face there again.

He waited until she had her shoes on. "Are *you* going to leave?" He meant him, them.

She swallowed the heart caught in her throat. "I have a lot of things to think about."

"You can't let this wreck us, Shana. There are more important things in life than sleep."

She looked resolutely unconvinced. "Remember who you're talking to."

"You've heard how sleep messed up *my* life. Why can't I help you?"

"Mine isn't curable."

"Then we'll deal with it."

She grabbed the legal pad from the corner of his desk. Gabe caught her shoulders in his grasp. "I won't give up, Shana."

She gave him the sweetest smile, pleading, heartbreaking. "That always worried me about you."

"If you're so worried, stick around."

She blinked away a sheen of tears. "I've got to go. For Hazel's sake. Wise practically murdered her right under our noses. I've got to get him out of that hospital."

"Merryweather may have already seen to it. I'm talking about us."

"We'll talk."

He didn't like the sound of that. But with Hazel's life hanging in the balance, he couldn't very well hold Shana prisoner until they'd settled things. Every instinct told him not to let her go.

He tucked her hair behind her ear, gently brushing her damp lashes with the back of his finger. "Why do I get the feeling I won't see you again?"

She swished her hair over her shoulder. The sassy tilt of her head fooled no one. "You're driving me home, remember? I'll be fine. I'll let you know when they've arrested Wise."

A warning pealed deep in his mind, a faint alarm he

knew he should heed. He dismissed it as paranoia. If she was in any danger, he'd have dreamed it.

He was putting a helluva lot of faith in something he'd spent years avoiding.

She kissed him, a hit-and-run peck on the cheek. "I'll call you from the hospital."

22

Shana put the finishing touches on her report. Her typewriter clattered with machine-gun speed. Her nerves jangled like the spare change in a hobo's pocket.

On the hour drive from Evanston to the hospital she'd reviewed all the facts. Pulling into the garage, she'd asked for a security escort to accompany her to her office. Gabe had insisted on it.

Gabe. She knew her humiliating demonstration would have to be faced sooner or later. She'd never expected sooner. She should have never told him she loved him. Although that sweet memory seemed like a century ago, it would make it harder for him to let her go.

He had to. She'd make him see that. Some night she'd fall asleep in his arms and lash out, kicking and punching until he pushed her away. No matter how sure she was of her course of action, her heart longed to put up the same fight. It conjured up Gabe's tense face when he'd dropped her off at her apartment, repeating his words. *"We can work this out. If you can accept my problems, why can't you accept yours?"*

She couldn't think about it now. Life-and-death issues required her full attention. For a few more hours she could pretend it wasn't over.

She pulled the paper from the typewriter. It made a ripping, ratcheting sound like something tearing inside her. She reached for the intercom. "Fiona, will you check on a patient for me? A Hazel Doe, admitted to emergency around one A.M."

She listened to the click of computer keys. The memory of Gabe's computer clicking softly in the night came back to her. She shut her eyes against the pain.

"She isn't listed," Fiona replied.

"They may have discovered her real name by now. Check for any patient admitted to intensive care, coma, barbiturate overdose."

"Intensive care," Fiona repeated.

Or the morgue, Shana thought.

Her mouth went dry. What if he'd killed her? While Shana and Gabe had stood ten feet away, he'd had a nurse administer an overdose. What was to stop him sneaking into intensive care and finishing the job?

Merryweather had said he'd take care of it. Then he'd gone into that office with Payne and shut the door. What happened after that was anyone's guess.

"Fiona, was anyone arrested here last night?"

"Not that I heard of. Wait a minute." Her disembodied voice carried over the intercom. "She's been released."

"She's what? The woman was in a coma."

"Says here she was transferred to a private clinic, north side. That's not so unusual."

Shana agreed. After his accident Brice Grier had requested transfer to a hospital closer to his home. "But who requested it?"

"This is interesting."

"What?"

"Merryweather did. He's listed as primary physician. Hmm. Good God, don't scare me like that!"

Shana had fled her office and raced down the hall. She leaned over Fiona's shoulder to see for herself.

"I could have told you over the phone," Fiona muttered.

"He knows. He knows who Hazel's husband is. He'd need the permission of a relative to send her anywhere else."

Fiona shrugged. "What's the deal?"

She slapped the desktop. "Why isn't he telling me?"

"I'm kind of in the dark too."

Shana set a hand on her shoulder. "No time. Thanks for staying."

Fiona swiveled her chair in a half circle, her knees bumping Shana's. "You don't think I'm missing this, do you?"

Their eyes locked. "Okay. Pull up Hazel's file."

Fiona led them through screen after screen, using the clinic's access code. "She has no file."

"Merryweather must keep it in his office." Shana knew the file cabinet. In the top drawer he kept canisters of special pipe tobacco. She'd teased him about locking up his precious reserve. Maybe he locked it for other reasons, such as preventing access to patient files he didn't want seen. "I'm going down there."

"Shana. When did you get in?" Merryweather looked surprised.

Dr. Payne's smile stretched thin as a razor cut. "Shana. I thought that was your typewriter I heard."

"I haven't finished speaking with Dr. Payne." Merryweather sighed. "If you could wait outside please."

She wasn't about to. She took two steps into the room, her legs quaking, her report shaking like a leaf in her hand. "Hazel's gone. Transferred. What do you know about that, Michael?"

Standing behind the barricade of his desk, he leaned forward, splaying his fingers across a slew of patient forms.

"You sent her to a clinic," she accused.

"Her husband requested it."

"Who is he?"

He shoveled the papers into a folder. Hazel's, she suspected. "Who is he?" she repeated.

"That's confidential."

"Also irrelevant," Payne said. He stood by the window, his skin paler than ever in the white winter light.

Shana shot him a look that would have made anyone else pause. "It's not irrelevant if her husband's been giving her sleeping pills."

"There's no proof of that," Payne responded.

She turned on Merryweather. "You're protecting him."

A sickly smile crossed his boyish face. "Dr. Payne is perfectly capable of taking care of himself."

"I meant Hazel's husband. He's been forcing sleeping pills on her, and you know it."

Merryweather didn't deny it. "As Payne said, we can't prove anything."

"Because of who he is, you won't reveal his identity. You've let him move her somewhere, somewhere he'll have control over her, somewhere they won't believe her stories either."

"I didn't know. I thought it could very well be dementia. Women of a certain age, no children, marriages gone stale—they often have trouble sleeping."

"Who is he, Michael?"

He stared at the paperwork, his eyes darting briefly toward Payne's perfectly shined shoes. "I can't say."

Shana knew he would have confided in her if Payne hadn't stood there watching over them.

Their committee chairman confirmed her suspicion. "Revealing a patient's identity to satisfy a colleague's curiosity would be a serious breach of confidentiality. Dr. Merryweather knows he'd get in a world of trouble breaking that faith."

Merryweather snatched a pipe from his pipe stand, gripping it as if he wished it were someone's throat.

"As long as we're clear on that issue," Payne murmured. He smiled at Shana. "Did you have anything else?"

"Yes." It was clear to her Michael had succumbed to political pressure to shield Hazel's husband. He'd never hidden the fact he'd do just about anything to keep his clinic going. But this—

She absorbed the disappointment like a blow. He'd been good to her, hiring her from Arizona, supporting her innovations, advising her to be less impulsive, less aggressive. She no longer knew what to expect from him.

Either way, she wouldn't fold before Payne. She'd left her glasses in her office. Lifting the single-spaced page closer, she read in a firm voice until she reached her conclusion:

"I believe Paul Wise tried to murder the patient known as Hazel Doe. I saw him sell her drugs on four. He ordered the sedative that put her into a coma. I believe the latter was not an honest mistake by a sleep-deprived intern, but a deliberate attempt to silence someone who might reveal his illegal activities."

Payne clapped. His hands made the damp sound of a seal's fins flapping. "She's got quite an imagination, hasn't she?" He strolled over, taking the paper from her hand. Idly scanning it, he frowned at every typo. "You should consider a career in writing, my dear. It's apparent you'll never be a secretary."

She snatched it back. "Michael?"

Payne turned, his hands in the pockets of his camel suit. "Dr. Merryweather?"

Michael nodded, sinking heavily into his chair.

Payne pushed the button on the intercom. "Send him in."

Shana stared at her mentor. Defeated, crushed, he propped his elbow on the chair arm, supporting his bent head with two fingers. "Just because you knew Wise doesn't mean you're responsible," she said.

Payne opened the door. "Come in."

Paul Wise stepped inside. Wiry, weaselly, the intern had done his pitiful best to look presentable. His stained lab coat was gone. In its place he wore a cheap-looking dog-eared sweater over a frayed white shirt collar. The long night weighed on him even more heavily than it had on her. The bags under his eyes were purplish-brown. His beady eyes matched the black stripes in his sweater.

Her attention diverted, Payne seized the report from her hand. "This young woman claims you sold drugs in this hospital."

"Never," Wise declared. "She's not gonna get me."

"I saw him," she said evenly.

"According to your own report," Payne interrupted, "you saw him hand a deeply disturbed woman a bottle of pills. You make no mention of money changing hands."

"They didn't have time."

"Michael?"

Merryweather flinched. The hateful stare he directed at Payne seemed to have more to do with the use of his first name than the patronizing tone. Deliberately modulating his expression, Merryweather's voice was almost numb. "There was no money involved, Shana. The drugs were legally prescribed."

"How can what he did be legal?"

"I'm not taking the fall for anybody," Wise said. "I was told—"

Merryweather cut him off with a look. "I prescribed them."

Shana stared at him.

"Hazel was my patient. She came to me, privately, regarding excessive sleepiness. She asked for something to help her stay awake."

"But you hate prescribing pills."

"I thought—" His lanky frame seemed to bend inward. "It's my fault. I thought, because of who she was, that we could get on her husband's good side if we helped her."

She darted a glance at Wise. "So what was he doing on four?"

"You know how skittish Hazel was about coming to the clinic. I asked Paul to meet with her. I couldn't be skulking all over the place."

"But he could?"

Merryweather met her eye. "There was nothing illegal, Shana. I prescribed diet pills to keep her alert—"

"And what about the sleeping pills?" Her voice rose. She flattened her palms on his desk as if to physically hold it down. "Did you give her those too?"

Ashamed, Merryweather looked away.

"Michael? Answer her."

He jerked when Payne spoke, as if a string had been pulled. "Her husband must have his own prescription. That could be perfectly legal too," he answered.

"Unless her forced her to take them," Shana said.

"We have no proof of that."

"We have a drug screen. Were barbiturates in her system?"

"She could have taken his pills without his knowledge. Spouses do that sometimes. They think what's good for the husband is good for the . . ." His voice trailed off. He didn't even bother to finish.

"Bullshit," Shana concluded for him.

Merryweather actually smiled. "I didn't think you'd buy that."

"So this is all *her* fault," Shana declared hotly. "Hazel takes her dear, sweet, innocent, but immensely important husband's sleeping pills, gets dependent, then comes to you for uppers to fight off the aftereffects. Diet pills. Which, of course, you were happy to supply."

"Not happy. Believe me, Shana."

"What about Wise?"

Nearly asleep on his feet, the intern swayed and snapped to attention when he heard his name. "I did what I was told. Why do I have to put up with this shit? My shift's over."

Merryweather ignored him, his gaze asking Shana to understand. "He delivered a prescription."

"He gave her an overdose that could have killed her!"

"It was an honest mistake," Payne said.

Shana whirled at the sound of that snake-oil voice. "I knew somebody would say that sooner or later."

Merryweather tossed his pipe on his desk in disgust. He rubbed his forehead. "Let it go, Shana."

She turned from him to Payne to the cringing Wise. "Honest mistakes? There isn't an honest thing going on here. If it's the last thing I do, I'm getting to the bottom of this."

"You have your wish," Payne replied. "It will be the last thing you do. I'm suspending you indefinitely."

She stepped back. "You can't do that."

"Your personal ethical conduct concerning a patient named Fitzgerald has been highly questionable to say the least. You came straight from his bed to answer an emergency call. Don't bother denying it, my dear, your cheeks had that lovely postcoital flush. I also believe there was a small bite on the side of your neck."

Shana's stomach lurched. Payne idly scratched the side of his neck. She kept her hands locked at her sides. "Gabriel Fitzgerald is no longer a patient at this clinic."

"In the nick of time, I'm sure."

"Let's stick to the subject here. Hazel Doe—"

"—was another physician's patient. You were out of line treating her, or failing to do so, without consulting Dr. Merryweather."

"He never told me he was seeing her."

"Nevertheless. By giving her ramblings credence you hurt her case considerably. The woman is sick, something you also failed to recognize. As a matter of fact, her behavior has been so erratic, her family is considering having her institutionalized."

"No." Merryweather stood, his face livid.

Payne deferred to him. "It's a possibility, that's all. I spoke to them myself this morning, after the transfer."

"I'm sure you did." Merryweather sat back down.

Payne paced between Shana and Wise, his pudgy hands clasped behind his back. "On a graver-note 'Doctor' Getz, you've leveled wild, inaccurate, and slanderous accusations against this fine young doctor. Drug-dealing," he said with a sneer. "Attempted murder."

"He ordered a sedative that almost killed a patient."

"A patient in dire need of sedation. She bit one orderly and assaulted two others. What would you have done? Sympathized? Listened?"

Everything she was sure of was coming apart, perspectives shifting in fun-house mirrors. Shana clung to her facts. "Paul Wise is severely sleep-deprived. Look at him. If we checked the records, we could probably find other incidents of mistakes he's made."

"Now who's getting off the subject?"

"He forgot to send Hazel's blood to the lab."

"Forgetting is not a crime."

"It is when the entire diagnosis waits on it. He chose to act despite the fact a sleep expert was on hand to advise him."

"Now she's an expert." Payne sniffed.

"You are." She pleaded with Merryweather. "You were there last night, Michael. Wise could hardly function. He was abusive, short-tempered, stressed out, completely inflexible. His mistakes weren't 'honest,' they were almost predictable!"

"Stop right there," Payne commanded. He crossed the room and set a hand on Wise's shoulder.

Smoldering gaze fixed on Shana, the young man flinched in surprise.

"It's well past the end of your shift, isn't it, Paul?"

"Two hours." He slurred the words. Hate and defensiveness were the only things keeping him going. "I could have been home by now if it weren't for this bitch—"

"That's enough of that," Payne murmured. He resumed pacing before Merryweather's desk like a prosecuting attorney, his hands clasped behind him. The gesture pulled his suit coat taut across his round body. He suddenly absurdly resembled Roly Poly, Pascewski's Fresh Kid.

Shana held back an hysterical laugh. She was bone-tired, her nerves frayed to the breaking point. This was a nightmare. No matter what she said, they had their answers ready. Her entire case was crumbling.

Payne picked her report off Merryweather's desk and ripped it to pieces. He sprinkled the white squares in the waste basket. Inviting a reaction, his sandy-colored brows rose on his egg-shaped head.

For a moment Shana got the creepy, crazy feeling they'd continue to slide all the way up his head like furry caterpillars.

"Having failed to convince anyone of your groundless drug charges against Dr. Wise, you're suggesting negligent behavior that could be grounds for the kind of lawsuit that could cripple this hospital. You're a loose cannon, my dear."

"I'm right."

He snorted. "It would be the first time today. I'll allow for the fact you've been under considerable stress: meddling in every department of this hospital, poaching one of Dr. Merryweather's patients. *You* misdiagnosed Hazel Doe. *You* failed to get her in for treatment. Unable to lay the blame on Wise, you're now accusing the hospital itself for your failures."

She turned to Merryweather. The room spun. "Michael?"

Payne held up a hand so white, it looked as if he powdered it with talc. "Nothing you've said so far has held up to reasonable scrutiny. Why should we listen to anything else you have to say? You may go."

"Michael?"

Merryweather stared bleakly at her.

Payne strolled importantly to the door. "Thank you for joining us, Dr. Wise."

The intern escaped, slamming his shoulder into the doorjamb in his hurry to get out of there.

"Get some sleep," Payne murmured. "You, too, Ms. Getz. You can catch up during your suspension."

She didn't budge. "I am not going to accept this."

"You have no choice. You're incompetent *and* sleep-deprived. Up and about at all hours of the night doing heaven knows what."

Like sleepwalking? Her stricken look helped confirm his suspicions. He walked out of the office.

Shana lowered herself into a chair, her legs so weak they wouldn't hold her any longer. "Why do I feel as if I've been hit by a train?"

"I'll talk to him," Merryweather said. Relieved at finding them alone, he reverted to the Michael she knew. "You got a little carried away there."

"With what? Being right?"

"Isn't that what usually gets you in trouble?"

"What about Hazel? What on earth were you doing prescribing for her? She was a mess."

He looked down, pulling open drawer after drawer. "I thought I could help."

"With more pills?"

"Here." He handed her a brochure. "Take this."

"The National Sleep Disorders Convention? What do I want with this?"

"It's in Hawaii. You'd have to go by Friday. Take a week. Give things a chance to simmer down here. By the time you get back I'll have your suspension reduced. It's all I can do."

"What about Hazel?"

"She'll be taken care of."

"In a clinic her husband's confined her to?"

"We can't determine what he's done until she's weaned off the drugs. When she can give us a coherent, credible account, then we can proceed against him. All of this will take time."

"And if the clinic treats her with more drugs?"

"Not all psychiatrists love prescribing." Merryweather

gave her another weak smile. "Don't worry, I can handle Payne."

For a moment she thought he meant physical pain. Maybe she was losing it. She should have waited before leveling her charges. She'd been impulsive, rash, her usual bull-dog, think-later self. And she'd gotten no support whatsoever from Merryweather. "I expected you to back me up."

"I'm sorry. I—I've made some mistakes here."

She rose to leave. He wasn't the only one.

"Shana? You weren't entirely wrong." He said it more to the bowl of his pipe than to her.

"If you believe that, you're more tired than I am."

"Maybe I am," he murmured as she closed his office door behind her. "Maybe I am."

She'd lost on every count. Every charge, every accusation had been parried, deflected, and ultimately dismissed by Payne. She'd been completely wrong about what she'd seen on four. How many other mistakes had she made, things she'd been sure of?

Like Gabe.

No, he hadn't done anything wrong. Unfortunately, she hadn't done anything right in so long, she wasn't sure of her instincts anymore. Her judgment couldn't be trusted.

Feeling like a fool for requesting a security escort in the middle of the day, she hung up her office telephone. She headed down the hall past Merryweather's closed door. Another failure. Obviously she'd miscalculated the depths to which he'd sink to save the clinic. Giving pills to the strung-out wife of a benefactor—

She shook her head. She didn't want to think. She found herself in the maternity ward, her hand on the large glass window.

"Shana. What are you doing here?"

"Can I hold one, Marilyn?" The abandoned preemies,

the children they didn't display to onlookers, were the only people in more pain than she was. If she could help one person, tiny and helpless—

"Sure you can," the head nurse replied. She surreptitiously glanced at her watch. Lunch hour wasn't even close.

"I know this is unusual."

"No problem. I'll get you a gown."

Defeat took the form of exhaustion, its waves rolling through her. She wanted to rest her cheek to the glass, to let the tears slide free, scalding and cleansing.

"May I ask what you're doing here?" Dr. Payne intoned.

Commanding one vertebrae at a time, she straightened her shoulders. Payne didn't frighten her anymore. She hated him for everything his hidebound, power-hungry view of hospital management had driven Michael Merryweather to do, what his shortsightedness had done to untold patients.

"Do you leave in this direction?" he asked.

"I volunteer here." She wanted to calm a child, to do one thing before she left that couldn't be misinterpreted by this man, twisted around.

"I'm afraid not," Payne replied mildly.

"What do you mean?"

"You're suspended."

"You can't suspend me from volunteer work."

"I can bar you from this unit. You'll leave now, unless you want me to call security."

"I already have." She would have brushed by him but the idea of getting close to his body repulsed her.

Payne accompanied her to the elevator.

"I can manage," she said tightly. She hated these ridiculous tears welling behind her eyes. She wanted out before Marilyn returned. She couldn't bear anyone seeing her humiliation, especially the nurse who'd taken her theories to heart, who'd respected her insights.

She closed her eyes and thought of Gabe. The first time he'd kissed her it had been outside these elevators.

Payne had been there too.

Bing.

She looked up, swaying slightly.

Payne steadied her, his hand on her arm. She tried taking it back. He held on until the doors opened. She had the nauseating fear he was going to board with her.

Instead he held the door open until she'd stepped on. He reached into his pocket. "If your lover has been keeping you up nights, might I suggest one of these?" He pressed a pill in her hand.

She stared down at it, too stunned to register anything but the brand name. Klonopin had never worked for her, although it was the first drug of choice for most parasomniacs. She almost said as much.

Then it struck her. How did he know she walked in her sleep?

The doors began to close. Her head jerked up.

Payne smiled as if reading her thoughts. "Dr. Merryweather and I are very close."

Staring at the closed doors as the floor dropped beneath her feet, Shana found herself dragging in breath. It hadn't happened. She must have dreamed it in a microsleep. Payne wouldn't dare hand her a sleeping pill.

The elevator shuddered to a halt. The doors opened on the basement linking Building C to the parking structure. Shana opened her clenched fist. The yellow capsule sat there, innocuous as a vitamin, evil as arsenic.

Bile surged through her. Her first instinct was to storm back to Merryweather's office. She'd accuse Payne of—of what? There was no proof. No witnesses. He'd claim she was turning her wild accusations against him now.

A security guard trotted toward her from the booth. "Are you the one who wanted an escort? I thought you were coming down from D."

"I have to get home." She practically ran up the slanting ramp.

The guard, a brush-cut former policeman with a pot-belly, tried to keep up. By the time they reached the third level, he pulled off his cap and wiped his forehead with a handkerchief. "You sure your car's up here? People make mistakes all the time."

Her recent life had been one big mistake. "There it is." She pointed to the end of the next row, the pill still clutched in her hand. She flung it away.

As they turned the corner, the guard veered to her right. "Excuse me a minute." He tapped on the window of a rusty Volvo with a smashed taillight. "Hey, buddy."

A man slept in the front seat, his head thrown back against the headrest, his mouth open. "Huh?" He started awake. Automatically lurching forward, he turned the key in the ignition. The roar of the engine helped him get his bearings. He glanced outside the car and caught sight of Shana.

"Wise."

His mouth twisted in fury. "Why don't you get off my back?" He rammed the car into gear and floored the gas pedal. Shana jumped out of the way as he swung into the lane.

"Hey, look out," the guard shouted.

The car peeled away.

"Idiot," he muttered under his breath. "One of them interns. Think they're hot sh—stuff."

Shana unlocked her car door, getting the quaking key in on the third try. "Thanks."

"You have a safe drive."

She had to get home. She wanted to lock her doors, hug her cat, close the blinds, crawl into bed, and sleep for a hundred years.

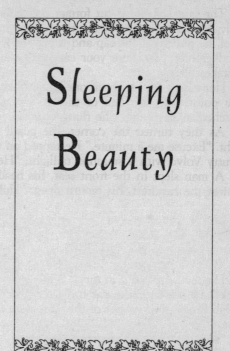

BOOK FOUR

Sleeping
Beauty

23

Gabe pounded on the door. Another minute and he'd break it down. Where was she? "Shana! Shana, answer me!"

He was frantic, furious. Fiona had told him Shana was at home. "On leave," she'd said. What kind of bullshit was that? Why hadn't she returned his calls? How did he know she hadn't been killed? If that intern was capable of poisoning one patient to hide his crimes, what would stop him from silencing Shana?

Calculating how hard to hit the door with his shoulder and from what angle, he shouted one more time. "Shana!"

The deadbolt slid back. The chain rattled. She peered out.

"What the hell is going on? Where have you been?"

"Sleeping."

"For two days? What the hell is going on?"

"I'm going to Hawaii."

"What?" He was sure her withdrawal had more to do with them than any crisis at work. He had a hundred arguments ready, all about her sleepwalking, how they could work it out, why she couldn't give up on them. He'd never expected Hawaii.

He stalked into her apartment, automatically scooping up the cat before Romper slithered through the door and escaped down the hall. "What's Hawaii got to do with anything?"

"You have to ask? It's two below zero outside." She turned her back on him, shuffling toward the sofa.

Gabe tossed Romper onto the nearest chair. He noted the pillows littering the couch, the half-empty mugs of cocoa and tea on the coffee table. Her ancient terry-cloth robe looked lived in.

Sinking onto the sofa, she balanced her elbows on her knees and held her hair back with both hands. The woman had been dragged through a wringer.

Gabe hauled himself through a similar gauntlet. He should have come sooner. The fact that she hadn't called hardly mattered. She looked like hell.

All right, he should be sympathetic, understanding, nice. Every fear he'd imagined had proven false; that didn't mean he knew what was going on. He raked a hand through his hair. All his one-sided arguments careened through his head. He was too wound up to play girlfriend. "This can't be because you slept at my place."

"I sleep*walked* at your place, remember?"

"I don't care. I told you that. There are worse things a person can do."

"Like swearing she saw a drug deal when it was nothing of the kind? Accusing interns of murder when they're just doing their jobs?"

Gabe snorted. "That guy was a mess and you know it. He called you a fucking bitch."

"I've been called worse." Payne had implied she was unfit to hold babies. Marilyn must have thought so too. When she'd gone to get Shana's gown she must have called him. How else would he have known she was there?

Shana crossed her arms over her middle, rocking

softly. She didn't know who to trust anymore. Even Merryweather had betrayed her. He'd told Payne about her sleepwalking. How could he?

How could she? She'd betrayed herself when she'd broken her promise never to sleep with Gabe. "You'd better go."

"Fat chance."

"I've got to pack."

"So you can run farther away?"

She stayed rooted to the sofa.

"What the hell is going on, Shana?"

"I've been thinking for two days and I still don't know. Somehow everything I thought I knew was wrong."

"Is Wise in jail?"

"For what? Playing delivery boy?"

"What about Hazel?"

"Gone. Transferred to another facility."

"This isn't making sense. I'm calling for pizza."

She managed a startled laugh. "What?"

For the first time in days Gabe felt the band of tension ease around his chest. He'd gotten through that dazed look in her eyes. "You don't need sleep. You might need a bath. You definitely need food." He sneered at the stack of frozen diet dinners in her freezer. Just as he thought. He punched in the number for the closest pizza company. "You want peppers on that?"

"I think you need to relax," she said from the living room.

He thumped the directory back onto its shelf. He loved her, dammit. Relaxation didn't enter into it.

Bits and pieces of the story emerged as they consumed the pizza. Gabe could tell she'd gone over the same territory time and again, obsessing over details, replaying scenes in her mind. Lighting on one incident, she'd delve into its implications before darting to another mystifying betrayal, another horrible miscalculation.

"Next thing I know, I'm out. Just like that."

"I don't see how Payne can suspend you."

"He can if Merryweather refuses to intervene."

"He said he'd get it reduced. Think he will?"

She lowered her gaze to the coffee table. "What if I've been wrong about everything? How do I know this is right?" She meant them.

Crumpling a napkin in his fist, Gabe had no instant answers.

Shana took his silence for one. Gathering her robe at the throat, she patted her hair, collecting the old mugs in the crook of her arm. "Goodness, I've wasted so much time. I have to pack. They sent the ticket over yesterday. I'm not usually so disorganized."

"Shana." His concern came a minute too late.

"Hawaii," she insisted, her voice resolutely cheerful as she shuffled toward the kitchen. "I really have to try that convention. Maybe I'll learn something. God knows I could use it. I couldn't help Hazel, I couldn't even get her to come in. I couldn't help you."

"You helped me."

"I'm a loose cannon all of a sudden. Even the babies are in danger when I'm around. He wouldn't even let me hold them."

The mugs thudded onto the counter. Tears rolled down her cheeks, her hand clamped to her mouth to stifle the sob.

Gabe dragged her into his arms. "It's okay."

She buried her face against his chest. It felt as if ice floes were breaking to pieces inside her. "He wouldn't even let me hold them."

"It's not your fault."

"I had it all wrong. Everything. I'm sorry. I'm so sorry." She owed the whole world an apology, for her pride and thoughtlessness, for rushing in where anyone else would think twice. For the babies. For Gabe, whom she loved more than all the world and whom she'd have to let go.

He drove her to the airport then insisted on parking instead of dropping her off. She didn't have the energy to argue. Lately she'd lost every argument she started.

"You don't have to wait," she said, for form's sake.

He scowled and carried her bags inside the terminal. Eyes forward, he stood in line. Completely impassive, he escorted her to the gate. He picked a wrinkled sports page off the black plastic seat and took a place beside her.

"Thanks for seeing me off."

He nodded curtly.

"You can leave now. I won't mind."

"I'm not going anywhere."

"Gabe."

"What?"

She darted a look at an eavesdropping woman who quickly buried her nose in her paperback. "You're getting stubborn," she murmured.

"Getting? Baby, I've been stubborn all my life." He'd defied time itself, fighting off sunrises and sunsets, naming the hours his body would rest.

She should have known. Just as she'd known their relationship would end sooner or later. He'd fought her on the sooner part back at her apartment. Three hours later, he still wasn't buying.

She set her hand on his arm. "Please," she whispered. "This is hard enough."

"You think I want your leaving me to be easy?"

"I need to get away. I need to find out why I went so overboard."

"You made a simple mistake on four. Anybody would have jumped to that conclusion."

"And all the others? Deliberate misdiagnosis? Attempted murder? I'm not saying it's permanent, Gabe. We can see each other when I get back. We can talk about us."

She'd be telling him they'd always be friends next. "So I shouldn't think of this as a breakup, just a suspension."

She winced.

He was being a son of a bitch. So what? He wasn't good at begging. It was usually the women in his life who begged to be let in, to be given a chance.

A staticky announcement brought people to their feet. Shana searched through her bulging briefcase for her boarding pass.

Gabe rubbed his eyes. The familiar itch of sleeplessness gathered there. A headache wound around the back of his skull like piano wire. "While you're in Hawaii thinking, do you plan to think about what you said the other night?"

"No."

He shot her a look. "So that's it?"

She touched his hand. "I know I love you, Gabe. That's one thing I'm sure of."

He gripped her fingers until he was afraid he'd hurt her. "Be sure of *me*, dammit. Us. I love you."

"I know. I'm just not sure there's anything we can do about it."

He dropped her hand. He wanted to pace up and down before the row of chairs, spitting out orders, laying down rules. *This is the deal. These are the terms.*

He drew in his heels before the old lady with the luggage tote rolled it right over his legs. "If I can live with my dreams, you can live with your sleepwalking."

"It isn't curable. I'm sorry."

"Stop apologizing, dammit."

"I'm sorry I can't be what you want me to be. I can't take drugs to make me 'normal.'"

"I never asked you to be perfect."

"I don't want perfect. I want to sleep like everyone else. To curl up next to you at night and not worry that I'll lash out, that I'll hurt you."

"And what you're doing now doesn't hurt?"

She bowed her head.

Gabe glared at the passengers meekly lining up along the wall. They were boarding the last rows. Her section would come up soon. No use waiting. Her mind was made up.

"I'll see you when I get back," she said, straining for some sort of compromise.

"Aloha." In Hawaiian it meant "hello" *and* "good-bye." He strode off without looking back.

Shana stood. Joining the line, she hoisted a shoulder bag that felt loaded with lead. She didn't cry. She didn't think. She just hurt.

He'd disappeared into the crowd so fast. He always did walk fast, the runner in him eating up the distance, the insomniac getting there and getting out before his energy deserted him.

She was the one who'd deserted him; her courage had failed. Maybe it had all been a dream. In her dreams she took risks, loved him without reservation. Maybe it was time she woke up.

Readjusting the strap on her shoulder, she slid her palm along it. Shame scurried through her like a mouse pattering across cold cement. She'd wanted to take that pill Payne had handed her so badly, she'd flung it across the garage. She remembered the sound it made when it hit the floor, drowned out by the roar of Wise's car engine. He'd nearly knocked her down.

She'd forgotten to tell Gabe that part. She drew a breath to speak. He was gone.

The breath shuddered out of her as she stared ahead. For a moment she wondered if Wise and the car had really happened. Maybe she'd dreamed that too. She'd seen so many faces in her dreams in the last forty-eight hours.

"Las Vegas?" a woman behind her asked.

"Hawaii."

"Lucky you."

Not really. She handed her ticket to the agent.

"I'm sorry, ma'am, but this plane doesn't leave for another forty-five minutes. This is Las Vegas, Flight 291. You want the Los Angeles, 315. It'll be up next."

"Oh, of course. I'm sorry." She sat back down. One by one people clustered in the doorway and said good-bye to their loved ones.

He wasn't coming back. Gabe wasn't going to come running out of that stream of people and pull her into his arms. Life didn't happen that way.

She needed time. Time away, time to put things in perspective. Time had healed her when Stephen left. It had healed her when David left. Men she'd trusted, men she'd thought she loved. None of them were Gabe.

That's because they hadn't had his problems, she thought reasonably. They didn't know what dreading sleep was like. They'd expected her to get better. Gabe accepted her the way she was.

People moved by on the concourse. Ideas flowed through her mind like a stream curling around stones, bubbling up, slinking away, returning in eddies, and pooling in cool, clear depths.

She'd never feared losing Gabe. She'd feared being rejected by him. The way she'd been rejected by Stephen. By David.

But Gabe was different. Determined, stubborn, hard as a rock, he'd never lost the ability to adapt. He'd adjusted to one tragedy after another. He'd stretched his sleep to the breaking point fighting his dreams.

Was that a man who flipped out over some thrashing in bed?

"I can't change," she said to herself.

He'd never asked her to.

Probably because he loved her, her conscience replied cynically. He treated her parasomnia as a quirk, not a personal failure.

Wasn't that what it was?

"You're a sleep therapist," she declared out loud.

People glanced over the tops of their newspapers.

She didn't care. The realization gripped her so strongly, she wanted to shout it. She wanted to lecture everyone there, herself first and foremost: sleep disorders were *not* shameful!

She'd told her patients that a thousand times. Had she listened? The idea of Merryweather betraying her secret to Payne had nearly crushed her. Why? Because it was shameful? Why was it even a secret? Confidentiality mattered, yes, but her "flaw" made her the specialist she was.

She clasped her briefcase to her chest, shoving her purse under her arm. Gabe had headed for the main terminal minutes earlier. If she caught up with him, she could tell him. If not, she'd call him from the plane. She loved him. They *could* work this out.

If he'd take her back. Gabriel Fitzgerald was one stubborn man.

She was more stubborn, especially when she believed in something heart and soul.

Gabe stared at the planes taking off. Lights drifted to earth like falling stars, comets burning out. Flares of blue, red, and yellow lined the runway. He peered across the field, picturing a small bonfire, people yelling, crowding the windows to see.

The hallway was nearly empty. A moving sidewalk hummed behind him. Instead of watching planes from the thirty-fifth floor of a penthouse apartment, he watched them from ground level inside the airport. He could have been nine all over again.

He'd said everything he could say, done everything he could. He hadn't prevented his parent's crash; he couldn't talk Shana out of leaving. With his parents he'd known what the outcome would be. He didn't this time. He was left twisting in the wind, wondering if she'd fly off and never come back.

He braced his outstretched arm against the window, the side of his fist creating a misty outline on the pane.

He wasn't normally a morbid man, but after worrying
about her for two days . . .

No way. She couldn't crash. He'd have seen it. He'd
have been warned.

He laughed, an ugly guttural sound that caused the
man next to him to edge away. Who'd have ever thought
he'd long for another dream, just a glimpse of how things
would end?

There was only one way to find out what the future
would bring; live it. Stay close to her. Never let her go. If
she was going to fly away, he had to be on that plane.

He had a talent for pulling strings. It had served him
well in the days when he was too tired, too grouchy, and
too damn stressed out to put up with lines and ticket
counters. He got his boarding pass by dropping one name
and writing down a private phone number. He watched
the ticket agent's eyes widen when she dialed it. "Yes, sir,"
she said.

Gabe was in.

He grabbed the ticket and ran for Gate B. He raced
past a courtesy cart with its flashing yellow light, a jani-
tor's mop handle, a two-year-old restrained by a harness
and leash who nevertheless toddled directly into Gabe's
path. "Shana!" he shouted.

He missed the kid. He nearly missed her. He'd been
focusing on the signs, the number of gates between him
and B-5. She'd been hurrying in the other direction, just
another traveler bustling toward her destination.

Her destination was him. He knew it the minute he
saw her eyes light up.

"Gabe." She dropped her purse, her briefcase, the un-
read magazine tucked under her arm. It wasn't easy keeping things pinned under one's arms while flinging them
around someone's neck.

Gabe crushed her to him. "You're not going anywhere."

"I'm going to Hawaii," she said between breaths. "I have to."

"So do I."

She pulled back, her mouth inches from his, her eyes the same wide brown caramel he remembered from that first time he'd seen her. This time they sparkled with happy tears.

"But you have work," she said.

"I'll be four hours closer to it. They've got computers in Hawaii." He angled his body even closer to hers, kicking the briefcase out of the way. "I want to be with you. I can't stand here and watch your plane go, not knowing what could happen—"

"Oh, Gabe. I'm sorry. I never realized. Your parents. I should have never let you bring me here."

"That isn't it," he insisted. "I don't want to lose you. Walk in your sleep, dammit. Talk, fly, turn into a werewolf, see if I care."

She blinked rapidly, a tear trickling between her freckles. "Hard to believe the most romantic thing anyone ever said to me is 'see if I care.'"

"I don't care. Not about sleepwalking, not about kicking. I want *you*, dammit. I love you."

"You're going to make me cry."

"You already are."

"Am I? Oh, gosh." She wiped her nose on the back of her hand. With a guilty glance, she reached inside his suit coat and snatched the handkerchief from his breast pocket. She waved it at him when she'd finished blowing her nose. "Nobody uses these anymore. You're very old-fashioned, you know that?"

"I suppose that's why I want you to marry me."

Her eyes dried right up. "You what?"

"Think about it. We've got the whole week in Hawaii."

"I, uh, already had a pretty full itinerary of things to think about."

"Then say yes and get it out of the way."

She stuffed his handkerchief back in his pocket. She wriggled out of his embrace. In her haste to stand on her own two feet she kicked her briefcase halfway across the hall. "That's the second most romantic thing anyone's said to me."

"I can think of better. Give me time."

"Time" seemed to be the magic word. He was asking for it, offering it. He wanted to spend all the time they had left together. "Marry me."

She bent to retrieve her briefcase, her purse rammed once more under her arm. "Get on the plane and we'll talk."

He held her hand the whole way. It was the only way to make up for his clumsy proposal. During the takeoff, the emergency demonstration, the in-flight snack, he held her hand. If the plane crashed, they'd go down together.

"Are you always so tense when you fly?" she asked.

"Are you always so tense when a man asks you to marry him?"

"I need my hand back."

"I asked for it."

"I want to unwrap these crackers."

"You're worried about crackers?"

"I'm worried about losing all feeling in my fingers. Let go."

"Never."

"I know that's meant to be a declaration of eternal devotion but—"

"But nothing. I mean what I say. I don't give up when something's important to me. As it stands, I haven't let too many things become important, mostly for fear of losing them. Correct that, for fear of watching them go. I won't stand by and watch you go."

"That'd be a little hard to do at thirty thousand feet." She suddenly drew in a sharp breath. "You're not saying you dreamed we'd cra—"

"No. I haven't dreamed anything in weeks. I don't know what's going to happen. I just want to be there when it does."

The attendant leaned over their first-class seats. Gabe's upgrade ensured they sat together. "Would you prefer red wine or white with your meal?"

"We'd prefer some privacy," he snapped out.

Shana had enough feeling in her hand to squeeze his. "He's a little testy," she said to the stewardess. "He didn't get much sleep last night. Sorry."

"Would you like a pillow, sir?"

"No."

"You didn't have to snap at her."

"And you don't have to keep apologizing."

"Sorry."

He speared her with a look.

Her grin could have lit the Loop.

"What's so funny?"

"I'm happy."

"Why? I'm screwing this up royally. My temper's shorter than a Doberman's tail, and I haven't slept in two days."

"And I've done nothing but sleep." She looked out the window and sighed. "Your insomnia is back with a vegeance. My career has all the momentum of a car stalled on railroad tracks. Why should I be happy?"

He studied her face, from the radiating lines around her smiling eyes to the slight twitch of her mouth.

"Maybe it's because I'm getting married," she whispered.

"You mean that?"

"Yes." She fitted her mouth to his, kissing him with a passion that brooked no doubts.

Gabe shoved up the armrest separating them, pulling her nearer. She was nearly on his lap. He didn't care; the closer the better. He signaled the attendant. "Make that champagne."

"Yes, sir."

Shana figured boot-camp drill sergeants heard fewer "yes, sirs" than Gabriel Fitzgerald. Limo drivers came running. The hotel manager fell over himself to supply accommodations despite the fact the hotel was completely filled with conventioneers and their families.

"There are cottages along the shore we reserve for certain guests. One is empty, sir."

"We'll take it."

Shana made eyes at Gabe when the manager turned his back. She whispered out of the side of her mouth. "Is this one of those things where, if you have to ask, you can't afford it?"

He leaned his elbow on the counter and grinned. "I wouldn't know. There aren't many things I can't afford." He was kidding. A little.

Shana smiled. A little. The implications of marrying an extremely wealthy man were making themselves felt.

A driver took them to the cottage to spare their precious feet a three-hundred-yard stroll. On the way Shana pushed the button that lowered the tinted windows. It was near midnight. In the dark her senses took on a heightened intensity. The aroma of hundreds of flowers wafted by, their petals rustling in a balmy breeze that gradually shaded into the whisper of the waves on a beach.

When the bellman and driver had gone, they stood on the veranda outside their cottage. Gabe settled his hands on her waist. Waves, invisible in the pitch-black darkness, rushed onto the sand and collapsed with a sigh. "This will be magnificent in the daytime," she said, sensing more than seeing the palms overhead.

"It'll be wonderful tonight too." His breath feathered across her cheek. His lips traced the line of her neck.

Warmth flooded her limbs. She felt as pliable as the sand, as drawn to him as the tide. A moisture like a flower's nectar collected at her core.

"Take this off," he commanded quietly.

The wool dress, so simple and warm in Chicago, hung like a hairshirt in Hawaii. She stripped it off. Standing in her slip and hose, she caught her lip between her teeth as Gabe's hands roved over her body. He treated her skin the way he treated the silk of her slip, tenderly, possessively, none too gently. She was his. He surrounded her in the velvety darkness, circling her like prey, like an object of art, first a glancing touch on her back, then a kiss on her breast. He was everywhere. It was as if the night itself had come to claim her.

She wanted light, shadows, and forms. She wanted to see the reverence in his eyes that she heard in his voice when he asked if she wanted anything.

"Only you," she said.

He didn't answer.

He didn't have to. He gave her all she asked. Clothes fell to the ground. Skin brushed skin. He stroked her thighs until she couldn't think. Her head lolled back when he cupped her, his fingers slick in her moistness.

A candle flame leapt high behind her closed eyes, the breeze caressing her like the glow of a black moon. Invisible fireflies danced beneath her skin. It was as if the sky wrapped her in its blanket, its pinprick stars alight inside her. Waves of desire washed the floor out from under her feet as if it were nothing but shifting sand. Gabe carried her to the bed.

"I can't see anything."

"Feel it." He nipped at her flesh, lapping honey.

She didn't want light. She was light. Sparks and flares went off behind her eyes. She reached for him. She wanted his body on hers, in her, his solidity and weight anchoring her to the bed.

This night was for her. He knew how to kiss her, what to do to make her quake deep inside. Everything they'd shared up to now told him what she wanted, what she loved. In the dark, in his arms, she felt more truly naked than any light could reveal.

He'd seen her fears, sat by her as she recounted her

failures. He loved her. That love gave him the right to plunder her defenses, strip her of her doubts, demand complete surrender and terrifying subjection.

In return he gave her unutterable joy, an incoherent ecstasy. He did it without words, without explanations or requests. He sank his shaft inside her, impaling her with agonizingly slow thrusts that made her sob for release. He held deathly still while she bucked beneath him, stealthy and sure while she writhed and panted, begging, climbing.

He slipped his hand between them, touching her, touching off a shower of fireworks that made her arch and cry out. Propulsive, driven, but so controlled every fiber in his body seemed made of tensile steel, he came with her. The climax broke through them simultaneously, waves of energy rocketing from one to the other then back, reverberating from earth to air, body to body.

They lay exhausted, their skin prickling in the dark with perspiration. Gabe took her hand and led her through the French doors. Her feet felt tender on the flagstones, alive to every grain of sand on the beach. She whispered his name.

He covered her lips with his fingers then his mouth. Her knees touched the sand. She kissed him back, his low moan lost in the undertow of the massive unseen ocean. Later, he washed her in the foamy crest of spent waves, their bodies sparkling, salty and clean, the sentinel palms standing witness to the first night of their marriage.

24

"Convention activities are on floors three and four."

"Thank you." Shana picked up her name tag and a manila envelope filled with schedules and copies of papers to be delivered.

Her hand shook slightly as she pinned on the badge. It didn't help that Gabe watched every move she made. Her body had thrummed since she woke up. Her nerves weren't much better. She'd woken beside him, her legs entwined with his, her cheek against his chest. His laser-blue eyes watched her intensely then too.

In the main lobby with people milling all around them, she felt unaccountably shy. The privacy of the cottage and the way they'd opened their hearts to each other had combined to unleash a passion she'd never experienced or expected. She wasn't sure how that new love translated to polite public behavior.

Gabe easily twined his fingers through hers. "Having second thoughts about this thing?"

She gave him a longing look. "We can't very well spend the week in bed."

"We could."

"I've got a convention to attend."

"Must be a laugh riot," Gabe muttered. "A hotel full of sleeping experts. What's their logo, a giant Z?"

"Some people take sleep *very* seriously."

"As seriously as you and I do?"

She couldn't resist running her finger along his jaw. She'd watched him shave that morning. If he hadn't chased her out of the bathroom, they'd still be there. "It's a growing field."

"And one of these days you're going to be recognized as a leading innovator in it."

"I don't know about that."

"I do. Now go on. Have fun. I've got some business to attend to myself. With the time change I can still catch the Japanese exchange before it closes."

"You'll need a computer."

"And a fax. The hotel can provide that. I read it in the room service list."

"While you were lying awake next to me?"

"I wasn't awake all night."

She caught her breath. "You slept?"

"With the couple hours I got last night, I might not need any this afternoon."

If he expected her to be happy to hear about his near-normal hours, she sorely disappointed him. "You're fragmenting your sleep again."

"I had better things to do with my time."

She flushed as a group of chatting conventioneers strolled by. Her body reminded her what some of those things were. "I need to go."

"See you later."

She stepped backward, teetering on her heels. She wasn't used to wearing pumps after the thick-soled nurse shoes she wore at the clinic. She wasn't used to saying good-bye to a man she'd spent the night making love with.

He reached out. Pretending to straighten her name badge, he let the backs of his fingers rest on her breast for a brief moment. "Later."

"Bye."

His kiss was neither too long nor too deep. There was no excuse for her legs to go wobbly. Then he said the words that made her heart expand in her chest like a flower opening to the sun. "I love you."

"I love you too."

She watched him stroll away. Another group of conventioneers walked by. An Indian woman in a light blue sari stopped to say hello. "Which sessions are you attending?"

Shana glanced at her program. "I think I'll start with the one on jet lag. I think I'm going to need it."

Gabe propped himself on an elbow, plowing through the jargon in one of the papers Shana had brought back from the previous day's session. A sick feeling sat in the pit of his stomach like a stone.

She breezed out of the bathroom, refreshed and ready for another four hours of lectures. Stooping before the mirror, she ran a brush through her gleaming hair.

Four days of salt and sun had brought out gold threads. A healthy pink flushed her cheeks. Her mid-winter pallor was long gone. Gabe figured he was responsible for at least part of that. The dab of makeup she patted under her eyes was definitely his fault. They'd made love every evening and into the night. When the convention allowed its participants an hour or two of freedom, he snuck kisses from her on the beach.

So why did he feel like a fraud? He tossed the paper on the bed.

"Boring?" she asked. She squirted solution onto her contact, ran it under the faucet, then popped it in her eye.

"Interesting." He lay back and clamped his hands behind his head, his feet balanced off the side of the bed.

The last four days he'd lived more normally than the last twenty years. They made love. They fell asleep in each other's arms. She didn't kick; he didn't stare at the ceiling. Admittedly, he rose early, about four-thirty or five A.M. He worked until Shana woke up. They had breakfast brought in.

When she left for the early sessions, he returned to work, making deals until the Japanese exchange closed, faxing the details to Brice.

He resisted his afternoon drowsiness by running for miles along the beach, exhausting himself in hopes of quieting his mind. It wasn't the dreams he feared; it was the future.

What if he couldn't keep this up? She thought he was cured. She took such pride in him. In Hawaii he was almost normal. What would happen when they got back to Chicago? When his hours were the opposite of hers? "Shana?"

"Mm?"

"What's rebound insomnia?"

She turned from the mirror. She'd stuck a gardenia in her hair. Daring and feminine, the wide-petaled flower erupted from her wild curls. She complained about the humidity and the ocean making them completely unmanageable. He found them irresistible.

Nevertheless, he kept his fists locked behind his head.

Slightly perplexed, she answered his question. "Rebound insomnia happens when someone's been using medication to sleep. When they stop, the insomnia can return worse than ever. You know"—she wagged her brush at him—"if Hazel had become dependent on the sleeping pills her husband gave her, then tried to stop on her own, say when he was out of town or something, rebound insomnia could have been responsible for her hallucinations."

Gabe noticed Hazel's name coming up more and more

in the conversation. For days Shana hadn't mentioned Chicago, Merryweather, any of it. Reality intruded in small glimpses, an occasional faraway look in her eyes, a frown of pain.

"Want to talk about it?" he asked.

She set the brush down, careful not to knock over her growing collection of beauty products. "I thought we had."

"I got some of the story at your apartment. You weren't terribly coherent."

She laughed. "For that I need notes, a chalkboard, and an audience."

"Like Merryweather, Payne, and Wise?" Gabe asked.

She walked to the French doors, her fingers playing across the curved knobs. "I thought you wanted to talk about rebound insomnia."

He didn't want to fail her, to fall back into old patterns. She said she wouldn't mind if he worked at night; she'd feel better knowing he wasn't there to be hurt if she kicked. But the way she curled beside him at night said different. He'd read the articles, the ones that said women preferred closeness to sex. It was hard to be close to a woman from the other side of the room.

He got off the bed, slinking his arms around her from behind, filling his nose with the gardenia's scent, the dusting of powder along her neck. "You want to tell me what really happened in Merryweather's office?"

She sighed. "Do we have time?"

He led her outside to the wrought-iron table beneath the flowering vines that covered the cottage's north side. The ocean spread before them. Billows of black and purple clouds built on the horizon. Rain would wash over the island around two o'clock then be gone.

Remnants of their lunch remained on the table. Shana poured sun-warmed orange juice from a jug to a glass. She sipped it the way a connoisseur savored vintage wine. "Fresh squeezed."

"Kind of like you."

She laughed. "I've been enjoying this so much, I've hardly thought about Chicago."

He covered her hand with his. "We can't stay forever."

"We could."

"Any sleep clinics in Hawaii?"

"Half the conventioneers have already checked that out."

"Start a new one."

"And leave my problems behind me?"

"Unsolved."

"I can make a difference, Gabe."

"You made your point. You stated your case."

"And got shot down in flames."

"Whose side are you on?"

"Yours. Always."

She sat in the shade, watching the clouds. Gabe peered at her from the sun. After minutes of silence, she spoke. She told him about the scene in Merryweather's office, the mistakes she'd made, the accusations that flew back in her face. She told him about Wise pulling out of the garage so fast, he nearly ran her down.

Gabe was glad he had a glass in his hand, something to strangle.

"He was just angry."

"I bet." He glared at the slash of color as two racing sailboards dashed past their cottage. Something still didn't add up.

"I have to go back, Gabe."

Shana never gave up a fight, not when she believed in something. "But if no one did anything wrong, who do you fight?"

"I want to find Hazel first. I need to know if her husband was drugging her against her will or if all these problems were in her head."

"And if he's not the culprit?"

"I don't know."

"What about Merryweather? He prescribed those pills."

"A lapse in judgment. It's understandable. That clinic is his life. I've broached a few ethical boundaries myself." She looked across the table at him. "Loving too much can do that to people."

Gabe spread his fingers so she could twine hers through. Their palms rested together.

"We could take the afternoon off," he murmured.

She gave him that shy grin that made his blood heat. To think she could feel shy after what they'd shared.

"Today's the final session," she said. "Oh, and we've been invited to sit with Dr. Rice at the luau. His wife's a pediatrician; they're a lot of fun."

"Pediatrician, huh? What did she think of your theories regarding preemies and light?"

"How did you know I'd tell her?"

"Good guess."

"She wants me to send her an outline so she can institute a similar system at her hospital."

Gabe frowned, gripping Shana's hand in his.

Affronted, she laughed. "Is that bad?"

"I don't like the idea of your going back to St. James'."

"I need to."

"Why should you be the black sheep of the department when you could be a star in anyone else's? There must be contacts you could make here. Other places you could work."

She shoved her chair back, padding barefoot into the bedroom. She slipped on her pumps and fastened her watch. "I went to St. James' precisely because the clinic was so raw. I knew getting things done would be an uphill climb. I wanted the challenge. If I wanted to fit right in I would have stayed in Arizona."

"Why didn't you?" He leaned his shoulder up against the doorjamb.

She sashayed over. "One morning I realized I could name twenty varieties of cactus. Besides, they didn't have any good bakeries." Her smile faded as she thought ahead. "I want to take some time after the convention's over."

"Not from me."

She rested her hands on his chest. "No, not you. I want to write up my notes. Coherent ones this time. I have to know where I went wrong."

Gabe drew the flower from her hair. "It wasn't here."

After each morning's session she came down the path from the hotel, plucking one perfect flower for her hair, for him. She wore it through lunch. When they forgot their food and made love it got lost in the sheets. It didn't matter: when she left the cottage she'd be prim and professional, and he'd be watching her go, twirling the flower in his hand.

"How do I look?"

He scanned her dress and blazer. "Flora would be proud."

"Think so?"

He caressed her cheek with the silky petals. "It's eight degrees in Chicago, not counting the wind-chill factor."

"Don't forget dinner. Seven o'clock."

"I won't."

She didn't come back after the final session. Gabe found out why at the luau. Reclining on a mat, his shorts and shirt formal enough for the final night's social activities, he idly watched a woman walk down the beach toward him.

She wore a light blue sarong strewn with golden flowers. Her shoulders milky white and bare, her chest bound by folds of brightly colored cloth, the garment moved with her. The long skirt wound around her ample hips, a calf showing with each step. A glimpse of thigh flashed when the breeze kicked up off the water.

Gabe had covered those thighs with kisses. Slowly getting to his feet, he sensed people staring. His stillness had drawn their attention. The statuesque beauty effortlessly reclaimed it for herself.

A gusty breeze, warm as a lover's breath, made her hair

stream behind her. It resembled the flames of the torches planted in the sand. Gabe strode past their shimmering heat waves. "You look like the fire of the volcanos wrapped in the arms of the ocean."

It was a miserable attempt at poetry. She didn't mind. She knew full well the power she had over him. She slipped her arms around his neck, her breasts rising in the silky fabric. Her kiss sizzled like the torches. Who cared if fifty sleep therapists gathered behind them?

"This is the last night with these people," he rasped out. "We've got the next two days to ourselves."

"And the nights?" Shielded from the group, she ran her hand down his waist to his thigh, gripping his rear end in her hand.

He stiffened. She'd never been a small woman. Fleshy, filled out, she was a feast no luau could compare with. He filled his arms with her. "We can leave early."

She nuzzled his cheek.

His voice nearly cracked. "Like now."

She ran a fingernail down the beating vein in his jaw. "Later. I want you to peel me a grape, big boy." Her arm linked through his, they strolled toward the group. Head high, barefoot, she stepped onto the woven mats covering the sand. "Dr. Morgenthau."

A neat little man with a Hitler mustache jumped up. He hastily smoothed the twenty-four hairs shellacked across his bald spot. "Dr. Getz. So good to see so much of you. I mean, to see you. So much."

As if speechless awe were her due, Shana smiled and moved on to the next. "Dr. Alberts. Tina. Jean-Paul."

Jean-Paul kissed her hand.

Gabe scowled.

Shana handed Gabe a seafood canapé, oblivious to the impression she made.

Gabe watched the women size her up. Her genuine warmth quickly won them over. Like him, they realized she wasn't a flame intent on attracting moths. She focused her attention directly on him.

When the main course arrived, everyone settled into place. Some crossed their legs Indian-style, others reclined. Gabe did everything but swagger to his spot beside Shana. He claimed his territory by leaning over to sniff the flower in her hair. Her own honey-sweet fragrance attracted him. He wanted to kiss her bare shoulder, to taste her flesh—

"Gabe."

"Hm?"

"I'd like you to meet Dr. and Mrs. Hornsby."

A circle had convened on their corner of the mat. He cleared the rust out of his throat. "Nice to meet you."

"Drs. Matthew and Sheila Rice. Oh, Dr. Morgenthau, I guess you can fit in here." She scooted closer to Gabe. "And this is Mr. Feingold, he's an attorney."

Gabe shook hands with each.

"Mr. Feingold," Sheila Rice said, "I heard your session on malpractice was excellent today."

His gold tooth gleamed, reflecting the orange hues of the early evening sky. "Thanks."

Forced to make conversation, Gabe asked how malpractice applied to sleep disorders.

"If you promise someone they'll sleep, and they *don't*—" The lawyer raised his palms to the sky. "Even implied promises can get you in trouble."

"People will sue over anything," Mrs. Hornsby said with a laugh. "Believe me, we've been through it."

"I'll say," her husband agreed.

"Our hospital, for instance," Matt Rice put in. "We're a small teaching hospital and we've been fighting a major malpractice suit for three years."

"Over what?" Shana asked.

"Internships."

Gabe was in the middle of passing the crab dip. He and Shana traded a quick look. "What about them?" she asked lightly.

"Our residency program requires first-year interns to

work the typical crazy hours. Get 'em used to the strain. That's the idea anyway. As it happens, we also have a sleep clinic on the premises."

"Which proves what?" Gabe asked.

"That *'we should have known better!'* " Rice and his wife said in tandem.

The group laughed. A few ruefully shook their heads.

"The jury said that because we have people on staff who know how debilitating sleep deprivation is, every one in the hospital should have known it."

"But it's the clinic's job to make it known," Shana argued.

"Yes, it is. To a point. But if hospital personnel know sleep deprivation is bad, and we allow interns to work all hours, the hospital can be found negligent if the intern ever makes a mistake."

Shana glanced at each person, saving her reply for Feingold. "Maybe the hospital *is* negligent."

The lawyer held up two bread sticks in the form of a cross. "Sacrilege, sacrilege."

Shana smiled but stuck to her guns. "A sleepy doctor, inexperienced, under stress . . ."

"I'm not saying you're wrong," Feingold allowed. "From what I've learned at your convention here, letting a doctor operate without enough sleep is like letting him operate on two or three beers. In theory, every member of a hospital's staff should get a good night's sleep. Of course, I know cardiologists who smoke like chimneys too."

"Maybe the residency schedules should be changed," Shana said.

"Ever try making waves in a giant bureaucracy?" Morgenthau asked.

"Actually, yes."

Everyone smiled except Gabe. He saw where this was headed. Even if she'd been wrong about everything else, Shana knew Wise was sleep-deprived when he misdiagnosed Hazel. It wasn't an "honest" mistake, it was a bad system.

He caught the gleam in her eye. She intended to change it.

The dancing, the grass skirts, the sunset, all lingered like the wine and the salty film clinging to their skin. By the time they said good night to her colleagues and walked down the beach to their cottage, Shana was miles away.

"My notes," she murmured. "I know I packed them." She'd rescued the handwritten copy from her office before leaving St. James.' She hadn't looked at it since. "I'll join you in that swim in a minute. I just want to jot something down."

"I bet you do."

Standing by the bedside table, she tapped the pen against her notepad. An embarrassed flush colored her cheeks. "Heard the wheels spinning, eh?"

"Spinning wheels tend to get you in trouble."

"Only when I'm right. Hey."

He took her in his arms, hips swaying as music played far down the beach. "There's a lot of Hawaiian culture in the hula. Every gesture means something."

"I'm sure you're an expert by now."

"I studied tonight's demonstration very, very carefully."

"Should I be jealous?"

"You were busy talking to your friends."

"The schedule for interns is horrendous. Truck drivers can't work those kinds of hours. Some utilities send electric linemen home after sixteen hours work no matter how bad the storm. People need sleep. The more vital their jobs—"

"The more important the fight."

"I have to, Gabe, I can't stand by."

He held her body to his. "Stand by me."

She rested her cheek to his. Their lips met in a knowing kiss.

"That's one of the things I love about you, you know."

"Do you?" she asked.

"You've got two days to make notes. Your nights belong to me."

"Is that a promise?"

"That's a fact."

"Okay." She tapped her pen against the glass top of the wrought-iron table. Court was in session.

Gabe sat to attention. "What have you got?"

She peered through her glasses, the chain bouncing slightly against her bare collarbone. Gabe had rubbed sun screen on those shoulders an hour earlier, not counting the other lotions they'd tried the night before. Nevertheless he tugged her chair back into the shade.

She focused on her legal pad. "I know why Merryweather and Payne are in on this and why they both tried to block me from going after Wise. Fear of malpractice."

"You're sure."

"They knew he was sleep-deprived. They were there that night. If it got out that his judgment was impaired, Hazel's husband could shut us down with a lawsuit. Ergo, they suspended me. To save the clinic they'll do anything they can to discredit me." She slapped the pad down triumphantly.

"I thought you wanted the clinic to survive?"

"I want patients to survive. What do you think the numbers are on interns making mistakes due to excessive sleepiness?"

"I'm sure you'll tell me."

"I don't know. Yet."

He grinned. "I was waiting for that."

Shana paced the edge of the flagstones. Tiny puffs of sand shot up from her bare heels with every step.

"I've got a question," Gabe asked.

"Shoot."

"If keeping interns up all hours is bad for them—"

"Uh-huh."

"—and bad for the patients they treat—"

"Uh-huh."

"—then why have the system at all?"

"Tradition. I'm serious. No better reason. I've button-holed every doctor still here and called others around the country. No one has a better explanation."

He'd heard her on the telephone. While he'd dealt with Japan and Singapore, she worked the phones, asking questions, leaving messages.

"The old guard claims young doctors have to get used to being up all hours during an emergency," she said. "Fine, although I claim a well-rested person would function even better. The real problem comes along when people are deprived of sleep *for no good reason*. They get groggy. Mistakes happen. Anything less than life-threatening gets lost in the shuffle."

"Like Hazel's drug test."

"Exactly."

"How are you going to get around Payne?"

"How do you mean?"

"If he suspended you to prevent you bringing up Wise's sleepiness, how're you going to make your case? Who are you going to make it to?"

"Payne may be in charge of our committee, he's not the head of the hospital."

"Go over his head?"

"It'd help if I had Merryweather behind me. And a computer."

"A what?"

"A doctor in Massachusetts is sending me some statistics. If I can get on the computer at St. James' I can track the number of mistakes attributed to interns. Then I can correlate that with how many hours they'd been working when the mistakes occurred. There's only one problem."

"What's that?"

"To find out their hours I need to get into Payroll."

Gabe peeled the rind off a sun-warmed orange. "That's no problem."

25

Back in Chicago, Shana hardly noticed the damp March cold that had replaced the frigid chill of February. She checked her apartment, giving Romper a hug and kiss he quickly wriggled out of. Miffed at her prolonged absence, the cat sat on the mantel grooming himself while she bundled into a warmer set of clothes and headed out again.

She made the round of bakeries, thanking Aunt Shayna for watching her pet, handing out Hawaiian trinkets, suggesting the whole family get together for dinner next Sunday—she and Gabe had an announcement to make.

Arms filled with loaves of bread and boxes of cake, she raced to the hospital, intent on beginning her research. She plopped the chocolate torte on Flora's desk. "For being such a good friend."

"Think again." Flora hung up the phone, snapping a chunky gold earring back in place. "Merryweather's not here, and I've found out nothing about this Hazel Doe."

"Thanks for trying. I'll do some snooping of my own. Have you got the keys to the lab? I need to use Fiona's computer."

Flora sat back, crossing her arms over her ample bosom. "I don't know if I'll give 'em to you. What happened with you, girl?"

"I had a run-in with Merryweather *and* Payne. Payne suspended me, Michael rescinded part of it. It had to do with this patient—"

Flora halted her with a huff. "I meant you. You look wonderful. Vibrant, healthy, alive." She stopped short. "Loved. If Hawaii does all that, Richard's getting me a ticket tomorrow."

Shana colored a pretty pink. "It wasn't all Hawaii."

Flora chortled. "I knew you'd come to your senses. That Gabriel man."

"We're getting married."

Flora's mouth fell open. She threw her arms around Shana, nearly smothering her in a hug. "Didn't I say I'd see you married? Good Lord, you've got to get outta here."

"Is Payne coming?"

"You've got shopping to do!"

"Not just yet." Shana laughed. "I want to look some things up first."

She fastened a suspicious gaze on her younger colleague. "What are you into now?"

"I have some questions about hours worked. Got any ideas on how I can snoop around in Payroll?"

"You can't even get into the computer."

"Flora, I have to."

"You can't. Your codeword was changed."

Despite the added color in her cheeks, Shana felt unaccountably pale. She sat down, the dingy walls closing in, the bad light making her feel dizzy. "They banned me from the computer too?"

"Michael told us at the last staff meeting. We're all getting new passwords. Some security thing. You get yours when you come back."

"And he's the only one who knows it."

"Payne is."

They'd stopped her before she'd even started. Shana peered at the yellowed paint near the high ceiling, the crack in the plaster, the nicked and scarred old desk Flora used. "Sometimes I hate this place." She sighed.

"It has its rewards." She placed her hand on Shana's shoulder. "DeVon Johnson's been looking for you."

"Ha. That's a reward?"

"Your talk about deep-sea diving helped him adjust to that CPAP machine. He wants to thank you."

"The minute it stops working he'll want to punch my lights out."

"Give the man a chance. Trust your abilities, girl, you saved a life there."

"And nearly lost Hazel's. I'll be on the lookout for him."

"You do that. Meanwhile, let Fiona and me take you to breakfast next week."

She stopped in the doorway. "You know, there is something you could do for me."

"Name it."

"It's a favor. A big one." She closed the door to Flora's office, unaware of the man at the end of the hall watching and listening.

Gabe laid the Chinese food out luau style on the low marble coffee table in his living room. Shana wriggled in next to him on the floor, keeping her toes warm by snuggling them under his thigh. She leaned forward for a sweet and sour kiss.

"How was your day?" They spoke in tandem.

Dipping a shrimp, Shana pointed it his way. "You first. How'd you sleep today?"

"Got a couple hours this afternoon."

"Jet lag."

"It'll settle down. I planned to work most of the night." It was his way of warning her.

If his work bothered her, she didn't show it. "Your day was better than mine. Oh, remind me I have a cake in the car."

"I'll have the doorman send it up. What happened at the hospital?"

"I couldn't get in."

"They changed the locks on your office?"

She looked impressed and chagrined by turns. "Luckily they didn't think of that."

"Did they arrest Wise?"

"Not that I know of."

"I don't like the sound of that."

"I'm safe here. Problem is, they've locked me out of the computer. I can't find anything out if I can't see the timesheets."

He picked up the plate of peanut chicken. "Follow me."

In the bedroom, she pulled her chair up beside his desk. "What's this? On line take-out service?"

"Computer security, Grier/Fitzgerald. Also known as Jeffrey."

Shana watched a reply magically appear on the screen after Gabe typed a few commands. "Who's Jeffrey?" she whispered, as if the invisible respondent could hear their conversation.

"Jeffrey's a skinny kid we hired straight out of college. Works all hours. He's got a closet-size office off a back hall and access to absolutely everything. People call him a hacker."

Her eyes widened. "You're not into computer fraud?"

"We transfer massive sums of money across continents every day of the week. We've got to safeguard them for our clients."

"Hence Jeffrey."

"He can uncode anything and go anywhere."

After a brief explanation from Gabe, Jeffrey got Shana

into St. James' antiquated data base in under half an hour. A graphic of a Rolling Stones backstage pass appeared on the screen with the magic words ALL ACCESS printed below.

"You're in, Dr. Getz."

Shana forgot any scruples about snooping through the files long distance. She pulled her chair up to the screen. "I can't believe you did that."

"What are friends for?"

She gazed into Gabe's eyes with pure adoration. "You're wonderful."

"I'll tell Jeffrey you said thank you."

"Don't tell him how." She twined her arms around his neck, kissing him until the peanut chicken was long forgotten. The blinking screen tugged at her attention.

"Want to reheat that dinner or forget it?" Gabe asked, his voice sultry and low.

Shana bumped his chair with her hip. "Scoot over. What I really want is to see where this leads."

So did he. He'd pictured beds, fireplaces. The only sheets Shana wanted were worksheets. "Give me a couple hours?"

Gabe poked the peanut chicken with a chopstick. "Take all the time you need."

He wandered into the living room, amused at the way the tables had turned. Now he was the neglected lover, sitting on the sofa while the computer keys clacked into the night.

He cleared the coffee table, depositing the boxes on the kitchen counter. A stack of pink While You Were Out messages waited for him. He'd copied them down from his answering machine earlier. It was an old habit, writing his messages as he listened to them. It had helped immensely in the days when he was so groggy, he forgot things in minutes.

The first was a call from Brice asking for information about some deal they'd hammered out a week ago. He tossed it. The second message requested a detail on the

Samoan deal. He folded it; a sign to double-check it when he got on the computer. The third had been from Aurora. She'd had a nightmare, sorry to disturb him. Nothing important.

Office call. Office call. He'd see to that one later if Shana ever got off the computer.

The last message was from Aurora again. Rereading it, he remembered the sound of her voice on his machine. She'd had an edge of concern totally different from her usual blasé tone. "Could you call me back? Anytime. I had the strangest dream. Really different. Call me?"

He reached for the telephone then glanced up. Shana might not like him calling another woman. A pencil clamped between her teeth, she was too intent on her search to notice. Gabe chuckled and dialed. Eddie answered.

He left his name and hung up. He'd talk to Aurora tomorrow. He folded the note and stuck it in his pocket.

At dawn he shut down his computer just in time to turn it over to Shana. "Now how'd Jeffrey do this?" she asked.

He got her up and running. It was the least he could do after the love they'd shared the night before. In his bed, his home. He wanted her to feel totally comfortable there. He busied himself making her breakfast. She kissed him good-bye and promised to do the dishes.

He cruised down to the office to say hello. Every trader glanced up, as shocked to see him at this hour as they were to see him whistling. He leaned in his partner's office door. "Brice, how's the arm?"

"The Vampire walks in sunlight. How novel." Brice gripped his hand with both of his. "You're lookin' good, pal. How was the big island?"

"Surprisingly small."

Brice sniggered. "Never got out of the room, eh?"

"We're getting married."

The leer changed to a beaming grin. "All right!" Brice threw his arms around Gabe, clamping him in a bear hug. "You son of a bitch. Guys, hey, listen up! Fitzgerald's getting married."

The brokers stared dumbfounded. One or two nodded, another grinned and waved halfheartedly. Telephones tucked to their shoulders, eyes glued to their screens, they quickly returned to business.

"Greedy hotshots," Brice grumbled. "Wait'll they fall in love. If they ever get over making money, that is. Tell you what, bring her over. Peg and I'll make you a meal."

"She's a little wrapped up in work right now."

"I never thought you'd do it."

"I was a little gun-shy."

"Gun-shy? Try sleep-shy. I never thought you'd shake whatever kept you up all these years."

Whatever it was, he hoped it never came back.

"It was weird." She didn't ask where he'd been or how he was. Aurora heard Gabe's voice and launched into a retelling of her most recent dream. "I was in the parking garage at St. James' and this woman's walking along and there's this guy. It was just like when I see little kids getting lost, totally real but somehow different. Scary. Like a nightmare."

Reclining on the sofa, waiting for her story to unfold, Gabe pulled a pillow out from behind his back and balanced it on his lap. It was nearly noon, his bedtime. Elbow canted on the back of the sofa, he watched Shana in the other room. The green glow of the screen reflected in her glasses. She'd been working all morning, feverishly compiling stacks of data, citing instances of every mistake committed by an intern who'd worked in excess of eighteen hours.

Gabe didn't mind. It struck him as curious how much he liked the clacking of keys in the background, the sense of someone else there. He'd suggested she bring the cat over. Extra clothes were piled on the corner of the dresser, others crowded his closet. She wasn't just a girlfriend staying over. It was becoming her home.

All the same, their hours hadn't meshed the way he'd hoped. He napped on the couch rather than distract her in the bedroom. That should settle down when her suspension was over and life returned to normal.

He pictured normal. Him sleeping all day while she worked. Her sleeping at night while he worked. A split shift like theirs would come in handy if they had kids.

He thought of the sleepless nights most parents had after a baby's birth. Shana probably had something to say about that. When the time came she might set up a class at the clinic for new parents adjusting their sleep schedules to the needs of a baby. With their cockeyed hours, he and Shana would do just fine.

"Then he came up behind her."

"Who did?"

"Are you listening to me?"

He readjusted himself on the sofa. Aurora had been droning all through his reverie. "I missed the last part. Say it again."

"I was in the parking garage."

"I got that."

"It was like one of the real dreams, I felt as if I were really there. But it was scary too. I don't usually have both at once. I mean, my real dreams are always so real-life and this—"

"What about it?"

"I was there, feeling it, seeing it. The cold. The damp. Her shoes didn't make any sound on the cement but then neither did his."

"Whose?"

"The man following her. We were both behind her, me watching, him waiting. He had a pipe in his hand. She started to run, then she turned like it was okay. But she was scared, I could see it. She started to say something. He hit her, dropped the pipe, and ran."

"Did you call the hospital and see if there'd been a mugging?"

"Nothing's happened, I checked. Like I said, though, this was different. There was this sense of impending something."

"Impending doom."

"Yeah." She laughed. "Sounds pretty melodramatic when you put it that way."

"Tell you what. Call Security at the hospital and tell them you were leaving the parking ramp and felt as if you were being followed. Maybe they'll beef up patrols."

"That sounds like a good idea."

Easier than convincing them she dreamed the future. Not that Gabe put much faith in her recounting. The dream was days old; the signals mixed. Its nightmare touches lacked the matter-of-fact quality typical of her predicting dreams.

He hung up the telephone. The next time Shana went down to the hospital he'd take her himself. Just in case.

He walked into the bedroom, pausing to kiss the top of her head. He kneaded her shoulders as she typed in a search command. "How's it going?"

She sat back, her eyes shuttering closed. "That feels wonderful."

"So do you." He kissed her hair.

She smooched the air. "Almost finished."

"Think so?"

"I've accumulated enough sloppy mistakes to scare anyone. This system will get us sued out of existence if we don't change it and soon."

"Think Payne will listen?"

"Someone has to. Remember the Hippocratic Oath; 'First Do No Harm.' When the board sees what errors the system leads to, they'll have to change it. If they don't, the lawyers will change it for 'em."

"Litigation to the rescue."

"Strange bedfellows."

"Speaking of which."

She stroked his hand where it rested on her shoulder. "Will my typing keep you up?"

He unbuttoned his shirt. "I think the jet lag's hitting home. I'm going to crash for a few hours."

"Sweet dreams."

He crawled into bed. Romper leapt up to see what was going on. He curled into a ball by Gabe's knees. Shana grinned at them both from the desk. She came over and tucked the blanket under Gabe's chin. Her hand strayed appreciatively over his shoulder and down to his chest.

Gabe brought her palm to his lips. "You've got work to do."

"I couldn't have done it without you."

He fluffed the pillow under his head. "I could say the same."

"I don't want to keep you awake."

"Then stop looking at me that way."

She smiled. "I love you."

"I know."

Shana reluctantly withdrew to the waiting computer. The letter she intended to present to the board needed one more rewrite. She'd run it by Merryweather first. If he was willing to join her crusade to change the system, she'd leave it up to him whether or not they informed Payne or went directly over his head.

Uneasy, Shana turned in her chair. She watched Gabe's eyes drift closed. His arm was slung above his head, the pose she recalled from the videotape the first time he slept in the lab. She wondered if he still had that tape. They'd watch it when they got old and remember . . .

She grinned at her straying thoughts and turned back to the computer. This time, before approaching anyone with her theory, she'd have an iron-tight case. She was going to shake things up, make real changes. Patients like Hazel would never be placed in danger again.

She wondered how Hazel was doing. Flora hadn't gotten anywhere calling clinics. Shana pushed a few buttons on the computer. She wondered if St. James' kept a directory of other hospitals in the area. Yes. She scrolled down the screen. Names, addresses, and phone numbers. But how would she know which one Hazel had been transferred to? She'd never found Hazel's file on the computer. She didn't even know her full name.

She went looking under ambulance billings. A patient transferred from intensive care would have been sent by ambulance to another facility. She called up February eighteenth. No records for a Hazel Doe.

She scanned the destinations. North Side Convalescence Center. That sounded good. The only patient transferred on that date had been named—

Her hands froze on the keyboard. The name stared back at her, the cursor blinking like a bomb about to explode.

The telephone rang. Shana nearly jumped out of her skin. She grabbed the receiver, swinging around to see if the ring had woken Gabe. "Yes!"

"Is that how you answer the phone?" Flora asked. "What number is this anyway?"

"I'm at Gabe's. I'm using his computer. Flora." She gulped. "I think I've come across something very important."

"You're telling me. Guess what I found in Merryweather's files?"

"You got in?"

She lowered her voice. "You asked me to, didn't you?"

"It's too dangerous. You don't have to—"

"Too late. I snuck in when he was at the department-head meeting. Guess what your mystery patient's real name is? Guess who her husband is?"

Flora read off the name from the filched report. Shana read along with the information on her screen. "He had her transferred to prevent us finding out," Shana said.

"What are you going to do about it?"

"I'm coming down there."

She hung up, her hand shaking so hard the receiver clattered into the cradle. She printed out her report; the conclusion would speak for itself. Switching off the computer, she scribbled Gabe a note. She'd written so many to herself in the last few days, she was nearly out of paper. It was no longer a question of mistakes made by drowsy interns. This was deliberate evil.

She set the note on the pillow beside Gabe. Stopping there, she longed to kiss him. Loath to wake him, she brushed the air near his ear with her lips. "I love you. Don't ever forget that."

The puddle of melted snow splashed dirty brown as Shana's car swerved into the parking garage. Careening around the third level, she passed DeVon Johnson. His glowering demeanor registered instantly. She didn't have time to talk. She drove around the next tight corner and the next, finally finding a parking space. Gathering up her briefcase, she trotted to the stairs. Who cared if they were deserted and dank? She had to get to Merryweather's office—now.

Her tennis shoes made no sound in the hallway of the Sleep Disorders Clinic. She'd taken no time to change her clothes. In jeans and a baggy sweater, she knew she'd present a less than impressive picture. The data she'd gathered would have to speak for her. She knocked on Merryweather's door and went in.

Flora stood beside his desk, her arms folded, her brow furrowed. "What does this mean, Michael?"

Shana thudded the briefcase onto his desk. "That's what I'd like to know. If you don't want to discuss it here, I suggest we go see Payne. Coming?"

Gabe had no sense of waking. The taste of chalk on his tongue, the sound of blood rushing in his ears was all he needed to know it had been real. He'd seen the garage,

lit with the sickly glow of sodium lights. Water trickled
down the floor from wet car tires. Dried salt outlined the
evaporated puddles in white, like the silhouetted body at
a crime scene. The place smelled of exhaust and burned
rubber, mildew and cement. The images chilled him to
the bone.

He sat on the edge of the bed, rasping his cheeks with
his half-closed fist. It couldn't be.

Aurora's dream. That's what it was. A woman striding
through a parking garage. A man with a pipe. Aurora
put the image in his head and he'd dreamed it—but with
all the details, the palpable reality of his foretelling
dreams.

He'd watched Shana striding through the garage, her
steps rapid but muffled. A van. A man in its hulking
shadow. Closing in on him, she hadn't noticed the steps
behind her. She backed into a doorway, whirling at the
last minute.

Gabe rubbed his eyes until they ached. He couldn't see
the face, only the image of the arm upraised, the sound of
a thud, blood congealing on the cement.

He pulled on his slacks, a sweatshirt, anything close at
hand. He saw the note on the pillow. "Fuck!" She'd
scrawled it so hastily, she'd written it in shorthand. The
only word he recognized was the name Hazel. He felt the
urgency of her writing come through the paper, the dot
beneath the exclamation point poking through the other
side like braille.

He crumpled it and shoved it in his pocket. He had to
get to that garage.

26

"I think we should talk to Payne now, don't you?" Shana was proud of the chilly certainty in her voice.

They'd left Flora to guard the clinic. Merryweather dogged her steps. If they went straight to the administration building, they might find Payne still there.

Shana took the stairs, cutting through the garage linking the two buildings. The sight of Payne's shiny bald head brought her up short. "Why, Dr. Payne, we were coming to see you."

He blinked, a reptile caught in the light. "I was just on my way to speak to Dr. Merryweather. Surely your suspension isn't finished?"

"You are." She sensed Michael hanging back. She'd have to face this on her own. She squared her shoulders. "Is there any chance you were going to ask Dr. Merryweather about your wife's progress?"

Payne resisted darting a glance Merryweather's way. Unmoved, his flat gaze rested on Shana.

"She knows who Hazel is," Merryweather said.

"Margaret Hazel Payne," she recited. "Age fifty-seven. Address—"

"I know the address."

"You were in the emergency room that night because Michael called you."

"I had a right to know. I am her husband."

"Does that give you the right to have her transferred to a private clinic so no one will find out who she is?"

"I have every right to see she receives the best, most personalized attention."

"I'd say she's had all the attention from you she could handle; sleeping pills forced down her throat, sexual attention—"

"That's enough."

"It was too much. She cracked. Before she did she found a doctor who'd listen."

"She found Merryweather—or rather, I asked him to treat her. Confidentially, of course. No one was to know my wife had a problem."

Merryweather looked sick. "Payne came in," he confessed. "He said his wife was having mental problems."

"Like bruises on her wrists?" Shana asked.

"She hid them. I never saw them until that night in the emergency room. That's when I began putting two and two together. She'd complained of drowsiness, nothing more. I thought amphetamines might help temporarily. I didn't know she was combining them with barbiturates."

"Combining?" Shana said. "She was fighting off the effects of what he gave her, trying to resist him—"

"I didn't hear about the Sandman until you told me. She never confided that."

"Because she knew you were in league with him."

"No."

"Yes, Michael."

"She told me some things," he admitted. "Toward the end, just before she went to see you. By then she was thoroughly dependent, irrational, incoherent. I threatened to stop the amphetamines. That's when she told me why she needed them. Given her condition, I didn't know whether to believe her or not. I refused to renew the prescription. That was months ago."

"But you told me—"

"I told you Wise delivered them on my instructions. In the beginning that was true. The last few months he's been acting on his own. I didn't realize it until you told me you'd seen them on four."

"Why didn't you stop him?"

"How? How could I have him brought up before a review board without revealing everything?" Merryweather glared at Payne. "I was trying to convince her to check herself in. Payne didn't want that—not even if continued dependency cost his wife her sanity. That's why I encouraged her to see you. I thought you could do more."

"And when I tried you got in my way."

"If you'd checked her in—"

Shana leveled a contemptuous gaze at Payne. "If I'd checked her in, the Sandman would have checked her out at the earliest opportunity."

Payne accepted her glare the way he'd watched their argument, with a bland smile on his face, a chilly distance in his eyes. "Indeed I would. My wife requires full-time psychiatric care."

"Your wife needs to get off the drugs so she can confirm what's happened. In a matter of weeks we should be able to interview her."

"If you can find her. I've been unhappy with the results at North Side. I'm thinking of requesting another transfer—"

The threat brought Merryweather side by side with Shana. "Stop it now, Payne."

"We'll get a restraining order," she said.

"I'll testify to the abuse," Michael added. "Hazel has a sister you forced her to break off contact with years ago. She'll get power of attorney to handle Hazel's affairs."

Payne remained as unruffled as an ice-covered pond by their threats. "Shana Getz, a disgruntled employee serving a suspension for making wild, unsubstantiated accusations, joins together with a staff psychiatrist who admits to treating a patient outside of channels, misdiagnosing her, misprescribing for her, and generally damaging a severely troubled woman. This woman may never be able to relate a coherent, much less believable story regarding her months of treatment. In the meantime her doctor has admitted allowing an intern to sell her illegal drugs. What do you think your chances are of convincing anyone of these slurs?"

Michael stammered something about being pressured.

Shana gripped her report. She'd hit Payne from a completely different angle. "I have here enough evidence to get your precious hospital closed down, Doctor. You knew the intern treating Hazel was sleep-deprived. Michael knew it. I knew it. And yet you allowed Wise to go on working on your wife. You wanted to limit the number of people who had contact with her ravings. When he almost killed her, you suspended *me* for telling the truth."

"And this is your tawdry revenge?"

"This is my intention, Dr. Payne. Unless you give us access to Hazel, I'll release this information."

"That's blackmail."

"It's the truth. What about all the other people Wise treated the night Hazel was admitted? The intern schedule must be changed."

"I don't see what that has to do with our discussion."

Stepping as close to him as she could stomach, Shana lowered her voice. "This is more than Hazel's case. If you don't change the schedule these interns work, I'll send this information to every malpractice attorney in town. When they realize we knowingly allowed interns to function under these conditions, that we *impose* these conditions, your beloved hospital will be bled dry by lawsuits."

"This is beside the point."

She handed him the report. "We may be too late for Hazel. There are other patients we can save."

"You've overlooked one other option, Dr. Getz."

"There are none. With a sleep clinic on the premises you can't pretend you didn't know the effects of sleeplessness on performance."

"Exactly." Payne turned to Merryweather. "That's why you shall vacate your office by five this afternoon."

"What?"

"The Sleep Disorders Clinic is shut down as of today. If anyone accuses us of negligence, we can rightfully claim we had no idea." He help up the report. "No one will ever see this so-called data."

"You can't do that," Merryweather argued.

"I shall immediately present Ms. Getz's case to the board. They'll agree with me: your department is a dangerous liability that opens St. James' to a host of legal claims."

"You can't do this," Merryweather shouted.

"Stop me."

"Look, you son of a bitch."

"No, you look, Michael. Thanks to your care, your clinic, my wife ended up screaming in an emergency room, hallucinating and psychotic. I may bring charges of malpractice against you myself."

Merryweather towered over him, shaking like a scarecrow. His body rail-thin, his clothes shuddered on his frame as if a gale blew through him. "You drugged your wife for sex, you bastard. You've abused her for years. I'll testify—"

"And then we'll put Wise on the stand. To keep his job I'm sure he'll say each delivery was at your request. Including the illegal ones."

Shana watched the fight drain from Merryweather. As Payne's threats cut the ground out from under him, his voice grew tighter, his gestures halting. "Now wait. Let's talk about this."

Payne raised his hand. Beads of perspiration clung to his slick brow. Nothing else had changed. While Michael paced, measuring the dimensions of the cage Payne had erected, his nemesis planted his feet evenly on the floor.

Payne owned this hospital. He'd tenaciously accumulated positions on every board, every committee of consequence. He had power, influence.

They had nothing but threats.

Below them, in the lowest depths of the garage, a car screeched into the entrance. Someone shouted at it to halt. The brakes slammed on. Angry words were exchanged, commands given. The wheels spun as it took off again. Shana almost smelled the rubber burning.

Whatever emergency was happening below had nothing to do with them. The whine of the climbing car as it swerved around each tight corner nearly drowned out the sound of footsteps approaching. Shana turned. The color of DeVon Johnson's bright orange parka caught her eye.

Flora had said he wanted to see her. Unfortunately this discussion wasn't for public consumption. She waved him away. Undeterred, he kept coming. He held a package in both hands.

Agitated, Shana glanced at Merryweather and Payne. Her heart sank to her stomach like a stone when she heard the anger in Michael's voice alter to anxious pleading.

"You can't shut us down. We have patients—"

"You'll have no more access to this hospital or its facilities. The lab equipment will be disbursed—"

"You can't do this!"

"Watch me."

Shana trotted down the slope toward Johnson. "Please, Mr. Johnson, could you come back later—"

Merryweather's raised voice snapped her head around. "You can't do this to me. This is *my* clinic! I started it from a piece of paper, a presentation to your goddamn board—"

Satisfied that his threat was doing its work, Payne strolled past Merryweather to the staircase that led to Administration. "By the time you fight the closure you'll be a former employee conspiring with a suspended one to blacken this hospital's name. Good day, Doctor." The door clanged shut behind him.

"Dr. Getz?"

"Just a minute, DeVon."

"About that machine you wanted me to wear to sleep."

That was probably it in the flat box, smashed to pieces like their clinic. She raced back to Michael.

His shoulders heaving, the breath wheezed in and out of his lungs. He smoothed a hand across his hair as if he could iron out the curls if he flattened it enough, as if they could iron this all out. "Get away from me."

"It'll be okay, Michael. We'll go over Payne's head. I have a copy of the report. If we get to the board first—"

"It's over. It can't be. I have to do something." His head jerked left and right. He scanned the garage floor as if he'd find the answers scattered there. "We have to stop him."

"Michael, listen to me."

"I should've never listened to you. This is *your* fault."

She stepped back as if slapped. "Mine?"

"Why couldn't you keep your mouth shut? I told you I could handle him! If it weren't for you I'd have my clinic. He's shut us down!"

"Who says he has that power? We can talk this over. Report it."

"To whom?"

DeVon edged closer.

Bearing down on the black man, Michael screamed at both of them. "We're closed! Tell him that, why don't you? We're out of business! Go home."

"Michael."

"Get away from me!" He flung Shana across the lane. She bounced off a car trunk, landing with a thud on the cement floor.

DeVon dropped his package and rushed forward. "Are you okay?"

More shocked than hurt, she nodded. "I'm all right."

The clang of the metal door reverberated in the empty garage. Merryweather was gone. The sound of that hot-rodding car filled the garage with its whine.

She got her shaking legs under her. DeVon took her arm. She forced a crooked smile. "Please disregard this little scene. It's an internal affair. The clinic will not go under."

"It shouldn't. Not after the way you helped me." He rushed to where he'd dropped the box. "Ever since you told me about how to see that machine, to use it as a life-line instead of some contraption—"

Shana held up her hand, dismayed to see grease smeared on her palm. A car swerved around the final corner. "DeVon, I don't have time, really, I—"

He drew his massive shoulders back. "I need to thank you, Doctor."

Behind him, the car slammed on its brakes. She turned toward the stairwell. She had to find Michael, to calm him down before he did something crazy.

She backed toward the door. "I appreciate you wanting to say thank you—"

She whirled at the thud of a footstep behind her. The force of the blow struck her like a bolt of lightning. She staggered into the garage. The sound of a crack ricocheted off the walls, unsynchronized, seconds late. Maybe it was the car door, she thought vaguely. A numbing blackness crowded in around the edges of her vision.

She concentrated every inch of her willpower to keep her eyes open. It didn't work. The floor came up to meet her, the cement strangely soft beneath her cheek, the cold comforting, welcoming. A lead pipe rolled past her, ringing in the deadly still garage.

Gabe slammed on the brakes. When he'd come around the corner she'd been backing toward the stairwell, trying to escape. The hulking man in the orange coat had completely blocked his view.

He leapt out of the car and elbowed Johnson out of the way. Shana crumpled, falling in slow motion. "What have you done to her?"

"That man—he hit her. He hit her."

There was no man. The garage was empty except for them. Shana lay ashy pale. The blood trickling along the cement was garish red in comparison. The color faded. Gabe blinked. The whole world was turning gray.

"Shana." He threaded his fingers gingerly through her hair. "Shana, baby, you okay? Talk to me."

DeVon Johnson mumbled something about a man, a pipe. He kept pointing under a van. "There, man. He hit her. Just came out the door and hit her."

"Shana, talk to me. Wake up, honey."

"I couldn't move, man. I never thought—"

He wasn't prepared. The words mocked him, repeating over and over in Gabe's head. He'd wasted precious minutes stalking around the apartment convincing himself it was Aurora's dream, not his. He should've reacted quicker, not thought—

"Baby, come on. I'm here. Open your eyes."

"Don't move her." DeVon pulled the pipe out from under the van. Scuffling over on his hands and knees, he shoved a box before him, ripping it open as he talked. "Put this under her head. Use this." He shoved something white at Gabe.

He ignored it. How could he not hold her? He wanted to pull her onto his knees and rock her, repeat all the things he'd heard her tell the babies in the womb room. He couldn't just leave her there on the cement. It was damp. She'd catch cold. He dragged her limp body into his arms.

"Security's comin'," DeVon said, motioning to some noise behind them. "You're in a hospital, man. They'll see to her right away."

"Why'd you do this?" His voice grated. Talking to DeVon instead of the sleeping Shana, he sounded like another person.

"I didn't touch her."

"You were here. You hated her. You've hated her from the start."

"No, man, you got it wrong." He raised from a crouch, his fingers splayed on the cement like a racer waiting for a gun to go off. "I didn't do nothing! Don't say that."

Two security men had already heard it. They grabbed him by both arms and slammed him against the van's door. He shouted curses at them, wrestling until they kicked his legs out from under him. Facedown on the cement, he lay spread-eagle beside Shana.

Gabe gathered her to him, shielding her, wiping sticky hair off her blood-smeared cheek. "It's okay, baby. It'll be okay."

Gabe followed the stretcher through the tunnel of fluorescent lights and endless hallways. Only when they wheeled her into the emergency room did the color begin seeping back into his vision. He saw the ugly green of the curtains that divided the cubicles, the white of the nurses' uniforms, the blood soaking his sweatshirt where he'd cradled Shana's head. The T-shirt in his hand had bright blue stitching.

DeVon Johnson had shoved it under Shana's head as a pillow.

Gabe dropped it on the floor.

Nobody moved him. Not the nurses gathering around, not the doctor shining a penlight in Shana's eyes. The intern lifted her lids, asked her questions. Getting no response, he talked to the personnel around him, shouting jargon, speaking in a code Gabe didn't understand.

"Excuse me." A nurse elbowed him out of the way. "We need you out of here."

"No."

"You don't want to see this."

He stayed. They forced tubes up her nose. The doctor

commented favorably on her gag response when they shoved another down her throat.

Gabe wanted to tear his face off.

"Relative?" the intern asked a nurse busy strapping an IV to Shana's arm.

"Don't know," the nurse replied.

No one asked him. They kept working on her.

"I want an experienced doctor," Gabe announced. "A neurosurgeon. A specialist in skull fractures."

The young doctor glanced up, snapping off his latex gloves. "We're taking her to intensive care. She'll get the best care we've got."

They wheeled out the gurney. Gabe followed.

"This yours?" the doctor called after him. His loose grip let the T-shirt unfurl.

A poem had been embroidered on it in flowing blue script. Gabe recognized the four lines at a glance. It began with the words "Now I lay me down to sleep."

They'd taken Shana directly from intensive care to an operating room. Merryweather had arranged for a neurosurgeon he knew to operate. "This guy's the best," he assured Gabe.

Unable to summon any words, Gabe nodded.

"How long has she been in there?"

"Over an hour," he croaked.

"This is all my fault. It's all my fault."

A policeman came in. "We've got a man in custody. We'll need you to identify him."

"DeVon Johnson?" Merryweather asked.

"That's the name."

"He was there," Merryweather said to Gabe. "Shana went to talk to him."

"Were you there?" the policeman asked.

Merryweather nodded. "Me, Dr. Payne, Shana. We were—having a discussion. Johnson came toward us. Shana went to talk to him."

"Did he seem belligerent?"

"No. He had something in his hands."

"A pipe?"

"A package."

"The shirt," Gabe mumbled.

The policeman picked up the T-shirt where someone had dropped it on a chair. " 'If I should die before I wake/I pray the Lord my soul to take.' In your opinion, does that constitute a threat?"

Merryweather shook his head impatiently. "He wanted to thank her. He was a patient."

Gabe shot Merryweather a look. "You mean he didn't hit her?"

"According to Flora, she saved his life."

Gabe scowled.

A black-haired Irishman, the policeman smoothed his dense mustache and thought. "If he had attacked her, why would he stick around to help until we got there?"

Gabe wracked his brain for images from the dream.

"Did you see anything else when you drove up?" he asked for the tenth time.

He'd seen an upraised arm, a doorjamb. Johnson had been wearing a bright orange parka. "The man who hit her wore beige. A camel-hair jacket."

"You're sure."

He'd seen it in a dream. "I'm sure."

The policeman flipped his notebook back a few pages. "That fits. The suspect claims a sixtyish bald Caucasian went into the west stairwell then came out again with a lead pipe in his hand. He hit the deceas—the victim in the doorway, then dropped the weapon and ran. He was wearing a beige suit, white shirt, and brown tie."

Merryweather looked to Gabe. "Payne."

"Where can we find him?"

"Anywhere in the hospital," Merryweather declared. "He's a doctor here."

The policeman sighed and shut his notebook. "He's

also got an hour head start. That means he could be anywhere, including O'Hare."

Gabe heard nothing more. The doctor emerged from the operating room. "How is she?"

He tugged his face mask to his chin. "The skull fracture we knew about. What we can't predict is the amount of swelling in the brain."

"What does that mean?"

"We'd like to try something. It's not an uncommon procedure. We need permission. It involves inducing a coma."

"Inducing?"

"By deliberately keeping the patient unconscious, we can minimize brain damage. I'm talking a few days, seventy-two hours at the most."

"And then what?"

"Then we wait for her to come out of it on her own."

"She will come out of it," Gabe demanded.

"She should." He wasn't making any promises. He signaled a nurse over. "Can you have Dr. Creager explain this in more detail to Mr. Getz? I have another operation scheduled at Children's—"

"This isn't Mr. Getz, Doctor."

"Hm?"

The nurse looked at Gabe as if he were an imposter. "The patient's mother and uncle are on the way. This man is no relation."

"I called them," Gabe insisted. "I'm her fiancé."

"Only immediate relatives are allowed in this area, sir."

He wasn't going anywhere.

"Sir, we may have to call Security if you won't go—"

Merryweather gripped Gabe's arm. "Wait a minute. Who ordered this? Who told you he didn't belong here?"

"The nurses' station was informed—"

"Did Payne call down?"

The nurse looked from Gabe to Merryweather to the policeman. "Dr. Payne said I should ring him when Mr.

Fitzgerald left. He wanted to drop in on the patient himself."

A bloody fury surged through Gabe. "Where is he?"

"He said to ring him in the sleep clinic."

"Come on," Merryweather shouted at the policeman.

"I'm staying here," Gabe said. Anyone who tried to get near Shana would have to go through him first.

27

Seventy-two hours passed like a dream. People came and went. Shana's condition didn't change. Doctors showed him X rays, CAT scans. They told him the procedure was working, the swelling kept to a minimum. They couldn't tell him how much damage the blow itself had done until she woke up.

He couldn't sleep until she talked to him. "Shana? Wake up, honey."

It had been a full day since the treatment ended. She should have woken up. He talked to her, telling her everything he knew or remembered. "They know Payne did it. They still haven't caught him." If he hoped that knowledge would shock her into opening her eyes, it failed.

He turned when the door opened. Her mother entered. "They gave me another hard time." Sylvie Getz sighed. "I told them you were engaged. You belong here."

"Thanks, Mrs. Getz."

She set her shopping bag at the end of the bed with a

sigh. "In that case don't you think you should call me Ma?"

He tried to smile. It died when he saw the way she stopped short of actually looking at her daughter. She fussed everywhere else, touching the cart at the end of the bed, sliding her hand along the rail. She rubbed the sheet between her fingers to test the softness. "They give them pajamas like that?"

"I brought them from my place. She likes plaid."

Sylvie straightened the flowers on the side table.

"You can talk to her," Gabe whispered.

"Oh no. I wouldn't want to wake her."

He stared at Sylvie's back. "Go ahead. Ask her what she's doing in my pajamas."

The older woman flushed. She still wore her hairnet from the bakery. She came straight there every afternoon. Like Gabe, she'd be there no matter how long it took. Unlike him, she still hadn't talked to her daughter.

"Go ahead," he demanded. "Shock her, yell at her, tell her a joke. The doctor says she can hear. She knows we're here."

Folding the sheet beneath Shana's breasts, her mother glanced at the bandages around her forehead. Her chin trembled. "They shaved her hair."

"Just in back. Don't worry, Shana," he teased, his voice grating, "you got two beautiful curls, one left, one right. Just like Goldilocks. The rest'll grow back."

Her mother floated her fingers over the surface of that golden hair. "Her hair always grew so fast."

"Grows."

"Yes. She can style it nice and short someday. Something she can take care of."

"That's the idea. Hear that, babe? We're doing makeovers."

Sylvie glanced from her comatose daughter to the desperate man with the four-day beard and the crazy hope in his eyes. "You're taking good care of her."

"She took good care of me. I wouldn't be where I am today without her."

He was in a hospital room praying for a miracle.

If she could hear, he'd talk. He'd read, sing, pray, anything to get through to her. Somewhere inside that dream world she had to know they were pulling for her. "Did you bring the books?"

Moving from the bed to the bag, Sylvie dug out the children's books. "I don't know what you want with them. Even the grandchildren have outgrown them."

"Shana likes them." He opened to the first page of the first book Sylvie handed him. He sat in the chair he'd sat in for four days. He gripped Shana's limp hand. "Once upon a time in a forest near a castle, there lived a boy and girl named Hansel and Gretel . . ."

He didn't sleep. He watched. Any flicker, any sign. Her hand lay cupped in his, her fingers cool, her skin dry to the touch. Every now and then he thought he felt a movement. Every time he waited for another. It never came.

"Shana?" His voice was sandpaper, his beard ragged stubble. In the bathroom off the private room he'd arranged for her, he splashed his face with water. "I'm not going anywhere. Hear me? Twenty years of insomnia has to be good for something. If there's one thing I know, it's how to stay awake."

He patted his face dry and draped the towel over the end of the bed. "I thought you *wanted* me to sleep."

No reaction.

He went back to his vigil. It was evening on the night of the fourth day. He hadn't slept a wink. The familiar leaden feeling weighed him down, a pounding behind his eyes like a jackhammer, an ache between his shoulder blades he recognized like an old friend. His face felt like sagging clay. He wasn't going anywhere.

She looked so peaceful. With nothing but the small overhead lamp casting its pool of light, she could have been in a coffin. He imagined organ music playing in the background.

Maybe it was the strain around the eyes that reminded him of his mother, the agony of her last weeks. Sleep had eased all that. Erased it. Her head was propped on a pillow that should have been satin, pleated, and gathered. The bed needed a lid, something he could close.

Stepping farther into the room, Payne wanted to whisper "rest in peace." The man sleeping in the corner might hear. He stepped very quietly closer.

The pills in his pocket would dissolve in the water glass. She might drink it in the night or first thing in the morning. In a perfect world, the man in the corner would lift her head and encourage her to drink it. She'd never wake up again.

"Kiss her good night," his grandmother said.

"No!" The little boy wrestled to escape the looming coffin, the lifeless body.

"Say good-bye."

He broke three pills into the glass, stirring it with his finger. He licked off the moisture. A bell for summoning the nurse hung from her headboard. Its thick plastic-coated wire would have made a wonderful restraint. Ever since he'd discovered the pills, they'd hardly needed the restraints to make her play dead, hold her perfectly still.

He'd kept them anyway. He liked them.

He ran his hand down the cord. It would have been wonderful tying her with the very bell she might have used to summon help.

She opened her eyes. He held his breath.

Hazel's mouth formed a scream. She clamped it shut, lips trembling, as if they were at home, as if she had to hold it in. He'd trained her well.

He lifted the sheet to her chin. "The Sandman's here."

She grappled with him, her eyes wide, terrified, the scream trapped in her throat. She clutched at his wrists, the bones in her hands so puny, so breakable. Not like the silence; she'd keep silent forever. Betraying him would mean revealing her shame, soiling her beloved dignity.

Holding a pill between his thumb and forefinger, he pressed it to her mouth. An involuntary grunt escaped her. He listened to the whisk of her head tossing on the pillow. "Take it."

The man in the chair shifted.

"Lie still," Payne commanded.

She refused, kicking and gasping, working up the energy to scream at last, to break free. He couldn't let her do that. He had to put her to sleep forever.

He covered her face with the pillow. It muffled everything, solving everything, like closing a coffin lid. They'd done that to his mother. No one seemed to care that she couldn't breathe, couldn't move in there. *Say good-bye.*

"No!" A force threw him against the wall. Lights sliced through his eyes. Men in uniform stormed in. The dozing security guard had leapt to his feet, mashing Payne's face against the wall as he wrenched his arms behind him. Forcing him double, he bent the bald man over the end of the mattress, cuffing him while his wife screamed and screamed.

She climbed to the head of the bed, her knees raised in a fetal position, her feet kicking at the bedclothes, anything to keep from touching him. Her voice echoed down the halls of the convalescent home. "I'm awake! I'm awake!"

"How is she?"

Gabe spun around. "Morning, Flora." Day five.

"Can she have visitors?"

"She can hear you."

Flora took that as fact. She walked up the side of the bed. "Child, you wake up now, you hear? This man of yours is about dead with lack of sleep. You've got a job to come back to and patients who need you."

As if to prove the point, Fiona and Merryweather slipped inside the door. "Hi, Shana."

"Hi, Shana. We've decided to hold the staff meeting in here this morning," Merryweather drawled. "No sense letting you out of the loop."

He pulled his pipe out of his pocket. Flora set down a folder. Fiona clicked a mechanical pen.

"I brought a couple of your files myself," Merryweather explained to Shana. He set them on the end of the bed. For twenty minutes they discussed their cases in low voices. Gabe held her hand, waiting.

Finally Merryweather glanced at his reduced staff. "I think that's all we have for today."

Fiona excused herself.

Gabe blinked his gritty eyes. He realized Flora had been holding Shana's other hand all this time. "You do good work," she said to her friend. "Don't you give up on us now."

Merryweather cleared his throat, staring into the black bowl of his pipe. "Payne's in custody. I don't know if you heard. With DeVon Johnson as a witness they've got a good case against him. Added to that there's the testimony we've been getting from Hazel. She's willing to talk now. Her sister's come to stay with her. As for me, I've been thinking of resigning—"

"Hush," Flora commanded.

Gabe looked to Shana for any reaction.

"I'm sorry," Merryweather said. "We'll talk about it later."

"We've got just one more thing," Flora said to Shana. She waved at the tiny window in the door.

Fiona escorted DeVon Johnson and his wife, Shirlee, inside. DeVon sent a wary glance Gabe's way.

Gabe stepped up to him and shook his hand. "I didn't know about Payne. I saw you and thought—"

"It's okay. The wife and I, we wanted to thank her. She saved my life."

"Mine too," Gabe added.

"We're praying for you both," Shirlee said.

"That's what the shirt meant," DeVon explained. "A prayer was Shirlee's idea. 'Now I lay me down—' "

Gabe cut him off. "She isn't going to die."

No one dared contradict him.

"Of course not." Shirlee placed her hand on his arm. "Love never dies. That's what God is about."

"He wouldn't give her to me then take her away. He wouldn't warn me—prepare me—" Gabe's voice caught.

People looked away. Not Shirlee. She was the one who'd always believed him, from the first time he'd talked about his dreams in Shana's group sessions. He got a grip. "All those dreams, they led me to her. They can't take her away too."

"You stay faithful and God will provide."

He wasn't going anywhere. "I think we've had enough," he said finally. "She needs to rest."

It wasn't much of a thank-you for their stopping by. No one seemed to mind.

"You need sleep too," Flora told him. "I can stay with her."

"I'm not leaving."

She didn't press him. When he had to find the strength it was there, it always had been, a kind of steel that wouldn't allow him to break. He had to stay awake. That's all there was to it.

"You snooze, you lose." He'd lost his parents that way. He couldn't fail Shana. One of them had to stay awake. That was the deal. While Shana slept he'd stay awake and watch over her. Somewhere along the way he'd promised her that.

· · ·

Nurses came and went. Doctors assured him it sometimes happened this way. The body could be healing itself.
Could be.

They tried coaxing him out of the room, lecturing
him. They brought in a cot he ignored. Sylvie Getz, Uncle Karl, Brice, and Peg came to spell him and ended up
sitting beside him.

He'd close his eyes for seconds. Intense dreams came
and went in microsleeps. His head jerked up. He remembered other dreams, old ones. Years ago, not long after his
grandmother had died, he'd dreamed his mother was leaning over him in bed, humming a lullaby. He was a child,
she was tucking him in. She told him he'd done the best
he could.

He'd woken up knowing they forgave him for the
crash. The catch was, he'd never forgiven himself.

You snooze, you lose. He wasn't losing this time.

Maybe the dreams prepared you, Aurora had said.
They'd prepared him to go without sleep, for years if need
be.

He took Shana's hand in his, opening the first book
on the stack. " 'Sleeping Beauty,' " he croaked. "You with
me, babe? One of your favorites."

She didn't respond.

He squeezed his eyes shut until the tears came and
dried up again, until lights flickered behind his lids like
sparklers. He opened them to the harsh white light of the
overhead lamp, the white of the sheets, the soft green of
the negligee her mother had brought.

"You look like a princess," he told Shana, unable to
concentrate on the blurring words. People used to call him
a vampire. He wasn't a vampire anymore. "I don't know
how long I can do this."

She didn't respond.

He traced the lace neckline scooping to her breast. He

leaned over and kissed her cheek. He hated the idea every kiss could be a good-bye. "I love you."

No response.

He opened the book again. " 'Once upon a time, there was a kingdom and a princess was born.' " He dropped it in his lap. If she needed a prince, he'd be a prince. "You just gotta help me here, Shana. I can't do this alone."

Was she listening?

He laid her hand on the bed, placing the fingers just so. He had to stretch. His back creaked, his neck was stiff. He walked to the door and turned out the overhead light. Returning to the pool of night-light, he held her hand. He threaded his fingers through a lock of her hair, leaned over, and kissed her lips. "Help me with this."

When he opened his eyes he looked into the soft brown eyes he'd known forever, understanding, caring, faintly amused.

"Shana?" He was dreaming. If he closed his eyes, he'd lose it.

"Hi."

He gripped her hand.

"You look awful."

"So do you." He curved his arm around her bandaged head, afraid to touch anything but her hand. The slightest movement might wake him up. "Are you okay?"

"I'm fine." A little sleepy-eyed, a little drowsy, she closed her eyes.

Gabe's heart scraped into his throat. "Shana?"

Her lips curled in a sleepy smile. "You didn't finish the story."

At that moment he couldn't have said where the book was, much less how the story ended. "Want me to call the doctor?"

"He said I'd be okay once I woke up."

"You heard that?"

"I don't know. I remember it."

"Do you remember me telling you I love you?"

Eyes closed, she smiled. "Kiss me again and I'll see."

He kissed her, his lips dry and chapped. He cupped her cheek.

She moved her head on the pillow. The bandages rasped against the cotton. She wrinkled her forehead and tried to look up. "Is my hair that awful?"

"No worse than usual."

A wider smile. It changed as she really looked at him, love transforming into concern. She drew her hand down his stubbled cheek. "You need a shave."

"I know."

"And some sleep."

"I will."

"When?"

"When I know you're not going anywhere."

"I'm not going anywhere."

"Let me call the doctor."

The medical team came and went, every question answered to their satisfaction. "She should make a total recovery," Dr. Creager told Gabe. The doctor leaned over his patient. "Is there anything else you need?"

She gestured weakly at Gabe. "Tell him to get some sleep."

"I thought that was your specialty, Dr. Getz."

She grinned. "Come here, you."

The room cleared out. Gabe sat beside her.

"Remember all the stuff I told you? People need sleep the way they need love."

"I'm not leaving you."

She brooked no argument. His Shana was passionate about sleep, his sleep in particular. "Then get in bed."

He hesitated.

"Afraid I'll kick?"

He was afraid if he slept, he'd wake up and find her gone.

She opened her eyes. "I love you."

"I love you."

"Sleep with me."

He stretched beside her on the mattress. Balanced on his elbow, he looked down on her.

She found his hand and rested it on her breast. She accepted his kiss. Pressing his head to her shoulder, she stroked his hair. "I love you. Gabe?"

He didn't reply. He was sound asleep.

Terry Lawrence makes her home in Traverse City, Michigan, where she enjoys a career as a full-time writer. Her published works include novels, short stories, and poetry. A community theater enthusiast, she has also authored a play, *To Jerusalem*, which was produced in March 1995.

THE VERY BEST IN CONTEMPORARY WOMEN'S FICTION

SANDRA BROWN

____28951-9 Texas! Lucky $5.99/$6.99 in Canada ____56768-3 Adam's Fall $4.99/$5.99

____28990-X Texas! Chase $5.99/$6.99 ____56045-X Temperatures Rising $5.99/$6.99

____29500-4 Texas! Sage $5.99/$6.99 ____56274-6 Fanta C $4.99/$5.99

____29085-1 22 Indigo Place $5.99/$6.99 ____56278-9 Long Time Coming $4.99/$5.99

____29783-X A Whole New Light $5.99/$6.99 ____09672-9 Heaven's Price $16.95/$22.95

TAMI HOAG

____29534-9 Lucky's Lady $5.99/$7.50 ____29272-2 Still Waters $5.99/$7.50

____29053-3 Magic $5.99/$7.50 ____56160-X Cry Wolf $5.50/$6.50

____56050-6 Sarah's Sin $4.99/$5.99 ____56161-8 Dark Paradise $5.99/$7.50

____09961-2 Night Sins $19.95/$23.95

NORA ROBERTS

____29078-9 Genuine Lies $5.99/$6.99 ____27859-2 Sweet Revenge $5.99/$6.99

____28578-5 Public Secrets $5.99/$6.99 ____27283-7 Brazen Virtue $5.99/$6.99

____26461-3 Hot Ice $5.99/$6.99 ____29597-7 Carnal Innocence $5.99/$6.99

____26574-1 Sacred Sins $5.99/$6.99 ____29490-3 Divine Evil $5.99/$6.99

DEBORAH SMITH

____29107-6 Miracle $5.50/$6.50 ____29690-6 Blue Willow $5.50/$6.50

____29092-4 Follow the Sun $4.99/$5.99 ____29689-2 Silk and Stone $5.99/$6.99

____28759-1 The Beloved Woman $4.50/$5.50

Ask for these books at your local bookstore or use this page to order.

Please send me the books I have checked above. I am enclosing $____(add $2.50 to cover postage and handling). Send check or money order, no cash or C.O.D.'s, please.

Name _____

Address _____

City/State/Zip _____

Send order to: Bantam Books, Dept. FN 24, 2451 S. Wolf Rd., Des Plaines, IL 60018

Allow four to six weeks for delivery.

Prices and availability subject to change without notice.   FN 24 7/95